AGENT OF ROME

THE

IMPERIAL
BANNER

First published in Great Britain in 2012 by Hodder & Stoughton
An Hachette UK company

First published in paperback in 2013

1

A CIP catalogue record for this title is available from the British Library.

ISBN 978 1 444 71489 0

Typeset in Plantin Light by Palimpsest Book Production Limited,
Falkirk, Stirlingshire

Printed and bound by CPI Group (UK) Ltd, Croydon CR0 4YY

Hodder & Stoughton policy is to use papers that are natural, renewable and
recyclable products and made from wood grown in sustainable forests. The
logging and manufacturing processes are expected to conform to the
environmental regulations of the country of origin.

Hodder & Stoughton Ltd
338 Euston Road
London NW1 3BH

www.hodder.co.uk

AGENT OF ROME

THE

IMPERIAL BANNER

NICK BROWN

HODDER

For Anne

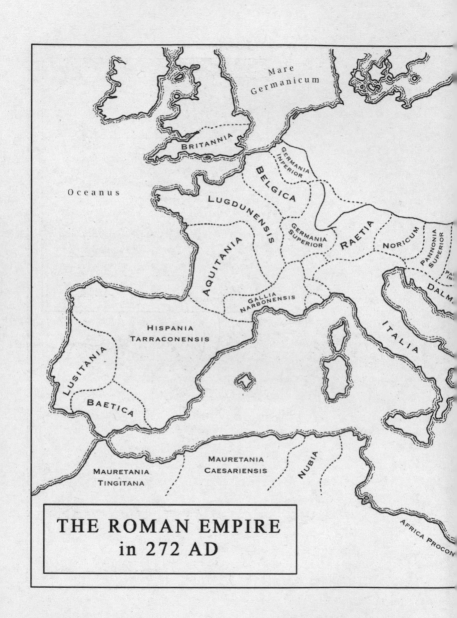

Mare
Germanicum

Oceanus

BRITANNIA

GERMANIA
INFERIOR

BELGICA

LUGDUNENSIS

AQUITANIA

GERMANIA
SUPERIOR

RAETIA

NORICUM

PANNONIA
SUPERIOR

PAN
INF

DALM

GALLIA
NARBONENSIS

ITALIA

HISPANIA
TARRACONENSIS

LUSITANIA

BAETICA

MAURETANIA
TINGITANA

MAURETANIA
CAESARIENSIS

NUBIA

AFRICA PROCON

THE ROMAN EMPIRE
in 272 AD

DACIA

PANNONIA
INFERIOR

MOESIA
SUPERIOR

MOESIA
INFERIOR

THRACIA

MACEDONIA

Pontus Euxinus

ASIA

GALATIA

CAPPADOCIA

CILICIA

MESOPOTAMIA

R. Euphrates

SYRIA
COELE

PHOENICA

Desert

Mare Nostrum

ARABIA

CYRENAICA

AEGYPTUS

Miles

0   200   400   600

Antioch

Seleucia

Beroea

Chalcis

Anasartha

Apamea

Androna
Seriane

Emesa

Tripolis

Palmyra

Damascus

■ - City
● - Town

- High
ground

Miles

0   30   60

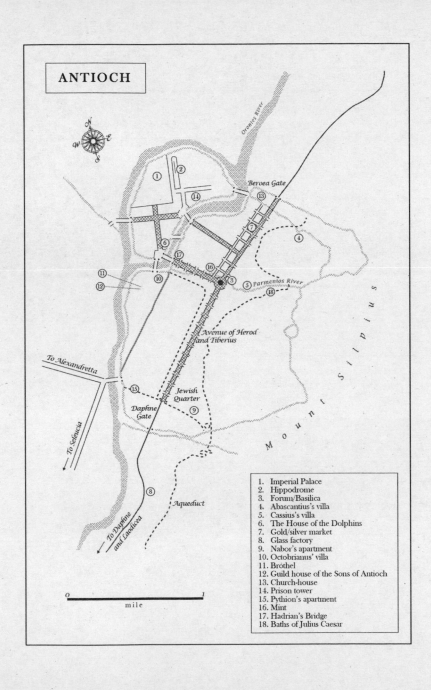

ANTIOCH

1. Imperial Palace
2. Hippodrome
3. Forum/Basilica
4. Abascantius's villa
5. Cassius's villa
6. The House of the Dolphins
7. Gold/silver market
8. Glass factory
9. Nabor's apartment
10. Octobrianus' villa
11. Brothel
12. Guild house of the Sons of Antioch
13. Church-house
14. Prison tower
15. Pythion's apartment
16. Mint
17. Hadrian's Bridge
18. Baths of Julius Caesar

Orontes River

Beroea Gate

Parmenios River

Avenue of Herod
and Tiberius

Mount Silpius

To Alexandretta

Jewish
Quarter

Daphne
Gate

To Seleucia

To Daphne
and Laodicea

Aqueduct

0   mile   1

MONEY

Four sesterces (a coin made of brass) were worth one denarius.

Twenty-five denarii (a coin made partially of silver) were worth one aureus (partially gold).

TIMES OF THE DAY

The Romans divided day and night into twelve hours each, so the length of an hour varied according to the time of year.

In autumn, in Syria, the first hour of the day would have begun at approximately 06.15.

The seventh hour of the day always began at midday.

The first hour of night would have begun at approximately 18.45.

Colonia Pietas Julia, April, AD 271

Indavara was ready when they came for him. He had just finished the last of his exercises and his muscles felt warm, his mind sharp. He had to be prepared; there wouldn't be much time once they took him up.

A bolt snapped and the door opened towards him, revealing Capito's full girth. A ridiculous black wig sat atop his large, oval head. Behind him, the latest whore – a plump beauty – looked on curiously, fingering a necklace. Capito winked at Indavara and waited for the guards to enter. Ducking their heads and lowering their knotted wooden clubs, the men took up position either side of the door. The older of the two, Bonosus, was Capito's chief guard and brother-in-law. Not for the first time, Indavara noticed the blotches of dried blood that stained the top of his club. Capito had to turn sideways to move inside the cell.

'Ready, my boy?'

Indavara could smell his perfume. He said nothing.

'Didn't I tell you I'd be true to my word? "Twenty and out," I said. And you alone have made it this far. I'm proud of you. Do you believe that?' Knowing there would be no reply, Capito continued: 'I shall miss these little chats, one-sided though they've been. You know – whatever happens today – we shall probably never see each other again.'

Indavara stared blankly at him.

'I imagine you'd like to kill me,' added Capito, before glancing speculatively at Bonosus.

'Him too, I'm sure.'

Indavara was careful to show no reaction whatsoever.

'Those eyes of yours. Cold fury. Mars himself made flesh.' Theatrically, Capito put a hand to his ear. 'Do you hear them, Indavara? They await you. They have come in their thousands. I have something very special for you this time. Very special indeed. Come!'

Indavara snatched a final look at the cell: his home for the last six years. Though he hated the place, he knew now he would miss it. Next to the thin straw mattress were the few items he could truly call his own: a wooden mug, a spoon and a bowl; a spare tunic and two blankets. All that was missing was the tiny figurine of the goddess Fortuna a woman had thrown to him after his tenth fight. It was now tucked inside his tunic, where he'd kept it for every fight since. He believed it had brought him luck.

Bonosus, Capito and the girl disappeared up a dank stone staircase. Two more guards joined the other behind Indavara as he strode through the cell-block. He paid little attention to the shouting and singing from above, but was grateful for the encouraging comments from his fellow fighters, all of whom stood by their doors, faces pressed to the bars.

Indavara nodded to each man but he was more interested in seeing who else had been taken up. Capito had purchased four fighters from the northern provinces earlier that month and Indavara's stomach turned over as he realised all were present except Auctus, a big brute who fought with the classic combination of trident and net. Auctus's reputation had preceded his arrival in Pietas Julia by several days; it was said he had won more than thirty contests. Indavara was at least grateful for the one mercy it seemed Capito had granted him: he wouldn't have to fight a man he knew.

One guard moved ahead of him and up the second staircase at the end of the cell-block. As he ascended, Indavara recalled all he'd gleaned from his fellow fighters about Auctus – the five tips he'd memorised.

Patient. Quick off both feet. Uses the net mainly to distract. Never throws it. Goes for the head with the trident.

The four men stepped up into a wide, square tunnel, just five yards behind the southern gate. Two grim-faced legionaries stood there, each armed with a spear.

Indavara flexed his arms and slapped his hands against his chest. Between the legionaries he saw a distinctive figure standing in the spring sunshine. Centurion Maesa was one of a handful of men with sufficient bearing and authority to address the crowd. Recently, he had taken to acting as host and umpire. His booming, sonorous tones were unmistakably martial.

'Silence!'

Maesa spun on his toes to face the other side of the arena.

'Silence there!'

Capito settled into a cushion, one hand on the girl's ample waist. His seat was just above the podium, where assorted luminaries surrounded the governor and his staff.

The arena at Pietas Julia had begun life as a timber construction three centuries earlier but now the impressive dimensions of its limestone walls made it one of the largest amphitheatres outside Rome. Even at four hundred by three hundred feet, however, it was just half the size of the Colosseum. The arena was accessed by four main gates and eleven access tunnels and could hold over twenty thousand spectators.

Capito surveyed the crowd with a satisfied smirk. There was barely an empty seat and those around him were an eclectic mix: young bucks still hung over from pre-fight parties, city bureaucrats relaxing after a long morning's work, affluent merchants with family, friends and assorted hangers-on. Then there were the lower classes, those with tickets issued free of charge; enjoying rare hours of leisure courtesy of the governor.

Pushing away the cup of wine offered to him by the girl, Capito wondered when the city authorities would finally reach an agreement with the sailors who were supposed to operate the shading system for the arena roof. They were currently on strike. He caught the eye of a nearby slave wafting a palm branch.

'Put your back into it!'

Wiping sweat from his eyebrows, Capito elected to take the drink after all.

A tall, balding man in an immaculate toga two rows down turned round and waved. He seemed utterly unaffected by the heat.

'What'll it be then? Wolves, I expect – a pack perhaps?'

Capito shrugged. He had let slip certain titbits designed to build yet more anticipation for the afternoon's contest.

'No, it's a big cat,' said another man. 'Someone saw it being unloaded.'

Capito held up his hands. 'All will be revealed!'

His jovial expression slipped quickly. Arranging for the purchase and delivery of the beast had cost him a small fortune. It had been captured just a week earlier, fed nothing, offered only a cell-full of clothes from executed prisoners to accustom it to the scent of human blood.

Capito suddenly felt hot breath on his neck.

'All arranged as instructed.'

He turned and smiled again, allowing any watching eyes to believe he was glad to see the squat figure now sitting behind him.

'I told you to stay away today,' he hissed, trying to ignore the chunk of meat lodged in the man's beard.

'Just checking that all promises will be kept. I cannot afford for this to go wrong.'

Capito managed to maintain the grin, conscious of the sea of faces behind him. Ideally, he would have used someone more discreet but the slave-trader was in desperate financial straits and had been more than happy to play his part. Their scheme was simple. A colossal amount had been staked by the people of Pietas Julia on Indavara surviving and winning his freedom ('sentimentalists' Capito called them) and their bets had kept the odds favourable. Using five proxies, he and the trader had bet a huge sum on Indavara's death. If successful, they would each net over ten thousand denarii.

'Do not concern yourself,' Capito replied. 'All good things come to an end. And this particular good thing is about to meet his.'

'He had better, fat man. He had better.'

Capito hadn't heard such venom in the slave-trader's voice before, nor had he previously taken much notice of the curved dagger he carried at his belt. Conjuring a final grin, he turned back towards the arena.

Maesa had just finished the formalities: greeting the honoured guests and thanking various gods for blessing the city and its inhabitants. The centurion was clad in full officer's regalia: white tunic lined with gold braid, crested helmet and scarlet cloak.

'Now the main event of the day. For six years, this man has fought time and again for his life within these walls. He has shown great courage, skill and ingenuity. He has seen off countless foes: both man and beast. And on this day, he will either die or claim his freedom. Who can doubt that this man – slave though he is – exemplifies the Roman virtues of strength, intelligence and triumph over adversity. I am certain that if he succeeds, he will enjoy – fully – the benefits of victory.'

Maesa gestured to a group of women next to the podium, provoking shrill shrieks and a low rumble of laughter from the men. Women were traditionally banished to the top tiers but the governor's predecessors had enjoyed observing their interactions with the fighters. Local custom now dictated that a hundred or so of the most voluble were admitted to a small, low-walled enclave.

'Today, our warrior faces his destiny. Will he die like a dog in the dirt, or leave this arena victorious, head held high, a free man?'

Now the noise really began to build. Some applauded or chanted, others beat home-made drums or took off their sandals and slapped them against the stone flooring.

Once the southern gate was unlocked, the legionaries and the trio of guards moved aside. Vitruvius was one of Capito's more reasonable and independent employees – a lanky young lad with a mop of brown hair. He nodded and said something, but Indavara couldn't hear it above the noise.

7

One of the older guards obviously took exception to what Vitruvius had said and swatted him across the back of the head. The other guard cursed at him too but when they looked away the young man mouthed the words again, and this time Indavara understood.

Good luck.

'Victor of nineteen contests, conqueror of thirty-six men. Governor Actius Lucius Vanna and our esteemed Organiser of Games, Gaius Salvius Capito bring you . . . Indavara!'

Shrill trumpets rang around the arena; twenty thousand people watched the compact, stocky figure amble into the sunlight. Regular observers had noted the developments in his physique since his first appearance as a teenager. The broad shoulders and thick neck had always suggested a propensity for bulk and this had been supplemented by endless hours of training and meals of barley gruel that added a protective fatty layer. Yet even those who had seen Indavara fight only once knew that the impression of immobility was purely that. Though he would never make a great runner, his raw strength and surprising agility were matched with a rare quickness of thought that invariably gave him an advantage even over a lighter, defter foe. Watchers were also always struck by the young man's near-supernatural air of stillness and composure. Whatever his occupation, from the most perfunctory walk to the most desperate struggle, he projected an unyielding, elemental solidity.

Scarcely an inch of his dark skin had survived unscathed. Aside from the brand upon his shoulder that identified him as Capito's property, his hands, wrists and forearms were a mass of scars, welts and bruises in differing states of repair.

At various times, he had fractured both wrists and both ankles. His arm had also been broken close to the shoulder, his leg just below the knee; but thanks to Capito's surgeon he had suffered no long-term effects from either. He had lost count of the broken ribs, knowing only that in cold winter air or when he breathed hard, he felt shards of pain in his chest. His only permanent disability had been sustained in his third fight: an opportunistic slash from a long cavalry sword that had taken off half his left ear. He recalled looking first at the slick stream of blood running down his chest, then the mangled piece of flesh lying close to his foot. His opponent had also been badly wounded and the governor had determined the contest a draw. Both men lived to fight another day.

Since then Indavara had allowed his thick, black hair to grow out and now a low fringe hung just above his wide, pale green eyes. To Capito, and others who knew men of his kind, their washed-out, lifeless quality was familiar. Indavara had seen them recently too, in a metal mirror used by the surgeon. He could hardly believe they were his.

He came to a stop ten yards beyond the gate and bowed in four directions. He had no weapon yet so he simply held a clenched fist high.

Groups of youths yelled and whooped and leapt in the air, punching each other or matching the clenched fist. Others carried flags with supportive slogans or surprisingly well-rendered likenesses. Women screamed at him and blew kisses.

Capito watched the aristocrats gleefully rubbing their hands together and exchanging excited smiles. The depth of support for Indavara never ceased to surprise him, because he had never come across a fighter less disposed to play to the crowd. Initially, his efficient, direct style had not endeared him to the mob. Not for him the ostentatious flourishes that many fighters employed to win the favour of the watching masses. He had been booed for his first seven or eight fights and a certain faction still maintained a stubborn dislike of his brisk, functional method.

But as time had passed, and Indavara survived battle after battle, outwitting and outfighting whatever was thrown at him, he had slowly won over the crowd. His status had been secured through dogged determination and unstinting resilience.

Capito admitted to himself that he would miss days like this.

★

Indavara examined the scene in front of him. Two thick ropes had been stretched across the sand, dividing the arena in three. Just in front of him was a barrel. There was another in the second section and another in the third.

As he had demonstrated a certain gift for resourcefulness, Capito had decided that – 'for the sake of entertainment' – Indavara would not follow the traditional path of specialising in a specific combination of armour, equipment and weaponry. In fact, for the last eight contests, his allotted weapon hadn't been revealed until he entered the arena. He imagined that inside each barrel he would find a different weapon for each stage of the contest.

In the middle of the first section was a square wooden structure fifteen yards long and ten wide. Mounted above it was a narrow, rickety bridge composed of rope and small timbers that could be accessed by steps at both ends. The 'box' was one of Capito's favourites. Indavara was almost relieved to see it; he'd suspected the vicious old bastard might choose it and had managed to fit in several practice sessions.

The second section of the arena was completely empty. The third – closest to the podium – housed the hatch for the lifting platform. It was powered by a team of twelve slaves and could raise loads of up to a thousand pounds. For now, however, the third section was also empty, except for a small deer carcass by the wall which someone had neglected to remove after one of the hunts from the morning show.

Maesa raised his hand again and waited for silence, then gestured towards the eastern gate.

'To our first opponents then. Two examples of the type of scum and villainy the city fathers wish to banish from our streets. These fiends were arrested just two days ago. One robbed a respected citizen, leaving him bleeding in the street; the other stole valuables from a temple.'

Maesa shook his head as the crowd vented their disdain.

'Let us hope that our warrior can ensure justice is done.'

Encouraged by the short swords of the legionaries, the two criminals shuffled into the arena, drawing hisses and boos. Both men were struck by a volley of low-value coins, bottles and foodstuffs. Only a few sharp words from Maesa and the prompt action of some soldiers in the stands restored order. The criminals were escorted to the other side of the box, directly opposite Indavara. One man – the younger and taller of the two – was bearded and well-built. Given his appearance, Capito had chosen to characterise him as a barbarian, equipping him with a heavy double-bladed wood axe. He remained defiant, shaking his fist and cursing at the crowd. The other man already looked beaten. Bony and slight, he could barely raise his eyes from the ground. The iron spear he held in both hands was dragging in the dirt. Indavara named the criminals Axe and Spear.

A weak cheer greeted the arrival of Bonosus and three of his guards. All now wore full military-style armour and heavy bronze helmets; and they were armed with seven-foot cavalry lances. With such weaponry and protection, the four of them could take on any animal or gladiator; as well as deter any thoughts of escape.

Indavara had resolved to make no such attempt. Even in the unlikely event that he could clear the arena, his face was so well known within the city that he would be picked up again in hours. He would not waste either mental or physical energy on false hope; he knew how Capito's mind worked, and he knew he would face his greatest ever challenge this day. He had accepted his fate.

Bonosus stepped into his line of sight and gestured towards the barrel. Indavara glanced across at Axe and Spear, now deep in conversation on the other side of the bridge. Axe was doing most of the talking. Judging by their body language, Indavara guessed they didn't know each other. That was good. He walked over to the barrel and looked inside, and at first he thought it was empty. Only when he leaned over the edge and reached into the shadowy depths did he realise there was something at the bottom. It turned out to be a tiny dagger: little more than a three-inch blade sandwiched between two lengths of wood. It looked like the kind of home-made weapon a boy might carry.

Bonosus made no attempt to hide his amusement as Indavara stared disbelievingly down at the blade. The chief guard then signalled to the criminals to raise their weapons. Spear just about managed to get his in the air. Axe, however, spun the weapon around his head with some aplomb. Bonosus indicated that it was Indavara's turn.

Shaking his head, Indavara held up the blade, unsure if the crowd would even be able to see it. The immediate chorus of booing suggested they had. Bonosus and the other guards withdrew to form a perimeter around the box.

Maesa's expression suggested he shared the crowd's opinion but he nonetheless waved to Indavara and mouthed: 'Ready?'

Indavara nodded.

The centurion ignored the criminals and faced the podium. 'It is time! Time for the first clash of this contest! Let the battle begin!'

Axe and Spear looked across at the man they would have to kill, then at each other.

Indavara moved up to the box and saw that the interior hadn't been changed. Fixed to the base were hundreds of pointed objects spaced about five inches apart: sword blades and spear-tips, shards of glass and upturned nails. Indavara had seen several men perish by falling from the bridge and none of them had died quickly. Close to the base were gaps in the wood to drain the blood out.

He examined the knife again. Despite the ridiculous size, it was well-made. If he could get close enough, he could kill with it. Bonosus sent two of his men towards Indavara but he didn't need any encouragement; experience would favour him on the bridge. Two strides and a neat leap carried him up on to the steps and prompted a burst of applause.

Bonosus and another of his men moved towards Spear. He looked all set to protest but then Axe stepped in front of him. With a word to Spear, he held the weapon in one hand and climbed up the steps on to the bridge. The crowd reaction was mixed. Some commended his bravery, others mocked his arrogance. Spear walked away to Indavara's left, around the corner of the box.

So that was to be their tactic: to attack him from two sides. He started across the bridge, knowing he had to judge his speed carefully. He didn't want to appear too adept, but he had to move far enough to draw Spear up on to the box behind him.

The bridge was moving now, an unpredictable rippling motion that swiftly focused the mind. Axe held his weapon out in front of him, advancing slowly with carefully chosen steps.

Indavara stopped close to the centre of the bridge, then looked over his shoulder as the crowd yelled a warning. Spear had just climbed up on to the box. Fabricating indecision, Indavara now switched his gaze between his opponents as both moved towards him. Axe was three yards away. He shouted at Spear to hurry up. Indavara turned again and saw that Spear had taken two shaky steps on to the bridge. Precisely where he wanted him.

He spun round and ran back across the bridge as fast as he dared, arms out to steady him.

Spear froze, eyes wide.

'Don't turn!' yelled Axe. 'Keep your spear up! Don't turn!'

But Spear had already turned. One of his feet slipped between two timbers. Shaking his leg free, he reached the edge of the box just as Indavara hurled himself chest first into his back.

The smaller man was driven into the air, then into the ground. Winded and helpless, he'd barely raised his head before Indavara punched the knife twice into the side of his neck. He then dropped the blade and grabbed the spear.

It was a heavy weapon – and not designed for throwing – but the distance was short and he had to catch his second opponent before he could reach safety.

Axe was still tottering back towards the edge of the box when Indavara let fly. The spear-head caught him on the flank; a glancing blow, but enough to unbalance him. Axe toppled backwards and his heavy body thumped down, impaled on the viciously sharp objects below.

Instinct turned Indavara around but he needn't have worried. Spear was pawing at his neck, vainly trying to stem the flow of blood. Indavara took a moment to wipe the knife clean on the man's tunic then left him where he lay. He walked past the box but didn't look inside. He knew Axe was still alive though – he could hear him whimpering.

Even though both men would certainly perish from their wounds and there was no need for the governor to make a decision, custom dictated that Indavara bow to the podium after the victory. But he simply stalked towards the second barrel. Today, he would fight precisely as he wished.

The thunder of the crowd faded as Bonosus's men finished off the criminals. The bodies and weapons were removed. Maesa reappeared from the western gate. He offered exaggerated applause to Indavara and waited for something approaching silence.

'Such intelligence! Such skill! Still, this was a poor class of foe. Now our warrior must face a giant enemy with a formidable reputation. From distant Germania, fighting with trident and net, and with a record of victory in forty-one contests, let us welcome to the arena . . . Auctus!'

The northerner couldn't possibly have prepared himself for the onslaught of abuse that greeted him as he strode out from the eastern gate. He kept his head held high and his expression neutral as bread and fruit rained down upon him. His long stride soon took him out of range and, after the noise died down, a few cheers could even be heard, some of them rather high-pitched.

Auctus could hardly have looked more different to Indavara. He was six inches taller, long-limbed, fair-haired and blue-eyed with high, pronounced cheekbones and an angular jaw. His left shoulder and upper arm were wrapped by thick padding; and this was covered by a section of bronze scale armour that began at his collar and stretched down to his elbow.

Held high in his left hand was the trident: a six-foot wooden pole topped by three barbed iron spikes. In his right hand was the net. Indavara had scoffed when he'd first seen one, but now knew how deadly they could be. Fully nine feet wide, the net was weighted around the edge by lead weights or, as in this case, polished stones. Indavara had seen them ensnare swords, trip a man from twenty yards, even take out an eye. He wondered what inadequate weapon Capito would provide this time. Any type of spear or sword would do; the longer the better.

Auctus had just noticed the female attention. He wandered towards the enclave and swung his net languidly above his shoulder, as if to catch the women. This was too much for one young girl who flung herself at the parapet and had to be restrained by her friends. With a slight grin, the northerner strode back across the rope and back into the second section.

Indavara reached the second barrel. This one was not shaded from the sun and he could easily see the bottom. He realised he had fundamentally underestimated Capito's determination to see him die. The barrel was empty.

Maesa took up a position midway between the fighters. He watched Indavara turn away from the barrel and stare down at the tiny dagger.

'There's nothing inside!' announced the centurion. 'A cruel twist of fate!'

'Cruel! Cruel!' thousands of voices replied. Others hissed at Capito, outraged that their hopeful wagers now seemed so unlikely to pay off. Capito waved away the noise and insults and dodged a bunch of grapes aimed at his head. As the barracking died down, he noted something an untrained ear would miss. Beneath the seething indignation was the buzz of animated conversation. Deep down, the mob wanted to see Indavara tested; to see if he could survive this.

Maesa conducted a cursory examination of Auctus's equipment, then hurried over to Indavara. There was only the knife to check. The centurion lifted Indavara's wrist to show the dagger once more to the crowd, prompting more boos. Auctus walked slowly towards Indavara, narrowing the gap to about five yards, then stopped.

'And now our warrior must face the second of his three tests. Who will triumph? Who will be defeated? Indavara against Auctus! Let the battle begin!'

The northerner held the trident level with his waist, grip about halfway down the pole. Indavara noted the thick, gnarled veins that chased up his forearm. Holding the heavy weapon up with one hand was difficult, and wielding it in battle for any length of time required great strength. The German gathered the ropes of the net together in his right hand and cast a professional's glance at the tiny knife, its blade barely visible above his opponent's fist.

They circled each other until Indavara was facing the podium. He darted forward, prompting Auctus to take a pace back and loosen his grip on the net, ready to use it if his opponent charged.

But when the attack never came, the German took his turn to advance. Indavara held his ground, settling into a low, fighting stance, ready for a move from either hand. Auctus centred the trident and stepped forward again, training the three spikes on his enemy's neck. Indavara still didn't move, even as the northerner released the folds of the net.

Just three yards separated them when Auctus made his first lunge with the trident. Indavara took a step left and ducked below the high thrust. He saw the net swing but was caught out by Auctus's speed. A stone caught the front of his shin; a stinging blow that would have halted a man unused to ignoring pain.

Auctus recovered the net and instantly closed the space again. Indavara was next to the rope – the limit of the fighting area. If he crossed it Bonosus was sure to poke him back into the second section with his spear. So he scuttled right, then backed towards the centre, the German following warily. Indavara could see he would be difficult to unsettle. He executed the basics well and always kept his body and weapons correctly aligned.

Aside from a few loudmouths, the crowd was quiet, expectant. This clash of champions was one for enthusiasts.

Auctus took the initiative again, eyeballing his foe as he strode towards him. Indavara bounced up and down on his toes and waited. His options were limited; he needed time to see what Auctus could do before he tried anything.

The German jabbed the trident forward again, simultaneously swinging the net at his enemy's knees.

Indavara shuffled backwards, avoiding both attacks.

Auctus pressed on and repeated the move. Indavara leapt to his left, sure he was clear of both net and trident.

But then Auctus twisted his wrist and swung the net upward. Indavara felt rope brush his neck, then a shuddering crack as one of the stones caught him under the chin.

Blinding white flashed into his eyes. He staggered back, reeling as the pain bloomed higher. His eyes cleared; and he saw the trident-head coming at him.

He pushed off to his right, dropping into a neat double roll that took him clear. Springing back to his feet, he looked up as the German marched towards him, yelling in a language no one else in the arena understood.

Indavara realised that the blow had pushed his teeth up into his tongue. The thumbnail-sized chunk he had bitten off was sliding around in his mouth. He spat it out, along with a glob of bloody spittle.

With the trident held high, his arm bent at the elbow, Auctus swung the net in ever wider arcs ahead of him.

Indavara retreated, heels scuffing the sand. He had a move in mind, but to pull it off he would need to slow that net-arm. Mindful of the rope, and Bonosus's men lurking behind him, Indavara crabbed right, quickly accelerating into a trot.

Auctus dropped his grip to the centre of the net and a swift flick of the wrist sent it spinning towards Indavara's feet. It struck the ground just as he jumped but then bounced back up, ensnaring a foot. He fell headlong into the dust.

Women screamed. Men bellowed warnings at him.

With not a single glance at the onrushing northerner, Indavara cursed his fellow gladiators – *Never throws his net?* – and sat up. He reached for the rope and the single stone pressed against his foot. The stone came away easily, leaving only two criss-crossing ropes wrapped tight. Indavara tore at them, then looked up.

Auctus was five yards away.

At last the rope slid off, and Indavara scrambled to his feet. He would have taken the net himself, had the trident-head not been so close.

Auctus drove the weapon at his enemy's neck.

Indavara threw himself backwards and twisted away from the trident.

A single spike hit, tearing a gash in his shoulder.

Auctus slowed himself, spun around and plucked the net from the ground before Indavara could react.

The wound was small but deep. Beneath the torn fabric of his tunic, Indavara could see dark and pale tissue. He wondered if Auctus kept his weapons clean. The wound wouldn't kill him; infection might.

From the crowd, the traditional chant: 'A hit! A hit!'

The German was in no mood to tarry. Taking only a moment to shake sand from the net, he adjusted his grip on the trident, and stalked towards his fellow gladiator once more.

Indavara took care to move slowly, and winced with every movement of his shoulder. He swapped the knife to his left hand for a moment, so that he could wipe the sweat off his right. When he returned it, he realised he might have a way to slow that net-arm.

Auctus stretched his arms wide like two great wings and closed on his prey once more.

The crowd were quiet again; their man was in trouble.

Indavara spat out more blood, tried to ignore the fiery pain in his shoulder, and awaited his foe.

Auctus jinked from side to side, offering half-jabs and feints. His next real swing of the net whistled past Indavara's left ankle. Then the trident shot forward.

Jab, swing. Jab, swing. Auctus was grinning and talking; he seemed to be enjoying himself.

Another jab.

Indavara threw the knife to the ground.

Confusion was just beginning to register on Auctus's face as he swung the net. It slowed him down.

Indavara darted down to his left and managed to grab the edge of the net.

Auctus hauled it back; but Indavara didn't resist, instead flinging what he held up and to the right. The net whipped high into the air and landed on the trident-head, catching two of the spikes.

Ducking under the tangle, Indavara launched himself at Auctus.

With both hands occupied, the German was defenceless as Indavara's swinging right forearm caught him under the jaw, knocking him clean off his feet. Auctus fell backwards, pulling the net and Indavara with him.

They had barely struck the ground when Indavara wriggled free of the net and hammered a fist down, splintering Auctus's nose. Despite the transformation of the middle of his face into a pulpy mass of flesh and bone, the northerner managed to keep functioning. His scrabbling fingers reached for the trident.

Indavara was not about to give up his advantage. Forcing his weight down, he wedged his elbows into the German's armpits and gripped his foe's neck with both hands. He'd used the choke hold before and knew it to be immensely difficult to dislodge.

That didn't stop Auctus trying. He punched Indavara in the head, then clawed at his neck; but he couldn't inflict enough pain to loosen the thick fingers digging into his throat. The German spasmed his back but he couldn't shift his foe.

Indavara had lowered his head to avoid the flurry of blows and by the time he looked up, Auctus had hold of the trident. Pain pulsed through Indavara's shoulder as he channelled all his strength into his hands and squeezed tighter. He couldn't let go now.

Auctus moved his arm as high as he could, holding the trident-head over Indavara's back. Indavara shook him, trying to dislodge the weapon, but Auctus knew it was the only chance he had left. Gritting his teeth, Indavara pressed harder still, watching his fingers turning white. Auctus was doing well for a man who couldn't breathe.

The crowd yelled warnings that became a single cry.

Auctus plunged the trident between Indavara's shoulder blades. The barbed spikes sliced easily through the tunic, sank into the skin, then tore at the flesh as the pole tipped backwards.

Indavara was still screaming when he let go and pushed himself up. The trident slid off his body.

Auctus's eyes were pink, his face and neck scarlet; and bulging veins ridged his forehead. But with both hands now free, he reached for his enemy's neck.

Indavara swatted his hands away and slammed his right elbow down on to the German's forehead, pummelling his skull into the ground. Something cracked.

The crowd roared.

Unsure whether Auctus was still alive, Indavara stood up and grabbed the trident.

Bonosus and his men hurried towards him, to ensure that the governor give the decision this time.

But Indavara was more interested in the burning rents in his back and shoulder than convention. With a one-handed jab, he buried the trident in Auctus's chest, then watched as the northerner's mouth fell open and his eyes rolled up into his head.

The crowd quietened. Bonosus looked around apprehensively; he had failed in his duty. This second breach of protocol turned eyes towards the podium. Sensibly, the governor waited. Shouts of approval – begun by Indavara's most ardent followers – grew swiftly into a tumult. Before long, the governor and those around him were applauding too.

Capito, now standing against the parapet, gestured for Bonosus and the other guards to follow Indavara towards the third section. He wished he was closer, to see how badly his fighter was injured. It was always so damned hard to tell with the rare few like Indavara; those who could not only take damage, but continue to fight long after most men would have fainted or given up.

Capito couldn't resist the urge to turn round. The slave-trader had moved to a spare seat just a few yards away. His face was set in a stony grimace.

A teenage slave arrived.

'Are you ready for the platform now, sir?'

'Raise it.'

Indavara touched his back. The trident holes were an inch deep; and a thin stream of blood issued steadily from each one. He twisted his body from side to side, then bent back and forth. The pain was no worse; it seemed there was no serious damage.

As he crossed the second rope, an enterprising supporter with an impressive throwing arm lobbed a gourd of water. It landed in the dust at Indavara's feet. He picked it up, removed the stopper and drank, idly watching as Auctus's body was carried away. He sloshed the remainder of the water over his wounded shoulder and back. The cheers reached a crescendo as he held the gourd up towards the supporter.

The messenger had reached the bowels of the arena, and now the order was given to raise the lifting platform. Sand slipped down over the edges of the five-yard-square gap created by the opening of the hatches. Then began the slow, creaking grind of the winches as the slaves set to work.

Indavara would have liked to avoid giving Capito the satisfaction of seeing him check the third barrel but he had to look. There was nothing there of course. He lashed out: a straight, solid kick that knocked the barrel on to its side. Facing a man with such a knife was one thing; facing a wild animal was another.

He watched the luminaries on the podium get to their feet, as eager as the rest of the crowd to see what would appear from below. The cage rose past him, covered with a huge grey sheet. Bonosus and his men closed in around it. When the platform reached the level of the arena, locking planks were hammered into place. The arena was quiet again. Indavara could hear the hurried breaths of the slaves below. Bonosus neared the cage and placed a single hand on the sheet.

Maesa began his final speech: 'Again our warrior has overcome great odds! Again he has triumphed! But now he faces his final challenge. The beast inside this cage is all that lies between him and freedom.'

Maesa halted for a moment, waiting for the cheers to pass.

'And what of this animal? It was captured just one week ago, in the high mountains of Dalmatia. A beast nine feet long, weighing over five hundred pounds. Within its mouth forty teeth, upon each paw claws three inches long. Behold . . .'

Bonosus pulled the sheet away.

'The bear!'

The crowd noise surged, then stuttered as they saw what Indavara faced.

The immense animal could hardly move. It had been forced to sit up on its hind legs – there was no space for it to settle on all fours. Indavara could not imagine how they'd forced it into the cage, though the small patches of glistening red on its light brown fur gave him a good idea. The bear was slobbering, and repeatedly knocking its head against the thick wooden bars; so hard in fact that one of them was coming loose. Then the beast poked its nose out, shiny nostrils flaring as it sniffed the air. The other bears Indavara had seen in the arena had been half this size: young or old; weak or diseased. But this one seemed in peak condition, with thick layers of flesh over its massive limbs.

Indavara looked despairingly at his blade. Yet more boos and jeers swept around the arena.

Capito sat down, thus making himself less of a target; the missiles aimed at him had become larger and more solid. Two young men tried to force their way over to him and had to be restrained by legionaries. Even some of the nobles shouted abuse. Capito shrugged.

Indavara was five yards from the cage. The side facing him was hinged at one end and functioned as a door. There was no lock, just a thick chain wrapped tight around the poles. Bonosus ordered two of his men to take it off. As they warily approached, the chief guard provided a distraction, poking his spear through the side of the cage and prodding the bear.

The animal growled a warning, then tried vainly to turn round. It pawed at one of the bars, claws scraping away slivers of wood. The anxious guards were making a poor job of loosening the chain.

Indavara suddenly felt a sick dread. Events had overtaken him. The legionaries were locking all the exits except the northern gate, the escape route for Bonosus and the guards once the bear was free. The only real cover he could use was the box. But it was a good thirty yards away.

The chain finally slid to the ground and the men pulled it free. Bonosus barked an order and they swung the door open, then hurried away. With one last jab, he turned and ran after them.

The animal swung a paw at the side of the cage, crushing one of the poles. It bucked backwards and then – realising it was free – half fell on to the sand.

Indavara backed away. He wanted the crowd as noisy as possible, but they had quietened so much that he could hear Bonosus still shouting orders as he neared the gate.

The bear righted itself, ran its nose into the dust, then looked up. Its beady eyes came to rest on Indavara. Then it ambled towards him, huge shoulders rolling above its head.

Indavara stayed absolutely still.

Teeth bared, lips trembling, the bear loosed a roar. Then it charged.

Indavara turned and bolted back across the second section as another wave of noise engulfed the arena. He had no idea how fast the bear was moving. He was aiming for the far corner of the box.

He saw his shadow flashing across the sand to his left.

Fifteen yards to the corner.

Arms and legs pumping, he sprinted along the side of the box. Ten yards. Five.

The noise was deafening. He readied himself to cut right, then glanced left again. A massive dark shape bore down on his shadow. He would not make it.

23

Indavara brought his hands up over his head and dropped to the ground.

The animal couldn't slow itself in time. One front paw struck Indavara and the bear tripped, flying over him, landing heavily in the sand, claws scraping the ground as it slid past the box.

Indavara was up quickly. He had taken a heavy impact on his back but felt only the sting of the trident wounds. Checking he still had the knife, he retreated back past the box, watching as the bear rolled over, shook itself down and got slowly to its feet. He looked inside the box to see if there was anything he might use as a weapon but there was nothing – not even a loose sword blade.

The bear sniffed its way over to where Spear had died.

Indavara glanced towards the northern end of the arena and realised instantly he had to get back there. He jogged backwards, eyes trained on the box; then crossed into the second section and moved left towards the eastern wall.

He was vaguely aware of people screaming his name, others shouting encouragements and suggestions, but this noise didn't register. He knelt down in front of the deer carcass. He had seen enough dead animals to know there was something here he could use. Just as he grabbed one of the rear legs, the bear's great head emerged from behind the box.

Looking down for as long as he dared, Indavara used the dagger to make an incision just above the deer's ankle bone. He dug around until he could see the tendon. Then he made another deep cut just below the back of the knee.

The bear was lumbering towards him now, nose close to the ground.

Indavara gripped the tendon, cut it away from the flesh, and pulled the pale stringy length from the leg. Then he stood, and calmly sliced more skin and hair away as he backed towards the cage.

The bear changed direction to follow him. What he feared more than anything was another charge. There was nothing but open ground behind him; the cage was too far away.

But the beast had picked up the smell of the deer and it now lolloped towards the wall. With only a cursory glance at Indavara, it sniffed the leg, then licked at some blood.

Still moving backwards, Indavara finished stripping the tendon. It was eight inches long, not as strong as it would be after days of drying but strong enough, he hoped. He tucked it and the dagger into his tunic.

As the bear stuck its snout into the deer's torn belly, Indavara reached the cage. The pole that the animal had struck was so broken as to be useless. The one next to it, however, was in good condition. Better still, it had come loose at the top; all he needed to do was get the bottom free. He wrapped both hands around the pole and twisted it from side to side, levering it away from the nails holding it in place.

The blow that had sliced off the top half of Indavara's ear had affected both his hearing and sense of balance. Over time, his sense of balance had somehow corrected itself but his hearing remained impaired. He could make out sounds to his left but they were often dulled and indistinct.

And so when someone in the crowd threw a bottle over the parapet, striking the bear's back, and sending it careering away towards the nearest living target on which to vent its rage, he didn't hear the thumping impacts of the huge paws. Though most within the arena saw the animal charge, their astonishment at its speed struck many of them dumb. Only a few managed to shout a warning in time. They saved Indavara's life.

He had almost wrenched the pole free when he turned. With one last heave, he threw himself to the ground just as the bear leapt.

The beast made a belated attempt to swipe at him but couldn't halt its charge. It crashed headlong into the cage, crushing most of two sides and knocking the entire structure end over end. Hardly seeming to notice, the bear raised itself up on its hind legs to its full height, towering over Indavara. Its whole body shuddered as it unleashed another roar.

Indavara was back on his feet. He clamped both hands on the pole and held it up in front of him.

The bear dropped to all fours and plodded towards him, snarling and salivating.

Indavara lowered the pole so that it was level with the bear's head. He retreated slowly, jabbing it forward as the animal pursued him. But its speed caught him out again, and one sweep of a paw struck the pole. Desperate to hang on to it, Indavara was knocked to the ground.

The bear lunged at him. Two claws tore flesh from his right calf. Crying out, he leapt to his feet and suddenly he was running again.

Every step jarred his wounded leg. His chances of outmaneuvering the bear had just dropped from minimal to non-existent. So he took the only option left. He ran towards the barrel he had earlier kicked over and darted inside, dragging one end of the pole in with him.

The crowd were confused. Some applauded their hero's resourcefulness, a few booed what appeared to be cowardice, others were disappointed that their man seemed beaten.

The bear was also perplexed. It circled the barrel, occasionally turning to lick the wounds on its neck.

As the moments of inactivity passed, people sat down and began to talk. Bonosus opened the northern gate and led his guards forward. They took up position behind what remained of the cage and watched as the bear neared the open end of the barrel, sniffing and peering warily inside. It retreated for a moment, then pawed lightly at the pole. There was no sign of Indavara. A hefty nudge from the bear's head spun the barrel around. Another shunt sent it rolling towards the wall. The bear trotted after it.

Hundreds of people swarmed to the parapet as the barrel gently collided with the wall. Legionaries pushed their way to the front to stop any more interventions.

Running its snout across the barrel, the bear moaned, then growled, frustrated it couldn't reach its prey. It rose up on its hind legs once more and a swat from its paw loosened one of the iron bands that held the planks together. The bear struck the barrel again and again, blows of such prodigious strength that in moments the other band was loose, and the barrel began to disintegrate.

The legionaries above had their work cut out trying to restrain the crowd, some of whom were ready to risk a blow from a sword pommel if they could somehow aim a missile at the animal and help their man.

The bear ambled around to the open end of the barrel and poked its head inside.

The wooden base at the other end flew off into the sand. A foot appeared, then a leg. Indavara wriggled free of what remained of the barrel and pulled himself clear, dragging the pole with him.

Except it was no longer a pole. It was now a makeshift spear, with the dagger lashed to one end by the length of tendon.

Those above were the first to notice. Cheers rippled around the arena.

Indavara moved sideways until the sun was directly above him. The bear trotted forward, wary of the pole swinging from side to side. Indavara waited until the animal seemed transfixed, then raised the pole high. Following the shining blade upward, the animal was momentarily blinded by sunlight.

Indavara took his chance. Lowering his grip, he darted two steps forward and drove the makeshift spear into the bear's chest. The dagger sank in as far as the handle. The beast yelped and shrank backwards.

Indavara pulled the pole free. The bear recovered itself and plodded forward. Indavara held his ground and jabbed for the eyes. The tiny knife missed them but sliced down the centre of the broad head, darkening the fur with blood. The bear stopped, then lunged forward again. Curved claws raked the underside of the pole but the weapon held together.

Indavara stayed on his toes, constantly shifting across the glaring sunlight, trying to confuse the bear further.

Now he used the other end of the pole as a club, smashing it twice against the bear's head. He caught an ear, and the animal seemed stunned for a moment. So he spun the pole over, then swept the makeshift spear towards its face once more, cutting across the smooth skin at its snout. Blood ran down into its eyes and dripped from its nose.

Enraged, the bear charged. Though Indavara had forgotten the pain in his injured leg, it buckled under him. He stumbled, and had only the time to get the pole up in front of him as the bear went for his throat.

The jaws snapped shut on the pole, splitting it in two. The bear twisted in the air and one great paw caught Indavara on the chest, slamming him to the ground.

He landed badly on his wounded shoulder, and knew a rib or two had gone. The dagger-end of the pole had landed close by but he found he could hardly move. The previously isolated points of pain on his body had fused into a pressing layer of agony that suddenly overwhelmed him. He knew with absolute certainty that at any moment he would feel teeth sink into his neck. For the first time that day, he could make out individual voices in the crowd. They implored him to fight, begged him to move. He wondered if the figurine was still secure inside his tunic. He wondered if the woman who'd given it to him was there.

He could not move.

Then he realised his eyes were shut. And when he opened them, he was looking at the bear, stretched out on the sand a few yards away. The animal couldn't see him. Blood was streaming down its face, forming puddles in the sand. It was blinking and pawing uselessly at its wounds, sniffing, trying to find him with its nose.

Hope returned, and with it a little strength. Indavara breathed in as much air as he could and got to his feet. He pulled the knife from its lashing and closed both hands around the tiny handle. Planting his feet close to the bear, he drove the blade down into the top of its head.

The beast moaned. Its eyes were glassy and still.

He stabbed the blade down again, into where he guessed the brain might be, then twisted it. The blade snapped off in his hand, and he collapsed to the ground once more.

He sat there, dwarfed by the vast mass next to him. Had there

28

been another weapon close at hand he would have struck again at the beast; plunged another blade into its skull, cut at its mouth, its eyes, its heart.

But the moment passed. And as the bear's great head finally slid into the dust, the rage dissolved. And he felt a kind of kinship for this poor, magnificent thing, forced to fight for its life for the amusement of others. And then something he had never felt after dispatching a human foe. Regret.

Capito was stunned by the noise. All around him people were leaping and shouting and crying. He turned, looking for one particular face. The slave-trader pointed at him, drew a finger across his neck, then disappeared into the crowd.

Indavara was dimly aware of Bonosus and the other guards around him. He struggled to his feet again. Blinking into the sunlight, he turned until he could see the northern gate. Then he felt inside his tunic. The figurine was there. He pulled it out and held it tight in his hand.

The guards made way as he limped towards the gate. The crowd began to throw money. Coins peppered the sand around him.

Indavara hardly noticed. He was occupied by a single thought. *Get to the gate. Get to the light.*

Centurion Maesa was already up by the podium, gathering the legionaries to restrain the hundreds rushing for the parapet above the northern gate.

Young Vitruvius was waiting for Indavara by the tunnel, holding some bandages he had torn from a sheet. The gladiator walked straight past him but the guard managed to hang the remains of the sheet about his shoulders. It stuck to his sweat-soaked body.

A small group lined the cold stone walls of the tunnel; more legionaries, pedlars waiting for the departing crowd, cleaners waiting to tidy up. Vitruvius hurried ahead and told the gate-keeper to open the second gate. Beyond lay the city streets.

For a moment, Indavara forgot the pain. He gazed at the golden glow ahead of him. This light seemed different to the light in the arena. Brighter. Warmer.

Vitruvius swung the gate open.

Indavara didn't miss a step. Tears slid down his filthy, bloody face as he passed beyond the iron bars.

Through the gate. Into the light.

I

September, AD 272

'I slaughtered three elephants and a giraffe in the arena on one day; and I was killed by a wrestler who strangled me in the bath.'

'Commodus, sir.'

'I'm detecting an air of boredom. Perhaps you tire of "Guess the emperor".'

'Not at all, sir. My turn: I once served a meal of six hundred storks, then ate every brain myself with a tiny golden pin.'

'Easy. Our old friend Elagabalus.'

'Quite right, sir.'

'Ah. Look there, a light. That must be it.'

Cassius Quintius Corbulo and his servant Simo had been riding south since morning. Night had brought a chill to the air and both men kept their cloaks clasped tight around their shoulders. The road was wide and well used, its edges marked by low banks of stones. To their left lay the sullen emptiness of the Syrian steppe; to their right a lake, its moonlit surface stretching far into the distance. There were few villages here, just the odd house built close to the water, usually attended by a small boat or two. Aside from the soft plodding of the horses' hooves and the thump and rattle of heavily loaded saddles, the only sound was the melodic chirrup of some unseen bird.

The ride was the last stage of an exhausting three-week journey. The letter demanding Cassius's return to Syria had made it clear his presence was required immediately. Departing from Cyzicus on the northern coast of Asia Minor, they had secured passage across the eastern end of the Mediterranean to Seleucia, the port that served Syria's capital, Antioch. A messenger had been awaiting them at the dock with a second letter summoning them south. They had hired horses and set off, journeying past the cities of Apamea, Larissa and Epiphania, staying in a selection of less than salubrious inns.

Approaching the city of Emesa on the sixth day out of Antioch, they turned east and passed right through the middle of a battle-field. Here, three months previously, the Emperor Aurelian had led his legions against a force of seventy thousand Palmyrans, finally smashing Queen Zenobia's military might. His army had then marched east and besieged Palmyra itself. The city now lay in Roman hands, the rebel queen on her way back to Rome in chains.

A rather overdramatic merchant's wife had told the two travellers that the sand of the battle-site was stained red as far as the eye could see, that an eerie sense of dread pervaded the land for miles around. Cassius and Simo had noticed neither. Anything of value had already been claimed by the victors or opportunistic locals. All that remained were the rotting corpses of thousands of Palmyran cavalry horses, still providing food for a colony of buzzards.

Two more days of riding had taken them into the middle of the bleak steppe. The instructions in the second letter directed them south from the Palmyra road, to the lake and an isolated inn – their final destination.

Cassius and Simo dismounted and led their horses towards the light. Cassius winced as he walked. His buttocks and thighs were sore, his back unspeakably stiff. He felt sure he would find dark purple bruises on his thighs later, and welts where sand had rubbed against his skin. He had never ridden so far, so fast.

Both men stopped. The light had moved. They soon realised it was a lantern, being carried towards them at speed. The horses tugged anxiously at their reins as the lamp-bearer approached. He turned out to be an unkempt, swarthy individual who perused the new arrivals with red-rimmed eyes.

'Your name?'

His Greek held a thick local accent.

'Corbulo.'

'Come.'

The man turned and hurried back towards the inn.

'A fine welcome,' muttered Cassius as they followed.

Once through the gate, the Syrian turned left towards a two-storey building of clay brick. Opposite was a stable block. The horses inside stirred, disturbed by the new arrivals. A young lad stumbled out of the darkness, wiping sleep from his eyes. He closed the gate, then came over and took both sets of reins.

'Careful,' Simo told him. 'They're tired.'

A dim light emanated from the doorway where the Syrian now stood. He gestured for them to enter. With Simo the customary three paces behind his master, they followed the man inside, ducking under a low beam into a smoky parlour.

Passing a stone staircase, they came to a wide bar stocked with all manner of bottles and amphorae. A large, bald man – presumably the innkeeper – sat there asleep, double chin resting on his chest as he quietly snored.

Opposite the staircase was a hearth surrounded by tables and stools. A raven-haired teenage girl knelt by the fire, taking logs from a woven basket. She turned to look at the men as they entered and Cassius caught sight of a fair, if rather rustic, face. Once she had checked that the innkeeper – her father perhaps – was still asleep, she gave a welcoming smile.

'I think I might warm my hands,' said Cassius, making for the fire.

The Syrian blocked his path. 'He's upstairs. Doesn't have all night.'

'I'm not entirely sure I care much for your manner.'

'His orders. Not mine.'

Cassius glared down at the man, then made his way back to the stairs.

'Not you.'

Cassius turned to find that now Simo's way had been barred by the Syrian's beefy arm. He poked the ruffian in the back.

33

'I've had about enough of you, my man. Who gave you the right or rank to inform an attendant of mine where he can and can't go?'

Before the man could reply, a deep, authoritative voice rang out from above.

'Actually I did. Please forgive Shostra there, he's yet to master a single social grace. Won't you come up? There's a mug of hot wine here for you.'

Cassius hesitated a moment, then shrugged. 'Perhaps you can rest by the fire for a bit, Simo.'

'I think I shall help the lad with the horses, sir.'

'As you wish.'

Simo departed. Cassius shot the Syrian a final glare then made his way up to the first floor. To the left was a cramped corridor leading to two more rooms. To the right was a space similar to the parlour below except that instead of a bar there were two wooden booths built against the wall. The single occupant was sitting in the far booth, his body angled towards the hearth.

The man who had summoned Cassius back to Syria; a man Cassius knew only by name and reputation.

As he entered, Aulus Celatus Abascantius stood up to greet him. He was of middling height but considerable width, especially in the heavily pock-marked face. The thinning hair was a curious mix of brown and grey. He looked about fifty but might have been a decade younger. As they gripped forearms, Cassius examined his extraordinarily tatty tunic and sandals.

It was hard to believe that the fellow before him was the Imperial Security Service's top man in Syria. Cassius knew the agent was regarded as something of a maverick but he hadn't expected him to so closely resemble a provincial merchant.

Abascantius ran a similarly inquisitive eye over the young man in front of him. Even after more than a week in the saddle, Cassius suspected he looked rather good. Thanks to Simo, his bright red tunic was fresh on that morning – finest Egyptian cotton. His boots were brand-new, bought especially for the trip. His thick military belt and the thinner, diagonal strap that held

34

his sword in place were also in good condition, the latter largely because it had been so rarely used. His light brown hair was well cut, his skin clear and perfumed. Of the many things Cassius appreciated most about Simo, the foremost was the Gaul's ability to maintain high standards in trying circumstances.

Abascantius sat down again and gestured to the bench opposite him. Cassius had no wish to sit close to the man but by the time he'd folded his rangy frame under the table, their knees were almost touching.

'Latin or Greek? Which shall it be?'

Cassius found the question odd. His Greek was fluent but officers of the Roman Army rarely used anything other than Latin.

'Up to you, sir.'

'Latin, I think. I need the practice.'

Abascantius switched languages.

'Perhaps I've been here too long.'

He took up an iron pot from close to the fire and filled a large wooden mug with steaming wine. Cassius pulled it closer as Abascantius topped up his own drink. The spices smelled good.

'Well, young Master Corbulo, it's taken me quite a while to track you down.'

Cassius had his answer ready. 'I can see how things might look, sir, but after what happened at Alauran, General Navio offered me a position with him. I remained with his staff when he was transferred to Cyzicus.'

'Transferred. An interesting choice of word. Demoted might be more apt.'

'I'm not aware of the intricacies of that situation, sir.'

Cassius tried not to look at the cluster of pale moles on Abascantius's left eyelid.

'You are aware though, I presume, of the events that have occurred in this province since your departure?'

'Of course.'

'And at no point did it occur to you to notify the Service of your new post, or your location?'

'It did, sir. But there was no one in Antioch for me to report to, what with the revolt. You yourself were . . .'

Abascantius leaned forward over the table. Cassius shifted back, not only because of the whiff of meaty breath.

'My location was, and is, no concern of yours. Do you know how many men the Service has this side of Cyprus? Eleven, including myself. Eleven men to guard the interests of the Empire and the Emperor. Eleven, though we should have had twelve. And all because you decided to take yourself off to sunny, peaceful Cyzicus!'

Well before the tirade was finished, Cassius had decided to stay quiet. It certainly didn't seem worth mentioning that the Palmyrans had actually got dangerously close to Cyzicus. Humility seemed the best option.

Abascantius stared at him a while longer, then the expression suddenly softened. He stood up and took his mug with him, knocking the table and spilling some of Cassius's wine. Abascantius looked down at the fire, his grinning face lit by the orange glow.

'I've waited a long time to say that. But I must admit I can't help admiring your gall. I doubt there's many of your rank between here and Rome who escaped action in the last two years. I suspect that week in the desert was more than enough for a fine young gentleman like yourself.'

Cassius looked down at the floor as Abascantius continued.

'Quite a triumph though. News of it spread right across the province. Outnumbered five to one, and it all came down to a duel between a guardsman and a master Palmyran sword-hand. What a tale!'

Cassius shrugged. 'Hardly mattered in the end, sir. The enemy took the fort a few months later anyway.'

'But you raised the spirits, Corbulo. Navio and his cronies made much of your victory. I dare say it bought him another few weeks. Clearly he was grateful.'

'I won't deny I was happy to find a way out of Syria, sir.'

Abascantius tilted his mug towards Cassius's chest. 'They gave you the silver medal, didn't they? Why don't you wear it?'

Cassius replied quickly. 'That battle was won by better and braver men than me. I do have the medal. But it's theirs, not mine.'

With a faint smile, Abascantius drank his wine.

'I have another question for you. Was she worth it?'

'Who, sir?' Cassius asked, though he knew.

'The magistrate's daughter. Welcomed you with open legs, by all accounts.'

Cassius felt his face reddening.

'Sorry,' said Abascantius unconvincingly. 'The provinces roughen one so.' He paused, tapping his fingers against the mug. 'Surely you must have known it would get back to Navio eventually?'

Cassius had known that. He had always known he was taking a massive risk that night in the governor's garden. Still, he thought of it almost every day, and couldn't quite bring himself to condemn his choice. He had found Marta alone, well away from the rest of the party-goers. He had been after her since arriving in Cyzicus. She was pretty rather than beautiful, but both elegant and voluptuous – a combination Cassius had never been able to resist. He really should have known better; it was the second time an ill-advised dalliance had set in motion a chain of events that had led him to Syria; and into danger. He stared gloomily down at the wine.

'Navio protected you,' Abascantius continued. 'Once I found out where you were, I wrote to him several times, but never once received a reply. You must have become quite useful to him.'

'Perhaps.'

'Oh, I'm certain of it. He's not the only person in Cyzicus I wrote to.'

Abascantius picked up a poker and shifted the burning logs around.

'Womanising aside, you were well thought of there. Some considered you a touch precious, arrogant even, but you completed your duties well. You refused the offers of several patrons and made no attempt to endear yourself to any particular faction.'

Cassius reddened again. Abascantius's sources were alarmingly accurate.

'And when the general called on you for some . . . special duties, you did very well. That's from him, by the way. Only when you disgraced yourself with the girl did he become amenable to the prospect of your departure.'

Abascantius paced in front of the fire, the poker still in his hand.

'Officially you were in charge of supply procurement and pay but on three separate occasions you solved some rather thorny issues for him: a hole in the accounts that led all the way to the top of the treasury; an arsonist you collared in less than a day; and a murderer you finally identified after personally interviewing every urchin on the city's streets. Quite the investigator.'

'I simply did what I was asked to do, sir.'

'The thing is, Corbulo, I have some able men under my command here – crafty, tough, unpleasant men. But they're all ex-legionaries. Not what one might describe as university material. Now – two years ago – when I heard I'd been given some cowardly young dolt simply because his father wanted to keep him out of trouble, I was less than enthusiastic. In fact, I was inclined to send you to the nearest available legion as a rank and filer. But it seems that you are not entirely unintelligent, and that you have a knack of getting to the bottom of things. Better still, your face is not known in these parts. I can make good use of you.'

'I don't know what you have in mind, sir, but—'

'We'll get to that.'

Abascantius hesitated a moment, then jabbed the poker towards Cassius. 'It sounded like you were about to protest then, Corbulo. I advise against it. You have absented yourself from the Service for over a year and a half. Chief Pulcher knows I've found you but it's up to me how I present your story to him. One explanation might be an administrative foul-up: lost orders, a miscommunication perhaps. You weren't with us but you were doing your duty nonetheless. Happens all the time. Perfectly feasible. After all – there was a war on.'

Abascantius tilted his head from one side to the other.

'Another explanation might be plain, simple, good old-fashioned desertion. The wilful neglect of a soldier's sworn duties. Also happens all the time.'

Abascantius replaced the poker by the fire, returned to the table and stood over Cassius.

'So which is it to be?'

'The former sounds preferable, sir.'

'Infinitely, I should say.'

Abascantius moved closer.

'Do you know how I have spent the last two years, Corbulo? Riding. The Palmyrans pushed us back a thousand miles, then we pushed *them* back. The lines could change in days, hours. And all the while, someone had to keep the governors and the generals and the Emperor advised of what was happening. And then do their bidding; even though they disagreed more than they agreed. And every single day there was someone to see, something to do, somewhere to go. Riding, riding, riding. I'm getting old. My stomach gets fatter and my arse just gets bonier – so I don't like to ride.'

He pointed at Cassius. 'You owe the Service, Corbulo. And you owe me. You should be grateful that I am offering you a chance to redeem yourself.'

Cassius slid off the bench and stood. Even during his most relaxed, peaceful periods in Cyzicus, he had always known this moment would come. He pressed his tunic down and nodded formally to Abascantius.

'What is it you require of me, sir?'

'We'll get to that. First we shall eat.'

II

Midnight was long past when Cassius finished his meal. It was simple but tasty fare: cold lamb with bread and cheese, then some dried pears and pistachio nuts – one of his few pleasant associations with Syria. Abascantius had wolfed down his food, then disappeared downstairs. The young girl had brought up wood for the fire, but Cassius had felt too morose even to strike up a conversation. Simo came later, carrying their saddlebags. The Gaul announced that the horses were settled for the night, then set about preparing the rooms reserved for them – the two chambers on the other side of the stairs.

Cassius pushed his plate away just as Abascantius returned. The agent was clutching a leather satchel and a long object wrapped in cloth. He thumped both down on to the table as he reclaimed his seat opposite Cassius.

'To the matter at hand then. You must consider what I will tell you most secret. On occasion you may have to disclose parts of it – then you must use your own judgement. Understood?'

'Yes, sir.'

'In Antioch, on the last day of this month, I am to meet with Marshal Marcellinus and the four members of the city's council. Like most of our esteemed military men, Marcellinus despises the Service and – for various reasons – me in particular. He's been given complete autonomy over the eastern provinces and will tolerate my involvement only because the Emperor charged me with one important task.'

Cassius found it hard to imagine Aurelian entrusting any job whatsoever to the dishevelled character in front of him, but he reminded himself that Abascantius had been in Syria for more than a decade. He had served under four emperors and outlasted three governors. Perhaps his appearance worked to his advantage; it was difficult to overestimate him.

'Aurelian left for Rome as soon as he'd finished treaty negotiations with the Persians. Gifts were exchanged, a few clauses agreed; all remarkably smooth. With the Palmyrans taken care of, the last thing we need is another conflict with our old adversaries to the east. Now, most of Zenobia's treasures went with the Emperor – some thirty cart-loads I'm told. All that was left in Palmyra was a cache of jewels, trinkets, silver and gold for the provincial coffers in Antioch. It was to be returned inside one large cart, packed in barrels. But one of the barrels contained something more valuable than the rest of the booty put together. It is a flag, but no ordinary flag. Does the term Faridun's Banner mean anything to you?'

'The Persian imperial standard.'

Abascantius nodded approvingly. 'Very good.'

'One of my neighbours in Cyzicus had a fine library, with several translated tomes on the rulers of the east.'

'What else do you know?'

'Not much. Faridun was an ancient king. A hero who embodied the virtues of courage, justice, nobility and so on. A familiar tale.'

'Indeed. And a sacred one to the Persians. They believe the standard represents their destiny, their fate. I've never seen it myself but apparently it's a great purple thing of the finest silk, with jewels the size of apples. It's been carried at the head of their army since the time of Ardashir I. But when Odenathus of Palmyra's forces overran Ctesiphon ten years ago, his armies looted the city and took the flag back with them.'

Abascantius paused to take another swig of wine.

Cassius nodded. 'Let me guess: the return of the banner is part of the treaty.'

'A crucial part. And a secret one. I'm told that only a few men close to the royal family even know the flag was taken by the Palmyrans. We think they may have been using a replica; the people certainly don't know of the loss. The young Emperor, Hormizd, is desperate for its return. His position is far from secure and he's paranoid that the truth will come out. A closed ceremony is being planned for the day after my meeting. Marcellinus is to hand the flag over to Hormizd himself. Without it, the Persians won't sign the treaty.'

Abascantius looked at the ceiling and rolled his tongue around his mouth.

Cassius said, 'I presume that the banner is not where it should be.'

'The cart should have left Palmyra twelve days ago. In command was my senior man – Gregorius, accompanied by ten hand-picked legionaries. They were to travel in local garb, just another merchant's load on its way to Antioch. There is a good road, but he planned to use a quieter route. Should have taken them eight days. But there has been no news, no sighting, no reports. The men, the treasure and the banner have disappeared.'

Cassius leaned back and exhaled. 'I hardly need ask what you expect of me.'

'Actually I originally had something else in mind for you, but it seems the gods have delivered you to me at a fortuitous moment.'

'Sir, I don't know why you imagine I might be suited to such a task. Surely you yourself—'

Abascantius held up a hand. 'The loss of the banner is my responsibility, yes. And believe me, I will do my part. But you must understand how it is here. My face is known on every street and in every inn and barracks from Seleucia to Dura. The legionaries call me "Pitface", and they – along with many of the locals – would no sooner divulge anything useful to me than eat their own shit. You, on the other hand – a fresh-faced young gentleman from outside the province – should fare much better.'

Abascantius tapped the satchel. 'I have an authorisation here for you, signed by Chief Pulcher. And there's this.'

Abascantius reached over to the covered item and removed the cloth. What he held up on the table could easily have been mistaken for a weapon: it was a three-foot length of solid silver topped by a spear-head, with two circles beneath hung with golden thread. Just below the circles was a square iron badge, engraved with the emblem of the Governor of Syria.

'These are carried by every senior agent in the Service. It identifies you as a member of the governor's staff and entitles the bearer to certain privileges. While in possession of it, you hold a rank equivalent to a centurion; you may use way-stations and the imperial post; and you can requisition troops when you need them. There are fewer than a hundred of this particular type in existence. This belongs to Gregorius. He left it with me.'

Cassius took the spear-head and laid it down on the table. 'I hope I get a chance to return it to him.'

'Look after it, and don't be afraid to use it. I suggest that you avoid mentioning me if at all possible; pretend you've been dispatched straight from Rome by Chief Pulcher.'

'Marshal Marcellinus knows of the theft?'

'Not yet, though I may have to inform him at some point.'

Cassius could understand his reluctance. The Emperor's deputy would surely be delighted to hear of a ready-made reason to discredit Abascantius. Emperors had been using the Service to spy on the army for years, the main reason why most military men regarded its agents with such contempt. Though the strength of the bond between Aurelian and Marcellinus was well known, the fact that the Emperor had used Abascantius for this assignment reinforced a historical truth: the Service had a far better record of loyalty to Roman emperors than the army did.

Abascantius sighed loudly. 'I fancy the ultimate solution to this may lie in Antioch, so I shall return there tomorrow. Aside from myself, Gregorius and Prefect Venator – who supplied the legionaries – the only men who knew about the cart were Marcellinus himself and the four members of the council. He swore them all to secrecy – on pain of death if I know him – but I've little doubt one of them is involved somehow.'

'In a theft of imperial property?'

'Stranger things have happened. The council may resent my interest in their personal affairs but at times like this it becomes extremely useful.'

'And what of this Gregorius? Isn't it possible that he—'

Abascantius shook his head vigorously. 'Not a chance. His loyalty is not in question. Besides, he's worked for me long enough to know the consequences of betrayal.'

'How much were the contents of that cart worth?'

'Not including the flag – over ten thousand aurei.'

Cassius blew out his cheeks. It was an astronomical sum – enough to buy an army or a fleet of ships. 'Sufficient to risk the consequences of betrayal then.'

'You don't know Gregorius. I do. He would have taken every precaution necessary. He has never let me down.'

'What about the legionaries he used, couldn't they have decided to do away with him and take the treasure for themselves?'

'I gave strict instructions. They were to be strangers from different cohorts: none of the men knew each other. They were all to be Italians, decorated veterans only, each personally recommended by their centurions. No, the answer doesn't lie there.'

'What about locals? Brigands? There must still be Palmyran soldiers scattered all across Syria.'

'They were to travel only at night, they were to—' Abascantius abruptly halted his explanation. 'Do you think I didn't consider all this?' he yelled, slamming his hand on to the table. 'Do you think I was born yesterday?' He stared at Cassius, bloodshot eyes wide.

'Of course not, sir. My apologies.'

Abascantius took a few breaths. The impact of his hand had sent the satchel to the far edge of the table, close to the window. He dragged it back towards him and smoothed the edges down. Then he placed it carefully in front of Cassius, shifting it around until it was parallel with the side of the table.

'I make no claim to be infallible. You are right to put such questions. And now you must seek some answers.'

'Sir, I should explain that I do not really consider myself a man of action. I have been in battle, yes, and I took on the odd criminal case for the general, but any group well-informed and well-organised enough to carry out this theft represents a considerable threat. What am I to do if I actually track them down?'

'In the first instance contact me – but that will take time. Remember that you can take command of any nearby units if you need them.'

'That entitlement sounds impressive on paper, sir; the reality might be somewhat different.'

'I am also providing you with some additional help: a professional bodyguard, also from outside the province. Bit dense but he knows how to handle himself. He was on a job for me in the north but should be down here by now. You are to meet him the day after tomorrow, at an inn called The Goat's Leg. It's in the village of Galanea, just south of Palmyra – run by an old ex-legionary. Close by is the encampment of the Fourth Legion; they're stationed there to deter any chance of an uprising. I suggest you go straight to Prefect Venator.'

'Does he know about the theft?'

'Not yet. You will have to tell him.'

Cassius rubbed his brow.

'Don't worry. Venator's a good old-fashioned aristocrat, I'm sure you'll get on fine. I doubt Gregorius told him much of his plans but he used his men so he may have let something slip. You have to start somewhere. Chief Pulcher has a saying: "Someone always knows something."'

Abascantius pushed the leather satchel towards Cassius.

'For you. Information. If you've any more questions, you'll need to be up early; I shall head off soon after dawn. I suggest you do the same – you've another long ride ahead of you.'

Abascantius stood. He glanced thoughtfully around the room for a moment, then ran a hand across his paunch.

'The handover ceremony takes place in nineteen days. I don't even want to think about the consequences of Marcellinus having nothing to hand over. Goodnight, Corbulo.'

'Goodnight, sir.'

Cassius sat motionless as Abascantius left and made his way downstairs. He eyed the satchel and was struck by an almost irresistible desire to throw it into what remained of the fire. A cool draught whispered through the shutters and across the back of his neck. He shivered, then slowly shook his head. He felt numb, overwhelmed by what he'd heard.

There had been time to get used to the prospect of a return to Syria, of working for the Service; but nothing could have prepared him for the magnitude of the task he'd been charged with. How he wished he'd never heard the name Abascantius. It would have been far more convenient if the accursed man had somehow perished during the Palmyran revolt. The loss of the banner was his fault, yet now he expected Cassius to tidy up his potentially disastrous mess? If it couldn't be done, Abascantius wouldn't be the only one to suffer, he was sure of that. And who did he have to help him? Some brute of a bodyguard he was sure to detest.

With one elbow on the table, hand propping up his chin, Cassius took a deep breath and tried to find a way through the mass of thoughts about what he faced; but his tired, addled mind soon gave up, and in the darkness he closed his eyes.

He drifted back to Cyzicus – to the idyllic atrium at his villa on the edge of the city, where he'd often look out beyond the grey-barked fig trees to a village well and watch the people come and go. He would get most of his work done by lunchtime, then spend the afternoons there with books from his neighbour's library. He had reintroduced himself to the works of the great orators and was determined to take up his aborted legal career if he ever made it back to Italy.

The villa had been his sanctuary, a poor second to his family home in Ravenna, but a sanctuary nonetheless. And when he wasn't reading Cicero or Cato or Plutarch, there were the letters from his family. Those from his mother and sisters were welcome but it was the missives from his father he would tear open, desperate for signs that his ire had dimmed. Recently, there'd been a few intimations that he'd begun to forgive Cassius's indiscretions, but not one suggestion that he might release his son from military service: reverse his demand that Cassius serve five years.

Cassius had always known that was unlikely; his father was not one to go back on his word. He was a compassionate and loving man, but a true Roman patriarch, and he ruled his family with an iron hand. So when Cassius had disgraced himself with his aunt's serving girl, Corbulo senior had taken swift, decisive action. His errant only son would – like his father – serve in the military, where he would learn the value of discipline and the paramount importance of doing one's duty.

Recently there had been talk of a visit home, largely from his mother, but Cassius knew that once he set foot back on Italian soil, he would not be able to bring himself to leave again; and that would mean yet more disgrace.

He had resolved simply to live day by day – endure the weeks and months as best he could. All his family and friends knew what he had done, the price he had been asked to pay; and if he wished to return and regain their respect, he would have to see out the five years. There were still two and a half to go.

The truth was, having somehow evaded death during the siege of Alauran, he had been lucky to avoid further danger for so long. There was a strange kind of relief at being found out. To return home with tales only of a comfortable life in Cyzicus would have been its own particular kind of shame. His family still knew little of what had happened at Alauran; he had tried to write an account of those events a dozen times but the words simply never came.

Cassius stood. The darkness seemed suddenly oppressive. He picked up the satchel and the spear-head and looked down at the glowing embers of the fire. Small lumps of charred wood lay beneath a large log that had somehow failed to take light. As the moments passed, more of the embers holding the log in place burned away, until it suddenly thumped down, expelling charcoal and dust from the grate, extinguishing the flame.

III

Cassius hadn't slept well since leaving Cyzicus; and that night he didn't sleep at all. Even if the revelations of the evening hadn't been enough to occupy him, there were in any case sufficient alien sounds to keep him awake. Not the low wheeze of Simo's snoring – he was well used to that – but the night-time breeze created an eerie whistle as it brushed through the reeds and lapped the water against the bank. Worse still, Shostra and the innkeeper stayed up most of the night: drinking, singing and laughing. Cassius might have quietened them down if he'd thought there was any possibility of him actually falling asleep.

He rose shortly after the sun, deciding his time was better spent examining the materials Abascantius had given him. Knowing he would need Simo on good form in the next few days, he decided to let him sleep. Leaving his boots at the end of his bed, he pulled on his tunic, grabbed the satchel and headed downstairs. No one else was up.

He found a nice spot around the back of the inn where a path ran close to the water. He sat back against the rear wall and looked out at the lake. It was incredibly wide here; he couldn't see the far side. A flat-bottomed boat was marooned on reeds just in front of him. Eating bright green weed from its hull were a duck and four chicks.

Cassius opened the satchel. First out was a bundle of papyrus papers held together by twine. The first sheet gave what he presumed to be Abascantius's home address in Antioch. The second consisted of some notes on Gregorius: his full name, a physical description and a code word he would recognise. The third sheet was the letter of authorisation from Chief Pulcher in

48

Rome, complete with his personal seal. The fourth named the bodyguard and gave instructions for his payment; Cassius was to give him a quarter when he met him, Abascantius would give him the rest later. The fifth sheet was a manifest of the cart's contents: a list of the trinkets and jewellery, totals for the number of gold and silver ingots. Cassius made a few quick calculations and a mental note. On the sixth sheet was a sketch of the Persian banner, on the seventh some renderings of specific pieces from the hoard.

The eighth sheet was folded over twice and made of thicker, more durable papyrus. It was a map of Syria – in fact one of the best maps Cassius had ever seen – with all major settlements and roads marked. In one corner was a date: the map was just a few months old; and it bore the emblem of the military cartographer's office. Like most army maps, natural features were represented by icons next to main roads, never as impediments to Roman routes. Using his thumb for scale, Cassius calculated that Palmyra was about forty-five miles away.

There was also a smaller sheet: a receipt with space for Cassius to mark his name. It stated that the heavy bag at the bottom of the satchel contained one hundred silver denarii. Cassius took it out and weighed it in his hand. The money would certainly prove useful but he was worried about carrying it around the wastes of southern Syria with only Simo for company.

The big Gaul didn't lack courage, but – like Cassius – he simply wasn't the warrior type. There wasn't an animal or human alive he wouldn't help if he saw them in distress. Cassius had even noticed his depressed mood on the days he'd had to kill a chicken for dinner.

He replaced the money and the papers in the satchel and put it to one side. Smiling at the chicks as they paddled around the boat after their mother, he rested his head back against the wall and closed his eyes. After a while he heard voices from the courtyard: Shostra and the innkeeper, then Simo, then Abascantius. He listened. He listened until he had to admit to himself that he wasn't just listening: he was hiding, and this thought propelled him to his feet. He had hidden long enough.

———8———

Abascantius was taking breakfast with the innkeeper. They were sitting on a low bench, picking at plates of fruit, idly observing the stable-lad cleaning a saddle. A line running across the court-yard split shade and sun.

Cassius had sent Simo up to pack. He handed the signed receipt to Abascantius, who tucked it into a small purse at his belt.

'Sir, I've a couple more questions.'

Abascantius touched the innkeeper's arm and nodded towards the stables. The Syrian obediently wandered away.

'Well?'

'Where was the flag was being kept before Gregorius took charge of it?'

'It had been hidden in a crypt under an abandoned temple. Apparently some centurion found it.'

'And this cart . . .' Cassius chose his words carefully, even though the innkeeper was out of earshot. 'Its . . . contents . . . would be unusually heavy. You're sure he planned to use only the one vehicle?'

'Yes, just the one. But you're right – it would have to be on the large side. You might be able to use that.'

'And if I pressed you for an opinion, sir? Who do you believe might be responsible?'

Abascantius had been about to eat a date but he now put it down and leaned back against the inn wall.

'I have some thoughts, but I shall not share them with you now. I do not wish to prejudice your work. A good investigator must approach these things with an open mind. Anything else?'

'Not at the moment, sir.'

Abascantius stood and went inside. Hooves clattered against the courtyard flagstones as the lad led a horse from the stable. Simo then exited the inn, both arms laden down with saddlebags.

'Sir, I've also arranged some food and water for the road.' He nodded at the satchel. 'Shall I take that?'

'No, I'll keep hold of this.' Cassius slipped the thick leather strap over his shoulder. 'Have you settled up?'

'No need,' said the innkeeper as he passed them, 'Master Abascantius has taken care of it.'

'Ah. Can you have a look at this for me?'

The innkeeper dutifully followed Cassius to a sun-soaked corner of the courtyard. Cassius pulled the map from the satchel and held it up against the wall.

'Where exactly are we?'

The innkeeper pointed to the northern edge of a large, unnamed lake. 'Here.'

Cassius moved aside to avoid close contact with the man's protruding stomach.

'Best route to Palmyra?'

'Keep to the lake track for two miles then bear north-east and you'll soon pick up the main road again. Should pass the boundary line about midday.'

'Boundary of what?'

'The territories of Emesa and Palmyra. It's just a line of stones running north to south. Good marker though. There are mile-stones too.'

'Might we make it before sundown?'

The innkeeper bobbed his head from side to side. 'Not much rain recently. You've two good horses there. Might do it, I suppose.'

'Accommodation?'

'There are a few inns. Army way-stations too. Not sure if they're back up and running though.'

Cassius and Simo had passed several of the way-stations since leaving Antioch. They were typically converted houses or inns with stables, manned by a few legionaries and slaves. Their main function was to facilitate the imperial post but some had lodgings for officers and men passing through. Cassius had seen a few burned to the ground, others had been damaged and defaced. Only a few had been reoccupied.

Despite Zenobia's defeat, Roman control of the province was far from complete. The large cities were once more at heel, but it would take months to fully restore order, transport, trade and communications.

'Anything else?' asked the innkeeper.

'No.'

Shostra and the stable-lad had two horses saddled and ready to leave. It wasn't difficult to see which was Abascantius's animal: the stallion was tall and stout, with a glossy black coat.

Its owner returned. He and the innkeeper stared admiringly at the horse and exchanged comments in Aramaic. Abascantius now wore a light, hooded robe over his tunic; and there was something rather disconcerting about the way the hood framed his broad, puffy face.

'Last chance then: any more queries?' he asked Cassius as Shostra attached the last of their saddlebags and the lad opened the gate.

'Just the one, sir. What if I don't get anywhere? What if I find out nothing?'

'Have a little self-belief, Corbulo. You're the hero of Alauran. Start acting like it.'

With an ironic grin, Abascantius took his reins from the lad and mounted up with surprising agility. He gestured for Shostra to ride out first, then caught Cassius's eye again.

'If you need an added incentive, I should perhaps remind you that the Service is also responsible for running military prisons. I understand there's a vacancy at a quarry outside Thessalonica. Two and a half thousand Goths live and work there, guarded by a garrison of just three centuries. The last governor was killed in a riot. Chief Pulcher's after a young, thrusting type to replace him. Feeling more inspired now?'

'Yes, sir.'

'Good. Only eighteen days until the handover now. Don't waste a moment.'

With a warm smile for the innkeeper, Abascantius tapped down on his horse's flank and rode out of the courtyard.

———◆8◆———

The track that ran along the lake was of smooth, compacted earth, and Cassius and Simo made swift progress. Insects hovered over the reeds and the water, and occasionally swept by or followed the horses for a while. The temperature was perfect for riding: the two men wore only tunics, their skin cooled by a thin morning mist.

The horses seemed well refreshed after their night's rest. They were both fine animals, hired at considerable expense. Cassius's was the larger of the two, a rangy grey; Simo's a stockier chestnut. They were both mares, and seemed to get on well, occasionally nudging each other as they walked along side by side.

Cassius glanced across at Simo. Though he worked all day long and never seemed to eat much, the Gaul was a heavy man, and he'd added several pounds during their time in Cyzicus. Cassius was convinced he'd lost a few of those already, just as he had during their last trip to the Syrian interior. He wondered how much of it was down to exertion, how much to anxiety.

Like all slaves, Simo was expert at concealing his feelings. Since their departure, he hadn't given a single inkling of what Cassius felt sure must be profound disappointment at having to leave their settled life in Cyzicus, or betrayed his fears about what this sudden change in their fortunes might bring.

'It seems that once again you must share in my bad luck, Simo.'

The Gaul sat a little higher in his saddle, and flicked at a fly buzzing around his head. He said nothing.

'I did say the good times couldn't last, didn't I?'

'You did, sir. You did.'

'You miss it, I dare say? The villa, the other staff. Your life there.'

Simo straightened his tunic sleeve and smiled blandly. 'When you purchased me from Master Trimalchio I understood that I would share both fortune and misfortune alike, sir. Such is the lot of a slave.'

'Ever the diplomat, Simo. Ever the diplomat.'

Buying Simo the previous winter had almost bankrupted Cassius – and he'd also needed a hefty loan from his father – but he believed the investment was worthwhile. He could forgive the Gaul's occasional unexplained disappearances and his strange obsession with helping others, because he looked after him fantastically well. Skilled, bright, loyal slaves were hard to find.

Though he would never admit it, Cassius felt a modicum of guilt for what he had put Simo through. The Gaul had been a respected deputy to his first master, a valued part of the merchant's business, but all that had ended two years ago when Trimalchio had generously lent him to his old comrade's errant son. Within days, Simo found himself at a remote desert fort, facing hundreds of rampaging Palmyran rebels alongside Cassius and the rest of the garrison.

Those few terrible days aside, however, once they'd arrived in Cyzicus with General Navio's retinue, life had been good. Now, though, they were pretty much back where they started. Simo knew about the indiscretion that had led to his master joining the army but Cassius wasn't particularly keen to explain that a similar 'moment of weakness' had landed them in this new predicament.

'If it makes you feel any better,' he said, 'having one's destiny dictated by the whim of others is a concept I am well able to understand.'

'I suppose we all must do our duty, sir.'

'Quite.'

'I gather we are bound for Palmyra, sir?'

'Indeed. Our task can be summarised simply enough: we are to embark on a treasure hunt.'

By noon, they had passed twelve milestones on the Palmyra road. Many of these had been defaced by crude graffiti: first by

Zenobia's triumphant warriors, more recently by passing legionaries eager to mark newly reclaimed territory. As they were making good time, Cassius decided to stop for some food.

'Here, Simo, some shade for our meal. We might find a trough for the horses too.'

Cassius coaxed his mount off the road and down a slope towards a ramshackle farmhouse. Leaning back in his saddle as his horse descended, he saw that the settlement was made up of two mud-brick buildings. The rear of the smaller one had half collapsed. A startled goat bolted from under its timbers and scampered round a corner.

Cassius and Simo followed the animal into a courtyard. The damaged building was a stable. Next to it was a longer, larger structure. The stable was empty, but tethered to the doors were two saddled horses and a third yoked to a cart. Wary of the interlopers, they shuffled anxiously and strained against the ropes. The cart was half-full with dust-covered sacks.

'Wheat, sir.'

Cassius nodded. On the back of the cart was a metal plate, identifying it as the property of the Second Cohort, Fourth Legion. Cassius looked again at the empty stable, then at a line of washing hanging across one corner of the courtyard.

'What is it, sir?' asked Simo.

They heard what sounded like someone kicking a door. Then a woman's cry, suddenly muffled.

Both men looked at the building ahead. There was only shadow beyond the low windows. Of the two doors, one was shut. The other, wide and made of thin timbers, was slightly ajar.

At Cassius's signal, they dismounted quietly. To their right were the remains of a long-abandoned plough. Cassius gestured for Simo to follow and led his horse over to it, looping the reins around a heavy iron bar. Tightening his sword belt, he nodded at one of his saddlebags.

'Bring the spear-head,' he said. 'And be ready with your dagger.'

Cassius again examined every window in turn, then started towards the open door. The whole courtyard was covered in

55

wheat dust. Ahead of him was a jumble of footmarks. He was five yards away when the door flew open. A young, smiling legionary walked out.

'Good morning!' he said, stumbling as his scabbard slapped against his leg. 'Good morning, sir,' the legionary added, noting the colour of Cassius's tunic. 'How are you?'

Cassius looked past him into the gloom. 'Name?'

The man could barely stand upright. Blinking into the sun, he pawed at his clammy face.

'Give me your name, soldier.'

Simo was now at Cassius's side. The legionary slowly transferred his gaze to the Gaul, then back to Cassius.

'Your name?'

The legionary shook his head.

Cassius indicated that Simo should watch the man, then walked past him.

'Hey!'

Before the legionary could move, Cassius bellowed at him, 'You stay there!'

Though he hadn't been a field officer in Cyzicus, Cassius now had two years' experience of dealing with junior ranks and he had perfected a deep, imperious tone for such occasions. He imagined his theatre teacher back in Ravenna would have been most proud.

The legionary did as he was told.

Cassius entered the building. Inside the cool, murky interior was a grain press: a large stone slab with a roller mounted on one side. To his left was a closed door. He saw movement in the shadows to his right. He gripped his sword handle but didn't draw the blade.

'Come out of there at once.'

First to appear was a tiny old woman, little more than four feet tall. She was barefoot and clad in dusty robes. She received a hefty shove in the back from the second figure, an older legionary with a thick beard and very little hair. The old woman fell to her knees and began wailing in Aramaic.

56

'Outside. Now,' Cassius ordered.

The legionary fixed him with a stare, then nonchalantly joined the other man.

The old woman was still on her knees and still wailing. Cassius took another quick look around then walked outside, past the men. He could smell the wine on them. He went and stood next to Simo once more.

'Will *you* give me your name?'

The second soldier was at least able to formulate a reply. 'Caesar. Julius.'

The younger man giggled.

'What are you doing here?' Cassius asked.

'Grain requisition.'

The second legionary reached into his belt and offered Cassius a scrappy sheet of papyrus. Cassius came forward and took it. An order for the grain had indeed been scrawled by one Optio Rullus.

'Well, since I now know the name of your legion, cohort and optio you may as well give me yours.'

The older legionary took a breath before answering. 'Nennius.'

Then the younger man spoke up. 'I'm Papus.'

'You have your grain. Why aren't you already back on the road?'

'Just taking a little break before the return journey. You know how it is.' Nennius offered what he clearly believed to be an engaging smile.

'Tell your friend to come out,' Cassius said calmly.

'Sir?'

'Your friend. There are three of you here.'

Nennius looked over at the horses. 'No, sir, that mount is a spare.'

Cassius nodded at the building. 'I saw all the footmarks in there. He's behind that door to the left. With the daughter, I expect.' Cassius pointed across the courtyard. 'The old woman didn't hang the clothes on that high washing-line.'

'You're wrong, sir.'

'Let's see, shall we?'

Cassius took two steps before Nennius blocked his way. Papus sidled into position behind him, hand on his sword pommel.

'I tell you you're wrong,' repeated Nennius.

'Do you know what that is, legionary?' asked Cassius, aiming a thumb at Simo.

The Gaul held the spear-head up. It took Nennius a while to process this new development. He looked back at Papus. The younger man shrugged.

'I see you do,' Cassius continued. 'Tomorrow I am to meet with the commander of your legion, Prefect Venator. I'm sure he'll be most interested to hear of this encounter. Optio Rullus too.'

Now Nennius moved his hand towards his sword.

Cassius swiftly decided on a different approach.

'However, if you three get on your horses and leave at once, this need go no further.'

Nennius let out an anxious sigh. Papus – at least aware that he was too drunk to make a decision – shrugged again.

After what seemed an eternity, Nennius nodded slowly, then scratched at his nose.

'Come out, Vulso!'

Cassius heard a door open inside, then soft footsteps. The tall, wiry legionary who appeared was carrying his boots in one hand, his belts and weapons in the other. His state of inebriation seemed to be somewhere between the other two. There were livid scratches on his neck and face.

'Morning,' Cassius said evenly. Another thing he had learned in the last two years was the value of civil formality, even when dealing with infantrymen.

Cassius would have preferred to take on the other two than Vulso alone. Despite the drink, Cassius noted the immaculate state of his belt and scabbard. He looked like a man who loved his weapons; and men who loved their weapons usually loved using them.

'You lads were involved in the fighting, I expect,' Cassius said. Silence.

'Emesa? Immae?'

'Both,' said Nennius.

'And quite rightly you feel entitled to a little reward. Fair enough. But that's what whore-houses are for. I'm sure Palmyra has its share.'

Vulso nodded towards the building. 'You haven't seen her.'

'To the victor the spoils, sir,' offered Nennius.

'The spoils of war do not extend to indiscriminate rape. Not among the armies of Rome at least. But if you go now, you have my word that news of this will not reach your superiors.'

Nennius and Vulso exchanged glances, then shrugged. Vulso bent over and put his boots on, then he and Nennius walked away towards the stable.

'I don't get a turn?' asked Papus.

'I didn't even get mine,' Vulso replied over his shoulder. 'Was hard enough to get the feisty little bitch on the ground.'

It seemed to take forever for the three legionaries to mount up. Whenever they exchanged a word, Cassius feared one of them was pointing out that it was two against three; that they could easily do away with the young officer and his servant, then do as they pleased and hide the evidence of their crimes.

But after a few wary looks at Cassius, they eventually rode out of the courtyard.

As soon as the cart disappeared, Simo hurried into the building. Cassius led both horses over to a trough by the stable. He was sweating heavily. He looked down at the moist cotton under his arms. He hated sweating.

Once the horses had had their fill, he took a drink from his canteen and went to fetch Simo. Behind the door was an empty storeroom. The old woman was kneeling over the girl, Simo beside her. The girl was indeed pretty, though no more than thirteen or fourteen; and Cassius realised that she was in fact the old woman's granddaughter. Her face was marked around her mouth, her nose bloodied. She was whimpering; and when she caught sight of Cassius, she pulled her knees up under her chin and wrapped her arms around her legs.

'Come, Simo,' said Cassius.

'She needs help, sir,' said the Gaul.

'Her grandmother can help her.'

'Just a few moments more, sir.'

'No. Not one moment more.'

Simo spoke a few more words of Aramaic, then stood. Cassius was almost outside when the old woman scuttled after him, threw herself at his feet again and grabbed his tunic. Simo put a hand to her shoulder and spoke to her but the old woman wouldn't move, instead twisting the material in her hands, staring up at Cassius as she pleaded.

'Simo, just tell her we can do no more for the girl, we must—'

'She's not talking about the girl, sir. She asks you to recover the grain. Those bags are all they have. Months of work. She doesn't know how they will survive. They—'

Cassius couldn't believe Simo was bothering to translate the old crone's every word.

'Get her off me, damn you!'

Simo grabbed both the old woman's shoulders but her grip was surprisingly strong. Cassius tried to drag his legs free but she still wouldn't budge. Only when he gripped both her hands and wrenched them away could he finally move.

'By the gods!'

Cassius's kick almost knocked the door off its hinges. It bounced back and narrowly missed him as he stalked outside.

'Get on your horse, Simo. We are leaving.'

Cassius strode over to his mount and leapt up on to the saddle. After a couple of steps it veered left, earning itself a vicious kick.

'Why I must be dragged down into the shit like this I will never know!' Cassius hissed between clenched teeth.

Simo was hurrying towards his own steed, the old woman not far behind.

Cassius caught sight of the young girl. She was on her feet, holding on to the door to keep herself up. Cassius hadn't noticed before, but mounted above the entrance were three stone carvings; religious icons placed there to protect the home and the people within.

'Your gods have failed you,' he muttered bitterly.

He yanked the reins and kicked down hard, sending his horse charging round the stable and up the slope.

IV

They passed the boundary line in the middle of the afternoon. Later, as the sky darkened around them, Cassius had long realised they wouldn't reach Palmyra. The road remained eerily quiet and – apart from a few merchants heading west – the only other traveller they'd encountered was an imperial courier. He had charged round a bend, his galloping steed kicking up swathes of dust, only stopping because of Cassius's frantic waving. Pausing for a few breathy words, the courier advised them to seek shelter at an occupied way-station on the road about ten miles west of Palmyra.

Now, as they urged their weary mounts up a hill, Cassius hoped that the smudge of light ahead was coming from that very building. He looked back at Simo. The Gaul's horse had earlier turned a hoof on a stone and was now limping up the slope, Simo dragging it along by the reins. Cassius sat up straight, tightened his grip and concentrated on keeping his steed away from the road-edge.

The final moments of the journey were interminable, and when they finally dismounted, he let out a mighty breath.

'Thank Jupiter that's done.'

The way-station was built of smooth limestone blocks. On each side of a solid-looking wooden door were shuttered windows. Hanging from a hook was a lantern that cast a faint yellow glow.

Cassius flicked his reins over the saddle and approached the door, cursing with every painful step. He knocked and waited. A small hatch slid open and a square of young, narrow face stared out at them.

'Who's there?'

Simo held up the spear-head as his master spoke.

'Cassius Quintius Corbulo, Governor's Office. I'm to meet with Prefect Venator of the Fourth Legion tomorrow and require lodgings for the night.'

Beckoning fingers appeared so Simo brought the spear-head closer. Peering at the badge, the man made a neutral sound then withdrew. Two bolts were drawn and the door opened.

The legionary standing before them was a skinny individual whose belt hung loosely around his waist. One of his boot laces trailed along the ground as he walked past them into the middle of the road. He looked east, then west.

'Sorry, sir. Can't be too careful out here. Legionary Gerardus, First Century, Fifth Cohort, Fourth Legion.'

'You here alone, soldier?'

'No, sir, Durio's inside but he's laid up with bad guts. We're here for another two days before a new shift arrives. Let's get the horses seen to, shall we? Stable's round the back.'

Gerardus took the reins of Cassius's mount.

'Would you like to go inside, sir?'

Cassius was momentarily taken aback by such friendliness and efficiency.

'Certainly.'

'Please bolt the doors, sir.'

Gerardus led the horse around the side of the way-station, closely followed by Simo.

'What's going on?' asked a weak voice as Cassius went inside and locked the door behind him. He walked over to the man lying under a blanket next to the hearth. Despite the wide chimney, the well-stacked fire was giving out a lot of smoke.

'Legionary Durio, I presume?'

With a panicky look at Cassius's tunic, Durio pushed the blanket away.

Cassius held up a hand. 'Stay where you are, man. I can see by your colour you're not up to much.'

'Thank you, sir.'

Cassius looked around and realised the night's accommodation would be basic. There was not one piece of furniture and the earthen floor was covered only by a thin layer of reeds. In one corner was a collection of rusting cooking pans and some firewood. Leaning against the wall behind the door were two spears. The legionaries had laid out the rest of their equipment on a cloak: a saw, a pickaxe, some goat-skin bags for water. They had at least kept the place tidy. Cassius glanced down at an iron pan next to the fire.

'Any food going?'

It seemed an age since he and Simo had sat by the side of the road to down a hasty late lunch.

'Actually yes, sir. We cooked up some barley and beans for dinner. Plenty left.'

'Sounds delightful.'

With the horses dealt with, and an area in the back room cleared for the travellers to sleep in, Gerardus and Simo joined Cassius and Durio by the fire. As there were no chairs, the Gaul brought in Cassius's saddle for him to sit on. Despite a few spices added by Simo from his portable supply, the lukewarm stew remained stubbornly tasteless.

'How was it, sir?' asked Gerardus as Cassius put down his empty bowl.

'The best that can be said of it is that it filled a hole. I suggest you stick to soldiering, and plan on finding a good wife to take care of matters related to the kitchen.'

Gerardus chuckled good-naturedly. He did seem determined to ingratiate himself. Cassius guessed this wasn't just sycophancy. With his fellow sentry incapacitated, the soldier was glad to have some company. He had already regaled the visitors with more details about the attacks on army units. Though no one knew for sure, it was generally assumed that Palmyran irregulars were responsible. In one incident, legionaries had been able to fight off the raiders without loss; in three others, men had been wounded and killed. Cassius was grateful that Gerardus had soon moved on to a different and rather more momentous topic: the siege of Palmyra.

'So you were both there?' he prompted.

'From the first day to the last, sir. The legion was called down from Zeugma many months ago. Three cohorts went west to join up with the Emperor. We arrived just as the main force approached the city. What a sight, sir!'

Cassius nodded, passing his empty mug to Simo, who instantly refilled it from a jug. Behind the way-station was a cistern that provided a good supply of water.

'Five legions, sir, imagine it. They'd lost thousands at Immae and Emesa, hundreds more from harassing attacks on this very road, but what a sight! More scarlet and gold than I've ever seen in one place; and ranks and ranks of Persian archers; auxiliaries from every province you can think of; and, most fearsome of all – Palestinian club-men. Big brutes every one, their weapons studded with all manner of bolts and spikes.'

'And this tale of the mouthy Palmyran defender? It's true?'

'I saw it myself, sir. A man called out from the city walls, insulting the Emperor. One of the archers asked if he would like the man silenced. The Emperor said he would. A few legionaries provided the Persian with cover and he advanced to within three hundred feet or so. The Palmyran had kept up with his insults but then he was silenced for ever – the archer fired an arrow straight into his mouth! What a noise came up from our lines. I knew then the city would be ours, sir.'

Cassius had the feeling Gerardus had already told the tale a number of times. Durio turned over and started snoring.

'And what of Zenobia? You saw the queen?'

Gerardus tutted. 'Not a trace. They say she was taken by our cavalry during the night, while riding for Persian territory. Apparently she hoped to persuade their king to come to her aid. When the city folk heard she'd gone, the fight went out of them. A few days later it was all over. I did hear something though – from a cook friend of mine – he knows a scout who's a cousin of one of the cavalrymen. He got a look at her.' Gerardus shrugged. 'Nothing special, he reckoned.'

'How disappointing,' said Cassius. 'One would expect a woman who had caused that much trouble to possess at least one redeeming feature. I take it things have settled down now?'

'I suppose so, sir, yes. There was a great exodus from the city but once they realised only Zenobia and her cronies would be harshly punished, many decided to stay. We've even seen a few return.'

'And apart from these raids, the city is peaceful?'

'For the most part, sir. The prefect has begun sending men back to Zeugma. The Third Cohort left last week, to get things in order before the rest of the legion returns.'

'And what of the fabled treasures of Palmyra? I'll wager you and the rest were eager to get your hands on some booty.'

'No such luck,' said Durio, suddenly awake, propping himself up against the wall. 'A few gold coins were handed out to the officers. Nothing more.'

Cassius decided to dig a little deeper.

'One would be entitled to expect something a bit more exotic, what with all those Palmyran victories in foreign lands?'

'All went west with the Emperor,' said Gerardus.

'I can't imagine the Governor was overly impressed,' replied Cassius. 'Surely the province deserved a share.'

'You'd know more about that than us, sir,' observed Durio. His comment seemed to remind Gerardus of the status of their guest. The legionaries stayed quiet. An officer from the governor's staff might easily be with the Security Service, and soldiers knew better than to say too much to a 'grain man'.

Cassius elected not to push his luck, especially as it seemed unlikely he'd get anything else useful out of them.

'I'll check the road again,' said Gerardus, heading for the door.

'And I shall retire for the night,' Cassius announced. 'Simo, prepare the water, would you?'

Wrapping his hand in a cloth, Simo removed a large kettle from a spit over the fire and took it to the back room.

'Tell me, Durio,' Cassius said as he stood up, 'ever heard of an inn called The Goat's Leg?'

The legionary beamed. 'Of course, sir.'

'It's in a little village, isn't it?'

'That's right, sir. Galanea – just south of Palmyra.'

'Quiet little hostelry then, I imagine?'

Durio chortled. 'Not quite, sir. Roughest bar this side of Antioch.'

'Ah.'

'No place for a gentleman like yourself, sir.'

'Wonderful.'

As Durio settled back down below his blanket, Cassius followed Simo next door.

'I shall enjoy this,' he said, undoing his sword belt and lowering it to the floor. Next off were his boots, then his main belt and finally his tunic. He stood well away from the blankets that would serve as beds, and watched Simo as he wetted a cloth.

'I feel utterly filthy.'

'I can imagine, sir,' replied Simo as he ran the cloth across his master's chest. 'Perhaps we might find a bath for you tomorrow.'

'I live in hope. Nasty business this morning.'

It was the first time Cassius had mentioned the incident with the three legionaries. Simo – now attending to his master's shoulders – took his time to reply.

'Evil, sir. Simply evil.'

'That kind of thing is to be expected at a time like this. Even so, not the sort of treatment likely to win over the locals.'

'I cannot imagine what possesses people to commit such acts, sir.'

'Well, it's in your nature to think the best of people, Simo, but the army does not always attract the most wholesome of characters, and not everyone shares your preoccupation with the well-being of others. I've spoken to you about it before, and yet you will persist with trying to help every poor unfortunate we encounter. I'll remind you again: charity is for Jews and Orientals.'

'Might I speak freely for a moment, sir?'

'As long as you hurry up. I'm getting cold.'

'Sir, you went to help those women without a second thought. Are our attitudes really so different?'

'Do you know what I should have done, Simo? I should have kept on riding. I am on imperial business. We might easily have fared a good deal worse with those three thugs. And who would have benefited then?'

'You did the right thing, sir, I'm sure of it.'

'Well, I'm happy to know you approve, Simo, but think on this. Another hour and we would have missed the whole thing. And who's to say they didn't find another poor girl somewhere else?'

Simo put the wet cloth aside and picked up a new one.

'You don't think your words might have brought them to their senses, sir?'

'Your naivety is endearing, Simo. Listen here: life is hard. I think we've both seen enough to know that. The world is too big and too cruel for the actions of well-meaning men to make much difference.'

'Perhaps their superiors could get those men back on the straight and narrow, sir? I suppose that's not possible now.'

'You mean because I gave my word I wouldn't report them?'

Simo didn't see his master grinning. He was down on his knees, vigorously rubbing away at the dirt caked on Cassius's legs.

'You know I'm not one to give an oath lightly but circumstances have changed, Simo. I am now in the employ of the Imperial Security Service and am therefore expected by all and sundry to be a lying, underhand scoundrel. I wouldn't want to disappoint anyone.'

V

It was quite astonishing to ride through a largely barren wasteland for more than a week, then look down upon the lush, dark green carpet of palm trees that surrounded Palmyra.

From Cassius's position high on a ridge, he could easily make out the Damascus Gate, where travellers arriving from the south or west entered the city. Down low to his left were more of the tomb towers that dominated the approach and where he and Simo had encountered a legionary patrol. The men had assured him that the path over the ridge was the quickest route to the village of Galanea.

From the Damascus Gate, a grand colonnaded avenue cut a crooked line eastward, embellished by vast arches and tetrapyla. Halfway along the avenue, on the northern side, was a high, imposing building book-ended by domed towers, which Cassius assumed to be Zenobia's palace. Further east was an even larger edifice, one he recognised from a sketch in one of his neighbour's books. The massive Temple of Bel honoured a Babylonian god long worshipped by the Palmyrans. It was easily the largest structure in the city. Though surrounded by a vast courtyard, its angular bulk dwarfed dwellings whose size decreased according to their proximity to the main avenue. Beyond the temple was a mile-wide lake where the subterranean waters that sustained the city broke the surface.

'Impressive,' Cassius said, though Simo was too far behind to hear him. He turned to the south. 'Almost as impressive as that.'

The encampment of the Fourth Legion was huge. Though Cassius knew precisely how such a settlement was created, how it was organised, and how swiftly it could be dismantled, he had never seen a legion-sized camp in the field. At moments such as this, he felt proud to be Roman.

The northern perimeter of the camp was perhaps a mile from the city: a deep ditch reinforced by a rampart wall. There was a narrow entrance on each side of the square, and a two-hundred-foot space between the wall and the first lines of tents. This space – a defensive buffer that kept everything valuable out of range of burning missiles – was empty apart from a few horses grazing on what little grass was left. The centre of the camp was remarkably uniform: rows of large, pale tents divided by wide avenues. Beyond the eastern perimeter, a cavalry unit drilled their mounts.

As if eager to share the view, Cassius's horse nosed him in the shoulder. He pushed it away and looked south beyond the encampment. A wide track marked by darker soil led from the Roman camp to the village. People could be seen travelling in both directions.

Puffing hard, Simo dragged his injured horse to the brow of the ridge. Cassius glanced at the animal.

'Will it make it down to the village?'

'Yes, sir.'

'Will you?'

'Of course, sir,' said Simo, straightening up and trying to control his breathing.

'Good, because we need to keep moving.'

Cassius squinted at the sun overhead, then started away along the snaking track that ran down to Galanea.

If not for the lame horse, they would have made good time that morning. Despite his blanket bed, Cassius had slept well and had awoken to find Legionary Durio up on his feet and feeling much better. He joined the others for breakfast and helped Gerardus and Simo with the horses. Cassius made no further attempt to extract any information from the pair and they remained cordial – if tight-lipped – until their visitors went on their way.

Of the two sets of legionaries from the Fourth Legion he had encountered since leaving Abascantius, Cassius hoped that those at Palmyra would be more like the second group than the first.

On the outskirts of the village they passed a few mud-built hovels occupied only by children playing at war. Cassius somehow lost the main path and they had to pick their way through several abandoned sets of foundations and assorted rubble before finding the main street. It was lined by large, two-storey buildings of cemented stone. Two veiled women emerged from an alley to their left, carrying woven baskets. They hurried past, heads down. A trio of local men rebuilding a courtyard wall stopped their work to inspect the strangers.

'Good morning,' Cassius said in Greek. 'There's an inn here – The Goat's Leg?'

One man looked as if he was about to reply, then turned to the others and said something in Aramaic. They all laughed, then continued with their work.

Cassius shrugged and pressed on. The street widened out into a square occupied by a few dozen legionaries and villagers. Traders had laid out their wares around a big date palm that leaned alarmingly to one side. Beyond the tree were two roads: one led east, the other south. Cassius stopped beside a smaller tree and looped his reins around a branch. Simo did the same, then stood with hands on his hips, breathing heavily.

'We shall at least both be a good deal fitter after this affair,' Cassius said as he reached for his canteen. 'Stay here. I shall try to find this inn.'

Ignoring the curious glances that greeted him as he walked towards the traders, Cassius sipped from the canteen and nodded to any of the legionaries who looked his way. Even when off-duty, they were easily spotted, with their short hair, thick military belts and hobnailed boots.

Whatever the villagers' attitude to their Roman occupiers, they clearly weren't averse to profiting from trade with the soldiers.

As well as food and clothing, there was glass and fine ware, building tools, firewood, blankets, sheets, cushions, riding equipment, and the ever-present local trinkets and cheap religious icons. Several legionaries were involved in protracted bouts of haggling. One of those looking on was a soldier carrying two folded sheets and chewing on a bread roll.

'Morning, legionary,' said Cassius.

'Sir.'

'Can you tell me where I might find The Goat's Leg?'

'You sure you want to go there, sir?'

'Yes.'

'Because that's a soldiers' inn, sir. Not an officers' inn.'

'Just tell me where it is, man.'

The legionary pointed to the southern road.

'Down the hill there, sir.'

Cassius headed off down the slope and gestured for Simo to follow with the horses. There were only six buildings on the street, three on each side, and it soon petered out into a dusty, palm-lined path. The inn was easily the biggest structure: three storeys high with an arched doorway. On either side of it were amateurish murals showing wine jars and girls wrapped in vine leaves.

Cassius caught a glimpse of watching eyes from a window and in moments a straggly-haired woman of about fifty had appeared at the doorway.

'Hello, handsome. Looking for some local hospitality?'

'Possibly.'

Cassius stopped and waited for Simo to catch up.

The woman moved aside to allow a bulky, large-headed man out, who then stalked down the steps and crossed his arms. Tucked into his belt was a thick cudgel.

'Don't mind him,' said the woman, switching to Latin.

'Quite the linguist,' said Cassius.

'I know a Roman officer when I see one. Not that we get many down here. My husband's an ex-legionary. Why don't you come in and meet him? We've got dancing girls and the finest selection of wines this side of the city.'

'A moment, woman. Will your man watch the horses for us?'

'Stable's closed. And you'll have to leave your weapons with your servant, or at the door. And you must buy at least one drink.' She pointed to a worn papyrus sheet mounted in a frame. 'Rules of the house.'

Cassius turned to Simo and shook his head as he undid his sword belt.

'The delights of the provinces. This won't take a moment, Simo. If the man I'm supposed to meet is here we shall depart at once, if not I shall leave a message and we'll head up to the camp.'

Cassius touched his tunic just above his belt, checking that the small bag of money he'd counted out that morning was there. The rest of the coins were in his saddlebag.

'Perhaps you should wait down there,' he suggested. Beyond the final house was a patch of unused land where Simo could remain safely out of sight.

'Very well. Careful in there, sir.'

Cassius removed his dagger and handed it to Simo with the sword belt. Greeted by a smile from the woman and a frown from the doorman, he stepped up through the doorway. Nearby was a large wooden chest with a few sheathed swords and daggers inside. Four bows (too long for the chest) had been leant against the wall, along with four quivers. The woman bustled ahead of him and pulled back a heavy curtain. Although he could hear voices, Cassius was surprised to find the room empty. There was a bar but no furniture.

'We're using the back room. Fire.' The woman pointed to the hearth. Black streaks of soot covered most of the wall and roof. 'Take your cape?' she asked.

Cassius shook his head as he undid the clasp himself and dropped the cape over his arm.

'Just through there.' She pointed at an open door, then returned to the window and took up some sewing.

Cassius walked warily through the doorway. There were two groups inside. Gathered at the bar directly in front of him were

73

six dark-skinned men with long, black hair. Auxiliaries, Cassius guessed; probably Cilician or Galatian. They were talking to an older man behind the bar. A couple of them threw a quick glance towards Cassius then returned to their conversation.

To the right, four men sat by an empty hearth, too occupied with three serving girls to notice the new arrival. They were all fair-haired and broad in the shoulders and chest; certainly the owners of the bows. Also auxiliaries – Celts perhaps.

Cassius waited for a moment to see if anyone might come forward but not one of them had given him a second look. In any case, he was certain they were all soldiers. He checked the tables to the left; they were empty.

Continuing to the bar, he kept well clear of the auxiliaries and sat down on a stool. There was a shrill call in Aramaic from a hatch. The barkeep nodded a greeting to Cassius, then picked up two steaming wooden plates. He delivered the food to the men then returned to Cassius, slapping his hands down on the bar. He had a weathered, ruddy face and an unusual mark on his chin; Cassius couldn't decide if it was a dimple or a scar.

'Good-day, sir. Not seen you in here before.'

'Just arrived.'

'Which cohort you with?'

'None. I'm with the governor's staff.'

'Is that right? I'm Telesinus. I own this place.'

'Ah, yes. I just met your wife.'

'Still out there, is she?'

'Yes.'

'Not been struck by lightning?'

'No,' Cassius answered with a curious grin. 'Why?'

'I've been begging the gods for twenty years – it has to happen one day.'

Cassius laughed; and wondered how many times a day Telesinus trotted that one out.

'What are you drinking, sir?'

'Well, I don't really have the time but I suppose I must follow the rules of the house. Half and half. Something decent. Hot.'

'Coming up.'

Telesinus wiped his hands on his apron and selected a wine bottle from a long shelf, then tipped some into a wooden mug. Finding the hatch untended, he reached inside and topped the wine up with hot water.

'There you go, sir – a light Galician. Some sausage? Goes well.'

Cassius investigated the plate Telesinus had retrieved from behind the bar. The meat looked edible but his policy was always to let Simo make or choose his food.

'No thank you. Listen, I'm supposed to be meeting someone here. Any strangers been in?'

'Just you,' said the owner with a grin, moving off.

Though he didn't want to leave Simo alone outside for long, Cassius took a moment to enjoy being still. He sampled the wine. Bitter but passable. He glanced over at the auxiliaries and saw a legend engraved on one of their mugs: *Fill it up again!* Judging by their inability to form coherent sentences, Telesinus had obliged. Cassius felt a light touch on his shoulder, and turned to find one of the serving girls beside him.

'Hello,' she said in Greek. Her voice was soft, her accent hard.

'Hello.'

Cassius looked her up and down. She was about his age: slim and pretty, and wearing a tunic short enough to reveal a shapely pair of legs and tight enough to outline a fine pair of breasts. If not for her dirty fingernails and the faint whiff of sweat, Cassius might have found her rather attractive. She ran a finger along his forearm.

'I'm Sabina. What's your name?'

'Cassius.'

Thanks to one of his more free-spirited uncles, Cassius had a little experience of such hostelries; and the girls who worked there. He was certain she would offer more than table service if the price was right. Sabina brushed her left breast against him.

'You smell nice, Cassius. And I like your hair.'

'I'm sure I look a complete mess. I've been on the move since breakfast.'

'You look fine to me.'

Despite a pang of guilt about what his mother would say if she could see him, Cassius admitted to himself that it was rather nice to have a little female company.

'How tall are you?' asked Sabina.

He shrugged. 'Tall.'

Over her shoulder, Cassius noted one of the auxiliaries nudge his friend. The second man looked annoyed.

'Hey!' he yelled. 'I gave you a good tip. Now you run off and leave me.'

Sabina rolled her eyes and spoke without turning round. 'That was an hour ago!'

'Get back here, you cheeky cow, or you'll not get another!'

Cassius moved his head forward so that the Celt couldn't see him speak. 'And people say northerners are coarse . . .'

Sabina giggled and ran a hand across his knee.

'What's that?' demanded the auxiliary.

Cassius leaned back and kept a straight face as he took another sip of wine.

'Not bad this,' he said, holding up the glass to Telesinus.

'You'd best hurry, girl!' shouted the Celt.

Cassius removed Sabina's hand from his leg and nodded towards the auxiliaries. 'Perhaps you better—'

'I'm staying here!' she yelled, spinning round and placing a defiant hand on her hip. 'Where I can talk to this nice *Roman*!'

The Celt, whose chiselled features were surrounded by an unruly tangle of sandy hair, glared at her.

Cassius caught his eye, then shrugged.

'Pah!' With a dismissive wave, the Celt turned back to the table and refilled his mug.

Sabina smiled gleefully. 'Good. Now we can talk. Will you buy me a lemon water?'

'Very well.'

Sabina leaned over the bar and ordered it. 'Honey too, please.'

Telesinus reached for a clean glass.

Cassius nodded towards the Celts again. 'Looks like he's given up. You know these bowmen have remarkably strong wrists. I suppose if he can't find any pleasure with you, one of his friends can oblige.'

Sabina's throaty laugh was so obviously tinged with mockery that Cassius knew instantly he had made a mistake.

Stool legs screeched as the Celt sprang to his feet.

'What was that?' he demanded, striding towards the bar. 'What did you say, Roman?'

'Calm down, Estan,' said Telesinus.

Cassius turned to the Celt, who had stopped a yard away. He really was quite large: as tall as Cassius, with a remarkably sturdy chest and a thick neck. Intricate, dark green tattoos snaked up his forearms.

'You said something about me. Admit it.'

'Not I,' Cassius said, with what he hoped was an appeasing grin. 'Please, let me buy you a drink.'

Estan hunched forward, eyes locked on Cassius. 'Tell me what you said.'

'Just a common joke: there's a Greek, a Carthaginian and a—'

The Celt poked Sabina in the shoulder. 'You tell me.'

'Why should I?'

Estan plucked a silver denarius from a bag attached to his belt and held it up to the girl's face. The other Celts and the serving girls had gathered behind him. Even the six drunks had quietened down. Sabina looked at the coin, then back at Cassius.

'Don't,' he said.

'Keep your mouth shut, girl,' warned Telesinus, walking around the end of the bar.

Sabina shrugged and took the coin. Then she told the Celt what Cassius had said.

The dark auxiliaries erupted into a fit of hysterics.

'You silly little bitch,' Cassius snapped.

Estan breathed in sharply through his nostrils and raised himself to his full height. One of his fellows spat on the floor by Cassius's feet.

'Now wait a moment,' Cassius said. Before he could move,

77

Estan swung a boot at the high stool. As it flew away, Cassius dropped like a stone, catching his head on the bar and landing heavily on the floor. Rubbing his head, he got to his feet and backed towards the other auxiliaries.

'You men, I am an officer of the Roman Army. You must help me.'

One of the soldiers stood and saluted. 'At once, sir!'

Cassius was all set to move behind him when the man sat down again and bellowed with laughter. The others joined in.

Cassius pointed to his tunic. 'I am an officer. It is your duty to assist me.'

One of the men tilted his mug towards the Celts. 'We know them. We don't know you. We're not Roman.'

'I command you to help me.'

'Somebody hear something?' replied one of the men.

'Not me,' said another.

'You haven't heard the last of this,' Cassius told them.

'You won't be in a state to tell anyone anything,' said one of the Celts.

Telesinus moved in front of Cassius. Sabina was now crying. Her employer pushed her over to where the other girls stood.

'That's enough, Estan,' he said. 'You—'

Telesinus never finished the sentence.

Estan barged him aside, stomped forward and drove both hands into Cassius's chest, propelling him across the room. Cassius's legs buckled as he hit a table, flew over the top of it and landed in a heap next to the wall. Though his shoulder now blazed with pain, he forced himself up straight away. He had to stay on his feet; if they got him on the ground he was finished. He reached instinctively for his dagger, then remembered it wasn't there.

Why had he said that stupid quip? Why?

He glanced across at the door.

'No you don't.'

One of the Celts blocked his way.

Cassius held up his hands. 'I apologise unreservedly. It was a harmless joke.'

'How you Romans love to mock us,' said Estan. 'We're good enough to kill for you and die for you but not good enough to earn your respect.'

Telesinus intervened once more. 'That'll do, Estan. You've had your fun.'

'Skinny here seems very interested in how strong we are. I think it's time for a little demonstration.'

Cassius decided to make a dash for the door anyway. He had barely taken a step before Estan grabbed his left arm and swung him back against the wall. The Celt gave an order in his own language and two of the others darted forward and took hold of Cassius. With a sly smile, Estan bent down and picked up Cassius's cape from where it had fallen to the floor. He stretched it out, doubled it over, then began twisting the ends. Cassius tried to shake himself free but now both his arms were pinned to the wall.

'I have money,' he said, nodding down at his belt.

'So have I,' said Estan. 'I don't want your money. What I want is for you to understand the consequences of insulting the men of Caledonia. When this is done, I think you will.'

Estan had finished twisting the cape and he now looped it over Cassius's head, crossing the ends in front of his neck. The other men took an end each and kept one hand on Cassius's shoulders.

Cassius knew he had to call for help while he still could.

'Simo! Simo!'

Estan nodded. The men pulled tighter and the cotton cut into Cassius's neck. He tried to draw breath but no air came. He reached for the cape but Estan sent a knuckled punch straight down on to his right wrist. Cassius would have cried out had he been able.

Estan spoke again. The pressure eased.

'Now listen. There is something I want you to say: "My name is Skinny. I am a Roman and I am nothing."'

Through the fear and pain, Cassius was surprised to hear his reaction.

79

'By Mars you'll pay for this. I am an officer of the Imperial Army and I am here to—'

With a nod from Estan the two men pulled again.

'No, no, no,' replied the Celt. 'That's not what I said. You must repeat it exactly: My name is Skinny. I am a Roman and I am nothing.'

The cape slackened again.

'I am here to see—'

Estan slapped him. 'I might have to change your name to Stupid.'

Cassius coughed. Spit ran down his chin. Tears ran down his cheeks.

The Celts laughed, even as Telesinus again implored them to stop. Estan told the others to pull harder.

Cassius could feel the cape cutting into his skin. His windpipe felt like a stone being pushed into his throat. He was choking.

Why had he come in here alone?

Now he was going to die here. The cape bit at his neck. Black mist edged across his vision. He was choking.

'Do you have my money?'

Cassius didn't understand. *They didn't want money, did they?*

'Are you Corbulo? Do you have my money?'

It was a different voice; a new voice. *Who here knew his name?* Cassius wanted to speak but he couldn't.

'You Corbulo?'

The black mist was now a cloud. All the light had gone. He nodded.

'Do you have my money?'

Cassius nodded again. The pressure on his neck eased. Light flooded back into his eyes.

Behind Estan was a well-built young man with what looked like half an ear.

The fourth Celt realised quickly that the interloper was to be considered an enemy and attacked right away.

He lined up his foe and swung a boot.

Pivoting to his left, Indavara waited until the boot was sailing harmlessly past him then gripped the heel and wrenched it forward, pulling the Celt off his standing foot. The auxiliary slipped easily on the smooth stone floor and fell on his backside. Indavara stamped down hard on his groin, twisting his boot in for good measure.

The ensuing high-pitched scream was enough to bring Telesinus's wife and the doorman running in. Telesinus warned them to stay clear as Estan turned to face Indavara. The other two let go of Cassius and fanned out behind their leader.

The folds of the cape were still stuck to Cassius's neck. He was too busy pulling it off and sucking in air to notice much of what happened next.

Indavara had hated having to leave his weapons by the door but he was not slow to improvise. As the three men closed, he retreated and picked up a small but sturdy stool and held it in his right hand.

Estan muttered something; the three Celts advanced.

Wielding the stool above his shoulder, as if preparing to defend himself with it, Indavara swung it back then launched it at the man to Estan's right. It caught him high on the forehead with a sharp crack. The Celt staggered for a moment, mouth wide, then toppled like a felled tree, bringing down several shelves.

With a quick look at his injured comrades, Estan picked up a hefty chair and launched it across the room.

Indavara stuck two hands up and caught it.

To his credit, Estan didn't let this feat put him off. He charged.

Indavara flung the chair back – at the Celt's ankles. Estan tripped and stumbled, doubling over as he careened forward. Indavara took a single step and drove his knee straight up into the Celt's face, catching him full on the chin. Estan's head crunched to one side and he crashed to the floor, his body limp.

The fourth Celt looked down at his three fallen fellows, then fled.

The serving girls were all crying, hands on their faces. Telesinus, his wife and the doorman stood in a line, watching Indavara. The woman looked down at Estan.

'Gods, he's killed him, hasn't he?'

With a wary glance at Indavara, Telesinus knelt down by Estan. He put a hand to his chest.

'He's breathing.'

Cassius pushed himself off the wall just as Indavara's second victim dragged himself back against it. The man looked blankly up at him, then at the hand he had just placed on his head. It was wet with blood.

Indavara walked past his first victim. The man was writhing around on the floor, clasping his groin and moaning.

Indavara glanced at Cassius and gestured towards the door.

Cassius nodded; and they left.

VI

Cassius walked towards the encampment with his head down, ignoring the legionaries and locals they passed, wholly occupied with trying to ascertain exactly how much damage had been done to his neck. It still felt horribly constricted and there was a rasping pain when he talked. Despite the presence of this bodyguard (who at least seemed well qualified to do the job), Cassius wouldn't feel safe until he was inside the camp. He couldn't believe such a thing was possible so close to a legion base. He felt angry and stupid; and his hands wouldn't stop shaking.

A few yards behind, Simo and Indavara walked side by side, leading the horses.

'What about my money then?' Indavara asked for the second time.

Cassius had heard him the first time but elected to ignore him. Now he spun round.

'You, my man, bring new meaning to the word mercenary.'

Indavara shrugged.

Cassius turned to Simo. 'Didn't come to my aid until he was sure I had his silver. Quite happy to watch me being strangled. You'll be paid within the hour. Quick enough?'

Indavara shrugged again.

'That's settled then.'

—◆8◆—

The rear entrance of the camp was narrow – no more than twenty feet across. On either side were high poles bearing the square standards of the Fourth Legion. The flags were of black cloth, with the legend and a goat (Capricorn being the legion's symbol) embroidered in gold. Below the flags, four legionaries stood guard.

Cassius called a halt well short of the entrance, where local traders had been permitted to set up day-pitches selling snacks and drinks. Simo had already retrieved the spear-head and now offered Cassius his helmet.

'Crest's not straight.'

'Sorry, sir.'

'Come on, Simo, I'm about to meet a prefect of the Roman Army. I must at least try to look presentable.'

Cassius looked down at his tunic. It was still dirty from his encounter with the inn floor, the cape too. As Simo dealt with the helmet, Cassius glanced over at the bodyguard.

'What was the name again?'

'Indavara.'

'Unusual.'

Indavara left his horse and wandered away to investigate the food on offer.

Cassius noticed how shoddy his mount and gear were. The sides of the horse's mouth were cut and sore; a sure sign of a bad rider. The saddle itself was ancient and poorly maintained: in several places the cover was coming away from the wood. Upon one side of the saddle was a leather bag. On the other side were a water-skin, a bow case and quiver, and a five-foot fighting stave.

Indavara had reclaimed his main weapon – a short sword sheathed on a diagonal belt – on their way out of the inn. As he approached the traders, a group of locals broke up to let him pass. Most of the men were taller and older than him but their action was instinctive. Cassius had been too distracted to notice before but he now realised that there was something undeniably impressive about the man. He wasn't overly large, or exceptionally muscular; but there was something in the way he carried himself. Cassius had met many such men, most of them soldiers, but he didn't recall ever seeing it in one so young.

Indavara returned. He had bought a large pastry covered with nuts and honey and devoured it at speed, eyes scanning the encampment. Cassius pretended to turn away but continued to examine him. His face, though handsome in a rather agricultural way, was marked and scarred. His eyes seemed to possess a vacant, almost innocent quality. Cassius suspected he was rather stupid. At least that would make him more biddable. Brainless but tough wasn't such a bad combination for a bodyguard.

'What will happen?' Indavara asked, his mouth full of pastry.

'What?' Cassius replied irritably.

Indavara pointed back towards Galanea. 'Those men. What will happen?'

'To you, nothing. It is they who shall face consequences. Ah, about time.'

Cassius pressed his hair down and pulled the helmet on, then straightened his tunic.

'How do I look?' he asked Simo.

The Gaul hesitated.

Indavara spoke up: 'You have purple marks on your neck. And your face is very red.'

Cassius scowled at him, then raised his eyes skyward. 'I think I shall need another drink by the end of today.'

Though he'd never been inside a full-sized army camp, Cassius knew they were all constructed along uniform lines and had no difficulty finding the way. The prefect's quarters would be found at or close to the centre; traditionally the point from which the army surveyors marked out the rest of the camp.

The trio turned left from the entrance then followed a wide avenue northward. They didn't see a single unoccupied legionary. Inside a small stockade, a squad watched over two dozen doleful Palmyran prisoners. At a stabling area, a line of cavalrymen waited for their horses to be examined by veterinarians. Cassius reminded Simo to note the location. Another square of the camp was occupied by large wooden tables, where specialists repaired weapons, vehicle parts and all manner of other equipment.

A smart young tribune, identifiable by the narrow purple stripe on his tunic, strode past them on the other side of the avenue. The officer was walking very quickly, so fast that the two men behind him were struggling to keep up. He wore a long cape and tapped a riding crop against his leg as he walked. Perhaps three or four years older than Cassius, he exchanged a graceful nod with his fellow officer.

'Civilisation at last,' Cassius announced.

After a few more paces through the heavy, ploughed-up soil, he turned and spoke to Indavara.

'Why Abascantius thought it wise for me to meet you in that damned inn I shall never know. I should have had you come here.'

Indavara trudged on, head down.

'Not very talkative are you? Unless the talk is of money, that is.'

Indavara looked up. 'What?'

'I said you're not very talkative.'

Indavara tapped his mutilated ear. 'I don't always hear so well.'

'Ah.'

The queue outside the prefect's tent contained eighteen people. Cassius knew that because, after an hour of waiting, he'd already counted them three times. There was little else to do. He'd been determined to bypass the queue but a staff officer had intercepted him and taken him aside. After seeing the spear-head and Cassius's authorisation, he'd promised to let the prefect know of his arrival. Cassius had caught a brief glimpse of Venator inside the tent: a tall, lean man poring over a map table, surrounded by his staff.

The Palmyrans in the queue seemed to be a mix of priests, administrators and merchants, all waiting patiently, talking in Greek or Aramaic. The sky had turned grey and now a light drizzle fell. Those with servants and parasols made use of them, others took shelter under the awning at the front of the tent.

The staff officer reappeared. He politely negotiated the Palmyrans, avoided Cassius's gaze and headed north towards the main entrance. Cassius jogged around the queue and caught up with him.

'Excuse me. Any news?'

The officer turned round. 'The prefect will see you later this afternoon. He hasn't the time now. I'm off for lunch. Do you mind?'

'As it happens I do. This is a matter of the utmost importance. Just mention the name Gregorius to him. I assure you he will be most upset if he finds out you were obstructive.'

The question of seniority was complex. The staff officer – a man of about thirty-five – was well below the level of a tribune but the proximity of his position to the prefect afforded him considerable authority. Cassius was young but the spear-head – and his position with the Service – gave him added status. He decided on a retreat into good old-fashioned politeness.

'Please, sir. You know the Service doesn't occupy itself with trivial concerns.'

The officer raised an eyebrow at this but he seemed to appreciate the improvement in tone.

'I will mention the name. Prefect Venator will make his own decision about the importance of the matter.'

He returned to the tent. Cassius walked back to where the other two were waiting. He shook his head as he watched Indavara – surreptitiously counting up the coins he'd been given. Simo was examining his horse's injured leg.

'There's not much point you two staying here. Why not head back to the stables and get your mount seen to?'

Simo looked up and smacked his hands together to clean them. 'Yes, sir.'

'You can use the spear-head if they're uncooperative.'

'Corbulo!'

Cassius turned to see the staff officer beckoning to him. He hurried over and was all set to head inside the tent when the officer moved aside and Prefect Venator himself appeared. He gave Cassius the briefest of nods then turned towards the Palmyrans.

'Good afternoon to you all,' he said in immaculate Greek. 'Apologies for keeping you waiting. Please come in out of the rain. There are some refreshments in here for you. My men will answer any immediate questions you have. I shall return presently.'

With a politician's smile fixed on his face, Venator stood to one side while the Palmyrans filed into the tent. A young servant appeared next to him and began unfolding a large parasol. Venator waved it away.

'I don't need that.'

He turned to Cassius. 'You have your horse?'

'I do, sir.'

'We shall take a ride.'

The prefect, Cassius decided, was a thoroughly impressive character. He was at least forty, undeniably handsome; and the incongruous combination of thick black eyebrows and soft white hair somehow reinforced his authoritative bearing. He carried no sword and wore a long red cloak fringed with gold.

Another servant trotted forward with a big, pale mare in tow. The first attendant got a box on to the ground just in time for the prefect to use it as a step. Venator climbed up on to the saddle, then turned and glared at Cassius.

'What are you waiting for?'

'Ah, sorry, sir.'

Simo brought Cassius's horse over. By the time he had mounted up, the prefect was already on his way.

'I'll meet you here later, Simo,' Cassius said. He guided his horse on to the road then urged it into a trot until he caught up with Venator.

The prefect looked him over. 'They say you're getting old when legionaries start to look young. It seems the same applies to grain men. Are you one of Abascantius's?'

Cassius wasn't sure what to say. It all depended on the prefect's opinion of the agent. He doubted it would be particularly favourable.

'Not exactly, sir. I report directly to Chief Pulcher.'

'Do you now? Then I should be careful what I say.'

'Not at all, sir,' Cassius replied, trying to sound humble.

'How is the old rogue? Still wearing those awful finger-rings?'

Cassius hesitated; he didn't want to get caught in a lie.

'I wouldn't know, sir. I've never actually met him. I've only been with the Service two years. I was transferred here from Cyzicus. I believe the idea was to use an investigator from outside the province.'

'An investigator? And something to do with Gregorius. Are you about to make an already bad day worse?'

'I'm afraid so, sir. He, the men and the – shipment – haven't been seen since they left here.'

One of Venator's hands drifted from the reins and he began rubbing the back of his neck. They came to a crossroads. A tribune left a group of legionaries loading a cart and ran over to the prefect.

'Sir, might I have a moment?'

'Not now,' replied Venator sharply. As the tribune sloped off, he guided his horse across the avenue.

'Marcellinus knows?'

'Not yet, sir.'

Venator let out a long breath.

Cassius hadn't really thought about the prefect's situation, but as part of Abascantius's scheme, he might also expect to suffer the consequences if the banner couldn't be found. Men of his rank typically used their command of a legion as a stepping stone to a senate career. A connection – any connection – to such a disaster might set his political ambitions back years.

The prefect brought his horse to a halt by another line of tents. There was no one close by.

'What have you found out?'

'Nothing yet, sir. Abascantius is returning to Antioch to see if he can make any progress there.'

'He assumes the army has something to do with it, I expect.'

'He made no suggestion of that to me, sir. I think he just wants to find the treasure and the flag.'

'Oh, I'm sure of it. Marcellinus will have his balls on a skewer

89

if he doesn't sort this mess out. Mine too, come to think of it. And yours.'

The pain in Cassius's neck suddenly seemed to double. It was alarming to see this noble, powerful man reduced to such statements. Venator was staring blankly down at a large puddle next to his horse as the rain continued to fall.

'I remember once hearing some Persian prisoners talking about Faridun's Banner. It means as much to them as a legion standard does to us. More even. Gods – if it can't be recovered.' Venator shook his head. 'Abascantius. I should have known better than to help that fat slug.' He cast a wary glance at Cassius, as if regretting his words.

Cassius realised that he still didn't fully appreciate the reach and reputation of the Service. If a prefect acted like this around him, no wonder ordinary legionaries were so wary.

'What do you think of your superior?' asked Venator.

'He's quite a character, sir. I suppose "fat slug" makes a change from "Pitface".'

Venator gave a grim smile. He ran an eye over Cassius.

'I must say, you don't seem like the Service type at all, Corbulo.'

'Long story, sir.'

Venator's horse was startled by something and backed off the road. The prefect swiftly got it under control and spoke softly to the animal, gently patting its neck.

'What do you need from me?'

'Everything you know, sir. The treasure and the flag, the men recruited from you, Gregorius's plans.'

'The first two I can help you with. The third I cannot. You can thank your paranoid friend Abascantius for that.'

Legion quartermaster was the pinnacle of achievement for a Roman soldier. Typically lifers with twenty years under their belt, they had a range of responsibility second only to the prefect. They made hundreds of decisions a day and were responsible for an organisation with a larger population than most towns and a budget to match. They were both the heart and backbone of a legion; but as well as being the peak of a legionary's career, it was also the limit.

Only men from aristocratic families could expect to become tribunes or prefects. And though they were rarely avid supporters of the Imperial Security Service, the officers were political animals; and they understood the reasons for the Service's existence, perhaps even viewing it as a necessary evil.

Quartermasters – like most career soldiers – usually held a different view. They saw the Service and its agents as little more than unprincipled liars and cheats; shadowy figures who held dear none of the army principles of unity, dedication and loyalty. Within moments of meeting Quartermaster Lollius of the Fourth Legion, Cassius knew he would not be one to break with tradition.

'Corbulo,' announced Venator. 'He's with Imperial Security.'

'Good afternoon,' said Cassius as he gripped the forearm of the burly quartermaster. He was ready for the squeeze but struggled not to wince as the thick fingers dug into his skin. He'd had quite enough manhandling for one day.

'You shall of course cooperate fully and extend him every courtesy,' added Venator.

'Of course, sir,' replied Lollius coolly.

They were standing inside a large, stuffy tent close to the main entrance. Upon finding Lollius there, Venator had ordered the half dozen clerks outside so that they might have some privacy. Lollius had dealt closely with Gregorius so Venator wanted him present to answer the questions he couldn't.

The three men were surrounded by tables, most of which were covered with papers and writing equipment. Venator found himself a high-backed chair and sat down. Cassius and the quartermaster each located a stool.

'Begin,' said Venator, waving a hand at Cassius.

Slightly startled, Cassius realised he should have made a list of questions or at least brought Simo to take some notes. He nodded at a nearby stack of blank papyrus sheets.

'May I?'

Venator nodded.

Cassius took a reed pen, two sheets of papyrus and a wooden tablet to lean on. There was an awkward moment as he tried to get the ink flowing. Shaking the pen, he noted Lollius's disdainful stare. The pupil of the quartermaster's left eye was surrounded by red instead of white. Cassius forced himself to look away.

At last ink dripped from the nib. Cassius reminded himself not to hurry the discussion; he might not get this opportunity again.

'First, sir, how and when did the treasure and the banner come into your possession?'

'Neither went west with the Emperor because it wasn't with the rest of the booty at the palace,' answered Venator, slumped sideways in the chair. 'There's a big abandoned temple to the south of the Damascus Gate which the Palmyrans used as an armoury. We took it after the surrender but the treasure wasn't found for a few weeks because it was hidden in a secret crypt. After Aurelian had left. When, Lollius?'

The quartermaster consulted a thick, leather-bound tome: the legion logbook.

'August 15th.'

'If you say so,' replied Venator. 'You were there when Tarquinius found it, weren't you?'

Lollius nodded. 'We were looking for some storage space outside the city.'

Venator turned to Cassius. 'Tarquinius is a centurion from the Third Cohort. Good man. Sensible.'

'I'd like to see this crypt if possible,' said Cassius.

'Lollius can show you later.'

The quartermaster looked less than enthusiastic about doing so.

'And what happened then, sir?' asked Cassius.

'I notified Marcellinus immediately by coded letter, including a list of everything we'd found and a description of the flag. Then we locked the crypt and posted a permanent eight-man guard there. None of them knew what they were guarding.'

'I'll need to speak to this Tarquinius too.'

'Not possible,' answered Venator, straightening the golden edging of his cloak. 'His cohort's back in Zeugma.'

'Do you at least have a copy of his records here?'

'No. They'll be in Zeugma too.'

'I'm afraid I must explore every eventuality,' Cassius said quietly. The list of those who had to be considered suspects continued to grow. It now included Lollius, Tarquinius and Venator himself.

'I received a note from Tarquinius yesterday,' said the prefect. 'Confirming that he and his cohort had arrived safely.'

'And when did you hear back from Marcellinus?'

Lollius checked the logbook again.

'Reply received August 24th.'

Venator continued: 'He had found out what the standard was and discussed the matter with the Emperor. He said the Service was to deal with the return of the flag and the treasure. In the same pouch were instructions from Abascantius, saying this Gregorius was on his way.'

'And when did Gregorius arrive?'

'Last day of August,' said Venator.

Lollius nodded without checking the book.

Cassius made a note, as he had for all the important dates.

'Did anything unusual happen in the period between notifying Antioch and Gregorius's arrival?'

'Almost certainly, this is Palmyra,' said Venator, leaning back and crossing his arms. 'But nothing to do with this matter as I recall. We alternated the guard regularly. No one else was allowed inside.' He shrugged. 'I was away to the east a lot of the time.'

'We followed the marshal's instructions to the letter,' affirmed Lollius. 'A couple of days before Gregorius got here, Tarquinius and I wrapped up all the booty and packed it into small barrels. Low-value coins were scattered on top and the lids were nailed down. It took us a whole day.'

'Just the two of you, sir?' asked Cassius.

'I'd have liked to have given the job to some of the lads, believe me, but we were told not to involve any more men than was necessary.'

'How many barrels were there?'

'Eighteen,' stated Lollius, wiping his red eye, which was now weeping.

'And what happened when Gregorius got here?'

'He arrived early in the morning and I spoke to him right away,' answered Venator. 'He was desperate to see the flag. Had a sketch of it. We took him to the temple and he confirmed it was genuine. Then he told us he wanted to leave that night. Said he would provide the transport but that he'd need ten of our best men. Lollius here wasn't particularly happy about it but Gregorius had his authorisation.'

Cassius pressed on: 'There were certain criteria for the ten legionaries, I believe.'

'Yes, which we followed exactly,' replied Venator. 'Men who weren't friends, had to be Italians, veterans and so on. Harder than one might imagine.'

'And you chose them personally, sir?'

Venator gestured for Lollius to answer.

'I spoke to ten centurions at morning briefing, gave them the criteria and asked for a name by lunch. The names arrived. The men arrived later.'

'And they were told nothing?'

Venator answered: 'Only that they would be under the command of this Gregorius and that they might be away for up to a month.'

'I'll need to see their records, sir. And I'd like to talk to those centurions. Perhaps even friends from the ranks if there's time.'

'We can probably arrange that but I don't want a big fuss. We take men off for special duties all the time but rarely from different centuries. There will already have been talk of it. If you start dragging everyone in for questioning, it'll be around the entire legion by tomorrow, the auxiliaries the next day.'

'I understand, sir. I'll be very careful. Where did this cart come from?'

'The city somewhere,' replied Lollius. 'Gregorius didn't tell me. Probably a merchant's yard. It was a big old thing.'

'You saw it?'

'I walked the ten men up to the temple. Gregorius had told me to wait until nightfall. Curfew was still in place then. I helped them load up and—'

'Sorry,' Cassius interrupted. 'How did Gregorius seem?'

'Nervous. But then so was I, being in charge of all that.' Lollius chuckled. 'He even made me sign for it.'

'And the men?'

'Don't suppose any of them were too happy about the prospect of a march like that but they knew they were on triple pay.'

'Abascantius's idea,' added Venator.

Lollius continued: 'I walked with them as far as the Damascus Gate.'

'And what about the picket line? Sentries?'

'I checked the next day,' said Lollius. 'They passed our sentries out to the north-east a couple of hours later – an area of big estates belonging to some of the richer Palmyrans.'

'You have the names of the sentries?'

'I can get them.'

'Then we might at least be able to establish the direction they took.'

'I wouldn't be so sure,' said Venator. 'There are scores of paths Gregorius might have followed: nomad routes, herder tracks.'

'The cart would be heavy though, sir. They might have left a trail. Has there been a lot of rain since then?'

'Not much,' said Lollius. 'But there'll be more coming soon.'

Cassius couldn't think of any more questions. 'Well, thank you both. I think that's about—'

Venator stood. 'I must be going. Anything else you need – just ask the quartermaster here. He'll find you lodgings too. Come and see me at the end of the day.' Venator took half a step then stopped. 'One more thing, Corbulo. What happened to your neck?'

VII

Their lodgings turned out to be a large tent previously occupied by clerks of the departed Third Cohort. The rain had stopped, so Simo opened the flaps at both ends to freshen the musty air. A team of slaves had just delivered three small beds complete with straw-filled mattresses. The beds were sturdily built but rather short – about two inches too short for Cassius. He now sat on one, his bare feet on the sandy ground, a pile of thin wooden tablets and a sheet of papyrus on his lap.

Quartermaster Lollius had remained cooperative, if begrudgingly so. He had consulted with a senior clerk who was able to lay his hands on six of the ten legionaries' records. The others would apparently take longer to locate; the administrator was under-staffed and most of his men were with a tribune in the city writing up new tax laws. He had however promised to find all the records by morning. Lollius had then sent another man to tell the centurions who knew the men best that they would be interviewed the following day.

Each of the wooden tablets recorded the personal details of three or four legionaries: names, dates and places of birth, height, distinguishing marks and pay level. Cassius had already been through three of those chosen for Gregorius' group and found nothing of great use. They were indeed all Italian-born veterans with at least a decade of service and numerous decorations. Cassius had copied the information on to papyrus himself; he didn't want to miss anything. With three done, he decided to take a short break, then do the others before meeting Lollius; the quartermaster had agreed to show him the temple and the crypt before nightfall. He put the reed pen to one side and stared out at a line of muddy legionaries walking by.

'I wonder if he's found them yet.'

'What's that, sir?' replied Simo, busy unfolding blankets.

'Those men from the inn. Prefect Venator told me he'd have them in chains by the end of the day.'

'Isn't that what you want, sir?'

'Yes, of course. I just wonder what will be done with them.'

'And those other men, from the road?'

'Optio Rullus and their centurion have been informed. They too will face punishment.'

Cassius stood up and touched his aching neck.

'Leave it alone, sir. I'll only have to put on more cream.'

'Yes, yes, I know.'

Venator had also arranged for Cassius to see the legion's chief surgeon. The elderly Greek had examined Cassius's head and back and decided it was 'just bruising'. The damage to his neck was 'purely superficial', though the surgeon had supplied a jar of unguent to ease the pain where the cape had cut the skin.

'It is helping a little. Stinks though.'

'That'll be the vinegar, sir.'

Cassius looked over at Indavara. The bodyguard was facing away from him, unpacking the meagre contents of his bag.

'You certainly travel light.'

Indavara didn't react.

'I suppose I should thank you. You literally saved my neck.'

Indavara gave a brief look over his shoulder and nodded an acknowledgement.

Cassius glanced at Simo and rolled his eyes. He was curious what exactly this man had been doing for Abascantius. Before he could ask him about it, Indavara picked up his bow and quiver.

'Do you need me here?' he asked.

'No. But I will in an hour or so. Are you going somewhere?'

Indavara held up the bow. 'There's a range close by. Looked empty.'

'Do you have any documentation from Abascantius? An authorisation or something? In case someone asks who you are.'

Indavara reached into his bag. He produced a worn half-page of papyrus and handed it over. It was a simple written statement, confirming that he was a bodyguard in the employ of the Governor's Office of Syria. There was also a small stamp and Abascantius's signature.

'Are you a good shot?' Cassius asked, handing the sheet back.

'Not bad.'

'Make sure of it. I think we've had enough excitement for one day.'

Indavara left without another word.

'By Mars, he's hard work,' said Cassius. 'I've had better conversations with my grandmother's cat.'

Simo nodded as he continued to unpack. It always amazed Cassius to see just how much the Gaul could stuff into their saddlebags. There were his tunics, a toga, riding breeches, capes and hoods; wash-cloths, towels, sheets, a pillow; a spare pair of sandals, a pair of felt slippers; plus a rack of oils and lotions that Cassius also deemed essential.

'He is rather quiet, sir.'

'You didn't manage to get anything out of him?'

'Not a lot.'

'You saw the state of his horse's mouth, and his saddle?'

'I did, sir. I don't think he's had much experience of riding. I offered to help but he didn't seem too interested.'

'He seems a bit of a dullard, Simo. Handy with his fists though. Dealt with those big Celts easily enough. For the time being we shall simply have to endure his company.'

Cassius neared the small pile of clothes Indavara had left on his bed. He bent over and sniffed them.

'Gods! And his stench. I thought it was this stuff on my neck. Simo, be sure to keep this place well ventilated. Move my bed further away from his – we have the space. And don't forget to spread some perfume around before we retire for the night.'

The western quarter of the sky glowed orange and pink as the sun set over Palmyra. Cassius and Quartermaster Lollius marched along the middle of the road that led from the encampment to the Damascus Gate, with Indavara and Simo a few paces behind.

Cassius found it difficult to reconcile the scene in front of him with the image of the great siege conjured by Legionary Gerardus back at the way-station. The southern side of Palmyra was protected only by a six-foot mud-brick wall with many damaged sections; and there were no towers or fortified gates.

'The defences were like this when our forces arrived?' Cassius asked.

'Pretty much,' said Lollius. 'But their queen had tens of thousands of warriors in there. The city is large and spread out, and many of the people stayed. If we'd gone in there house to house it would have been a bloodbath. The Emperor played it well. A victory without a battle is the best victory of all.'

Lollius nodded to the right and the four of them turned down a narrower road that ran parallel to the city walls. At the end of it was a large temple. Two legionaries stood guard. A third shot to his feet when alerted by his fellows.

'Indeed,' said Cassius. 'The Emperor's policy of clemency does seem wise.'

'And he even spared the dogs this time.'

'What's that, sir?'

Although the question of rank was again complex, Cassius thought it circumspect to show Lollius the utmost respect.

'The first city to resist him was Tyana in Cappadocia,' explained the quartermaster. 'The Emperor was livid that the inhabitants had sided with the Palmyrans, so he swore he wouldn't leave even a dog alive. But then there were the usual negotiations and he ended up sparing the town just like he did here. The men were disappointed – they'd expected a good sack. So he told them he would fulfil his oath – and ordered them to kill all the dogs. They took it in good spirit and did so.'

'One way to keep the streets clean, I suppose.'

In front of the temple was a wide courtyard. It was overgrown with grass and weeds and in places bricks had been removed from the walls. In the centre of the space was a large altar. Carved into the middle of it were channels to drain the blood of sacrificed beasts.

'Whichever god this was dedicated to, he seems to have fallen out of favour,' remarked Cassius.

'I forget the name,' replied Lollius. 'There are so many out here and they all sound the same to me. I heard the followers belonged to a group that somehow offended the queen. Hasn't been used as anything other than an armoury for many a year.'

Though dilapidated, the temple maintained an imposing grandeur. The walls were constructed of huge limestone blocks; the front was dominated by four thick, weathered columns; and high, wide steps led up to a hefty wooden door. At the base of the steps stood the three legionaries, arms by their sides.

Lollius took a key on a chain from around his neck and threw it to the oldest of them.

'Open up.'

The quartermaster then looked at the man who'd been late getting to his feet.

'Name?'

'Legionary Decius Herius Faustus, sir.'

'Faustus, eh – the lucky.'

The legionary grimaced; he knew what was coming.

'Well, not tonight. If you want to lounge around like some slovenly easterner, I shall find you a useful occupation.'

Lollius looked back at the courtyard.

'You know what my wife makes me do when I'm home on leave? She has me pull up all the weeds on our terrace. Every tiny shoot. Right pain in the arse – the back too after a while. But that shouldn't be a problem for a young buck like you, especially after you've had a nice little break. Get to it then! I don't want to see anything green left in this courtyard.'

The legionary leant his spear against the nearest column, removed his helmet and bent down in front of the nearest clump of weeds.

After three failed attempts, the older legionary had finally managed to turn the key in the stiff iron lock. He heaved the creaking door open. Lollius took the oil lantern he had given Simo to carry and stepped inside.

'You two wait here,' Cassius told Simo and Indavara.

With only a high line of small apertures to admit the fading light, the temple was almost pitch black, and Cassius stayed close to Lollius as the quartermaster stalked along the central corridor, footsteps echoing on the flagstones. Cassius had expected a voluminous space but, as the light of the lamp splashed across the interior, he saw that each side of the temple was divided into small chambers. Every one was full. There were barrels stuffed with spears and swords, stacks of helmets and armour; even huge stone balls a yard across – ammunition for siege engines.

'Some of this was already here,' said Lollius. 'The rest we took off the Palmyrans after the surrender.'

At the end of the corridor was a steep set of steps that led up to a wide platform. To the right of the platform was a doorway leading to a large chamber. Cassius had seen this arrangement before in the eastern provinces. It was here that the cult image would be kept; the devotees wouldn't want the sacred object to be visible from outside. As he climbed the steps – still close behind Lollius – he could make out depressions made by the knees of prostrate worshippers.

The walls of the chamber were dotted with empty niches, and in the middle of the floor was a square gap with soil below; presumably a former resting place for another altar. Cassius followed Lollius over to the far left corner. Here, a dozen stone blocks had been piled next to a low arched doorway. Beyond the doorway, steps led downward.

'There was a false wall here,' explained Lollius.

Cassius cast a quizzical glance at the limestone blocks. They weren't as large as those in the exterior walls but would still be extremely heavy.

'How did you—'

'Lift one. You might surprise yourself.'

Lollius held the lamp over the nearest block.

'Go on. Try.'

Cassius gripped it with both hands and found he could easily move it.

'How in Hades?'

As he put the block down, Lollius drew his dagger and jabbed it into the stone.

Cassius jumped back.

'Easy, grain man,' said the quartermaster, twisting the blade before pulling it out.

'See here – it's wood. They plastered it or painted it somehow to make it look like limestone.'

Cassius leaned forward to examine the strips of wood on the dagger blade.

'Clever eh?' continued Lollius. 'Tarquinius spotted it; the colour's slightly different if you look closely. He'd seen something similar while treasure-hunting up north.'

'Sir, I don't mean to be impertinent, but do you really believe – and expect me to believe – that a soldier so adept at digging out booty found a crypt full of it, then simply reported it to his seniors without taking a single piece for himself?'

Lollius shrugged. 'For all you know, I might have done the same. One has to think of one's retirement at my age.'

Cassius stared at him. Then the quartermaster grinned. Cassius told himself to relax; in the grand scheme of things, it hardly mattered if he or this Tarquinius had nabbed a bit of silver or gold for themselves.

'Can we go inside the crypt?'

'You can. Scrambling down there Jupiter knows how many times almost did my back in.'

Lollius handed over the lantern.

'Go ahead, I'm sure you'll be fine. There haven't been any earthquakes this week.'

'Earthquakes?' Cassius stopped at the top step.

'Just tremors. I mean, enough to bring down this old place, but, no, nothing this week. Of course sometimes that means there's another one coming but . . . I'm sure you'll be fine.'

Fairly sure that the quartermaster was lying, Cassius descended the nine steps into the crypt. It was dank and musty, and in one corner, water dripped on to the floor. He could almost stand up straight.

He walked along all four walls (measuring the chamber at eight paces by five), studying the floor as he went. The lamplight sparked off something. He reached down and picked up a small brass coin. He held it close to the lamp. The obverse, which would almost certainly show an imperial portrait, was worn beyond recognition. The reverse showed what looked like two crossed swords and the end of a word he couldn't read. He glanced around the crypt one last time, then headed back up the steps. He found Lollius sitting on one of the blocks.

'What do you have there?' asked the quartermaster.

'A coin, old thing. One of those you used to cover the treasure with?'

Lollius peered at the coin, then shrugged. 'Probably.'

'Where did you get them from?'

'There was a load of them in one of the other rooms. Not worth a lot now. We used them all, I think – made sure the barrels were full up to the lid.'

'They all looked like this one?'

'No idea. We just threw them in.'

Cassius returned the lamp to Lollius and followed him out of the chamber.

'There are no other ways in or out?'

Lollius shook his head. 'None.'

They made their way down the steps and back along the corridor.

'So you brought the barrels into the crypt, filled them up, covered them with the coins, then left them in there?'

'Yes. Then on the night that Gregorius and the men left we brought them out to the cart in the courtyard.'

Cassius stopped short of the door so that the soldiers couldn't listen in. He spoke quietly.

'You said you walked with them for a while?'

'I did. The last I saw of them they were heading for the valley of the tombs. Bad omen, I suppose.'

'I'd like to follow their route, out past where this sentry last saw them.'

Lollius sighed. 'Very well. We'll go out first thing tomorrow, grain man. I'll bring the sentry along too. You should go and see the prefect now. He has a drink with the tribunes most evenings and he won't want you around for that. Too many awkward questions.'

Cassius followed Lollius out into the courtyard. They were met by the bizarre sight of Simo and Indavara helping Legionary Faustus with his weeding. All three of them stopped when they saw they were being watched.

Lollius frowned. 'Why are you helping him?'

'Yes,' added Cassius. 'Why *are* you helping him?'

'It's a big job, sir,' said Simo flatly.

'I like to keep busy,' said Indavara, shrugging.

Lollius shook his head, then marched away across the courtyard.

VIII

'Don't let that wine get too hot,' ordered Venator.

An aged servant hurried over to the brazier and moved the pan to one side. Cassius was standing in a corner with his hands behind his back, waiting for the prefect to finish some paperwork. He watched as the servant returned to the prefect's bed, and continued to dress it with freshly laundered cotton sheets. The bed was huge, with ornate wooden posts at each corner; and the tent was filled with other hefty items of furniture. Cassius wondered how many carts were needed to transport the prefect's belongings.

Venator dropped his pen, leaned back and yawned. He stood up and walked over to three couches that had been arranged in a U. Cassius followed him there and waited as the prefect kicked off his sandals and lay down, propping a fine red cushion under his head.

'Sit, Corbulo, sit.'

Cassius sat in the middle of a couch opposite the prefect and tried to look relaxed. Nothing was said while the servant moved two tables within easy reach and brought them each a cup of wine. The prefect took a long, slow sip.

'Ah, yes. My one real pleasure of the day. Well, anything to report?'

'I've started going through the legionary records, sir, but nothing stands out so far. Quartermaster Lollius has just shown me the temple. In the morning he's going to take me out on the Antioch road with the sentry who last saw Gregorius and the legionaries.'

'And any thoughts about what may have happened?'

Cassius had already decided to be honest and frank with Venator. Though the slim possibility remained that he or one or more of his men were somehow involved in the theft, his material help might prove crucial; and his experience and position made him a valuable source of advice.

'The way I see it, sir, there are three possibilities. One: someone who knew about the flag and the treasure arranged for the cart to be ambushed. The motive might be simple monetary gain or political advantage – if they knew of the banner's significance.'

Venator nodded. 'Go on.'

'Two: some other, unexpected fate befell them. They ran into Palmyrans, locals, who knows? Three: someone within the group is responsible.'

Cassius knew how Quartermaster Lollius would have responded to the last of the three alternatives but Venator was rather more circumspect. The prefect sat up a little higher and ran his fingers through his soft, white hair.

'I've little time for Abascantius but he's no fool. I can't believe he would assign such a task to a man he didn't absolutely trust. As for the legionaries, well, I've as many rogues in my ranks as any prefect – you yourself can attest to that – but the ten we gave Gregorius are not among them. Even if one or two found out what was inside those barrels and concocted some scheme, I don't see how they could have overpowered the others. These men are veterans. Heroes.'

'How dangerous are the lands between here and Antioch, sir?'

'Safer than they've been in several years, but there are Palmyran irregulars still scattered around, not to mention the odd gang of brigands between towns. It's possible Gregorius ran into trouble, but it would have taken a strong, well-organised force to get the better of them, I can tell you that much. Which leaves your first possibility.'

Cassius nodded and drank some wine.

'Someone with prior knowledge of the operation,' added the prefect. 'Marcellinus and the members of his council. Plus myself, Lollius and Tarquinius of course.'

Cassius decided he could conclude little from the cool manner in which the prefect had unabashedly named himself as a suspect.

'And the Service itself of course, sir. I'm not sure if Abascantius has involved anyone other than Gregorius and myself. And then there's the imperial post. I wanted to ask: how secure is it?'

'Well, code is usually used for important communiques.'

'How exactly does that work?'

'You really are new to all this, aren't you. Amandio!' The slave shuffled over to them. 'Bring me the largest box from the top shelf.' Venator turned back to Cassius. 'There is a standard cipher book with about two hundred different codes in it.'

Cassius had heard of these books but never seen one.

Venator continued: 'On one of the first occasions I met Abascantius, we agreed verbally which cipher we would use but made no written record of it. From then on, anything either of us deemed to be sensitive would be written in that code. Common practice.'

As Amandio returned with the wooden box, Venator directed him to Cassius. The servant placed the box on the floor and opened the lid. Inside was a single leather-bound book. Cassius picked it up and opened it. On each page was a different code: some used numbers assigned to letters, others used a formula or symbols.

'These books are all the same?'

'Yes. They're issued from Rome.'

'But anyone with a copy could simply go through all the codes – if they wanted to decipher a certain letter.'

'Yes, but they're very hard to get hold of. Plus the army and the Security Service vet and monitor the couriers very closely. There have been incidents in the past of course, but nothing in this province that I can recall.'

Cassius replaced the book in the box and the servant took it away.

'Sir, there might be another angle to all this. Some of Zenobia's people must have known about the contents of the crypt. If any of them are still at large, then they might be responsible.'

Venator thought about this for a moment.

'The queen kept much of her wealth with her; a good deal of it was captured at Emesa. The fact that the banner and the rest of the treasure were left here might indicate she didn't know about them.'

'Or that she did and they were being kept secret and safe – some kind of bargaining tool for dealing with the Persians.'

'Possibly.'

'And what of her courtiers, sir? Ministers? They were all killed?'

'Her most trusted aide was Cassius Longinus. I believe Zenobia tried to blame him and the others for instigating the revolt. They were all put on trial and executed.'

'But someone who knew of the banner may have survived, or passed on that knowledge.'

'If they already knew of it, why not recover the flag and the treasure earlier?'

Cassius shrugged. More questions. No answers.

'Sir, is there anyone left in the city who might be able to help us with this?'

'Some of those working with us now were fairly high up in the queen's administration. I'll make some enquiries tomorrow.'

The oil lamps flared and fizzled as someone entered the tent. Cassius and Venator turned to see Lollius lowering a flap of canvas. He looked hot and unhappy.

'You have them?' Venator asked.

Lollius nodded.

Venator stood and put on his sandals.

'Amandio. My cape.'

Shaking his head impatiently as the old man struggled with a drawer, Venator hurried across and took the cape out himself. He threw it over his shoulders and finished off his wine.

'Come, Corbulo.'

Venator stopped close to the entrance and selected a long leather riding crop from a cylindrical wooden case. Cassius had a good idea who might be outside. He felt sick. As he exited the tent behind the prefect and Lollius, six legionaries were just being dismissed by a tall centurion. Four soldiers remained, standing in a row behind three prisoners. The Celts were down on their knees, manacled at the wrists and ankles.

Estan looked up at Cassius. His pale eyes bored into Cassius's with unalloyed rage. His chin was bruised and one side of his jaw seemed to be hanging at a strange angle.

'I thought there were four,' said Venator.

'One of them fainted when we grabbed him out of bed,' explained Lollius. 'Apparently he caught a stool in the head from the bodyguard. He's in the infirmary under guard.'

'Sounds like you've got a good man there, Corbulo,' said Venator. 'Not that you should have needed protection from men drawing a wage from imperial coffers. This is definitely them?'

Cassius thought it unlikely that he would ever forget Estan's face but he double-checked the other two to make sure.

'Yes, sir.'

Venator turned back to the quartermaster. 'And what about the others from the inn – the auxiliaries who stood by?'

'Enquiries are being made, sir.'

Estan mumbled something.

Venator slashed the riding crop across his shoulder.

'Not a word, you dog! Not a single bloody word.'

Spit from Venator's mouth landed on Estan's face and on Cassius's arm. Estan bowed his head. The crop had torn straight through his tunic, leaving a livid welt on the skin.

Venator turned to Cassius. 'They'll face a proper tribunal later in the week. Flogging, I should think. But I didn't want you to miss an opportunity for recompense.'

Cassius was nodding, but all he could think of was what exactly the prefect meant by recompense.

'You men are Caledonians, I gather,' said Venator, now pacing slowly in front of them. 'Well, this man is an officer of the Roman Army. Which means he is worth ten of you. And which means that if you ever encounter him – or indeed any other officer – you should show nothing other than deference, obedience and loyalty. Clear?'

The other two Celts nodded. They had also been beaten about the face.

'Speak.'

'Yes, sir,' the men answered in Latin.

Estan remained silent and still, staring blankly ahead.

'By Mars, he's a stubborn one, isn't he, Lollius?'

'Like a mule, sir. Like a stupid Caledonian mule.'

'Well, we need to hear him say it too. Let's see if he can be persuaded.'

Venator handed Cassius the riding crop. The handle was warm.

Cassius took it, but he had his excuses ready. 'Sir, I would prefer to allow military justice to take its course. I thank you for taking this action on my behalf, but I—'

'On your behalf? No, Corbulo, you misunderstand. This is about discipline. Or rather indiscipline. They must be made to understand the error of their ways. They must be made examples of.'

Venator waved a hand towards the Celts. 'Go ahead. They tried to murder you, man.'

Cassius looked over at Lollius. There was a faint smile as he wiped at his weeping eye. The tall centurion was watching keenly too. Cassius approached Estan.

'Leave him until last,' ordered Venator.

Cassius moved on to one of the other Celts. The auxiliary bowed his head. Cassius tried to think of the inn, what they'd done to him, the pain. He tried to channel all the anger and frustration of the day, and suddenly he was lashing out, striking the man about the head and the shoulders.

'Come on!' yelled Lollius. 'I bet you hit your horse twice as hard.'

Cassius's next blow hit the man on the arm.

'Draw blood at least,' snapped Venator.

Cassius unleashed a final blow across the man's head. The Celt cried out.

'Better, better,' said Venator.

Cassius lowered the crop to his side. He couldn't bear to look at the man.

'Finished already?' Venator asked as Cassius moved past Estan.

'It's enough, sir.'

Venator bent over in front of the first Celt. 'Let's have an apology to the officer then.'

'Sorry, sir,' said the auxiliary.

This time Cassius made sure he put enough into the attack to keep it quick. He hit the second man hard three times; once across the head, twice across the shoulder. At the third blow, the Celt fell on to his side with a whimper. The centurion righted him by pulling him up by his hair. Cassius felt a thick bile rising up his throat. He coughed to clear it. The centurion laughed.

'I do believe he's going green.'

Lollius chuckled, as did a couple of the legionaries.

Venator held up a finger, quietening them all in an instant. He peered down at the auxiliary.

'Well, that's a quarter of what I'd give him but I suppose it will have to do.' He slapped the Celt across the nose and pointed to Cassius. 'Your turn.'

'Sorry, sir.'

'Good. You can take these two to the stockade now. Leave this fellow with us.'

The centurion ordered his men to get the prisoners on their feet, then the seven of them walked away along the avenue.

'Now, Corbulo,' said Venator. 'You are not to stop until we get an apology from this one too.'

From what he'd seen of Estan, Cassius dreaded to think what might be required to get him to cooperate.

'Sir, please. I'm not sure what purpose this serves.'

Venator frowned. 'You should be thanking me for this, Corbulo. You have caused us considerable inconvenience today.'

Cassius bowed. 'I do thank you, sir, I do.'

'I know you're not a real army officer but I think you need to face some harsh realities. The field is no place for half-measures. This man tried to kill you. What did you think we would do?'

'I don't know, sir.'

'We will get that apology. There are other methods we can use. Isn't that right, Quartermaster?'

'Tried and tested methods, sir,' said Lollius, tapping a thumb against the hilt of his dagger.

'You seem to prefer talking to doing, Corbulo,' continued Venator. 'Why don't you try to persuade him?'

Cassius could still not quite believe how the prefect had been considered and urbane one moment, thuggish and cruel the next. He took a breath, and locked eyes with Estan.

'Just say it, man. Save yourself the pain. Just apologise.'

'Not to you, Skinny. Never.'

Lollius laughed; Venator too.

Cassius lashed the Celt across the head, catching him just above his ear. Estan shut his eyes for a moment but then looked up and smiled. Cassius raised his arm high, and brought the crop down hard on his neck. He kept hitting him there, until Estan turned his head away; then Cassius shifted to his left, and swung the crop up into his face. The Celt's head snapped up, and Cassius unleashed a flurry of blows down on him, not caring where he struck him, as long as every ounce of his strength went into each blow. Only when Estan grunted with pain did he stop.

Cassius stood there, sweating, trying to think through the rhythmic pounding in his head. He was gripping the crop so hard that his fingernails were biting into his palm.

Estan's face and neck were heavily marked. The skin had opened up in several places. He was no longer smiling.

'Not bad, not bad,' said Venator. He looked down at Estan. 'Well, ready to speak yet?'

Estan spat on to Cassius's tunic.

Venator tutted. 'Tough son of a bitch, isn't he? Now I know why we never managed to conquer Caledonia.'

He nodded to Lollius; and the quartermaster drove a knee into Estan's back, sending him head first into the mud. Then he put the same knee between the Celt's shoulder blades, pinning him. He reached down and tried to grip Estan's manacled left forearm but the Celt was struggling.

'Help him there, Corbulo,' ordered Venator. 'Stand on his arm.'

'What?'

'Address me correctly, damn you. You heard me: stand on his arm.'

'Yes, sir,' Cassius stammered.

Lollius had drawn his dagger.

'Keep him still!' ordered the quartermaster.

Venator pushed Cassius towards them. Lollius bent Estan's arm towards him, so that the Celt's hand was in reach. Cassius placed his boot on the forearm.

'Stand on it!' Lollius yelled.

Cassius pressed down harder. Mud oozed out from beneath Estan's arm. He was still struggling.

Venator tutted again, then came forward and planted his foot on Estan's other arm.

'Do hurry up, Lollius.' He then called out to his servant: 'Amandio, get some more wine on, my tribunes will be here soon.'

Estan's face was flat against the mud, twisted towards Cassius. Lollius gripped the Celt's wrist with his spare hand.

'Just say it,' Cassius told Estan. 'Just say it.'

'Which finger, sir?' the quartermaster asked.

'Who cares? Just hurry up.'

Say sorry. Just say sorry.

Lollius pushed down so that the Celt's fingers splayed out in the mud. He placed the edge of the blade against the little finger. Estan was still trying to pull his hand free. Lollius dug in his knee. 'Hold still, damn you.'

He put the blade against the finger again.

Cassius squeezed his eyes shut.

Say it, say it, say it.

Lollius began to slice through the finger just below the knuckle.

'I'm sorry!' cried Estan. 'I'm sorry!'

Lollius stopped cutting. Cassius removed his boot. Lollius looked down at the finger. 'Only just into the bone. You might just keep it, Celt.'

The quartermaster stood up.

The first thing Estan did was to grip the mutilated finger with his other hand to hold it in place. Then he dragged himself to his knees, half his face covered in mud.

Cassius reached into his belt and took out the handkerchief Simo insisted on giving him every morning. He handed it to Estan, who took it and wrapped it around his finger.

'That wasn't so hard, was it?' said Venator. 'Back to the stockade with him, Quartermaster. And apologies for taking up so much of your evening.'

'Sir.'

Lollius hauled Estan to his feet by his tunic, then directed him on to the avenue and to the left. The Celt hobbled away, slowed by the shackles. Lollius followed, still taunting him.

Venator fixed Cassius with an imperious stare. 'Leave the crop just inside the tent. Amandio will clean it later.'

Cassius did so. When he returned outside, Venator nodded at the departing Celt.

'A lesson for you there, Corbulo. You'll not last long in the Service if you've no stomach for the rough stuff. How do you think your friend Abascantius gets answers when he needs them? Lollius and I are but novices in the dark arts of coercion compared to him.'

'Yes, sir.'

'Think on it. You're dismissed.'

Venator went inside. Cassius stood there for a moment, listening to the low hiss of the oil lamps, staring down at the hollows and lines where Estan had struggled in the mud. He walked to the avenue, turned right and started back for the tent.

What a day it had been. A terrible, violent day. And he knew it wouldn't be the memory of those Celts trying to throttle him that would stay with him. It would be the sight of himself – as if observed through another's eyes – whipping a kneeling, mana-cled prisoner until he bled.

Approaching a junction, he saw four tribunes coming round the corner. To avoid an awkward encounter and conversation, he ducked quickly out of sight, moving into the shadows of a cart piled high with tent canvas.

The tribunes were in good spirits as they headed for their evening drink with the prefect. Cassius stood still, waiting for them to pass; and he listened intently to their conversation. They were talking about art.

IX

Though not as green as Palmyra itself, the lands north-west of the city were more than fertile enough for farming. The road that led eventually to Antioch turned north after the Damascus Gate and was surrounded by fields, orchards and vineyards. It was one of the best maintained roads in Syria: fully twelve feet wide and built of square slabs of stone, with a narrow gravel track for pedestrians on either side. After more than an hour on this road, Cassius had seen just a handful of people, most of them close to one of the grand, sprawling villas they had passed. Few of the fields were being properly tended: some of the crops had spoiled, others were yet to be harvested. Even this quiet, affluent corner of the Palmyran empire had suffered the effects of war.

Quartermaster Lollius was ten yards ahead, riding alone. He seemed even more contemptuous towards Cassius after the events of the previous evening and had said nothing since setting off from the encampment just after dawn. Cassius rode alongside Indavara and the sentry who'd seen Gregorius and his group – a keen young legionary named Mico. Simo was back at the encampment. One of the legion veterinarians had decided his horse would not recover quickly, so he had to find a new mount.

Cassius watched a large group of people filing on to the road up ahead, bound for the city.

'Followers of Bel,' announced Mico.

At the head of the procession were four priests wearing high cylindrical hats decorated with woven images of the stars, the sun and the moon. The silent worshippers behind them ranged in age from six to sixty and there were as many women as men. Not one of them acknowledged the presence of the watching riders.

Half a mile further on, Lollius turned left and led them between the grounds of two villas. They negotiated a wide ditch then came to a small stone hut. Lollius shouted something and two legionaries appeared. They stood stiffly to attention as the four men dismounted and tied their horses to a fence. Lollius hurried past the two sentries. Cassius and Mico followed him.

'What are you doing?' asked the quartermaster. 'I'm going for a piss. It would take both of you to hold it for me, but after all these years of practice I can just about manage on my own.'

Mico and the other legionaries waited for Lollius to disappear behind the hut before they started laughing. Cassius wandered away from them and looked to the west. After a couple of miles, the patchwork of fields ran into flat, dusty steppe. He called Mico over.

'This is the edge of the picket line?'

'Yes, sir.'

Directly to the south was the edge of the city; they could still see the tops of the tomb towers. To the north, perhaps ten leagues away, was an undulating line of hills.

'So tell me what you saw.'

'It was the third hour of night. I was here with Colias.' Mico turned to check that Lollius was still out of earshot. 'We were both supposed to stay awake but as usual we took it in shifts. I went first. I saw these lights coming up from the south, parallel to the road. When they got close, I woke Colias and we went over to have a look. It was unusual – what with the curfew and everything.'

'So they must have turned off the main road earlier than we did.'

Mico nodded. 'There were about a dozen of them and a cart. I recognised a few faces.'

'They were carrying torches?'

'Two at the front, two at the back. This one fellow came forward and showed us his papers. Seemed a bit odd – them being out of uniform – but we saw the prefect's stamp and let them go on their way.'

Lollius returned from behind the hut, tightening his belt as he walked. He stood next to them, dabbing his weeping eye with a cloth.

'Now, this is most important,' said Cassius. 'Try to show me the exact direction they took.'

Mico got his bearings, then walked back to the hut. 'We were sitting inside here, looking out of the window. I reckon it was something like this.'

Cassius examined the direction of the legionary's outstretched arm then looked up at the sun.

'North-east. After how long did you lose sight of the torches?'

'Perhaps an hour.'

'We must try to find their trail.'

Lollius summoned the two sentries and pointed at Cassius. 'Do whatever this officer tells you. I'll man your post. Got any food?'

'Just our lunches, sir,' volunteered one of the men meekly.

'That'll do.'

As Lollius headed back to hut, Cassius asked him a final question.

'This cart, sir. How wide apart would the wheels have been?'

Lollius answered over his shoulder without stopping. 'Eight or nine feet.'

Cassius waited for the quartermaster to go inside then turned to Mico.

'You'd agree with that?'

'Yes, sir. Big one. And well-laden. Would have left deep ruts.'

Cassius called Indavara over. With a concerned glance up at the banks of grey cloud sliding in from the west, he led the four men out to where the fields ended.

'So you spoke to them somewhere round here, Mico.'

'About exactly here I would say, sir.'

Cassius dug the toe of his boot into the ground. There was a top layer of dark sand with pebbles and firm soil underneath. Cart-tracks would surely show – but the only marks visible were hoof-prints.

'Goats, sir,' said Mico. 'The locals bring them through here all the time, for grazing where the fields have overgrown – might have covered the tracks.'

'We must still look. Men, you are searching for a cart-trail – lines about eight or nine feet apart. Two horses towing it, men walking in front, behind or at the sides. Call out if you see anything.'

Cassius placed himself in the middle, then positioned Indavara and Mico to his left, the two sentries to his right. He stationed the men ten yards apart then ordered them forward, directly north-east.

After half an hour, they were a mile from the picket line. Cassius called the men together. All five of them had seen multiple trails made by boots or animal hooves but there had been no sign of carts. Either the marks had since been obscured, or they had simply missed them. As cloud continued to roll in above them, Cassius set the men back to work.

By the time another mile had been covered, his eyes were stinging from staring intently at the ground. Moments earlier, Indavara had called him over to a cart-trail. The wheel marks had been clear, maybe even wide enough; but they were accompanied by only a single set of hoof marks. It couldn't have been Gregorius's group.

Cassius called a halt once more, and shook his head as the others joined him. 'They must have come through here.'

'I'm sure of it, sir,' answered Mico.

'We shall turn back and check this area again. The further we go, the more likely we are to stray off their path.'

'Sir, I have an idea.'

Mico pointed to a dwelling a mile to the north. Smoke was rising from a chimney.

'Goat-herder lives there. Nice old boy – we bought some milk off him the other week. I'll wager he knows this area like the back of his hand. Can't hurt to ask if he's seen anything.'

'Go.'

With not a single new trail spotted, Cassius was about ready to give up by the time Mico returned. The news was good.

'We're in luck, sir. He was out on one of the old nomad tracks a couple of days ago – saw a trail. Noticed because he's never known anyone else use it. Says you can see the wheel marks clear as day. Two miles east of here.'

'He'll show us?'

'He's heading over there now. He'll want paying of course.'

Cassius saw a small figure walking quickly away from the dwelling. The Syrian waved.

'To the horses,' said Cassius, already running.

The two sentries were sent back to their post and a muttering Lollius rejoined Cassius, Indavara and Mico as they rode across the plain to meet the goat-herder. The old man had covered the distance with admirable speed. He was squatting by the side of a narrow track but stood and bowed when the Romans arrived. The left side of his body was covered with a bright pink rash from ear to ankle. He pointed down at the ground.

One wheel-track was very clear, the other less so. Cassius dismounted and paced out the distance.

'About right.'

'Looks like you've found it, grain man,' said Lollius, turning his horse around.

Cassius looked along the track. It ran as far as he could see, heading a little north of north-east.

'Has to be it,' he whispered to himself. A drop of water landed on his hand. He looked up; and two more drops splashed on to his face.

'Caesar's balls.'

Hunched low, with his thighs pressed against the saddle, Cassius held on tight as his horse charged through the palm grove. He'd already survived a couple of near misses with protruding roots, and – as the path took an abrupt turn around a tree – he only just avoided a local man carrying a barrel on his head. The Syrian might easily have been knocked flying but there was no gesture or shout of protest. Cassius grinned; there were some advantages to being an officer of the Roman Army.

Riding out to the east of the city to find Venator at least gave him a few moments' relief from what was becoming a monumentally frustrating day. The rain continued to fall – light but insistent – and Cassius found himself staring up at the sky every few moments, hoping desperately that the cloud would clear.

The decision to follow the trail was an easy one; his brief time at Palmyra had yielded nothing particularly promising and he could always return if the cart-tracks led to a literal or metaphorical dead-end.

Simo and Indavara were busy packing. With no idea how long they might be out in the desert, or where the trail might take them, Cassius had told the Gaul to buy enough food and water for a week. Lollius seemed relieved that he would no longer have to play babysitter, and had even agreed to procure a mount for the old Syrian, who had readily assented to act as their guide. He seemed most concerned about what he would do with his goats but had pledged to meet them back at the trail at midday. Cassius had spent the last hour looking for Venator. Nobody seemed to know where he was, and only after questioning a tribune had Cassius discovered the prefect was in fact out at the city's eastern walls, overseeing some construction work. He had also managed to fit in a visit to the clerk, who'd promised to get the remaining four legionary records transcribed on to papyrus immediately.

The palms began to thin out. Cassius slowed down and came off the path to avoid a pair of horses hauling timber. To his left was the south-eastern corner of the city walls – perhaps even less impressive than those to the west. Up ahead a massive crew of slaves were hard at work digging; three hundred men at least, scattered along a low ditch marked with poles and rope. There were Palmyran overseers there too, brandishing long canes as they patrolled the ditch. The only Romans in sight were officers: four centurions and two tribunes, standing around a table piled high with sheets of papyrus. They were listening intently to the seventh man at the table: Prefect Venator.

Cassius jinked his horse between cubes of basalt, then stopped and dismounted. The officers looked up as he approached. Venator – whose hands were planted on a big drawing – stopped speaking and turned round.

'It's important?' asked the prefect. As he lifted his hands off the table, the drawing rolled itself up and fell off the table.

Cassius reddened as the tribunes and centurions all stared at him. 'Yes, sir.'

Venator addressed his officers: 'Go and check your sections. We'll reconvene in an hour.'

The prefect walked over to one of the basalt cubes and sat down. Cassius tied his horse to a palm then hurried over.

'Well?' asked Venator.

'We've found the trail, sir. I've hired a guide and we'll follow it as far as we can.'

'You must be quick. The rain.'

'We'll be gone within the hour, sir.'

'What about those records?'

'I'll have them all before I leave, sir.'

'Good. And I shall try to find out what I can regarding what we discussed yesterday: the temple, the Palmyrans – who knew what.'

'Thank you, sir. And if you discover anything of note, anything at all—'

'I shall dispatch a note to you via Abascantius's address in the capital. Using the usual code – thirty-two.'

'Thirty-two, sir.'

Venator let out a long breath and gestured towards the workers. 'What a job. Marcellinus tells me I must keep the Palmyrans weak, yet the Emperor wants the city's defences strengthened now that it's once again a Roman possession. If the new walls are ever finished, I expect I shall receive orders the following month to tear them down.'

Venator ran a hand through his hair. Cassius wondered when it had turned white.

'Well, sir, I suppose I should—'

'Wait a moment, Corbulo. Last night – the auxiliaries. It was a surprise to you, I imagine.' Venator smiled. 'You believed me to be a gentleman.'

'It has been nothing less than an honour to meet you, sir.'

The prefect waved this away. 'Don't toady, lad. I get enough of that from my tribunes. You grain men don't enjoy a lot of advantages. Not having to worm your way up the promotional ladder is one.'

'I meant what I said, sir. Regarding last night – the fault lies entirely with me.'

'How old are you?'

'Twenty-one, sir.'

'You've only three years more than my eldest.'

The prefect folded his arms across his chest.

'What I saw last night was a young man struggling with himself. I know that struggle. Every officer who's ever worn the crest knows it. But that's the life. Dirty job after dirty job, and in the Service you'll get the dirtiest of the lot. I remember what my old prefect used to tell me – though they were still called legates in those days: "You're a Roman officer. And a Roman officer cannot be just one man. He must be two or three or four." There's truth to that. You think the man you saw last night is the same one who returns to his family on leave? Goes to the theatre with his wife and makes small talk with his respectable friends? Or the one who spends hours politicking with the bloody Palmyrans? Even the same as the one talking to you now? I'm not so keen on that man you saw last night myself. Don't like him much. But I know I need him. Just like you need the man who was giving that Celt a good hiding.'

Cassius looked down at the ground. The thought of it still shamed him.

'No, no. Head up, lad. Accept it. You need that man for this life. You must always take care not to *become* him, but you will need him. If you're to find this accursed banner, by Jupiter you'll need him. Don't be afraid to do what needs to be done. I for one will owe you if you see this thing through.'

'I shall do my absolute best, sir.'

'Good luck then. And keep that bodyguard close by.'

Having collected the newly copied records from the clerk, Cassius found Simo and Indavara waiting outside the camp's main entrance. Their mounts were heavily laden with water-skins, sacks of food, firewood and horse-feed. Tied to the back of Simo's saddle was a placid-looking pony: shortly to become the goat-herder's mount.

Cassius's own saddlebags lay on the ground. He dismounted and kept hold of the reins as Simo set about attaching them.

'Got everything?'

'Yes, sir,' answered Simo, grunting as he lugged one of the bags up.

'Spear-head?'

'Yes, sir.'

'Money?'

'Yes, sir.'

'All my papers?'

'Yes, sir.'

As a short column of cavalry trotted into the camp, Indavara looked along the road to the Damascus Gate and shook his head.

'What's up with you?' asked Cassius.

'I had a dream last night,' Indavara answered, his brow knotted.

'Congratulations.'

'There were animals.'

'Thrilling.'

Cassius knew where this was going; Indavara struck him as just the type to ascribe dire consequences to his nocturnal imaginings.

'Let me guess – owls.'

'How did you know?'

Cassius rolled his eyes. 'You dreamed of owls so there'll be storms on our journey. Nonsense. Maybe there will, maybe there won't. Your dreams have nothing to do with it. It's the will of the gods or whatever else controls these things. My aunt won't travel for a month if she dreams of moving statues. But she's a silly old woman. What's your excuse?'

Indavara frowned. 'I thought owls meant we would be attacked by bandits.'

'Ah, I've never heard that one but at least it's a bit more realistic. Yes, we may well be attacked by bandits. So keep your bow handy and your sword sharp.'

'We should at least wait until tomorrow,' said Indavara.

Cassius turned to Simo. 'By Mars, he's serious.'

Indavara shrugged. 'Just thought I'd tell you.'

'Hey you! You there!'

Cassius and Indavara looked up at a cavalryman who had stopped.

'You,' the man repeated, nodding at Indavara, 'you were a fighter, weren't you?'

Indavara turned away from the road and said nothing. As he fiddled with his saddle, the rider examined him a moment longer, then turned and called out to a friend, one of the last in the column.

'Here, Sita! Come and look! We've a famous fighter here!'

Sita brought his horse up next to his friend.

'Remember – Pietas Julia, wasn't it? A couple of years back.'

Sita was nodding. 'You're right, Ruso. It's him all right. I remember the ear.'

Indavara was doing a poor job of ignoring the men. In fact he seemed to be getting angrier by the moment.

'What's the name again, mate?' asked Ruso.

'Indavara,' answered Cassius.

The bodyguard shot him a glare.

'That's it!' said Ruso, slapping his hand down on his saddle. 'I doubled my money on him. Right tough bugger. So what you doing here, mate?'

Indavara shrugged.

Another cavalryman joined the duo. 'Did you say Indavara? Everyone the other side of Byzantium's heard of him. Won twenty bouts and his freedom. Killed a seven-foot German, then a bear – with only a dagger. My sister was there.'

'Well, well,' said Cassius.

Simo was now listening in too.

'Here, mate, show us a move or something!' said Sita.

'No, no, he's not that type,' said the third man. 'Just hard and quick. Crafty too.'

Indavara took up his reins, turned his horse around and walked away up the road.

'Come on!' shouted Ruso. 'Just a trick or something!'

'Miserable sod,' muttered Sita when Indavara was safely out of earshot.

The third legionary turned his attention to Cassius. 'Is he your bodyguard, sir?'

'He is.'

'Must be costing you a fortune.'

Sita grinned mischieviously. 'Just don't get on the wrong side of him, sir.'

The cavalrymen went on their way.

Cassius and Simo looked up the road. Indavara glanced back at them for a moment, then kept walking.

X

Following the trail turned out to be surprisingly easy. Gregorius had kept to the track and only on very dry, hard soil did the wheel marks become unclear. Simo knew enough Aramaic to communicate with the goat-herder, who seemed thrilled to have a pony to ride and kept up a good pace throughout the day.

As evening approached, the track edged past a mountain; the western flank of a range that stretched forty miles to the east. The steep sides of the crag were striated by horizontal bands of yellow, brown and black; and the top seemed to have been cut away, forming a huge escarpment.

Cassius looked up at a pair of broad-winged eagles, circling hundreds of feet above. He knew from his map that the Antioch road followed a pass through the mountains, then struck north for the town of Seriane. Gregorius's route cut between this range and a smaller one to the west.

As his decision to follow the trail seemed to have turned out well, Cassius's spirits had lifted throughout the afternoon. He'd even had time to read the records of the other four legionaries – some of the men who had walked this very path two weeks earlier. Again, nothing of note stood out: four more highly decorated Italian veterans and no reason to believe they were anything other than reliable, honest soldiers.

'Well,' he said, turning to Simo. 'They got this far.'

'Indeed, sir.'

Cassius had told Simo and Indavara only the basics. They knew nothing of the banner – only that they were following a group escorting a precious cargo.

'Would you like your cape, sir? It is rather chilly now.'

'No, no. I'm fine.'

Cassius looked at the sun. 'Another two or three hours of light. If we see another suitable building we'll stop there.'

Even though they were now venturing deep into the Syrian desert, there always seemed to be some kind of structure in view. They had already seen three hamlets and several isolated stone-built houses, all long since abandoned. There had been no time to arrange tents, nor was there space to carry them; one of these old buildings would have to provide shelter for the night.

Cassius nodded over his shoulder. 'I don't think our ex-gladiator friend is enjoying himself.'

Though they'd already noted his lack of riding ability, only now did Cassius and Simo realise just how uncomfortable Indavara was in the saddle. He constantly berated his horse, though he hardly ever struck it; and was often seen squirming around, unable to find a comfortable riding position. They'd both offered a few words of advice but it was evident he'd never been taught properly.

So now Indavara was walking, towing the horse by its reins, trudging along with his head down.

'It's quite common for gladiators to become bodyguards,' Cassius continued. 'Certainly explains a lot.'

'The scars, you mean, sir.'

'Not just that, Simo. His demeanour. He was probably a captured prisoner of war, or – if our bad luck's still with us – a criminal. Those men are kept alive only to fight. They are utterly brutalised. And he's not been out that long. Two years ago that soldier said he saw him in the arena. No wonder he struggles with the niceties of everyday life.'

'I suppose he must have killed many men.'

'There's no suppose about it. And with great efficiency judging by what I saw at the inn. Gods, to think we're to spend nights out here alone with him.'

'Do you really fear him, sir? He did help you yesterday.'

'Only when he knew he would receive his money. You must

keep our coins well hidden, Simo. Be on your guard around him. He may seem quiet, shy even – but don't forget what he is.'

A sudden gust of wind blew around the base of the mountain. Cassius shivered.

'I think I'll take that cape after all.'

As the sun sank close to the horizon, the track led past a small farmhouse. Its uneven walls were formed of dark basalt blocks. It might have been twenty years old or a hundred. As Cassius, Simo and the Syrian dismounted, the Gaul translated the old man's words.

'He says they stopped here too.'

Cassius examined the disturbed ground in front of the doorway. 'So I see.'

Recalling that Gregorius had set off at dusk (and had intended only to travel during the night) Cassius imagined they stopped at dawn; the darkness and the cart would have slowed them. The two parties had covered the same distance on the first leg of their journey.

He wandered inside the farmhouse. In one corner, close to the only window, were the remains of a small fire. The dusty floor was criss-crossed by footprints. Cassius imagined it must have been a squeeze to get them all in. Despite the gloom, he took the time to inspect every inch of floor while there was still enough light. He found only a few crusts of bread.

Outside, the Syrian was distributing fodder to the horses. Simo had removed his and Cassius's saddles and was unpacking them in front of the farmhouse. Indavara arrived, still on foot. He dropped the reins and left his horse where it was, then sat below the window and undid his boots.

After all the talk of his violent past, and his concerns about the man, Cassius decided he would feel happier if he could at least strike up some kind of rapport with him.

'I'll have to give you some proper riding lessons.'

Indavara pulled off one boot and examined a nasty set of blisters on his heel.

'I'm serious,' Cassius added, standing over him. 'I need you fit and fresh, and we've many a mile to go. You have to learn some time.'

'Not now.'

'Of course not now.'

'I mean I don't want to talk about it now.'

Indavara pulled off the other boot.

Cassius shrugged, then headed back inside.

'Well, a rude bodyguard I can accept. A lame one I cannot.'

Cassius grabbed two blankets and lay down in a corner while Simo brought in their gear. He thought again of the legionaries. So they all had spotless records. But what if they'd found out what they were guarding? A lot of men had died in the last few months. The campaign against the Palmyrans had been difficult and costly and – with the state the Empire was in – few legionaries could expect a peaceful life over the next few years. Had one of them seen an opportunity for a way out? And what of Gregorius? Had he been the one tempted or coerced into an act of betrayal? Perhaps they were all innocent; victims of some unforeseen raid.

Despite these dark thoughts, Cassius was weary and he soon dozed off, only waking when he heard the metallic clank of pans.

Outside it had grown dark. The other three were inside: Simo had an oil lamp lit and was taking food out of a sack; Indavara and the Syrian were setting up their beds.

'Ah, you're awake, sir,' said the Gaul. 'What do you think about a fire? Nice to have something hot – I've a pot of stew here. I can warm you some wine too.'

'I don't see why not. The other party did.'

'Perhaps that was their first mistake,' observed Indavara.

'Go ahead, Simo,' said Cassius. 'We've not seen anyone for hours.'

Simo nodded and reached into the little bag where he kept his fire-starting equipment. The old man said something, stood up and walked outside.

'He's checking on the horses,' explained Simo as he laid some kindling – dry grass and bark – in a circle next to his firewood.

'Tell him to make sure they're well roped,' said Cassius. As the Gaul did so, Indavara picked up his quiver and moved close to the oil lamp. He selected an arrow and began checking the shaft and feathering. Cassius sat down next to him.

'Those men said they'd seen you fight at Pietas Julia. That's where you won your freedom?'

'Yes.'

'How?' asked Cassius, looking on as Simo wrapped a square of char-cloth around one end of a knapped flint.

'It was promised that any fighter who survived twenty matches would be set free.'

'Twenty. That's a lot, isn't it?'

Cassius didn't know much about the games; his family rather disapproved of them. He shared their view that it was a barbaric practice but he'd always been curious about what went on inside the arena.

'It is,' replied Indavara.

Simo now brought out the fire-striker: a c-shaped implement made of iron.

'When was this?' Cassius asked.

'About a year and a half ago.'

'And how did you end up in Syria?'

At last Indavara met Cassius's gaze. 'Why are you asking me so many questions?'

Simo set himself, then brought the striker down against the flint. He got a good spark, but the char-cloth didn't take light and it eventually took him five attempts to get a flame. He delicately set light to the kindling and was soon adding the first pieces of wood.

Cassius answered: 'It seems we shall be spending a good deal of time together. Perhaps it would be nice to know a little about each other. You may ask questions of me if you wish.'

Indavara thought about this for a moment. He ran two fingers down the arrow's feathers to straighten them.

'At the inn yesterday. Why did those men attack you?'

130

'There was a misunderstanding.'

Indavara frowned. 'Must have been a big one.'

'It's complicated,' Cassius replied, thinking that a genuine explanation of what had occurred would make him seem extremely foolish.

Simo was now setting up the arrangement of iron rods that would support the spit above the fire.

'They can be dangerous,' said Indavara.

'Who? Celts?'

'No. Inns.'

'Occasionally.'

'That's why I had to leave Pietas.'

'What do you mean?'

'The inns.'

Exasperated, Cassius threw up his hands. 'Stop speaking in riddles, man. Explain yourself.'

Indavara frowned and rubbed the back of his neck but then continued: 'The inns. Every time I went in one, somebody would want to fight me.'

'Ah, I see – to prove themselves. Test you. You grew tired of it.'

'Yes. And I killed a man.'

Cassius only just managed not to look at Simo.

'Go on.'

'I didn't mean to. But there were four of them. I was in a corner. Nobody would help. Other people were betting money on who would win. Afterwards, the magistrate's men came looking for me.'

'So you left, headed east?'

'I used up what money I had to get to Byzantium.'

'And what happened there?'

'A man recognised me from the games. Said he had a job for me.'

'Abascantius?'

'No, someone else. I worked for him for a few months. He

131

recommended me to Abascantius. From Byzantium we went to Tarsus, then Aleppo. I had to guard a man and his wife at their villa. That job finished. Then I was sent to meet you.'

'How do you like it? The work?'

'Usually it's easy.'

'Apart from when you have to ride.'

Indavara shrugged. He replaced the arrow in the quiver, then took out another.

'How is it that you've never learned to ride?' asked Cassius. 'What about before? Were you taken as a prisoner?'

Indavara said nothing.

'I assume that's how you came to be a gladiator?'

Indavara ran his fingers along the arrow.

'Well?'

'How hungry are we all?' asked Simo. 'Sir?'

Cassius dragged his eyes away from Indavara, who was holding the arrow just inches from his face. Simo showed him a large glass jar full of stew.

'What's in it?'

'Lamb and vegetables, sir. Made just yesterday.'

'Plenty for me.'

Simo turned towards Indavara. 'Sir?'

'You don't have to call him sir, Simo. It's Indavara to you.'

Indavara seemed utterly uninterested in how he was to be addressed; he was staring at the stew.

'As much as you have.'

Simo emptied the entire jar into a deep pan, then hooked the handle on to the spit over the fire.

Cassius glanced at Indavara again. He thought about persisting but decided against it. At least he knew something now.

'So what about that riding lesson in the morning?'

Indavara was wrapping twine around the end of the arrow. After a while, he nodded.

day anyway.' He didn't want to appear indecisive but the body-guard was for once making sense. 'We'll only lose a few hours. And we can dry off at least. If we find nothing, we can head off in the afternoon. North it is.'

Simo walked over to the Syrian and pointed towards the village.

'I'm glad today finds you in a more communicative mood, Indavara,' Cassius said as he hauled himself back up into the saddle. 'Time for that riding lesson.'

Two hours later, under a clear sky, the bedraggled foursome guided their horses down a hill through a grove of olive trees. Below them, nestled in a bowl-like valley, was the main part of the village. The settlement showed no sign of planning whatsoever: multiple paths led off the main road and the houses all faced in different directions.

They came to a small hut. Carved into an outcrop of rock next to it was a wide, flat slab – an oil press. Scattered across it were hundreds of dark green olives.

A stout man in his forties walked out of the hut carrying a wooden pole. He had a thick head of jet-black hair and an equally dark beard; and he greeted the strangers with a curious glance that swiftly became an engaging grin.

'Here's an unusual sight,' the villager said in Latin. 'A Roman officer in lowly Ethusa.' He leaned the pole up against the press. 'What brings you here, sir?'

'Actually I'm looking for someone. A group rather. They may have passed through about two weeks ago. Eleven men escorting a large cart. Do you recall anything?'

The man shook his head. 'We've only had a few visitors since the Festival of Sol. A couple of wandering priests, a few pedlars and now you. Get caught in the rain?'

'Very observant,' Cassius replied sourly. It seemed they had wasted yet more time.

'Name's Dacien,' said the villager. 'Formerly Optio Dacien, First Century, Third Cohort, Sixteenth Legion.'

Cassius decided to be a little more polite. 'Officer Corbulo, governor's staff.'

'Somebody not pay their taxes?'

'Tax is not my concern. All I'm interested in is these men. Is there any other way through here?'

Dacien put his foot up on a rock. 'From the south?'

'Yes.'

'A couple of small tracks but nothing wide enough for a cart.'

'You've heard nothing of any strangers in the area at all?'

'No. But there's folk here with animals and property scattered all over. Somebody may have seen something.'

'Is there an inn? Somewhere we might dry ourselves, get some hot food?'

'We've not enough passing traffic here for an inn. It's mostly retired soldiers and local families.'

Dacien examined the four men, then nodded. 'But my wife can help you with hot food and a fire. For a coin or two of course.'

'Is your home close?'

Dacien glanced towards the village. 'Just there. That's all there is to Ethusa, by the way.'

Cassius gestured down the hill. 'Please.'

Dacien's home turned out to be one of the larger dwellings, right next to the main road. Outside, two young boys were playing with a young puppy by a puddle.

'Back so soon, Father?' cried the elder lad in Latin.

'We've got some visitors, boys,' said Dacien. 'They're a bit wet – need to dry out.'

Dacien, Simo and the old Syrian took the four horses behind the house. Cassius looked around. Among those observing the strangers were a pair of old women sitting on a bench and a trio of girls washing clothes in a barrel.

The boys were no longer interested in the puppy. The younger one hid behind the other as they stared up at Cassius and Indavara. After a moment or two, they summoned up the courage to approach Cassius. He disliked children and studiously ignored them. The boys passed him warily.

As they neared Indavara, he suddenly darted down at them with a mock attack. The boys jumped back, squealing and laughing; and one of them fell back into the puddle. Indavara helped him up; and for the first time since he'd met him, Cassius saw the bodyguard smile.

'Come in,' yelled Dacien from a first-floor window. 'Round the back.'

Running up the rear of the house was a staircase. Cassius led the way into a large, well-equipped kitchen. Dacien's wife was plucking a chicken. She eyed the visitors curiously.

'Some hot wine for our guests,' Dacien told her in Greek.

As his wife got to work, the ex-legionary pulled out a chair for Cassius. Cassius sat down then offered Dacien a denarius. He hadn't even a chance to take it before his wife plucked it from Cassius's hand. Dacien shrugged good-naturedly. The old Syrian laughed, then Simo and Indavara too. Even Cassius managed a smile.

'Give us your wet things and we'll dry them as best we can,' said Dacien, moving a wooden rack closer to the fireplace. As the others set about removing their outer garments, Cassius noticed the two boys peering around the doorway.

'Good to see you're educating them well.'

Dacien grinned. 'I speak Latin to them, Greek to the wife, and when I'm not around the three of them use Aramaic – what a mess.' He sat down on a stool opposite Cassius and nodded at the floor. 'Take those boots off if you want, sir, warm your feet.'

Cassius began to undo his laces.

'You needn't call me sir. Your army days are over.'

'You know what they say. Once a legionary . . .'

Cassius shifted his chair closer to the fire.

'You did your twenty-five years?'

'I did. Got my plot of land and the house five years ago. All pretty peaceful until the Palmyrans started kicking up a fuss.'

'You're glad to see the queen gone?'

'Of course. Good to have a proper army man as emperor too.

Stability – that's what we need. Though my wife would argue with me if she knew what I was saying.'

'She favoured the Palmyrans?'

'I think she just liked the idea of a woman being in charge.'

Cassius hunched over and stretched his hands towards the fire.

'The men we're looking for may have passed north of here. Are there any properties in that direction?'

'Not occupied ones. But you're in luck, in a way – being here today. The elders are holding a meeting at midday – village affairs. Boring as usual, I expect, but all the men will be there. Perhaps somebody saw these fellows you're after. I can't guarantee that they'll all be falling over themselves to help a Roman officer but I have a good name here. I can speak for you.'

'My thanks. I'll be more than happy to reward anyone who can help.'

'That's settled then.'

Cassius was used to being looked at. He was taller and more handsome than most men; and his skin was at least three shades lighter than most people east of Rome. He was also often required to wear an officer's helmet with a scarlet crest and – now – carry a three-foot ceremonial spear-head. Though neither was in evidence today, he was still being stared at long after the meeting had started.

On some occasions, the trappings of authority could be extremely useful. Rich, colourful clothing caught the eye and impressed the lower classes; and provincials in particular were often awed by anything that resembled a staff or rod, associating it as they did with the divine. But today Cassius wanted to seem as approachable as possible, and he was working hard to maintain a friendly, open expression on his face.

He'd hoped Dacien would speak right away but the village elders – a greying quartet who seemed to make their considered utterances at half speed – had insisted on waiting for a few latecomers. An argument had then ensued about the issues to be discussed; and this was only coming to an end now because everyone had been allowed their say.

At least fifty people – mostly men – had crowded into the courtyard of a house two along from Dacien's. The elders sat on chairs facing the rest of the villagers. Cassius and Dacien stood to their left, waiting their turn. Simo, Indavara and the guide were leaning against the wall at the back.

At last, Dacien was permitted to speak. He stepped forward and began.

Cassius made no attempt to understand the Aramaic; he simply observed the reaction of the locals. There were a lot of frowns, more interrogative stares for him and a good many hushed conversations. When Dacien finished a few of the men shook their heads or shrugged. No one raised a hand or said anything. The ex-legionary waited a while longer then walked back to Cassius.

'It may be that no one wants to speak *here*. They might come to us later.'

'Or it may be that nobody saw anything,' Cassius replied dourly.

'Are you sure you don't want me to take you out to the north – search for the trail?'

Cassius nodded at a large puddle in the corner of the courtyard. 'After that much rain? It lasted most of the night. The ground will be sodden for miles around.'

'Let's go back to the house. It'll take a little time for you to pack up. You never know, someone might come along.'

'The men I'm after were trying not to be seen,' replied Cassius. 'It shouldn't surprise me that they weren't.'

He and Dacien passed the rows of seated villagers. Indavara, Simo and the old Syrian followed them out under an archway to a paved area next to the house. Four teenage lads were sitting there, spinning coins to see whose would last longest. As Cassius passed them, two of the coins struck each other. One spun away and was caught. The other came to a stop by Cassius's boot. It took him moment to register the fact that he'd seen two crossed swords. He took another pace before stopping.

The others halted as he picked up the coin. It was thin, brass and very familiar-looking.

'Give me those others,' he told the boys.

Dacien translated, then took the coins and showed them to Cassius. None featured the crossed swords. Cassius delved into the little cloth money bag he kept tied to his belt. It took him a while to find the coin from the crypt floor; it was buried under the larger and heavier denarii. He compared it to the boy's coin. They were roughly the same size; but then again so were most sesterces.

The obverse of the new coin was again extremely worn, with only a trace of the Emperor's neck and chin visible. But above the swords on the reverse, part of a word could be seen. The crossed swords clearly symbolised a victorious battle but this design was common on many denominations from many periods. He needed to know which battle it commemorated.

He held it up to the light. Much of the lettering was worn but both the first and last letters were A. The fifth letter was an X.

'Artaxata – capital of Armenia. There were several battles there. But which?'

He looked again at the coin from the crypt. In the bright midday sun, he could just make out the last two letters of the Emperor's name.

'U – S.'

He showed it to Simo. 'You agree?'

'Yes, sir. U – S.'

'Are you trying to work out the Emperor?' asked Dacien.

Cassius didn't answer. He was searching his memory; remembering his history lessons, and a papyrus sheet covered with nothing but dates and emperors' names.

'That coin's at least fifty years old,' continued Dacien. 'Perhaps Macrinus? Pupenius? Balbinus? Could be any of them.'

'It could,' said Cassius. 'But I think I know which it is.'

He held up the coin again.

'See how small the U and the S are, how far they are around the side of the coin. A long name. Marcus Aurelius.'

Then he held up both coins. -

'These are actually over a hundred years old. They commemorate the capture of Artaxata under Marcus Aurelius. And when they were minted, they looked exactly the same.'

'So what?' said Indavara. 'I thought we were hunting men, not coins.'

'They had some of these with them,' replied Cassius. 'A lot actually. Dacien, ask the boys where they got this.'

The youngest lad spoke up.

'He says the river,' Dacien explained moments later. 'But he means the old water channel.'

'Where is it?'

'North-west of the village.'

'And when did he find it?'

'This morning. Says the rain must have washed it down.'

'How far away is this channel?'

'Two or three miles.'

Cassius clinked the coins together, then looked at Indavara and grinned. 'I'm glad I listened to you.'

XII

With the young lad running ahead, Cassius and his four companions rode over a low ridge and down towards level ground. They had packed up quickly and were only momentarily delayed by the boy's father, who'd demanded payment for his son's help. Only some harsh words from Dacien had stopped the rest of the local youngsters from trailing the party out of Ethusa. Cassius dropped back a little so he could watch Indavara. He had given him a few pointers that morning, and although the bodyguard had grumbled at almost every instruction, he was already sitting higher in the saddle and making better use of his reins.

The water channel was easy to see. It cut a line north to south across the plain in front of them. Two miles to the north was a small bridge; to the south the channel ran for a similar distance before disappearing under a large structure with half its walls missing. According to Dacien, this had once been a minor legionary fortress, abandoned over a century ago. As they reached the bottom of the slope, the boy spoke up and pointed at the channel.

Dacien called back to Cassius. 'Somewhere there. He's not exactly sure where.'

'You can send him home now,' said Cassius.

The lad looked disappointed when he was told; and he trudged back past them, head down.

Cassius brought up his horse a few yards from the channel. It was about six feet wide and four deep, lined by pale clay bricks. There was little more than a trickle of water running.

'It's upstream we're interested in,' he told the others. 'Towards the bridge. We are looking for any clue, however small – might even be another coin. Simo, you and Indavara take this side. Tell the old boy too. Dacien and I will cover the other side.'

Indavara frowned. 'How will you get your—'

'What a keen student you are,' interrupted Cassius. 'Already eager to see lesson number two. Observe!'

With a roar, Cassius kicked hard against the horse's flanks. As it charged away, he whipped the reins across the back of its head, feeling the wind in his ears. Despite the wet ground, he was confident the animal was strong and sure-footed enough. He yanked the reins left.

'Yah!'

They took off two yards short of the channel's edge but cleared it with ease. The horse landed solidly and cantered on before slowing.

'Good girl.'

Cassius patted the animal's neck as he guided it back to the channel; then let it settle into a walk while he kept his eyes fixed downward.

They had covered at least a mile before he saw something worthy of investigation. He dismounted and clambered down into the channel. There was perhaps half an inch of water flowing here; and floating on the surface were tiny pieces of something black. Cassius placed his hand in front of one and it stuck to his finger. He was still examining it when the others caught up.

'Cloth or some other material – burned to a crisp.' He waited a while but nothing more floated down. 'Probably nothing. Take my horse, Dacien.'

Cassius set off up the channel on foot, which not only gave him a better view of the water, but also provided a much needed break from riding.

Another half-mile, and he'd seen nothing but a few more of the black flakes. It was Indavara who saw the coin.

'There!'

The bodyguard jumped down, then picked it up and threw it to Cassius. Both sides were relatively unscathed. It was a different design, issued under the Emperor Septimus Severus. The obverse showed the Emperor himself, the reverse the prow of a ship.

'Not as old, but it could easily have come from the same haul.' Cassius put the coin in his money bag as he walked past Indavara. 'Well spotted.'

Cassius increased his pace. He spied more of the black flakes before eventually reaching an obstacle. Someone – probably the village children – had filled a section of the channel with branches. Cassius hauled himself out and waited for the others, who were now twenty yards behind. He looked north. The bridge was only half a mile away now and he saw there was something else in the channel just in front of it. The branches had obscured it before.

Shielding his eyes from what was now a bright sun, Cassius walked on, staring at the shape. It was dark and uneven, and big enough to fill the entire channel. Sunlight glinted off something metallic.

Cassius ran back to Dacien and took the reins of his horse without a word. He swung up into the saddle and swiftly pressed the horse into a gallop. As they sped north, his eyes never left the shape. Despite the wind generated by his speed, a sweet, sickly odour grew stronger with every step. By the time he neared the bridge and dismounted, he was no longer looking at one shape, but many.

The burned and badly decomposing bodies of at least ten men had been dumped into the channel. They lay on top of each other, bloated limbs obscenely intertwined. Underneath lay a stack of wood, only half of which had burned away: an unsuccessful attempt to incinerate the corpses. The briefest glance at the close-cropped hair and muscular physiques of the men was all the confirmation Cassius needed.

'Gods, the smell,' said Dacien when he arrived.

Simo and Indavara stared at the pile of bodies. The old Syrian backed away.

'Where's he going?' Cassius asked.

The goat-herder mumbled something.

'He's scared. Wants to leave,' said Dacien.

'We may need him yet.'

'I know this area better than he does,' said the ex-legionary. 'Why not let him go?'

The Syrian was still retreating, taking his pony with him. Judging by the muddy state of the ground, Cassius could see that the rain had been just as strong in this area. The chances of them picking up the trail again were negligible.

'Very well. Tell him to take his mount for the rest of his payment.'

Once told, the guide nodded to Cassius, then set off.

'Dacien, if you're willing, I'll need your help here. Some grisly work, I'm afraid.'

'I've seen enough to know you're a man who rewards those who lend assistance. Whatever you need.'

Cassius squeezed his nostrils between finger and thumb, as if this might somehow reduce the smell. He waved Simo and Indavara forward.

'I've already told you these men were escorting a precious cargo. They were legionaries. And there was one Service man with them. The coins were used to cover the cargo which was carried in barrels on the cart. Evidently they were attacked. We must try to work out how and by whom. Understood?'

The three men nodded.

'Let's get to it then. Simo, tether the horses together, then find the notes I took at Palmyra.'

Cassius pulled out his handkerchief and tied it around his neck to cover his nose and mouth. He led Indavara and Dacien back to the bodies.

'By Jupiter,' said Dacien. 'They could at least have burned them properly. This is barbaric.'

'Actually, it's most fortunate that they didn't,' said Cassius. 'We must take each body out and lay them up here. I must examine each one.'

The uppermost bodies were almost level with the top of the channel. Indavara took off his sword belt, placed it carefully on the ground and reached for the blackened ankle of the nearest corpse.

'Somebody help me.'

Cassius was relieved when Dacien stepped forward but

147

he reminded himself that he'd seen plenty of dead men before. He had picked them up and loaded them on to carts and buried them. He could handle this.

With Indavara holding one leg, Dacien the other, they heaved the corpse towards them. It slid over another, opening a wide rent in the dead legionary's side. The flesh peeled open, releasing a seething mass of white maggots.

Cassius staggered away and threw up. Two years suddenly seemed like a long time.

Simo approached the channel slowly, carrying Cassius's satchel. When he saw the full horror of what lay there, he covered his mouth with his hand and looked away. Cassius – drinking from his canteen – heard him recite a quiet prayer.

'Little late for that,' he said. 'Put my satchel down there. Then you'll have to help, I'm afraid.'

'Sir, I'm not sure I can.'

'The sooner it's done the sooner we can get out of here.'

With help from Dacien, Indavara hauled the corpse off the pile and on to the ground.

'Nothing to fear from a dead man,' he said evenly.

'Come on,' Cassius told Simo. He reached down and gripped the legionary's tunic at the shoulder. 'You take the other side.'

They dragged the body out of the way and laid it out flat. Indavara and Dacien were already on to the next one.

'Poor sods,' Dacien remarked. 'Looks like they never knew what hit them.'

Cassius reached into the satchel. He was fairly sure he'd be able to spot the legionaries (especially with the details provided by Venator's clerk) but what about Gregorius? Was his body there too?

Cassius unfolded the sheet describing the agent.

Height: Five feet, seven inches.
Build: Slim.
Eyes: Green.
Hair: Black, shoulder length.
Marks: Long diagonal scar, back of left knee.

The man before him looked taller than five foot seven, but his hair was black and quite long. He certainly couldn't be described as slim: he had the bulging calves and forearms of a Roman soldier. Then again, his build could have changed since the record had been made. Cassius lifted his left leg. There was no scar. He checked the right leg just to be sure. Nothing.

He and Simo dragged the next man over.

'By Mars.'

The side of the legionary's face had been seared by the flames. Most of his hair had been burned away. He was about the right height. One eye was closed, the other red, just like Quartermaster Lollius. Cassius couldn't tell what colour it had been. He checked for the scar again. Nothing.

By the time all the bodies were out of the channel, even Indavara was breathing hard. Cassius thanked him and Dacien and told Simo to fetch them some water.

'So what do you think?' asked the ex-legionary, nodding towards what was now a line of twelve. Cassius had examined each corpse and had already made some basic conclusions.

'The Service man isn't here. None of them matches his description. I can tell nine are legionaries. Short hair, light beards, muscular and with military tattoos. Plus several are still wearing their army-issue boots. Numbers four, five and eleven possibly not. Come and have a look.'

The three of them gathered in front of the fourth body.

'Ah, look here,' Cassius said, bending down and pointing at a rectangular area of lighter skin at the base of the man's throat. 'Where he wore his identity tablet.'

Dacien nodded.

'That's our last legionary,' Cassius added. 'So – five and eleven.'

Number five was the tallest man in the line by some distance. He was wearing one light leather sandal and a tunic. The bottom of the bloodied garment was charred. The blow that had killed him was a deep slash across his neck.

'Long hair. Slim. No tattoos. No tablet mark. Enemy,' said Cassius.

He moved on to number eleven. This man was shorter. His body had been heavily burned from the chest down and they could see the dent in his skull from a fatal crushing blow.

'No tattoos. No tablet mark. Enemy.'

Cassius looked down at the tangle of ash, firewood, clothing and weaponry littering the bottom of the channel.

'All that has to come out too.'

He decided he could at least take charge of this. He jumped down and began sorting through the debris. It was filthy work, and in moments his tunic was more black than red. Simo was soon there to help and when Dacien and Indavara weighed in too they finished quickly, leaving only a thick pool of bloody, ash-covered sludge. The smell was still horrific.

Cassius drank from his canteen as they looked down at the recovered items. First was a pile of swords. Dacien had already sorted through them.

'Not a lot to help here,' he said. 'All look like army issue to me.'

Cassius bent down and examined a few. They were all personalised with little touches but Dacien was right. In any case, he wasn't sure what they could learn from a sword. Next were the partly burned belts that had come loose and ended up at the bottom of the pile.

'Nothing much here either,' said Dacien.

Cassius moved on to the four stray boots they'd found. 'Army issue, yes?'

The ex-legionary nodded.

The last pile was of smaller objects: charms, amulets and three money bags containing a handful of coins.

'Right, let's take some time to think about this.'

Cassius led them away from the channel, only stopping when he could no longer smell rotting flesh. On those occasions he'd acted as an investigator for General Navio in Cyzicus, he'd found it beneficial to discuss such a situation, even if it was only with

Simo. Though the Gaul would sometimes say something useful, it was really just the process of airing his thoughts that helped Cassius see things differently or make some previously elusive connection. He pointed east.

'Let's suppose the legionaries came from there, well clear of the village. The Service man knew the area, so I expect he was aiming for the bridge. We must remember they were travelling at night. The raiders, whoever they were, obviously knew they were coming because they ambushed them here – the only place the cart could cross the channel for several miles.'

'And they must have done it very well,' added Dacien, 'to have only suffered two dead.'

'Which suggests they attacked in considerable force. These legionaries were all veterans. Even with surprise on their side I'd say the raiders must have numbered twenty at least – two to a man – to have overcome them so easily. They probably hid in the channel.'

'Under the bridge even,' said Indavara.

'Possibly – we must check there. Now the Service man isn't here. Which means they took him with them, probably alive.'

'Maybe he knew they were coming,' suggested Dacien.

Cassius raised an eyebrow. It looked like Venator had been correct about the trustworthiness of the ten legionaries but had Abascantius also been right about Gregorius?

'Then they burned the bodies but made a poor job of it, which suggests they were in a hurry. Possibly they wanted to get somewhere before daylight. So where did they go?'

Dacien shrugged. 'Before the rain, any route would have been easily passable.'

Cassius let out a long sigh. He glanced around at the dirty, sweaty faces of the others and knew how similarly weary he must look. Had the toil of the last two hours really been for nothing?

'Let's have another look at those two enemy,' he said, heading back to the channel.

'I'll check under the bridge,' offered Indavara.

Cassius went straight to 'eleven'.

'Help me turn him over, Dacien.'

Once this was done, Cassius knelt down and examined the warrior's legs. He saw what he thought was a tattoo, then realised it was just charred flesh. Then he inspected the man's tunic, or what was left of it. Cheap, thin cotton. It could have come from anywhere.

Indavara came out from under the bridge. He threw a boot up to Cassius, then pulled himself up out of the channel.

'Found it close to this end, must have fallen in there.'

Cassius examined the boot. It was unusually large and matched that worn by 'five'. He walked over to the body and dropped it by the bare foot. The boot landed on its side. The sole was covered in a thick brown layer and a few flecks of white. Cassius picked it up again and held it to his nose.

'Yuk.'

'Shit?' asked Dacien.

'Well done. And I thought I was the investigator.'

'What type?'

Cassius frowned. 'What type? It's not a fine wine.'

Dacien took the boot and sniffed it. 'Goat,' he said before handing it back.

'Well, I'm glad we've established that,' said Cassius. 'So our only lead is a man who once stepped in goat shit. That really narrows it down.'

He drew his dagger and scraped the sole of the boot.

'This stuff, however, might be a little more instructive.' Under the muck was a thin layer of the white substance. Cassius sniffed it. A faintly bitter odour. He knelt down and scraped at the other boot and again found the same white layer.

'Well, I lack your expertise as far as ordure goes, Dacien, but I know that smell.'

Dacien took the boot and sniffed it. 'What is it?'

'Quicklime. It's used in mining.'

'What kind of mining?'

'Iron and copper, mostly.'

'Copper? There are copper mines just north of here. The very name of the city—'

'Chalcis,' said Cassius.

'But there are scores of mines there.'

'Yes, but it's something. And a moment ago we had nothing. This fellow was probably near a mine not too long ago. And I can't think of a much better place to hide a big cart, or to use as a base for some criminal scheme. Whereabouts are the mines?'

'I don't know exactly. Mostly between Chalcis and Androna, I think.'

'How far is Androna from here?'

'A day's ride perhaps.'

'We wouldn't make it by nightfall?'

'You might – if you picked up the Antioch road.'

Cassius nodded. 'I'd like you to go back to the village. Bring out a couple of men who know how to keep their mouths shut. These legionaries deserve a decent burial.' He pointed at the money bags. 'You can keep all that as payment.'

'Fair enough.'

'We're leaving. I'm sure I can trust you to do the right thing by these men.'

'You can, sir.'

'My thanks for all you've done,' said Cassius as they gripped forearms.

Dacien bade farewell to Indavara and Simo, then started back towards Ethusa.

Cassius took a last look at the bodies, then at his filthy hands.

'Come, you two. I for one have had enough of this place. We ride north.'

XIII

'A sesterce.'

The innkeeper shook his head.

'Two.'

'No, sir.'

'Three.'

'No, sir.'

Cassius was surprised by the Syrian's lack of commercial acumen. Admittedly it was the middle of the night, but he was offering well above the odds.

The three travellers had arrived at the southern edge of Androna and been directed to the inn by four watchmen guarding the road. The innkeeper had opened up, summoned two lads to deal with the horses, then shown the latecomers to their rooms. He'd been cordial, welcoming even, but was now proving most reluctant to grant one particular request: Cassius wanted a bath.

The Syrian pursed his lips. 'It is not simply a question of money, sir,' he said quietly, anxious not to disturb his other guests. He, Cassius and Simo were standing outside their room at the top of the stairs on the first floor. 'There is no fire lit in the bathhouse. It will take more than an hour to warm enough water.'

'I don't care if it takes two,' Cassius replied. 'I'm not going to bed like this.'

He gestured to his dirty, bloodstained, stinking tunic. A loud yawn sounded from inside the room. Indavara was already undressed and in bed.

'Very well,' continued Cassius. 'A denarius.'

The innkeeper rubbed his brow. 'I have no intention of haggling, sir.'

'All right, forget the money,' said Cassius, not bothering to keep his voice down. 'I don't know if you've been keeping up with current events but Syria is once more a province of Rome. I am a member of the governor's staff and you are obliged by imperial law to assist me.'

The innkeeper rolled his tongue around his mouth, let out a final sigh, then set off down the stairs.

'Stubborn. Intransigent. Obstructive. And I see now that you also have a propensity for over-exaggeration. I doubt three-quarters of an hour have passed and behold – I am clean.'

The innkeeper, pouring steaming water from a bronze jug, said nothing. Cassius sat back against the lip of the bath and rubbed his forearms. Simo was kneeling behind him, wiping his shoulders with a sponge.

'Nice little arrangement you have here.'

The bathhouse was a domed brick building that took up one side of the inn's courtyard. The bath was five feet across, three deep and surrounded by fire-pits. The Syrian had two of them going, each heating a cauldron.

'You have all you need now, sir,' he said, putting down the jug and walking towards the door.

'Stay a while,' said Cassius. 'I need a little information.'

The innkeeper halted.

'Your name?' Cassius asked.

'Addra.'

'How long have you lived in Androna, Addra?'

'All my life.'

'Excellent. The watchmen told me there is an army officer here with a squad of legionaries. An administrator too.'

Addra nodded tiredly. 'They arrived last month.'

'I assume those are bath oils?' Cassius asked, nodding at a row of clay pots on a shelf. 'Bring one over. Something strong.'

As Addra complied, Cassius spoke to Simo over his shoulder. 'Gods, that smell. I believe it's still on me.'

'It may be me, sir,' answered Simo.

'Oh. Yes. Perhaps you can jump in after me, Simo.'

'Thank you, sir.'

Cassius held out his hands and the Syrian poured yellow oil from a narrow hole in the pot. Cassius nodded when he had enough and rubbed it across his chest.

'Where would I find this officer?'

'Further along this street. They've taken over another inn.'

'Good. Now tell me, what do you know about copper mining?'

Addra wiped sweat from his forehead as he leaned back against the bathhouse wall.

'I am an innkeeper, sir.'

'But copper *is* mined in this area.'

'Chalcis rather than here – to the north.'

'Who in Androna might know about such things? Traders? Smiths? Anyone from that area?'

While Addra thought about this, Simo took more of the perfumed oil and rubbed it into Cassius's hair.

'There is Karacha – supplies some of my fittings. Old iron-worker. He'd probably be able to tell you more. He's out on the eastern edge of town.'

'That's a start. You can give us directions tomorrow.'

Cassius closed his eyes as Simo rinsed off his hair.

'Is that all?' asked Addra.

'Yes. Goodnight.'

'Put the fires out before you come up,' Addra told Simo.

As he left, Cassius stood, then climbed out using the steps cut into one side of the bath. The roof was low; and he had to bow his head as Simo dried him with a towel.

'Another nightmare of a day. I was beginning to wonder if we would ever get here.'

'I'm not sure I shall ever forget what we saw outside that village, sir.'

'I feared from the beginning that those poor legionaries would not be found alive. At least I have something to report to Abascantius now.'

Simo lowered Cassius's sleeveless sleeping tunic on over his head, then slid a pair of light sandals on to his feet.

'There you are, sir. All ready.'

'I hope our room's well aired. How a man can take himself off to bed in such a state I shall never know. Tomorrow imperial business shall have to take its place behind a matter of greater urgency. First order of the day: a bath for Indavara.'

'Now tell me that doesn't feel better,' Cassius said as the bodyguard joined them in the courtyard for breakfast the next morning.

Indavara nodded, flicking water from his hair on to the table, before attacking a plate of bread rolls.

'Next thing we need to work on are table manners.'

By way of response, Indavara ignored the cutlery in front of him and grabbed a handful of soft white cheese.

'Gods, we should have put you in with the horses. It's lucky most of the other guests have already finished.'

Cassius had decided that a lie-in was well deserved, and there was only one other occupied table: a middle-aged merchant and his wife. The morning sun had warmed the courtyard nicely; and Addra's guard dog – a sandy, shaggy-haired beast – lay on his side at Simo's feet. The innkeeper had done a good job of avoiding Cassius but Simo had managed to get directions to the metal-worker's yard.

Indavara drank straight from the water jug and belched. Cassius shook his head.

'I don't think I can take any more of this. Grab what you want, bodyguard, we're leaving.'

Cassius extricated himself from the bench and table. As Simo would have to carry his cape and helmet, he put the spear-head into the satchel and swung it over his shoulder. Indavara grabbed two more rolls before following the others out of the rear gate and on to a side street. They turned right, then left on to the main road.

Considering recent events, Androna and its inhabitants seemed to be doing rather well. The road and pavement were in good condition, and walking or riding along them was a healthy mix of slaves, artisans and the rich. Although there were several ramshackle wood and mud-brick dwellings, most of the buildings facing on to the street were constructed of solid basalt blocks. A few even had colonnaded doorways and coloured glass windows. In a walled enclosure between two of the more impressive villas was a fine sandstone statue of a lion.

Cassius waited for a shepherd and his flock to pass, then led the others across the road. Outside the inn Addra had mentioned was a legionary. He was standing to attention by the time Cassius reached him.

'At ease. My name's Corbulo, Governor's Office.'

'Legionary Getha, sir. First Century, Second Cohort, Sixteenth Legion.'

Cassius knew that while Venator's Fourth Legion were in charge of securing Palmyra and the eastern frontier, three cohorts of the Sixteenth had been divided up and sent out to major settlements in central Syria. Their job was two-fold: first to gain information about the situation at each locale; second to re-establish Roman rule.

'Who is your commanding officer?'

'Optio Surex, sir. We have a clerk from the Governor's Office here too. Master Lucan.'

'Are either of them here now?'

'Optio Surex took a squad out on patrol at dawn, sir. I'm not sure when he'll be back.'

'And this Lucan?'

'Well, he is here, sir.'

'Good, take me to him.'

Cassius stepped towards the door but Getha didn't move.

'What's the problem?'

'Well, sir . . .'

'Is he still in bed? Drunk? With a woman?'

Getha nodded.

'Which is it, man?'

'All three actually, sir.'

'By Mars, what a state of affairs. You tell this Lucan character that I'll be back here to talk to him before midday. And he better be up – or his seniors will hear of this. Understood?'

'Certainly, sir.'

'By the way, you don't know anything about copper mining, do you?'

'No, sir.'

The iron-worker's abode was at the end of a dusty track; and beyond it lay only desert. In the middle of the fenced rectangle of land was a small house with a roofed workshop attached to one side. Hanging askew from a post next to the gate was a painted sign: *Iron*.

Just as Cassius put his hand on the gate, two dogs burst out of the house and raced across the sand. Cassius stepped back as they skidded to a stop. They were mongrel beasts, big-jawed and ugly. One barked, the other growled.

A bearded man of about sixty came out of the workshop. He shaded his eyes with his hand to peruse the strangers, then hurried over as fast as his bandy legs would carry him. He was wearing a thick leather apron over his tunic, and, as he came closer, Cassius noted his blackened, sinewy arms. The Syrian kicked one of the dogs up the backside. Surprisingly, this was enough to calm them both down.

'Karacha?'

The iron-worker nodded.

'You speak Greek?'

'I do.'

'Officer Corbulo, I'm with the Governor's Office.'

Cassius was getting used to the expression of fear and distaste that invariably greeted this statement.

'Don't worry – you're not in trouble. I just need information. I was told you might know something about copper mines in this area.'

The Syrian mulled this over for a moment.

'Will I—'

'Get paid? Yes, yes, will a couple of pieces of brass do you?'

Karacha undid the gate and gestured for them to enter. With wary glances at the dogs, they followed him to the workshop.

'I must just douse a fire,' Karacha said, hurrying to the rear of the building.

Cassius nodded at a high wooden table.

'Clear one end of that off.'

Indavara pushed the mass of crudely cast nails, handles, hinges and belt-buckles to one end, then Simo wiped away the worst of the dirt. Cassius reached into his satchel, pulled out the map, and stretched it out on the table. He pointed to Androna, then Chalcis.

'About forty miles north-east of here.'

Karacha arrived with his hand outstretched.

Cassius gave him one sesterce. 'Another when I've finished with you. First question. Quicklime is used in mining, yes?'

Karacha tucked his thumbs into the wide pocket on the front of his apron. 'It is. You push it into cracks, then wet it. It expands – opens fissures in the rock.'

'It's employed in iron and copper mining especially?'

'Usually.'

'Neither of which is done here.'

'Correct. In fact I've not heard of an iron mine in all of Syria. All you see here came from outside the province.'

'But there are copper mines – close to Chalcis, yes? Whereabouts?'

The Syrian jabbed a grimy finger towards the map. Cassius swiped it away.

'Don't touch it, man. Do you know how much one of these costs? So to the south of the city?'

'And to the west.'

'Are any of them close to the Antioch road?'

'Some. There's a track runs west off it about ten miles before Chalcis. Twisty turny old road, had to go past all the mines you see.'

'For transport.'

Karacha nodded.

'It's still usable, this road?'

'Trade pretty much died off during the war but I'd think so, yes.'

'So some of the mines might have been abandoned?'

'Oh, certainly. There are shafts up there older than me. Haven't been touched in decades.'

Cassius looked up from the map. 'Perfect: remote, quiet, but not far from the main road.'

He took a second coin from his money bag and handed it over. 'Thank you, Karacha. You've been most helpful.'

They found Lucan sitting at a long table in the parlour of the inn. He offered only a cursory nod as Cassius took up a chair at the opposite end of the table and stared at him. The clerk couldn't have been more than eighteen. His face was clammy and pale and he stank of wine. Before Cassius could say anything, a young girl came down the stairs and stuck her head through the doorway.

'Goodbye,' she said, before hurrying away.

Lucan looked sheepishly at Cassius, then at the spear-head he had just placed on the table.

'Good night?' Cassius asked.

'I wish I could remember.'

'Ah, the delights of life in the provinces. Simo, perhaps some water for young Master Lucan.'

Simo went over to a table in one corner of the parlour. He filled a cup and gave it to the clerk.

'Wine for me,' Cassius said.

Lucan flinched at the very mention of the word. Cassius smothered a grin.

'So apart from drinking and whoring, what exactly do you do here, young sir?'

Lucan took a breath and leaned back in his chair. 'Counting. I spend my whole time counting. How many people, how many trades, how many miles of good road, how much timber, how much grain. You name it, I count it.'

'Then you might be of some use to me. I'm looking for a group of men who may have passed through here. About twenty of them, with a big cart laden with barrels.'

Lucan shrugged. 'There's not been a lot of traffic.'

'But if someone had come here and traded some silver or gold, or—'

The heavy wooden door at the front of the inn smashed open. A legionary lurched into the parlour with his sword in his hand. He took a quick look at the other three men in the room, then grabbed Lucan by the shoulder.

'Get that surgeon. Two injured coming in.'

'What?'

'The surgeon. The local. Get him.'

Lucan followed the legionary outside.

Cassius downed his wine. He was almost to the door when another soldier hurried in. He was tall and muscular, and his helmet bore the horse-hair plumes of an officer.

'Who are you?' he demanded.

'Corbulo. Governor's Office. Optio Surex, I presume.'

Surex nodded, then pushed past Cassius.

'Clear this shit off the table.'

Simo grabbed the cups and the bottle.

'We'll need that water though,' added the optio.

The door into the parlour was narrow, and it took Surex and his legionaries a while to get the first wounded man inside and on to the table. Half of the arrow sticking out of his upper right arm had been snapped off. There wasn't a lot of blood but the head had sunk two inches into his flesh.

'Get some wine for him, someone – the strongest you can find,' said Surex as he checked the wound.

Simo touched Cassius's arm and shook his head. 'He should be kept awake. Whatever the pain, it's better to keep him conscious.'

Cassius had learned to trust Simo's judgement on medical matters. After his experiences dealing with injured soldiers two years earlier, he had pursued a keen interest in the treatment of disease and injury; and had built up quite a little library on the subject. When he needed money for books, Cassius always gave it gladly; he felt it was in his interest to do so. He tapped the optio on the shoulder.

'Surex, let my man treat him.'

'You think I've never dealt with an arrow wound before?'

From what Cassius had seen of soldiers, their knowledge of medical care was at best basic and at worst downright dangerous.

'Trust me – he knows what he's doing.'

Simo moved forward. 'May I?'

Surex looked at Simo for a moment, then backed away.

The Gaul asked the man's name and gave him some water. He asked one of the other soldiers to open the curtains to admit more light, then examined the wound.

'Move back, you lot,' ordered Surex. 'Give the man space to work.'

'That's a long bolt,' Cassius said, nodding at the arrow. 'Palmyran?'

Surex looked him up and down. Cassius knew exactly what the optio would be thinking: an ignorant grain man who'd got himself promoted away from situations like this, yet still felt qualified to stick his nose in.

'What would you know about it, Officer?'

'Actually, rather more than you might think.'

XIV

When Lucan returned with the local surgeon, Simo spoke to the man and they agreed on a plan of treatment. An hour later the arrow was out and the legionary bandaged up and resting. They hadn't been able to help the other wounded soldier. He had been struck twice in the chest, and was dead by the time the legionaries brought him in.

Cassius and Optio Surex stood in the street, watching as two men carried the wrapped body along the hallway to another room. The innkeeper and his wife looked on, horrified. Cassius turned round and observed the townspeople. A small, curious crowd had gathered earlier and though it had now dispersed, an air of unease remained. He wondered where their loyalties lay. To Palmyra? Rome? Possibly neither.

Surex paced up and down, clicking his knuckles. He had sent small squads to both ends of town to back up the watchmen and guard against any further incursions.

'So it was an ambush?' asked Cassius.

'We were on patrol a couple of miles east. They were behind an outcrop a few hundred feet from us. Just couldn't get close to them.'

'Archers?'

'Swordsmen too. At close quarters we could have made a fight of it but there was no cover. Lucky they didn't have horses.'

'You did well to get back with so few injured.'

'I've kept the lads training hard and we managed to outpace them, even carrying shields.' Surex shook his head and wiped away some of the dirt caked to the bottom of his tunic. 'Just don't have enough men here. Wouldn't know the war was finished, would you?'

'You think there's more of them out there? Enough to attack the town?'

'No idea.'

'What about the people here? They'd help you?'

'Some. We're on reasonable terms with the council.'

'What about reinforcements?'

Surex tugged at one of the thick tufts of hair on his chin. 'There are two centuries at Chalcis.'

'I might be heading that way. Perhaps I can deliver a message for you.'

'You're going to risk the road after this?'

'I don't have a lot of choice. Might I ask you a favour?'

Surex nodded.

'Can you ask your men about a large cart that may have come through here in the last two weeks? With a group of around twenty men.'

'I'll ask the lads who are here now.'

'Thank you.'

Cassius followed Surex inside. While the optio headed into the parlour, he continued through to the inn's courtyard. Here he found Simo, Indavara and Lucan. The clerk was sitting on a bench, hand propping up his chin, eyes closed. Cassius kicked the bench. Lucan's head dropped off his hand and he woke with a start.

'I think you need some activity, young man. I've a job for you. You two as well.'

Indavara now had his stave, bow and quiver with him.

'You can leave those here,' said Cassius.

'What about these Palmyrans?'

'I doubt they'll come into town. Walking around with all those weapons you'll worry the locals and it's going to be hard enough to get any cooperation now. Just the sword.'

'Don't blame me if things turn nasty.'

'If you really did kill a seven-foot German and a bear with only a dagger, surely you're not worried about a few provincial tribesmen?'

Indavara shook his head and put the weapons under the table. Cassius led the others back through the inn.

'Corbulo.' Surex stepped out of the parlour. 'None of this lot remembers anything. I'll ask the rest when I see them.'

'Please do. I need to make some enquiries in town. We won't stray too far.'

Having observed hundreds, probably thousands of servants over the years, Cassius knew how lucky he was to have Simo. As well as his faultless manners and numerous practical skills, the Gaul possessed one other useful attribute: he was good with people. With his warm, gentle character and friendly face, he seemed able to endear himself to almost anyone in a remarkably short period of time.

Cassius had made use of this ability several times while investigating in Cyzicus, recognising that Simo could draw out information that would never be divulged to him. Even if he wasn't in uniform, Cassius's voice and manner instantly marked him out as a gentleman and the lower classes were often wary of talking openly to anyone in authority. He was reluctant to rely solely on bribery and threats; Simo provided a useful alternative.

Leaning back against the edge of a well, Cassius watched the Gaul speaking to a pair of peasant women selling vegetables – his tenth such conversation in an hour. Lucan was back at the main road, asking passers-by if they'd seen anything of the men, the cart or its cargo.

Indavara, meanwhile, was exploring the marketplace, on the lookout for new foodstuffs to sample. Unseen by him but noted by Cassius were a group of teenage girls, following the bodyguard from a safe distance, jabbering and giggling. They were a rough-looking bunch: serving wenches stealing an hour off perhaps. Their tatty clothes and dirty faces reminded Cassius of that stupid whore Sabina, yet he couldn't quite shake off a nagging disappointment that they weren't following him.

'Anything?' he asked when Simo returned.

'Gossip mostly, sir. But one of their husbands has a stall selling trinkets and such like. He's at home ill today but she says he's not heard of anything new or unusual turning up. If anyone would know, he would – or so she said.'

'All right. I'm beginning to think they bypassed the town completely. We shall see if Lucan's discovered anything, then return to the inn. We've some preparations to make.'

---8---

Cassius stood by the window of their room at Addra's, watching one of his serving girls tidy some tables in the courtyard. She was no beauty but possessed the most wonderfully sleek black hair, and she moved with an easy grace not normally associated with one in her position. She tipped over a mug, then pulled a cloth from her belt to wipe up the water. Cassius indulged himself with a momentary fantasy about taking her up to a room, locking the door and spending the afternoon under the sheets. The moment was soon lost.

'Will this do, sir?' asked Simo. He'd returned to the room holding a thin belt.

'Let's see.'

Cassius raised his arms as Simo tried the belt.

As expected, Lucan's enquiries had also yielded nothing of interest so there was no reason to stay in Androna. Once Simo had finished packing they would leave; and Cassius had decided they would travel in disguise.

Simo and Indavara could go as they were, and Cassius needed only to make a few small alterations. He would dispense with his thick military belt and change his red tunic to a white one. The spear-head, his helmet and his scarlet cloak would be well hidden from any prying eyes.

The belt fitted well.

'I shall just go and pay Master Addra for this and the food and water,' said Simo.

Indavara was lying on his bed, staring into space.

'Packed up already?' asked Cassius.

The bodyguard nodded.

'Then we shall go over it again.'

Indavara rolled his eyes.

'Speak,' said Cassius. 'You've nothing else to do.'

Indavara replied in a tired monotone: 'You are Cassius Oranius Crispian. A man—'

'A *Raetian* man.'

'A Raetian man looking to invest money in mining now that the war is over. You're surveying the area south of Chalcis to check the state of the mines and see what work is going on. You've been in Syria for three weeks and have journeyed north from Palmyra where you were, er . . .'

'Checking on the caravan trade. Not bad.'

'Why do *I* have to know it? Nobody ever asks bodyguards anything.'

'Listen, if we run into a bunch of brigands or Palmyrans, we need to have our story straight. And remember – I am Raetian, not Roman. *Not* Roman.'

'All right, I'm not stupid. What about me? Where am I from?'

'By Mars, you've a gift for irony, Indavara. You won't tell me where you're actually from but you want me to make up an imaginary background for you. Don't concern yourself. Like you said: nobody ever asks bodyguards anything.'

Indavara reached into a sack of provisions and retrieved a handful of dried apricot.

'Do you ever stop eating?'

'So why did these Palmyrans attack the legionaries?' Indavara asked before sinking his teeth into a piece of fruit. 'I thought the war was over.'

'It is, and they were on the losing side. Our Emperor's army has defeated their beloved queen and taken her back to Rome in chains. Their dream of supplanting us here in the east is over. So they'd like nothing more than to take their revenge on any Roman soldier they come across. Which, despite the fact that we are supposedly back in charge of the province, is why we must now travel incognito.'

'So they like to use bows, these Palmyrans.'

'Very effectively, I might add. I've had first-hand experience.'

Indavara's attempt to cover his disbelieving expression with his hand was not entirely successful.

'I see you doubt me.'

Indavara shrugged and ate another piece of fruit.

Cassius looked out of the window. 'Well, I'll not pretend to be much of a warrior, but two years ago, when the Palmyrans first rose against Rome, I found myself at a place not so very far from here. And I saw enough action to last me a lifetime, I can assure you of that.'

He gazed beyond the sprawl of the town, at the dark, straight line that ran north across the barren plain.

'I'd prefer not to risk the road, believe me. But time is against us, and with every day that passes, the trail of the men we're after grows colder. We must take our chances.'

Dusk came as they passed through the outskirts of Androna. Washing was collected, children called inside, doors bolted shut. Smoke and the smells of cooking drifted out of the houses; and anxious, curious faces looked out at the unlikely sight of three travellers taking the road north in darkness.

Calling in at the second inn, Cassius had discovered that Surex was out checking on the northern sentries; and they came across the legionaries less than a mile beyond the last of Androna's dwellings.

The soldiers were gathered around a glowing brazier, drinking steaming wine from their canteens. They were well-equipped with bows and throwing javelins, and well-stocked with food and water. Two lookouts had been posted, one half a mile to the east, another to the west. Surex came out to meet Cassius as he dismounted.

'I've been round all the men now,' said the optio. 'Nobody remembers any big groups passing through. Nor any big carts.'

'No carts at all?'

'Only small things – donkey pulls. Locals.' Surex nodded at Cassius's tunic. 'I see you've dispensed with your officer's gear.'

Cassius shrugged. 'Seemed sensible in the circumstances.'

'Absolutely.'

One of the legionaries came forward and struck up a conversation with Simo. It turned out he was a close friend of the injured man and he and several others wanted to offer their thanks. As they spoke, Cassius and Surex moved to one side. The optio took a sheet of papyrus from behind his belt.

'My letter. The senior centurion at Chalcis is Volcatius Arius.'

Cassius took the note and put it in his satchel. 'If I'm unable to get there myself, I'll try to send it some other way. Do you know of a road that branches off to the east about ten miles short of Chalcis? Apparently it leads past the mines south of the city.'

'I remember it. I'd never come down this way before so I made my own map.'

'Did you see any traffic there? Any sign of activity?'

'No, but the road was still in good condition – passable.'

'That would be about forty miles from here, yes?'

'About that. There are milestones all the way.'

'So we might expect to arrive this time tomorrow.'

'If you pushed it. Probably later.'

'And any way-stations, inns?'

'Here.'

Surex led him closer to the brazier and reached inside his tunic. He pulled out a rudimentary map with markings made in charcoal. They knelt down, side by side; and Indavara wandered over to listen in.

'First way-station is twelve miles from here. Second one is at twenty-five. Neither is occupied though. We haven't the manpower.'

'And inns?'

'Several. But also empty. It's just too risky for people to come back and take them over with the Palmyrans still roaming around.'

Cassius looked north. 'This could be a very unpleasant trip.'

'At least the road is wide and smooth. You can ride without a light. But if you need to leave the road, don't go too far. There are these damned underground water channels criss-crossing this whole area, with vertical shafts leading down to them. You'll never see them at night – perfect for snapping a horse's leg.'

'Wonderful.'

The two officers stood and gripped forearms.

'Hope you make it,' said Surex.

'You too.'

XV

The cold night air chilled their hands and faces, until their fingers became stiff, their cheeks numb. And with the moon only offering its light on the rare occasion of a gap in the cloud, Cassius felt as if they were being drawn along some endless, black tunnel that narrowed with every passing mile. Though the road was indeed smooth underfoot, and the horses could ride side by side, they too seemed unnerved by the dark. Every clink of metal or tap of hoof seemed to reverberate outward, announcing their presence to whoever else had decided to brave the desert night.

They had missed the eighth milestone. Determined to see the ninth, Cassius stationed himself to the left of the road. Cradled in Simo's lap was Cassius's hourglass; only that afternoon the Gaul had adjusted it to account for the shorter days and longer nights of autumn. Exploiting a moment of moonlight, Simo checked the glass. The top half was empty.

'Fourth hour,' he said, turning it over.

Cassius rubbed his eyes. 'Where's this damned stone? Can't be far now.'

With no word of warning, Indavara pulled back on his reins. His horse lurched off the road with a snort of protest. Cassius and Simo halted their mounts.

'What are you doing?' demanded Cassius.

'Look there, ahead!'

Indavara pointed north. In the distance were several dots of orange light.

'Gods,' said Cassius. 'They must be moving quickly – I saw nothing a few moments ago.'

'We should get off the road while we have time,' said Indavara.

'Don't you remember what Surex said about those channels?'

'Then what do we do – wait for them?'

Cassius looked north again. Were the lights closer already?

'Simo, you wait here with the horses,' he said as he dismounted. 'We'll try to find a safe path.'

Once Indavara was off his horse and beside him, Cassius hurried off the right side of the road and down the shallow slope beside it.

'Keep a few yards between us,' he said. 'Slow and steady.'

The bodyguard did as he was told and when Cassius had counted fifty paces of even ground, they turned and ran back to the road. Cassius dragged his eyes off the lights as he took his reins. There were three torches; no more than a mile away now.

Indavara's mount was tossing its head around and puffing.

'That accursed thing better stay quiet,' said Cassius. 'Follow me. Don't stray off my path.'

With a last glance at the bobbing torches, he led the way. When the fifty paces were done, he gently brought his horse around. The others did likewise; Indavara to his right, Simo to his left. The bodyguard's horse was still unsettled, and as it strained against its reins, anxiety spread to Cassius's horse. He held its head close to him and stroked its neck. Indavara swore as his mount yanked him backwards.

They could hear the riders now; the percussive thud of hooves amplified by the stones below.

Indavara's mount began to sniff and snort.

'That bloody beast is going to do for us all,' Cassius hissed. 'Simo, you take it – might calm it down.'

Cassius muttered a prayer to Epona, goddess of horses, and held the reins while Indavara and the Gaul swapped positions. Either or both of the methods seemed to work because in moments all three animals were quiet.

'That's it,' said Cassius. 'Just a little longer.'

They stood in a line in the darkness, watching the road.

The riders approached. The first man was slightly out in front, torch held high.

Cassius's horse began to shuffle its hooves and back away from the road.

The first rider was past them now. There were four more behind him, two with torches.

'Keep going, keep going,' Cassius whispered.

Suddenly Simo was struggling to keep control of Indavara's horse and Cassius was hauled off balance by his own mount. He prayed again. All three horses were now snorting but the noise from the road was louder. Then Indavara's horse loosed a high-pitched whinny.

One of the riders cried out and stopped. The others halted too, then the man in front. Without the clatter of hooves, the quiet came suddenly.

'No, no, no,' Cassius breathed.

Indavara's horse whinnied again, then Simo's too.

The riders peered warily into the darkness. They leapt down from their saddles, conversing in hushed, urgent tones. The leader was last off his horse. By the time he reached the others, three were holding their swords, one was putting an arrow to his bow. The leader drew his own blade. Flame flickered across its polished surface. He spoke; and one man sheathed his sword and took charge of the horses. The other three gathered behind him. With his torch in one hand, sword in the other, he strode confidently off the road.

'What shall we do, sir?' implored Simo.

Indavara came close to Cassius. 'Take these,' he said, holding up the reins for Simo's horse.

'What?'

'I'll move off. Stay hidden. If things go bad I can catch them cold.'

'What? No, we—'

'I may be some distance away so if you want me to strike, put your hand to your mouth and cough loudly. Understood?'

'Wait—'

'Understood?'

'How do we explain the spare horse?'

'You're the talker. Think of something.'

Indavara forced the reins into Cassius's hands, then took his bow and quiver from his saddle. Eyes locked on the men, he retreated silently into the darkness.

Cassius decided there was now nothing to be gained by staying hidden.

'Come, Simo.'

He handed the Gaul the reins of Indavara's horse and led his own mount forward.

'Hello there,' he said in Greek.

The men stopped. Cassius continued on until he was only a few feet from them. The leader was the oldest of them, bearded, dark-skinned and wiry, and he smiled when he saw what he and his men faced. Strapped to his left arm was a small, round shield. Cassius had seen those before. Palmyrans. The archer raised his weapon. The bow was unusually long, the arrow too, and the tip was aiming straight at Cassius's head.

'Do you speak Greek?' Cassius asked, failing to stop his voice wavering.

The leader nodded. He held torch and blade high, framing his drawn, angular face.

'What are you doing out here?'

'Hiding, actually. We were told the road was dangerous.'

A flicker of amusement crossed the Palmyran's face. 'Can be, can be.'

Cassius nodded at the archer. 'Could you ask your friend to aim that somewhere else?'

'You have three horses, but there are only two of you.'

'A spare.'

'It's saddled.'

'I used it this night. My mount is tired.'

The leader spoke to the archer. The Palmyran kept his string half-drawn, but aimed the arrow at the ground.

'Who are you?' asked the leader. 'And why are you on the road?'

'My name's Oranian. I'm from Raetia. I'm interested in the mines north of here – looking for trade opportunities. I arranged several meetings in Chalcis but I was delayed, hence the night-time journey.'

'Raetian, eh? Sure you don't mean Roman?'

'Quite sure, thank you.'

'And him?' asked the leader, turning to Simo.

'My manservant.'

The leader walked past Cassius, passing within inches of him. The horses had calmed down but became skittish again as the sizzling torch came near. The Palmyran looked at the saddles and the gear. He said something in Aramaic to the others, then walked back to them. Cassius understood none of it and he turned to Simo, but the Gaul was staring at the four warriors.

'There's a tax for using this road,' said the leader.

'I see. How much?'

'It varies. From a few coins to . . . everything you own.'

Cassius noted that the other men made no reaction to this quip. They didn't speak Greek.

'I can be reasonable,' he replied. 'If you'll allow us to continue peacefully on our way.'

The leader nodded at his comrades. 'I don't see you've much room for negotiation. You've some fine saddles and bags there. Who knows what we'll find?'

He spoke to his men. The bowman raised his weapon again. The leader and the two swordsmen came forward.

Cassius was in little doubt about what would happen if they discovered the spear-head or his helmet.

'I'll give you twenty denarii,' he said quickly. 'I'm sure that would make this one of your most profitable nights.'

The Palmyran stopped a couple of feet away. Cassius felt the heat of the torch against his face. The man grinned.

'Twenty, eh? I bet you've at least double that tucked away somewhere.'

Cassius took a step backwards and handed his reins to Simo.

'Thirty. I'll give you no more.'

'Now I'm getting really interested,' said the Palmyran. 'I reckon you've a hundred at least.' He aimed his sword at Cassius. 'Where are your coins then?'

Cassius had already decided the maximum he could give away as a bribe before they set out. He had four bags, each of ten denarii, ready at the top of one of the saddlebags. He took them out and walked back to the Palmyran. The leader eyed the money.

'Forty,' Cassius said. 'Then you turn around, take your men, and continue on your way.'

The Palmyran spat on the ground. 'You don't tell me what to do.'

One of the other men spoke. The leader dismissed his comment with a wave of his sword.

Cassius could have given the signal then, but he reckoned there was one last chance to avoid bloodshed.

'I see you're not one to listen to reason. Perhaps this will change your mind. I lied. That mount is not a spare. It belongs to my bodyguard.' Cassius nodded over his shoulder. 'He's out there somewhere. He has a bow. And I'd be very surprised if – at this precise moment – it's not trained on you.'

Cassius was right about that.

Indavara was thirty paces away. His bow was half-drawn and the tips of his fingers were beginning to ache. His open eye was close to the string; the arrow was aimed at the leader's chest. Every time the men moved, Indavara would move too, ensuring he kept an angle on both the leader and the archer.

The moon was covered by cloud and he hoped it stayed that way. With both the darkness and surprise on his side, he had a good chance of hitting at least two of them before they scattered. Then he would have to go for the man on the road; he couldn't let him get away and bring others after them.

Corbulo and Simo would have to take their chances.

The leader took a step forward.

Indavara pulled the string back another two inches. His hand was beginning to shake. If the man made a move, he would fire, whether Corbulo gave the signal or not.

'You're bluffing,' said the Palmyran.

'No,' replied Cassius. 'I've not known him long, but the first time I met him he came to my aid and dispensed with three men equally as unpleasant as you appear to be without breaking a sweat.'

The leader looked past him, eyes boring into the inky black that surrounded them.

'But there are *five* of you,' Cassius continued. 'I suppose one or two of you might make it.'

Another of the Palmyrans addressed the leader but he ignored him.

'My offer still stands,' said Cassius. 'Forty. You can turn round and walk away. A good night's work.'

The Palmyran glanced back at the men, then out into the darkness again.

'Just take it,' Cassius continued. 'No blood need be spilled. We can all walk away from this.'

The leader's eyes narrowed.

Cassius got ready to move if he had to.

The Palmyran nodded at the bags. 'Forty it is.'

'Let me give it to you. I would advise against any sudden movements. He can be a little impetuous at times.'

The leader passed his torch to another man, then took the bags from Cassius. One of the other Palmyans smiled and laughed. With a last glance at Cassius, the leader turned and walked away. The archer seemed to protest and pointed back at the horses but the leader snapped at him and thrust his torch towards the road. After a few paces he opened the bags and showed his comrades the contents. The two swordsmen cheered.

Cassius and Simo were left suddenly in darkness.

'Well done, sir,' said the Gaul.

Cassius took the reins of his horse then watched as the Palmyrans mounted up and went swiftly on their way. Cassius's horse gave a whinny.

'Yes,' he said, 'you can make all the noise you want now.'

Indavara materialised in front of him. 'What happened?'

'I offered him forty denarii but he wanted to search our bags, so I told him you were out there with a bow aimed at him.'

'What? Why give away our advantage?'

'There are alternatives to violence, you know.'

'You were lucky.'

'Maybe. Well – I'm due a bit.'

'Insane,' Indavara muttered.

Cassius took the reins of Indavara's horse from Simo and threw them at him. 'Insane is people getting killed for no good reason. It worked, didn't it?'

By dawn, when the sun finally spilled colour into the sky, they reached the second way-station. All the doors hung open and everything of value had been looted, but there was enough straw in the stables for both riders and mounts to lie down in comfort. The horses were exhausted, and Cassius reflected that perhaps Epona had watched over them after all; it was remarkable that not one of them had sustained an injury during the night.

He didn't want to push the limits of her favour, so allowed the animals four hours' rest before setting off once more. He'd calculated that there would still be enough time to reach the mines before dark: they couldn't risk getting caught on the road at night again.

All through the afternoon, he gazed west, looking for some angular shape between the road and the limestone hills, but he saw nothing of the fort, nothing of Alauran. He knew from the map that it had to be close but he chose to say nothing to Simo and part of him was glad not to see it. That place, that time, seemed to exist entirely in its own space: and he felt that to revisit any part of it would diminish it somehow. He remembered those few days so clearly and he wanted to keep the memories as they were. He had made his peace with them, for he knew they would always be with him.

It became hard to tell who was most tired. As the hours and miles passed, Cassius felt himself tipping further forward in his saddle, and he lost count of the times he'd seen Simo's head snap up moments after he dozed off. Indavara, meanwhile, had spent more time walking than riding. Even he seemed weary now, cursing at his horse and tripping over his own feet.

It wasn't just physical exhaustion. The encounter with the Palmyrans had unnerved them all; and the scarcity of other travellers on the road was the surest sign that they were crossing dangerous territory.

They passed several mounds of stones by the roadside and Cassius explained to Indavara that these were 'Mercury's Heaps': honorific offerings for the god of wayfarers. Where there was no sanctuary or statue, a single stone added to a mound sufficed. Indavara took to throwing one on to every pile, and – when he could be bothered – Cassius did so too.

There was less than an hour of light left when they finally arrived at their destination. The road was marked by a collection of painted signposts giving distances and directions to various mines: *Golden Mine, Great Mine, Long Mine, Drusus's Mine, the Mine of the Antiochene Metalsmiths.*

'Thank the gods,' said Cassius. 'Here at last.'

Further along the road they could see a sign hanging from a pole and a sprawling heap of spoil. This turned out to be Long Mine, and they had barely passed the sign when an old man burst out of a shack and ran towards them, shouting in Aramaic and waving his hands. He was barefoot, wearing only a ragged tunic and a blanket tied round his neck. His beard was a mix of white and ginger, his face worn rather than wrinkled. Cassius couldn't age him; he might have been fifty or seventy. Judging by the feral look in his eyes and his vitriolic ravings, he was quite mad.

Simo tried to speak to him, but the old man wouldn't stop.

'He says the mine is his, sir. He has claimed it. We cannot set foot on his property.'

'Tell him—'

The old man was getting louder.

'Tell him to shut up.'

Cassius continued in Latin before Simo could translate.

'Shut up!'

But the old man only stopped when a dagger embedded itself in the ground between his feet. Indavara fixed him with an implacable stare and raised a finger to his mouth. The old man watched in silence as he dismounted.

'Simo,' Cassius continued, 'tell him that if he doesn't stay quiet, I'll have Indavara here tie him to that post over there and use him for target practice.'

Simo translated. The old man stepped away from the knife and nodded.

'Explain that we mean him no harm and we have no designs on his mine.' Cassius pointed at a second timber-built shack. 'We simply need shelter for the night. We'll move on in the morning. Now ask him about the men and the cart.'

As Simo began, Cassius slid down off his saddle and looked along the road. It bore right around the spoil heap then disappeared from view. If his hunch about the raiding party heading north proved correct, they might be close to getting some answers. If he was wrong, the efforts and trials of the previous day and night had been for nothing.

'Sir, he will give us permission to stay but if he sees anyone go near the mine entrance he'll strike them down at once.'

Indavara grinned as he pulled his dagger out of the ground.

'Terrifying,' said Cassius. 'Has he seen anything?'

'Four riders came past last week but didn't stop. Some time before that he did see some men with a big cart. He thinks they were slave-traders.'

'Here? I doubt it.'

Simo shrugged. 'I wouldn't take his opinions too seriously, sir.'

'How many of them were there?'

Cassius waited impatiently for the translation.

'Twenty or more.'

'Palmyrans?'

'He says no.'

'Why did he think they were slave-traders?'

'Because one man was being towed along on foot by a rope round his neck.'

'One prisoner,' said Cassius. 'Gods – it might have been Gregorius. How tall was he, this prisoner?'

'He doesn't remember.'

'What colour hair?'

'He can't remember anything about him. Just a man, he says.'

'All right. Last question. Which way were they going?'

No translation was needed this time. The old man pointed down the road, towards the other mines.

'Another salubrious locale,' Cassius remarked as he laid out a blanket at one end of the shack.

Indavara was sitting opposite him, sharpening his dagger with a flint. Behind him was a pile of rusting mining implements. Simo was outside, preparing dinner.

'Truly a treat to work for old Abascantius, isn't it?' Cassius added as he lay down.

Indavara didn't reply.

'Bodyguard, I spoke to you. Perhaps you could do me the courtesy of responding.'

'What? Oh, I don't care that much. I like being outside. All the open space.'

'I must say I was surprised you'd not heard of Mercury's Heaps; and I've not once seen you pray or make an offering since we met. Who are your gods?'

'I have only one.'

'You're a Christian? A Jew?'

Indavara shook his head, as if the words meant nothing to him.

'How unusual,' Cassius continued. 'Who is this single god?'

'Fortuna.'

Cassius laughed. 'Everyone prays to Fortuna. That's a given. There must be some others.'

Indavara looked hard at the dagger as he whipped the flint along the blade.

'All right then,' said Cassius. 'Why just Fortuna?'

Indavara pulled out the figurine and showed it to Cassius but said nothing.

'It's a bit on the small side; if Fortuna's the only god you pray to, you might want to show her a bit more respect.'

Indavara contemplated this.

'You weren't allowed many possessions, I suppose.'

'A woman threw it to me after a fight.'

Cassius propped himself up on one elbow. 'Ah yes – the wome They love you fighters, don't they? All that bare flesh and bloc letting. I've heard the more forward of them go to the cells at night. You had your share of visitors, I expect.'

Indavara looked at the ground.

Cassius chuckled. 'Relax. I'll not press you for details.'

Indavara carefully returned the figurine to its place beh belt and went back to work with the flint.

'What about your people's gods? After all you must h through, you've never asked them for help?'

Again receiving no reply, Cassius came to conclusion.

'You felt that they'd forsaken you, perhaps. Giver

Indavara stopped sharpening the knife for a moment and thought about this. Then he nodded.

◄—8—►

Cassius decided they could do without a sentry – that it would be better for them all to get a good night's sleep. Indavara reluctantly agreed but insisted on placing several empty bottles at strategic locations around the shack.

The 'mad miner' – as he was now known – had calmed down considerably when Simo had given him some food; and had even come over to bid them goodnight.

They lay in a triangle around some stones Simo had heated in the fire, Indavara closest to the door. Cassius observed how he kept his right arm outside his blanket, two fingers resting on the handle of his dagger.

'So, tomorrow,' he said. 'We need to check every mine on this road. If we see anyone, we stick to the story and go on our way. I'll take note of the location and if need be we'll return with legionaries from Chalcis. If not, we go inside and look for any possible trace of our prey. We'll leave at dawn, and make sure we're somewhere safe before nightfall. Clear?'

'Yes, sir,' replied Simo.

Indavara's only answer was a guttural snore.

'By Mars,' said Cassius. 'Just like a dog. When he's not eating, he's sleeping.'

XVI

They found nothing at the second and third mines. Cassius had expected to be rather more impressed but they were little more than holes in the ground surrounded by piles of sand, earth, rubble and rock. One shaft had been blocked off by criss-crossing timbers, another had caved in just a few yards beyond the entrance.

Halfway along the track that led to the fourth mine they came across a sign lying in the sand. There were two words upon it, etched in white paint: *Great Mine*. And when they reached the shaft itself, they saw the name was well deserved. It was the largest they'd seen so far, rectangular in shape and cut down into the earth at a shallow angle. Beyond the shaft was a huge mound of spoil that formed two great arms, also enclosing the road and two stone buildings, one of which had collapsed.

Once off their horses and sure they were alone, Indavara went to check the intact building while Cassius examined the ground in front of the mine. There were signs of activity but the rain had obscured anything so obvious as a footprint or wheel mark. There were, however, scattered streaks and patches of white. Cassius scraped up some of the familiar white dust with his dagger.

'Quicklime, sir?'

Cassius sniffed it and nodded. 'Tie up the horses. And prepare a torch.'

He walked down the short, sloping path that led to the mine. Outside the dark mouth were a stack of buckets and a pile of pick handles. It was impossible to see more than four or five yards inside but Cassius walked forward nonetheless – straight into a cobweb. As he pulled the wispy strands from his face, he felt the chilly breath of some subterranean breeze. The air smelled earthy, old. Cassius had never been in a mine before.

He walked back up the slope and met Indavara.

'Nothing,' said the bodyguard. 'Just an empty hut.'

Cassius pointed back at the mouth of the mine. 'This looks rather more interesting. Must be six yards across, three high.'

'More than enough for a big cart.'

'Exactly what I was thinking.'

It took Simo a frustratingly long time to get the fire going. He blamed damp char-cloth but Cassius was cursing him by the time he finally wrapped an oiled goat-skin round one of the pick handles and set light to it.

'You keep watch out here, Simo,' Cassius said as the three of them stood in front of the shaft. 'Indavara, you're with me.'

The bodyguard didn't answer. He was gazing wide-eyed into the gloom.

'What's the matter?'

'I've never been in somewhere like this.'

'Neither have I,' replied Cassius as he took the torch from Simo. 'And I don't know what we're going to find down there, so I need you with me. Draw your sword.'

'What about the spirits?'

'If you're so worried about spirits, best utter a prayer to your precious Fortuna.'

Sighing, Indavara drew his blade.

'Perhaps you'll need your cape, sir,' suggested Simo.

'We shan't be in there long enough for me to get cold.'

'These mines can run for miles, sir. And how will you find your way?'

'If the men we're after used this place, they had no reason to venture far from the main tunnel. Get the horses out of sight and watch the road. If anyone approaches, call down to us right away.'

'Yes, sir. Do be careful.'

Simo hurried away up the slope.

'Have you said your prayer?' Cassius asked.

Indavara shook his head.

Cassius was all set to ignore him and get going, but he wondered if a few words for Fortuna weren't such a bad idea. Epona had looked after the horses after all; and he might face numerous dangers in the coming days and weeks. He'd never been much of a worshipper, but life had been easier before: safer, more predictable. Things were different now. It certainly couldn't hurt.

'Allow me.' He clasped his hands, closed his eyes and began: 'Great Fortuna, goddess most high, we two humble travellers ask you to watch over us as we set forth into this dark place. We ask you to remember our offerings and prayers and we pledge to show our love for you when next we can. This man worships only you, so sacred are you to him. Our occupation is a noble one; we are engaged in a task that might keep peace in this land. Please grant us your favour, great goddess. Please grant us your favour.'

Cassius opened his eyes. Indavara's were still shut. Cassius tapped him on the shoulder.

'You should repeat that last bit.'

Indavara did so.

After only a few steps into the mine they spied the cart-tracks. Cassius paced out the distance.

'Eight and a half feet. This really might be it. Come on.'

The torch crackled as they strode into the darkness, and soon its glow caught the smoky wreaths of their cold breath. Cassius moved the light around, sometimes keeping it low so he could examine the ground, sometimes raising it high to check the roof.

He stopped and glanced back at the entrance. They were only a hundred feet inside but it already looked alarmingly small.

'What is it?' asked Indavara.

'Nothing. I just thought there would be tunnels or turns by now. On we go.'

Cassius hunched over, eyes fixed on the left-hand wheel mark. Occasionally, he would stop to check the walls but he found only niches for long-removed lamps. Indavara stayed a couple of paces behind him.

The wheel mark suddenly veered to the right. Cassius veered with it.

'Odd.'

Thoughts of why the track might suddenly change direction – and that he was perhaps walking too quickly – struck him just as his left foot slid down the lip of a vertical shaft.

'Gods!'

His foot gave way and he fell. His right leg, however, buckled under him and he landed on his knee, left boot still dangling in the air. Indavara grabbed his belt and pulled him away.

The torch fell to the ground and sizzled on the damp soil. As the flames flickered, Cassius snatched it up. Indavara knelt beside him.

'All right?'

'Yes. Just. Thank you.'

Cassius held the torch over the lip of the shaft.

'That was close. I thought the tunnels would go off to the side, not straight down.'

He stood up and walked carefully around the shaft. It was six feet wide and flush against the left wall. There were small hand-holds cut into the earth, and the remains of a rope.

'Right. Slower this time.'

Fifty feet further in, the tunnel divided. The main path continued downward at an even steeper angle while a second, narrower shaft bent away to the right. Cassius now realised that he was in fact following two sets of wheel marks, and both led along the smaller tunnel.

'They came in and out again,' he whispered to himself.

With a last look at the entrance, they continued round the bend, Cassius's gaze still trained on the ground. The lower and further they went, the softer and wetter the soil became, and the more obvious the wheel and foot marks; and as the tunnel widened out into a cavern, the ground became a muddy bog.

'Stay still a moment,' Cassius told Indavara, before twice traversing the twenty-foot width of the cavern. 'They may have been covered by the footprints but I see no more wheel marks beyond this point. I think they stopped here.'

'Look.'

Indavara pointed to the tunnel wall behind Cassius. There was a torch there, placed in an iron frame fixed to the wall. Cassius examined it.

'Used fairly recently, I'd say.'

They found six more of the mounted torches, and were able to light four of them. Indavara sheathed his sword and took one. The light seemed to bounce around the cavern; they could see the space quite clearly. Further on, it narrowed to a tunnel once more but before this were two small caves, one on either side.

They checked the left side first. Inside was a big wooden table with one broken leg resting on a slab of rock. There were chairs, stools and a chest too; plus some iron-framed buckets and two barrels full of green, putrid water. Indavara pulled open the lid of the chest. The rotten wood disintegrated and spilled the chest's contents – thick coils of hemp rope. Cassius knelt by the chairs, examining the area beneath the table.

'They sat here. Counting their treasure perhaps.'

'So that's what was in the barrels,' said Indavara.

'Among other things, yes. Doesn't look like they left anything behind.'

'They left this.'

Indavara pushed his sword tip into the muddy ground and levered out a brass coin. Cassius picked it up and scraped off the mud on the edge of the table. Before he had finished, Indavara found two more. They were all the same design; identical to the one from the Palmyran temple.

'Careless,' said Cassius. 'Very careless.'

'Perhaps they thought they had nothing to worry about; that no one could follow them this far.'

'Possibly. But all we've done will be for naught if we find nothing more here. Those cart-tracks vanish outside. We must keep looking.'

They found nothing else in the first cave. The second contained more buckets, a pile of rotting leather hides and a voluminous barrel of quicklime. They took half the chamber each, and examined the ground, the walls, even the roof; but there was nothing more to help them. The goat-skin on Cassius's torch had almost burned through so he swapped it with another from the cavern.

'This way.'

Cassius had to bow his head as they pressed on down the narrowing tunnel. With the additional light of the two bright torches, they were at least able to see further and walk quicker; and before long the light from the cavern was no more than a dim glow behind them. The walls were more rock than soil now; and the temperature had dropped dramatically.

Indavara stopped.

'What is it?' asked Cassius.

'I thought I heard something.'

'You're imagining it. All I can hear is my teeth chattering. Let's keep moving.'

'What if it was the spirits?'

'Calm yourself, bodyguard. We've not seen anything yet, have we?'

'I can feel them though. Their breath on my skin.'

'It's cold air, that's all.'

'Perhaps they're displeased. Perhaps they don't want us here.'

'Then we should stop dawdling.'

Cassius had counted forty paces more when they came upon a kind of crossroads, where a wider, perpendicular tunnel crossed the other.

'We'll take a side each. You to the left. Careful, there may be vertical shafts here too.'

This hunch was soon proved correct; Cassius came across one after just a few yards.

'Here's one already.'

'Here too,' answered Indavara.

Cassius was curious about how deep the shaft was, so he slid one of the burning branches out of the torch and dropped it. It fell so far that he couldn't tell whether it had hit the bottom or the flame had simply gone out.

'Indavara, watch yourself. They're very deep.'

'This one's not. I think there's something down here.'

Cassius hurried over to him. 'What do you mean?'

'The smell. Like before.'

Cassius knelt down next to him. The bodyguard was right. The smell of rotting flesh. Horribly, unmistakably human.

Cassius drew out another burning stick from his torch and threw it into the middle of the shaft. It landed about five yards down, on what looked like solid ground. They saw only soil before the flames went out. Cassius then took out a clump of branches and he made sure the whole bundle was well alight before dropping it. The bundle seemed to bounce off something before hitting the ground.

'Oh, gods. Look there – you see it?'

'A foot,' answered Indavara.

They were even able to make out toes before the flame died. Cassius sat down on his backside.

'By Mars. Another horror. I tell you, I'm not cut out for this job.'

'What now?'

'One of us will have to go down there. We'll need that rope from the cavern.'

'Not me. If the spirits are anywhere, there'll be down there.'

'What happened to "there's nothing to fear from a dead man"? That's what you said at the water channel.'

Indavara jabbed his torch towards the roof. 'That was up there. In the light.' He shook his head. 'I'll not do it.'

'For a hired man, you seem very definite about what you will or won't do. Isn't it the case that you should do whatever I tell you?'

'I'm not your manservant, or your slave. I get paid to protect you. No one said anything about this.'

Cassius looked down into the darkness. They had come so far. He couldn't falter now.

'All right then, will you at least fetch the rope?'

Cassius would have preferred to anchor the line to something solid but Indavara was confident he could take the weight. The bodyguard tested the rope, tied one end around his waist and dropped the rest into the shaft. He then dug out two holes with his boot, wedged his feet into them and sat down.

'Ready,' he said, both hands on the rope. 'You'll have to leave that here,' he added, nodding at Cassius's torch. 'I'll throw it to you once you're down.'

Cassius rubbed his brow. 'Gods, I need a drink.'

Indavara had stuck his torch into the ground by the side of the tunnel. Cassius did the same. He got down on his knees, legs astride the rope, feet hanging over the lip of the shaft. Gripping the rope with both hands, he lowered one leg. The wall of the shaft was compacted soil, but yielded enough for him to get a hold. He let his arms take his weight. The rope slipped a couple of inches.

'What are you doing?' he yelled.

'Just changing my grip. Go. You're fine.'

'Oh. Am I? Thanks.'

Making sure his feet were secure every time he moved his hands, Cassius slowly descended. Indavara kept the rope remarkably steady, and didn't even seem to be labouring. By the time Cassius's head was below the lip of the shaft, there was smooth rock under his boots.

As he continued downward, the combination of complete darkness and the ever worsening smell became almost overpowering. Thoughts flashed into his head of his fingers slipping and him falling into a pile of stinking, welcoming corpses. Gripping the rope hard, he stopped.

'You all right?' shouted Indavara.

'Just about.'

'You can't be far away now.'

Cassius's left foot was flat against the rock wall. He dangled his right foot and it brushed against something. He lowered himself further and the foot landed on solid ground.

'Made it.'

Cassius brought his left foot down. It landed on something

soft. The something crunched. Had he been in a state to care, Cassius would have been embarrassed by the noise he made then: a curious combination of whimper and scream.

'What is it?' yelled Indavara.

Cassius said nothing. He pressed up against the cold wall, not daring to move.

'Throw down the torch.'

'Where are you?'

'Just throw it, damn you!'

'I don't want to hit you.'

'Throw it, you dolt! I'm by the wall.'

The torch landed in the middle of the shaft by a bloated, blackened face streaked with livid veins. The mouth was horribly swollen, the lips like dark slugs. Thankfully, the eyes were shut. The dead man's hair began to smoke. The torch had set him alight.

Wincing, Cassius edged around the body until he was close enough to grab the torch; but by the time he removed it, the hair was burning. He had to scrape his boot against the head to put out the flames.

Cassius clamped a hand over his nose. He lowered the torch and forced himself to look at the body. There were no clothes to help with identification. The dead man was naked, and his belly and thighs had turned green. There were lacerations all over his throat. The unsinged hair was pale, colourless; there was no way of knowing if it had been black. Cassius couldn't even think about going anywhere near the eyes.

'Well?' asked Indavara.

'Wait.'

Cassius held the torch higher over the body, trying to guess the man's height. Five foot seven? Possibly. What about the scar? It was supposed to be on the back of his knee. Cassius knelt by the legs. The flickering light caught the black, polished shells of moving insects. They had burrowed into the body. Cassius retched, then felt his stomach burn.

Straightening up, he spied red marks on the rock wall where

he'd just been standing. At first he thought he might have made them himself and he checked his hands for blood. There was none.

He walked back around the body and held the torch close to the wall. The marks had been made with a finger, a finger soaked with blood; and they were not just marks, they were words.

A. Mallius Gregorius.

This man killed me.

Under the last phrase was a crude drawing of a hand. The thumb and two of the fingers were missing.

— 8 —

Cassius couldn't bring himself to touch the body, but he checked every other inch of the pit and found nothing more. Once back up the rope, he decided they could at least give the dead agent some kind of burial. Using their daggers to dig out sections of the compacted earth, they threw down enough to cover him.

After putting out the torches in the cavern, they hurried back towards the entrance; and once they were past the shaft that had so nearly done for Cassius, Indavara ran the rest of the way. Cassius maintained just enough self-control to resist joining him, but once outside he sucked in deep, long breaths – fresh air had never tasted so good. He took his canteen off his belt and drank while Indavara told Simo what they'd found.

Standing there, he realised he was developing a genuine hatred of the mysterious band of men they had followed across the Syrian desert. It was their treatment of the legionaries, and Gregorius in particular, that enraged him. The man had simply been doing his duty, acting on the orders of the Emperor; but he had been captured, dragged around like a dog, then left to die, naked and mutilated. Cassius shuddered as he thought of him passing his last hours alone there. Had he been a family man? Was there some poor wife – children even – awaiting his return?

Cassius felt guilt too. He'd questioned the man's loyalty yet it seemed that Abascantius's unswerving faith had been justified. Even as he lay dying, Gregorius had recorded a crucial detail that

194

might yet see his murderers caught. In a province where every other man was a sword-hand, two-fingered men were hardly unheard of, but it was something distinctive – something that might be remembered. A. Mallius Gregorius hadn't died entirely in vain.

They left the mine road a few miles south of Chalcis, aiming to pick up the Antioch road heading west. The desert was behind them now, and the landscape was changing. Ahead were the limestone hills and rich, fertile land of north-western Syria. With the raised road visible in the distance, they passed through untended fields now overgrown by sprawling bushes.

Between two of these fields, they came across a rectangular area cut into the ground: fifty feet long, twenty wide. The horses seemed unnerved as they stepped down on to the shale surface of the cut. To the left, at the far end, was a dark, curiously shaped boulder. Strewn around it were animal remains and decaying flowers.

'A sanctuary,' said Simo, as they dismounted.

'The rock has a face,' said Indavara, walking towards the boulder.

'Oh yes,' replied the Gaul. 'I've heard of these. Look – there's the nose.'

Cassius knew there were very few such sanctuaries without a supply of water and he wasn't disappointed. Behind the boulder was a wide stone basin full almost to the top.

'Thank the gods. This one in particular.'

He had been desperate to clean himself properly since exiting the mine but they had only enough in their canteens to wash his hands. Discarding his sword belt, he knelt beside the basin. He was about to splash water on his face when Simo arrived with two empty canteens.

'Please, sir. This place is sacred to whoever uses it. I don't think you should wash here. We might take some water out though.'

Cassius paused. There was no sense in angering any gods – even local ones – if it could be avoided.

'You're right. Do so.'

Cassius took his satchel and sat down on the fringe of the sanctuary, which formed a convenient bench. The horses had been let free to graze. Indavara lay close by, dozing.

Once Simo had washed his hands, arms and face, Cassius took out the map and spread it across his knees. Theoretically, the cart and its precious cargo could have been taken anywhere from the mine, but Abascantius had seemed sure someone in Antioch had facilitated the theft; and for anyone wanting to ship, sell or deliver the treasure or the flag, it was the obvious destination. In any case, he needed to tell the agent what he'd found. Using his finger for scale, he estimated the remaining distance to the capital. About sixty miles.

They covered twenty-five of those that day. The going was slow to begin with – the River Chalos ran south from Chalcis, and two hours were wasted finding a circuitous route through a marsh – but by midday they were on the Antioch road, heading straight for the capital. They ate lunch at an inn, and Cassius paid one of the proprietor's men to ride into Chalcis with Surex's letter. He hoped the optio would get the help he needed.

On hearing that this section of road was generally viewed as safe, and that there were occupied inns every few miles or so, Cassius decided that they would continue on until dusk. With the beating their backsides and legs had taken, he and Simo even spent a couple of hours on foot with Indavara.

When they finally bedded down that night, Cassius had cause to be glad of his exhaustion. For when Simo put out his lamp, he found it impossible not to think of cold, dark tunnels, and the fate of poor Gregorius.

XVII

They set off just after dawn, across the plain of Chalcis, through a tapestry of fields and olive groves demarked by low walls. There was no unworked land here; all the wheat had been harvested, and the olive farmers tended carefully to their crop. The road was busy too; the trio passed priests and merchants, pedlars and beggars. They lost count of the goat-herders and shepherds, and became used to the chime of the bells tied around their animals' necks.

Just after midday they met a century of the Sixteenth Legion marching to Chalcis. The centurion, a grey-haired veteran brandishing a long cane, was reluctant to stop but when Cassius told of him of Surex's predicament he ordered the men to rest and listened intently, pressing Cassius for a full appraisal of the situation at Androna. It turned out that he knew Surex well and his century had been ordered to Chalcis as reinforcements. He let the men get some water down, then led them off to the east at a prodigious pace.

Cassius turned round several times to watch the departing column. As a youngster he had loved to watch marching troops. He found the sense of power and purpose intoxicating, and had longed to be part of it. His father's ambiguity on the subject had confused him at the time; Corbulo senior had been proud of his son's yearnings yet wary of encouraging his only male heir to join the legions. But as Cassius grew older, his fascination with the army declined, replaced by his interest in academia and the fairer sex. But then circumstances (or, rather, his own misdeeds) had found him taking the oath after all. Training had been detestable, those few days at Alauran terrifying, then he had been in

Cyzicus, and now working for Abascantius; and in truth he had never felt like a proper soldier at all.

Cassius was a little ashamed by that, but he knew himself well enough to acknowledge he didn't have the stomach for the legions. He might have got by as a tribune – like the young men he'd seen with Venator at Palmyra – but overall he was better off with the Service. A soldier could find himself thrown into battle at any moment, his fate decided by a throw of the dice or the whim of the gods. Cassius could not live like that. It was already clear that working for Abascantius was rarely going to be anything other than difficult and dangerous; but he at least had a degree of autonomy. He would have to learn quickly, and he would have to deliver; but if he could make himself useful, there was a chance he might just survive the rest of his term in exile. And then life could begin anew.

They reached the edge of the plain that afternoon, and the road continued west through low, rolling hills. Close by was Immae, the site of Aurelian's first great clash with Zenobia's forces earlier in the summer, just weeks before the decisive battle at Emesa. Here the Emperor had defeated the forces of the Palmyran general Zabdas; and his wily tactics had already become the stuff of legend. Well aware of the formidable reputation of the Palmyran cavalry, Aurelian had instructed his lightly armed riders to fake a withdrawal, successfully drawing the Palmyrans into a long pursuit. The heavily armoured enemy were soon exhausted, and when the Romans finally turned on them, could put up little resistance. Few of Zenobia's warriors survived.

There was only one sign on the road that the battle had occurred so close by: a young trader with a stock of Palmyran swords, helmets and armour. Indavara took a quick look but didn't buy anything.

As afternoon became evening, the road descended through vineyards and yet more olive groves to the River Orontes. Though relieved to get there, Cassius was rather disappointed by what he saw. There was an impressive bridge with eight arches but water flowed under only one of them.

In front of the bridge were two large inns, one on each side of the road, busy with travellers seeking lodgings for the night. Simo hurried away to see about a room while Cassius and Indavara stayed with the horses.

They watched a man traverse the bridge, lighting lanterns. On the western shore, a group of fishermen packed up their gear and walked back across the river bed. Beyond them was a line of tall cedars, swaying gently.

'Not far now,' Cassius said. 'Ten miles or so to the capital.' He turned and looked at his horse. It was standing with its head bowed, eyes half-closed: a picture of misery. 'Poor thing. Looks just like I feel.'

Indavara nodded wearily.

'Yours seems a little happier though,' Cassius continued. 'Now that you're not pulling its mouth to pieces. You've improved. I see it.'

Simo returned quickly.

'One is full, sir, but the other has three small singles free on the top floor. It is rather expensive though.'

'No matter,' said Cassius. He left his horse for Simo and passed him on his way down the hill. 'A room each it is, gentlemen; courtesy of Master Abascantius and the Imperial Security Service.'

Once the horses had been stabled, Simo and Indavara took the gear up to the rooms. Cassius made straight for the front parlour, which opened up on to a grassy slope facing the river. He sat down at the only spare table – a solid looking structure with benches attached - and caught the eye of a middle-aged serving wench. The woman had to negotiate her way through a crowd of well-attired men, all carrying personalised wooden mugs. As she approached, Cassius tried not to look at her enormous, sagging bosom.

'Busy, eh?' he said in Greek.

The woman tutted. 'Guild of goat-skin bag makers. It'll be a long night. What can I get you, sir?'

'A bottle of something expensive. And some water. And three glasses.'

'Glasses?'

'You do have some, don't you?'

'We do, sir. Won't be a moment.'

When the woman returned with the wine, Cassius poured himself a full glass before she'd even taken the jug of water from her tray. And by the time Indavara and Simo came down, he was on to his second glass and feeling better than he had in weeks.

Surely the worst of the job was over. Abascantius would probably find something for him to do in Antioch but responsibility rested with the senior man now.

Simo looked aghast when Cassius poured wine for him and Indavara.

'It's all right, Simo, I can lift a bottle you know. Let us drink to small mercies: we have made it across the Syrian desert unscathed.'

The other two raised their glasses.

'And to great Fortuna, of course,' Cassius added, with a nod to Indavara.

'Lovely wine, sir. Thank you very much.' Simo grinned, and looked out across the river.

'You'll want to visit your father, I suppose,' said Cassius.

'If you could spare me for an hour or two, sir, I would be most grateful. Most grateful.'

'Of course. And not just for an hour or two.'

Simo put down his wine and bowed his head.

'What's wrong?' asked Indavara, glancing curiously at Simo, whose eyes were now wet.

'The poor fellow's not seen his family in two years,' explained Cassius, 'largely on my account. He's entitled to shed a tear or two.'

Indavara continued to stare at Simo. His expression was – as ever – hard to read, but it certainly wasn't sympathetic.

'What, you don't miss your kin?' asked Cassius. 'You never think of your mother and father?'

Indavara looked away, across the river. 'Just let me drink, would you?'

'Happy to,' replied Cassius, determined not to let anything ruin his mood. 'I shall do the same. And then – food.'

They dined well, starting with fresh bread, olive oil and goat's cheese, followed by thick black sausages served with an imaginative array of vegetables. By the time an unnecessarily large platter of fruit arrived, Cassius and Simo were so full that they contented themselves with a few dates, safe in the knowledge that Indavara would plough through the rest. He duly did so.

While emptying the second bottle of wine, Cassius and Simo began an extended session of 'Guess the Emperor'. Despite their assurances, Indavara insisted that none of the outlandish acts could possibly be true, though he did think the seal-skin coat Augustus had worn to protect him from lightning was 'probably not a bad idea'.

From the game they moved on to poetry and Cassius began by reciting a few lines of Varrius Rufus he thought apt. Simo – who could never be tempted into a recitation when sober – responded with an entire three verses of Valerius Flaccus. Though he rarely indulged, the big man took his drink well, and as usual didn't make a single mistake. Cassius continued with some Statius but quickly realised he'd overreached himself and cut the second verse short, hoping Simo hadn't noticed.

As it grew dark, lanterns were brought out to each table and the guildsmen struck up a song. Unable to keep pace with Cassius and Simo, Indavara switched to water and watched sullenly as they worked their way through a third bottle. With his arm round the Gaul's shoulder, Cassius tried to sing along with the guildsmen. One man staggered over to them, then thumped down on to the bench next to Indavara, opposite Cassius.

'Enjoying yourself?' asked Cassius in Greek.

The red-faced guildsman raised his mug.

'The goat-skin bag trade must be in good health,' continued Cassius. 'I'm surprised the inn still has any wine left.'

'We come here every September. Rain or shine. War or peace.'

It took the guildsman three attempts to open the purse on his belt. He took out a handful of silver coins and counted them.

'Good. I've got something left for next week.'

'What's happening next week?'

'The hippodrome and the arena are reopening.'

'Ah, I see. What's your team?'

'The Greens, of course.'

A man standing close by heard this. 'The Greens! The Greens!' he cried before tottering away.

The guildsman and Cassius laughed.

'I mean, they're not what they were – best charioteer was killed during the revolt – but they've still got a chance at the title.'

'And what of the games?'

The guildsman's eyes lit up. 'The governor's promising a hundred men on the first day alone – Palmyran prisoners of war. The crowd will love it. And then our local champion's taking on some big Nubian.'

'Really?' Cassius nodded at Indavara. 'My man here was a gladiator. Killed a seven-foot German and a—'

Indavara stood up, knocking the table and tipping over the bottle of wine. As Simo righted it, the bodyguard walked away towards the inn.

'Where are you going?' demanded Cassius.

Indavara stopped, and spoke without turning around. 'To bed. It's late.'

'No, no. We're celebrating. Sit down.'

Indavara went on his way.

'I said sit down!'

As he disappeared inside, Cassius shrugged.

'Doesn't know how to have fun – that's his problem.'

The Greens' supporter returned and grabbed his fellow by the arm. 'Come on, we're off down to the river.'

The guildsman took his drink and got up. With all the weight now on one side, the table tipped backward, dumping Cassius, Simo, several plates, the bottle and the glasses on to the grass.

'Oh dear,' said Cassius as he lay there.

'Time for bed, sir?' said Simo, removing a plate from his master's chest.

'Time for bed.'

XVIII

'Now that's what a proper city wall looks like.'

Ignoring the mass of people in front of him, Cassius gazed at the northern side of Antioch. The wall was twenty-five feet high, built of gargantuan limestone blocks, some of which were faced with triangular pieces of brick. Left of the Beroea Gate, the walls ran for half a mile then gave way to the tents and improvised housing that covered the lower slopes of Mount Silpius, the fifteen-hundred-foot peak that overshadowed the city. To the right of the gatehouse, the walls extended two hundred yards before meeting the Orontes. Here the river divided, running around the island connected to the rest of the city by five bridges.

'If only the walls were in such good repair all the way round, sir,' observed Simo.

'You can thank the Persians for that. They will insist on invading every few years.'

Cassius's role in an assignment that might help avoid future incursions from the east was too much for his wine-addled mind to deal with, so he instead admonished the two slaves manning the cart ahead of them. Their vehicle was full of manure, and they didn't seem to mind that every movement of their horses caused more of it to seep on to the road. Simo, meanwhile, had already pledged not to let his master ply him with wine ever again. Cassius had heard that before.

'Twenty at least,' said Indavara. 'Twenty carts between us and the gate.'

'Not for long,' replied Cassius. 'Follow me.'

The approach road sat atop a robust causeway that crossed the marshy, flood-prone plain to the east of the city. Cassius guided his horse down a short slope on to the soggy ground and set off along the right side of the road. Many of the waiting multitude cast annoyed looks but not one dared say anything. They were commoners in the main; it was midday, and most of the merchants or farmers with anything to sell would have arrived in the city hours ago. Cassius did however see two heavy carts carrying chunks of marble, and one loaded with big lidded barrels. Had another such vehicle passed the gates in the last few days? Had its precious cargo entered the city unseen?

The road narrowed to fifteen feet as it passed under the great arch of the gatehouse. Planted on the roof was a stone rendering of Romulus and Remus being nursed by the she-wolf. The gate itself – a monstrous spiked iron grid – hung from foot-wide chains high above the ground. Mounted on each of the gatehouse's two towers was a life-sized silver statue of the Tyche: the local goddess who, for the Antiochenes, symbolised both fortune and their city. Clad in long robes and a high crown, she held a bunch of grapes in one hand, a sheaf of wheat in the other.

Cassius dismounted close to the western tower. While waiting for Simo and Indavara to catch up, he put on his helmet and retrieved the spear-head. The waiting crowd were remarkably quiet and orderly; largely because of the dozen burly men patrolling back and forth in front of them. Cassius noted their weapons: clubs formed from tightly wrapped lengths of wood. These were the municipal magistrate's sergeants, responsible for enforcing the law and maintaining order. Beyond them, eight clerks sat at tables, interviewing entrants and collecting taxes. There were legionaries there too. One of them spotted Cassius and pushed some locals aside.

'This way, sir.'

'My men must pass also.'

Simo and Indavara – looking faintly embarrassed – led the horses up the side of the road past the crowd. An aged centurion strode out of the gatehouse. His left arm was withered and hung limply by his side.

'Morning,' said Cassius.

'Afternoon, I'd say. Turpo. I'm in charge here.'

'Corbulo, governor's staff.'

'I can see that. Come, you must sign in. Your men can go straight through. Sanga!'

Legionary Sanga escorted Simo and Indavara past the sergeants while Cassius ducked in to the gatehouse. Inside the cramped room was a desk piled high with papyrus and leather-bound books. One such book had been left open. A reed-pen sat in a bronze holder next to it.

'Name, rank, date and purpose of visit,' said Turpo. 'Oh, and time. It's the seventh hour.'

As Cassius filled out the book, a clerk came in from another door and began what swiftly became a fraught debate with Turpo about the tax rate for prostitutes being brought into the city. Cassius left the 'purpose of visit' section blank and waited for Turpo to dismiss the clerk.

'Centurion, do you record all the traffic that comes in and out – carts and such like?'

'Just for those bringing in goods. There's a flat fee for traders – per horse, cart or whatever.' He aimed a thumb at the gate. 'But this is all because the council want to keep everyone on the straight and narrow until things settle down. The Palmyrans changed all the rates and tolls but we're slowly getting back to normal.'

'You don't keep track of particular loads then?'

'Not usually. Just the money taken. Unless it's something unusual, or suspicious.'

'Would I be allowed to check through the records of the last few weeks? I'm interested in a particular cart that may have entered the city.'

'You would. If you had the right authorisation.'

'And who would I get that from?'

'Tribune Bonafatius.'

'Bonafatius. And what about other routes into the city?'

'There's the Bridge Gate and the Daphne Gate to the south. And a few tracks in over the mountain, but a heavy cart couldn't use those.'

'Much obliged.'

On the other side of the gatehouse, Cassius found himself at one end of the Avenue of Herod and Tiberius, the impressive colonnaded street that ran north-east to south-west through the heart of Antioch. The imposing double line of columns supported porticos on each side that covered a walkway almost as wide as the street.

If not for the crew of slaves hammering away at a plinth, the street would have been fairly quiet. The busiest part of the day had passed, and many of the city's inhabitants would be at home, eating and resting after a hard morning's work. A second gang of dark-skinned slaves appeared from a side street. Escorted by four armed overseers, they marched swiftly past Cassius and under the gatehouse. Indavara and Simo emerged out of the shadows behind them, the Gaul with a set of reins in each hand. He was smiling. Cassius took off his helmet as he wandered over to them.

'Glad to be back, I see.'

'Oh yes, sir. Yes indeed.'

'Lead on then.'

Cassius had aimed to arrive in the city around the middle of the day, hoping they might find Abascantius at home. He had already given Simo the agent's address; the Gaul had lived in the city all his life before working for Cassius and didn't take a single wrong turn. They headed east – towards Mount Silpius – and passed warehouses and granaries, bakeries and inns. Here, those without the luxury of an afternoon break laboured on.

The streets widened and acquired pavements as they moved into a residential area. They saw a large fountain with an ornamental pool and carved spouts for public use. But there was no water running and only a little in the pool; it would be several weeks before the aqueducts that fed the city were in full flow.

Abascantius's villa was a one-storey, stone-built townhouse, narrow-fronted but extending back a long way. It was surrounded by a cordon of high poplars and a six-foot wall. The entrance was secured by an iron gate. Next to it was a bronze bell hanging from a rope. Cassius told Simo to ring it.

As they waited, Indavara gazed at the quiet, well-maintained villas and the steep slopes above. Cassius put his hands on the bars of the gate and peered along the path that led to the villa. He could see no one; and the door was obscured by voluminous, purple-flowered bushes. The whole arrangement was very strange; he'd expected Abascantius to maintain a large staff – certainly enough people to man his own gate.

They heard a door creak open, then footsteps. Cassius instantly recognised the squat frame and grim visage of Shostra.

'Ah. We've got the right place at least.'

With not a word of greeting, Shostra perused each of the three men through the gate, taking a particularly long time over Indavara. He then turned on his heels and walked back to the house.

'Hey!' Cassius shouted after him. He turned to Simo. 'I really don't like that man.'

They heard voices. Shostra returned a few moments later. He produced a key from his belt and unlocked the gate.

'Master wants me and your man to go on to where you're staying – get the horses stabled and the house ready. You can go in.'

'Thank you so much,' replied Cassius. 'Go ahead, Simo.'

Once Indavara had removed his weapons from his saddle, Shostra led Simo and the horses away down the street. Cassius and Indavara walked up to the villa. Unsurprisingly, there was no one to meet them at the door. As they stepped inside the hallway, Cassius looked down at the multicoloured mosaic set into the tiled floor beneath their feet: *WELCOME*. He nudged Indavara and nodded down at it.

'Not so far.'

Indavara frowned.

'Can you read?' Cassius asked him.

'Ah, there you are! Come, come in.'

Abascantius had appeared at the end of the hallway. 'You two look stiff,' he remarked as they walked towards him. 'Not surprised with all that riding. Don't tell me you've been strolling around the city with that in your hand, Corbulo.'

Cassius looked down at the spear-head; he'd been holding it since the gate.

'Gods, you'll not be much use to me here if everyone knows who you are. Thank Jupiter it's late. Nobody important will have seen you at least.'

Cassius didn't particularly like the sound of that; it seemed Abascantius already had more work in mind for him.

They were standing in a large atrium with an air of faded grandeur. Under the rectangular opening in the middle of the room was a circular basin half full with rainwater. The sides of the basin had turned green. The few items of furniture looked new but the frescoes on two of the walls were in dire need of repainting and an extravagant mosaic – a trio of peacocks – had lost many of its pieces.

Abascantius looked Indavara up and down. 'And how was our monosyllabic friend here?'

'Monosyllabic,' said Cassius. 'We're having to educate him in the finer points of riding, eating and conversation but he's done his job well enough.'

'Good, good,' said Abascantius. 'We shall keep him on for the moment then.' He turned to Indavara. 'We shall sort out your money later. Wait here for now. Come, Corbulo.'

Abascantius looked even fatter than Cassius remembered him. As he followed him around the basin to the other side of the atrium, he looked at the rolls of flesh hanging over his belt, and his hairy, mole-covered calves. He really was a singularly unattractive man.

They passed along a corridor with a number of smaller rooms on either side then emerged into a spacious courtyard. Beyond was a neat orchard of apple trees and the rear gate. In the middle of the courtyard was a large, waterless fountain and – rising from its centre – a bronze statue of a bearded, contemplative god.

'Hermes or Dionysus?' queried Cassius.

'Palmyran,' Abascantius sneered. 'I keep meaning to knock it down.'

'You've not been here long then?'

'A month or so. The previous resident was a man who did

rather well out of the occupation. Gave up two of my best operatives to the Palmyrans. I had him . . . evicted.'

'I see.'

In front of the fountain was a marble table and two wooden
benches. Abascantius picked up a bottle of wine, topped up his
own glass and poured a full one for Cassius.

'So the Emperor's policy of clemency has its limits,' Cassius
said as he sat down.

Abascantius pushed the glass over to him. 'Exceptions can
always be made.'

One end of the bench was next to the wall of the fountain,
with two cushions propped up against it. Abascantius sat there,
glass in hand.

'What about Gregorius?' he asked. 'Do you know anything?'

Cassius found he couldn't keep his eyes on the older man.

'Yes, sir. Not good news, I'm afraid.'

Now Abascantius looked away. He took a long swig of wine.

'You may start. Leave nothing out.'

It took Cassius almost an hour to relate the events of the last
nine days. He did leave something out: the incident with the Celts
at Palmyra, and he made a mental note to tell Indavara to keep
quiet about it too. Abascantius listened carefully, sometimes
pressing Cassius for details. His wide, ravaged face remained
largely impassive until Cassius described what they'd found at
the mine. Cursing, he sprang up and kicked out at a chair. It
skidded away across the tiles and on to the grass. He stood still
for a time, then leaned over the fountain with his hands on the
surround.

'They'll pay,' he whispered through clenched teeth. 'By Jupiter
they'll pay.'

'Why do you think they kept him alive, sir?'

Abascantius backed away from the fountain. 'Sounds like the
legionaries fought on to a man, but Gregorius knew how important it was that he live – wait for a chance to escape, get word
to me. He was crafty. Resourceful.'

'He may yet have helped us, sir.'

'Indeed.'

'He had a wife?'

'No. And no children, thank the gods. But he lived with a woman. I shall have to tell her.' Abascantius looked down at Cassius and ran a thumb across his chin. 'You have done well, Corbulo, all things considered.'

Cassius agreed; but did his best to appear magnanimous.

'If I may, sir, I do have some ideas about how to proceed. This two-fingered man, obviously. And the gatehouse – they sometimes keep records of incoming traffic. Or the silver and gold markets. We might see if—'

Abascantius held up his hands. 'Wait. Wait a moment. Those matters should be followed up, I agree. But you're forgetting the council: the only men who knew of Gregorius's mission.'

'The only men apart from Venator, Lollius and this character Tarquinius.'

'Who probably took his share – whatever he could carry and safely keep quiet.' Abascantius shrugged. 'Good luck to him. Lollius too, if he did likewise. There's not a chance Venator's involved: he's been chasing a seat in the senate for ten years, and his family are the eighth or ninth richest in all the Empire.'

'Sir, I don't believe for a moment that Venator had anything to do with it, nor Lollius if I'm honest. But the man who sniffed out the treasure in the first place . . .'

'Assuming for a moment that a Roman officer would allow ten of his fellow soldiers to be killed, how would he organise such a thing?'

'I have no idea. But a haul like that would provide a powerful incentive. And attract a good deal of help.'

Abascantius didn't look convinced. 'If this Tarquinius was behind the raid he'd be long gone by now, and Venator himself told you he was back in Zeugma. I'm afraid you're missing the point, Corbulo. It's not about the trinkets or the silver or the gold. It's about the flag. What we must focus on is who's pulling the strings. I've only been back a few days and my resources aren't what they were, but I've made a little progress. We'll follow the council members day and night if need be, leave no stone unturned.'

'Who exactly is on this council?'

Instead of answering, Abascantius stared thoughtfully down at Cassius. 'Do you have a good toga with you?'

'Yes, sir. Why?'

'You can see the council first-hand. Act as my eyes and ears. Don't look so worried, Corbulo. After all those days in the desert I'm sure you'll enjoy a cultured evening with the great and the good of Antioch.'

'Sir?'

'You're going to a dinner party.'

The villa they were to stay in was another of those liberated from one of Abascantius's 'evictees'. Cassius knew he shouldn't have been surprised to hear the agent talk of such a thing in so dispassionate a manner, but it disturbed him to think what the man might truly be capable of.

Before he and Indavara left, Abascantius summoned three messengers and dispatched them to various locations. He told Cassius to meet him at the eleventh hour by Hadrian's Bridge, and that he should make himself as presentable as possible.

The villa was located half a mile south of Abascantius, closer to the centre of the city, in a similarly anonymous area. As Cassius and Indavara walked through the streets, Antioch seemed to reawaken after the quiet of noon. Glancing to the right, they caught glimpses of crowds and the grand buildings at the city's heart.

'Where's this big face then?' said Cassius.

According to Abascantius's directions, when they were level with a distinctive carving on the side of Mount Silpius, the villa would be dead ahead. As they emerged on to a wide road running down to the Avenue of Herod and Tiberius, Cassius's question was answered.

'Ah. Quite impressive.'

Carved into grey rock high above the city was a large male face with a smaller figure on one shoulder. The sculpture looked damaged or unfinished.

'So that must be it,' said Indavara, pointing forward.

The villa was smaller than Abascantius's but again well protected by a high wall and a sturdy gate. Running along the southern side of the house was a smaller river – the Parmenios – that flowed down from Mount Silpius into the Orontes.

The gate was open. They found Simo sweeping the path.

'Welcome, sir.'

The Gaul shook his head as he followed Cassius inside. 'There's so much to do. I shall have to get firewood, some cooking utensils, there's no water coming in; oh and—'

'Relax, Simo. You've the rest of the day to attend to all that. At least we have somewhere habitable to base ourselves.'

Inside the villa were a few basic bits of furniture but no decoration of any kind.

'It's terribly bare, sir.'

'Less for you to clean then. Where are the horses?'

'Stabled just down the road. Shostra said the man there is reliable. We may come and go as we please.'

Leading off from the atrium were four rooms, including three bedrooms. Cassius took the largest of them and told Indavara to take the room closest to the front door. Simo asked the bodyguard to help him with a few chores, and he seemed happy to lend a hand.

Cassius's saddlebags were already in his room, on top of a low but wide wooden bed. The only other furniture was a large set of shelves. Cassius pushed the saddlebags across the bed and lay down beside them. On the way to the villa, he had heard a slave announcing the start of the ninth hour, so decided there was time for a short nap. He was tired and hung over and couldn't possibly face the demands of civilised company without taking a rest. He listened to Simo ask Indavara to go and buy some water. Before he left, the bodyguard asked Simo about the rock carving.

'That's the Charonion,' the Gaul explained. 'It's more than four hundred years old. Built on the orders of Antiochus himself – the ancient king who gave the city its name. During his time a plague struck; a seer advised him that he should create a great image of Charon, the god of the underworld, to appease him and prevent further pestilence striking the city.'

'Did it work?' asked Indavara.

Cassius didn't hear the reply. He was already asleep.

XIX

Cassius arrived at Hadrian's Bridge before Abascantius, which gave him a few welcome moments to gather his thoughts. Two hours of sleep seemed only to have depleted his strength and he was troubled by the prospect of the evening ahead. He wasn't sure how one gained admittance to a dinner party without being known to the host; and he wondered what the agent wanted him to do.

Arms crossed, he leaned back against the rough wall of the bridge, a wide, arched structure that stretched a hundred feet over the Orontes. There didn't seem much need for a bodyguard at a dinner party, so he'd told Indavara to stay and help Simo.

It was strange – unnerving in fact – to be among crowds of people after all those days in the desert. He gazed at the thronging mass of pedestrians and carts moving in both directions. There was clearly some substantial building work going on somewhere; most of those returning from the island seemed to be labourers. More of the municipal magistrate's men were on duty, ensuring that pedestrians kept to the side of the road and clearing any dawdlers with a harsh word and the odd poke with their clubs.

Cassius turned round and looked down at the river, where a multitude of punts and skiffs vied for space with larger boats upon the calm, dark water. Some of the bigger vessels were manned by six or eight slaves pulling hard at their oars while their masters and mistresses lounged at the rear. Several of these boats were converging on a dock at the south-west corner of the island. Already moored there was a big, sea-going galley. Two lads were working at the top of the mast while the remainder of the crew scrubbed sails laid across the deck.

Beyond the dock was a huge, sprawling villa set in its own

gardens, complete with several fountains, a stable and a bathhouse. There looked to be some other private residences close by, but most of the island was taken up by public buildings: theatres, baths, civic offices, and – on the far side – the oval bulk of the hippodrome and the looming walls of the imperial palace.

'Don't turn. We should avoid being seen together.'

Abascantius and Shostra were suddenly by the wall to his right. 'Guests already arriving,' said the agent. 'We must be quick.'

Cassius nodded towards the big villa. 'I'm going there?'

'You are. The House of the Dolphins. But first I shall show you the council. Their meeting at the forum has just broken up so they'll be along soon. On the other side of the bridge turn right; there's a theatre next to the villa. Go inside and wait. I'll have someone fetch you. Go now.'

Cassius waited for a gap in the traffic, then darted through it and strode away across the bridge.

The high wooden doors at the front of the theatre were open. Cassius went inside and found himself in a spacious reception area lined by benches. Opposite the entrance was another set of doors, presumably to the auditorium and stage. On either side of the room were staircases leading upward. Two women were on their knees, cleaning the floor.

Cassius sat down on one of the benches. He hadn't been there long when a young boy – no more than eight or nine – came running down the staircase to the right. He took a momentary curious glance at Cassius, gestured for him to follow, then ran back the way he'd come.

The staircase spiralled up to a high second floor, and a gallery with an excellent view of the stage, currently obscured by scarlet curtains. The boy pointed to a room on the left side of the gallery then trotted away. Shostra was in the doorway, handing a few coins to an elderly, well-dressed man. Shostra ushered the man away and nodded inside the room. It was packed full of tables, benches and chairs.

'Over here,' said Abascantius, popping his head up above the jungle of furniture.

Cassius squeezed his way through, trying not to get his toga dirty. Abascantius was sitting on a chair in front of a small, iron-grilled window. There was a spare stool next to him. As Cassius sat down, the agent looked him over.

'Very smart.'

It was a hot afternoon, and though the toga was thin, the wool irritated Cassius's skin. He hadn't worn it since leaving Cyzicus, and felt rather self-conscious. Simo had also given him a wash and shave, then cut his nails and attended to his hair.

Abascantius grimaced. 'You are rather good-looking though. Tall too. Not ideal.'

'My mother would take issue with you on that,' said Cassius with a grin.

'You don't work for your mother.'

Abascantius pointed down at the street. Beneath them was the House of the Dolphins. Guests were arriving at the wide set of steps that splayed out from the main door. Cassius dragged his stool closer to the window to take in the full scale of the structure. It was truly enormous, with four atria and three separate courtyards.

'Your host is Kaeso Scaurus, one of the richest men in Antioch. His first party since the liberation of the city. Not that he and his kind particularly suffered, but most of them are relieved to be rid of the Palmyrans. His parties are infamous – more than a few of the city folk will be looking for an excuse to cut loose. Should be quite a night.'

'Were you invited?'

Abascantius laughed bitterly. 'Me? No. My presence would spoil the festival spirit – put the guests off their food. Ah, the man himself.'

Cassius peered down through the grille. A plump individual in an ostentatious purple and gold cloak was jogging down the steps. He had a round, ruddy face and a voluminous head of curly black hair. As two particularly decorous ladies disembarked from an open carriage, Scaurus bowed low, then kissed each hand in turn. He

217

turned his attention to their menfolk, smiling broadly and gripping their forearms with overt enthusiasm.

'Still trying too hard, I see,' said Abascantius. 'Will he never learn?'

'Something of an aspirant?'

'The very definition. Mother was a Jew, father a legionary. Made his fortune in slaves and money-lending. He's been trying to buy his way into the provincial assembly for years. Doesn't seem to understand that unless he marries into one of a handful of families or wins the favour of Marcellinus, those doors will remain for ever closed.'

'The same people hold power now? Even after the occupation?'

'Most were sensible enough to keep their heads down and their mouths shut – wait until the storm passed. Antiochenes are rather adept at that. A few ran into trouble with the Palmyrans of course, but I doubt today's guest list will be that different from a couple of years ago.'

Three ranks of spear-carrying cavalrymen had just arrived in front of the villa. Between them was a diminutive figure on a pale grey horse.

'Ah. The first of our council members. General Julius Ulpian, commander of the Antioch garrison.'

A swift boot from Scaurus sent a slave boy scurrying towards the general with a little box to help him dismount. As another slave held his horse's reins, Ulpian descended. Scaurus offered a hand but the general waved it away. As he made his way up the steps, a huge African legionary fell into step behind him. Ulpian removed his helmet to reveal a sparse head of grey hair and a lined, leathery face.

'He's old, even for a general,' observed Cassius.

'Sixty-five, I think. In truth, his has been a nominal title for the last few years. The Palmyrans let him stay, but every last century had already been withdrawn. He's got a full cohort again now though.'

'A suspect?'

'Possible but unlikely. He's had to watch himself ever since a nasty incident a few years back. He became obsessed with one of his tribune's wives, and was none too subtle about it. He was warned off several times, but couldn't help himself. Eventually he sent the tribune away on some pointless errand, then went round to his house and raped the girl.'

'Gods.'

'He tried to cover it up but it got back to me eventually. I told Chief Pulcher and he told the Emperor. Claudius decided that Ulpian could keep his job on condition he keep his nose clean until he retired. As far as I know, he has.'

'He was lucky.'

'It wasn't just luck. He's a war hero. Finest cavalry commander in the province in his day. Fought two wars against Shapur.'

'Then he must hate the Persians.' Cassius glanced at Abascantius. 'Enough to stop us signing a treaty with them?'

'I don't see it. Like you said – he's old. I doubt he has the energy for criminal intrigues. Probably more interested in getting his end away as many times as he can before he finally keels over.'

The procession of guests seemed endless. Some men came alone on horseback, their steeds swiftly removed by Scaurus's slaves. Women, couples or groups used open carriages drawn by mules. Others emerged from litters carried by four or six slaves, and one elderly lady arrived in a luxurious carriage complete with miniature marble columns supporting a purple canopy.

A crowd was developing in front of the villa: guests watching other guests arrive. Scaurus threw up his hands in dismay and corralled them back inside the house. One of his servants alerted him to another carriage pulling up and he hurried back towards the street, lifting the folds of his cloak as he descended the steps once more.

'This must be someone important,' said Cassius.

Abascantius leaned forward as a tall, slender man stepped grace-fully down to the ground before turning to lend his female companion a hand.

'Our esteemed governor, no less. I give you Titus Fabius Gordio. The politician's politician.'

'How so?'

'Not many men could manage to be governor before an occupation, during an occupation and after an occupation. He somehow managed to smooth the way with the Palmyrans and protect his consituents' interests.'

'An intelligent man, then.'

'They don't come much brighter. It's said that he charmed Zenobia into no end of concessions, and that she politely bade him farewell as she fled the city. And he's been able to hide the fact that he's in love with his clerk from his wife for more than a decade. I'm not sure which is the more impressive achievement.'

Gordio accepted Scaurus's low bow, then took his wife's hand. The elegant couple ascended the steps, nodding to the other guests.

'Could he be involved?'

'Up until a few days ago I would have said no, but some new information has come to light.'

Abascantius was evidently reluctant to explain further.

'But after surviving for so long,' said Cassius, 'what possible motive would he have to endanger the treaty?'

'None I can think of. But what if he is being manipulated by others – with motives of their own?'

'Blackmail?'

'It's all supposition at the moment.' Abascantius sat back and let out a sigh. 'Unless I have proof I daren't make a single move against him. He's close to Marcellinus, and we've crossed swords many times in the past.'

Abascantius nodded down at the street again. 'Here's number three.'

Next up the steps was a younger man in his thirties. He was alone, dressed modestly, with a pale green cloak over his tunic. He seemed somewhat out of place; bookish and reserved.

'Looks pretty harmless.'

'Procurator Gallio Novius Octobrianus.'

'He's done well to make procurator at his age. He survived the occupation too?'

'Positively flourished. He'd just been appointed deputy procurator when the revolt began. If what I've been told is true, he was quick to exploit the situation to his advantage. The Palmyrans compiled a list of troublemakers – those who would not accede to their authority under any circumstances. I've heard it said more than once that Octobrianus helped them compile it. One of the first names on the list was that of Docillus: the previous procurator. Octobrianus's immediate superior.'

'How convenient.'

'Quite. Many of the other men on that list didn't get out in time, and they were either removed from their posts or killed. Docillus was lucky. He left a week before the city was taken. A day or two before me, as I recall.'

Cassius turned to Abascantius.

The agent nodded. 'I was on the list too. Somewhere close to the top, I imagine.'

Cassius looked back at the villa. Octobrianus had disappeared inside.

'He may still have connections to the Palmyrans, then?'

'Possibly.'

'But how can such a man still be in charge of the city's finances? I understand the Emperor's attitude – a fresh start and all that – but if it's true Octobrianus deserves to hang.'

'You'll hear no argument from me. But the key word is *if*. I've heard about him and this list from three different sources; but none of them would speak openly of it, and there's no other proof. He covered his tracks too well. Another survivor.'

'Assuming for a moment that he's still in league with them, who of the Palmyran leadership remains? Zenobia is on her way to Rome and her lackeys were all executed.'

'True. And I've spent a good portion of the last few months dismantling their intelligence operation, but there may be individuals I don't know about – back in Palmyra or even here.'

'What would *they* gain from disrupting the treaty?'

'They may simply want the flag back; it gives them great power over the Persians as a bargaining tool. And in the long term, an alliance between the great powers on either side of them does little to advance their cause. The ultimate aim? Quite possibly the re-establishment of Palmyran rule. Look, I'd love to see that little shit Octobrianus on the end of a rope, believe me, but there's nothing definitive on him yet.' Abascantius shrugged, then gestured to the villa. 'You must also realise it's my job to know all their dirty little secrets. One can start to feel rather paranoid – that everyone is hiding something. But these are ambitious people. What was it Aristophanes said? *Under every rock lies a politician?*'

'Sir, I apologise if I'm speaking out of turn, but shouldn't the Emperor just get rid of these men? It seems to me they're all guilty of collaboration.'

Abascantius pointed at him. 'You are speaking out of turn, Corbulo, but I shall answer that in the interests of opening your eyes to a few political realities. You call them collaborators. But isn't every Roman who stayed here, to a lesser or greater degree? Should we have them all driven from the city? Don't forget the Palmyrans held sway here long before they decided to annex the province. People had to make choices; consider their families, their futures. And it's not as if Zenobia had them raping and pillaging. One might even argue that she wished only to rule the Empire, not to eradicate it. Was she so different to any other usurper?' Abascantius shifted in the chair. 'In any case, despite what people may think, the Service doesn't act solely on rumour and guesswork. We look for proof; and we must investigate every possible alternative.' He turned back to the window. 'Ah, there she is.'

'Who?'

'Your escort.'

'My escort? Where?'

'Wait a moment, here's number four. Quarto – the magistrate. See him there – the big fellow.'

'Big' was an understatement; the magistrate made Abascantius look svelte. He was a tall, broad-shouldered, bearded man, with a huge gut that wobbled beneath his tunic as he walked. His cloak was trimmed with silver thread, and he was holding a ceremonial version of the club his sergeants carried.

'What do you know of him?' Cassius asked.

'A crooked thug.'

'And a suspect?'

'Again, possible but unlikely. He's new to the city. Marcellinus appointed him three months ago. No genius, but he's sly; and a good choice to keep the commoners in order.'

'But if he's crooked, surely we can't ignore him entirely?'

'He's crooked in the sense that all magistrates are. Skims what he can from the market taxes, helps his friends get contracts. But he's served in three different cities without much criticism and he was a legionary for a decade before that.'

Quarto and Scaurus had just embraced, and the host sent the magistrate into the house with an affectionate slap on the back.

'Look at them. Like old friends. I'm told they've already forged a mutually beneficial relationship.'

'You're not giving Quarto much attention then?'

'Not at the moment. But he could be obstructive. I've already had a couple of unpleasant encounters with him. Typical ex-legionary: hates the Service more than most. I may have to dig up some dirt on him just to keep him out of my way.'

Cassius reflected on what he'd seen: the men Marcellinus trusted to govern Antioch and arguably the four most powerful men in Syria.

'So,' he said, 'a general, a governor, a procurator and a magistrate.'

'And one of them a traitor to Rome,' replied Abascantius, standing up.

'Or one of their staff.' Cassius got to his feet too. 'Or a wife, or a mistress or a slave. By now, any number of people could know about the flag and the treasure.'

'In theory. But Marcellinus swore them to secrecy – not

something to take lightly, given his reputation. If one of them broke their oath, they must have had a damn good reason to do it.'

Cassius glanced down at the villa. 'What exactly do you want me to do, sir?'

'First, nothing to draw attention to yourself. If asked, say you are a member of the governor's staff but no more.'

'Gordio knows I'm here?'

'Of course not. Technically, I should notify him but he has as little to do with me as he can. Try not to think of the Service as part of the army, or even part of the provincial administration. We stand alone, outside all that. It's what makes us unique.'

Abascantius took hold of Cassius's shoulder and turned him towards the window.

'Now listen. You are to watch those four, especially Gordio and Octobrianus. Look at their behaviour: who they're talking to, who they're avoiding; how much they drink; whether they look nervous or relaxed; whether they stay or whether they go home early. Your escort will be there to help you.'

'And where is she?'

'See there – the second carriage from the steps.'

Cassius could see only a fine head of hair, kept in place by a silver diadem.

'Lady Antonia. She's been most useful to me over the years. Charges a lot for her services but she's never let me down yet.'

The carriage arrived at the steps and Lady Antonia stepped down. She was shapely and elegant but Cassius then saw her face. She was old – forty at least! He did a poor job of hiding his disappointment.

Abascantius chuckled. 'Typical youth – underestimates the value of an experienced woman.'

'Don't tell me we're to masquerade as a couple? I'll be the laughing stock.'

'Actually you wouldn't be the youngest man ever to take her arm but no, you're her nephew, newly arrived to take up your post. You can agree the details between you. Hurry now – she has your ticket.'

Cassius turned to leave.

'Ah, wait a moment.' Abascantius reached into his belt and retrieved a pin shaped like a bow. 'Wear this on your toga. She will know you by it.'

XX

Cassius had seen his share of luxurious villas: scores in Cyzicus and his native Ravenna, even a few in Rome; but nothing could have prepared him for the House of the Dolphins.

Just beyond the main entrance was a reception room of immense dimensions and brazen splendour. The walls were faced with pink Egyptian granite, giving the whole chamber a faint red glow. The guests – three hundred at least – moved between life-sized statues cast in bronze and silver. Running along the floor from each wall to the centre of the room were paths made by immaculately rendered mosaics; mostly fish or other sea creatures. Where the paths met in the centre of the room was a high plinth, and upon it a spectacular white marble bust of Aphrodite, leaning down to touch a leaping dolphin.

Lady Antonia nudged Cassius and pointed at the tray being proffered to him by a servant. On the tray were glasses of wine. Antonia was already holding one.

'Good for your nerves.'

Cassius took a glass and shrugged. 'What nerves?'

Antonia smiled. She had met him outside with a convincing 'Hello, nephew,' before grabbing his arm and hurrying up the steps. They were the last guests to enter and the doors had just been closed behind them.

'Come.'

Antonia led him along one of the mosaic paths. Whatever her ancestry, it certainly wasn't Syrian. Her skin was as light as Cassius's, and her hair a kind of dark blonde. At five and a quarter feet she was what he considered to be the perfect height for a woman. She wore dark kohl around her eyes; and the blackness brought out a green just a shade darker than the emeralds embedded in the bronze viper circling her upper right arm. She was wearing a long, flowing stola, with a vibrant purple border at the neck. Remarkably slim for her age, she was also blessed with high breasts and a pert behind.

Cassius imagined she would have been quite lovely in her youth. It was a pity she was about the same age as his mother.

Antonia stopped next to the statue of Aphrodite, taking up one of the few free spaces in the room. She had a placid half-smile fixed on her face, and scanned the room as she spoke.

'Abascantius is becoming more inventive with his choice of operatives. You look every inch the fine young gentleman.'

'Is it beyond the realms of possibility that I am one?'

Antonia sipped at her drink and looked him up and down. 'Fine – certainly. Young – obviously. But a gentleman? In the employ of that toad? Unlikely.'

Cassius chose not to point out that she was also 'in the employ of that toad'. 'Then I shall do my best to convince you.'

'I look forward to it. Just let me do most of the talking. Starting now.'

'What—'

'Antonia, my darling!'

Cassius turned round to see a very overweight man waddling towards them, flanked by two fresh-faced servants.

'Festus, I've not seen you in an age.'

Antonia smiled as Festus kissed her hand. His gaze shifted to Cassius.

'And who is this striking young fellow?'

'May I present Cassius Corbulo. He has just arrived to join the governor's staff.'

'A pleasure. Hey you, over here!'

Festus intercepted a slave walking past with a tray. Upon it were several bowls of nuts and fruit. Festus took one full of almonds and offered it to Cassius and Antonia.

'Apparently they stop you getting drunk. My brother swears by them.'

The shrill tones of trumpets sounded from the other side of the room. The guests quietened as the quartet launched into a triumphal fanfare more suited to an imperial parade than a dinner party.

Scaurus strode into the reception room, head held high, arms clasped behind his back. His cloak had been removed to reveal a dazzlingly white toga. As the guests parted, he stepped up on to a wooden platform. Cassius noted that his body seemed to have been composed of two different halves, the cherubic face and barrel chest contrasting with the thin, almost spindly legs.

The trumpeteers finished. Scaurus waved his guests closer until he was surrounded.

'Our venerable host,' said Festus in a low voice, 'as self-effacing as ever.'

He, Cassius and Antonia found themselves at the back of the watching crowd. Scaurus waited for absolute silence, arms still behind his back. Cassius noticed another white marble bust by the far wall: it was of the host himself.

'Governor, friends, welcome – once more – to the House of the Dolphins.'

The guests broke into spontaneous applause. Scaurus returned the gesture and then quietened them down.

'How long I have waited to say those words. The dark clouds that have hung over this city have finally been banished. Our esteemed and beloved Emperor, Lucius Domitius Aurelianus, has freed us from the tyranny of the Palmyran occupiers. Now is the time . . .'

Scaurus's speech continued in this vein for what Cassius estimated to be a quarter of an hour. On at least three occasions, he had to turn to one of his slaves for a reminder of the next line. Cassius guessed the slave – almost certainly Greek – had written the entire piece. Scaurus's delivery was amateurish: stilted and monotonous; but there was some fine language and the sentiments of liberation and renewal met with an enthusiastic response. The host finished his address by announcing that the formal dinner would start in one hour. Until then the guests were free to roam as they wished; his house was their house.

'You've been invited to the dinner?' enquired Festus.

'Of course,' answered Antonia.

The big man looked rather disappointed.

'You shall have to excuse us, Festus. I need some air.'

Antonia grabbed Cassius's arm and dragged him away towards the throng following Scaurus out of the reception room. Stopping only to refresh their glasses, they moved through three more huge rooms, each faced with a different coloured marble. As the sun was out, most of the guests gravitated towards the wide sward of grass between the villa and the river. Two musicians were seated at opposite ends of the turf: a harpist and a flautist. A group of young men hurried over to the dock to inspect Scaurus's galley. Cassius noted the large bronze plaque on the vessel's stern: it was named *Radians*.

He then almost lost his glass when nudged by a man trying to avoid Scaurus, who'd just bounded out of the villa with four tall, fine-boned Ethiopian drummers in tow. He lined them up in front of the river and had them strike up a beat. The other musicians were forced to stop, and those guests who'd been enjoying them turned round to watch.

Scaurus clapped along and tried to get others to join in. Only his entourage and a few lively individuals did so. Undeterred, he leapt in front of the drummers and – with a ribald grin on his face – began to dance. Some of the guests simply laughed, others didn't know where to look. Governor Gordio and his party were doing their best to ignore the host's antics.

'Too early perhaps,' said Scaurus, bringing his mercifully brief performance to an end. 'Later you shall all dance with me!'

He grabbed a drink from a tray and disappeared inside. The drummers looked at each other and after a few moments stopped playing. Guests started to drift away to the river or the other musicians.

'Quite a character,' observed Cassius.

Antonia nodded towards the governor. 'They tolerate his

vulgarity only because of what he's done for the city. Without his slaves and donations, half of the buildings wouldn't have been rebuilt after the last Persian invasion.'

'And I understand he lusts after higher office.'

'I wonder if he really does any more. With displays like that he'll likely ruin any chance he had. Anyway, hadn't you better tell me what all this is about? Why are you here?'

'I'm not at liberty to discuss that, but we're interested in the four members of Marcellinus's council – the governor and the procurator in particular. Abascantius would like to know of any unusual or suspicious behaviour on their part.'

'That sounds disappointingly mundane.'

'Not at all. A matter of the highest importance.'

'It might be better if we split up. I'll see what I can find out about Octobrianus. Perhaps you can focus on the governor.'

'How? I don't know a single person here.'

Antonia moved so that Cassius could look over her shoulder.'See the two girls, the twins?'

'Yes.'

'Gordio's daughters. I'll have someone introduce you to them. You might hear something germane.'

Cassius wasn't concerned about talking to the girls, but the prospect of getting close to the governor unnerved him.

'I can try, I suppose. I'm not really used to this kind of thing.'

'I can see that. Just tread carefully. You assured me you're a gentleman. Now's the time to prove it.'

Lady Antonia was not one to waste time. She immediately recruited a friend named Drusilla and told her that Cassius was interested in meeting the young ladies. Antonia made her way inside, leaving Drusilla to escort Cassius across the lawn. Gordio's daughters and a third girl were listening to the harpist. Drusilla encouraged him by explaining that single young men of his class were few and far between; most had been called up for military or administrative duty outside the capital. The girls would be delighted to talk to him.

She was quite right; and before long, Cassius was standing next to the bench where the three girls sat, regaling them with tales of his trip across the Mediterranean. Drusilla listened politely for a while then left.

The twins – Julia and Junia – looked about fifteen; and they were utterly identical. Unfortunately, they were identically plump and nondescript; but Cassius didn't let this distract him. Like many of the plainer girls he'd met they compensated by being charming, and he soon found himself relaxing into cordial small talk. It was a pleasure to be among young ladies again and he amused himself by glancing at their cleavage, drawing identical shades of pink from their full cheeks. Their friend Clara was a few years older. She too was rather plain, and said very little; but her few contributions revealed her to be both circumspect and knowledgeable. Cassius was careful, and waited a long time to steer the conversation around to the governor.

He spoke to the twins of how difficult their father's job must be and how his peerless reputation had spread all the way back to Rome. The girls accepted the compliments politely. Cassius pressed on, ruminating on the pressures and difficulties of the job, but the girls couldn't be cajoled into anything even remotely useful, responding only in bland generalisations. It was becoming a one-way conversation, so Cassius moved on.

He asked about Zenobia; and the three girls suddenly became animated. They took it in turns to tell him what they'd seen of her and – though careful not to suggest any kind of admiration – it was obvious Zenobia's beauty and charisma had made a lasting impression on them all. When the talk turned to her fate they became quieter, almost sad, and – not for the first time – Cassius felt regret that he wouldn't get a chance to see the fallen queen in the flesh.

Interesting though all this was, Cassius had made no progress.

He looked around for Antonia and was about to make his excuses when a slave announced dinner.

——8——

For about two-thirds of the guests, this signalled the end of their involvement in the evening's proceedings and they were guided to the door by Scaurus's numerous servants. The remaining guests – about a hundred – congregated outside the dining room.

Feigning interest in a wall dotted with antlers and tusks, then a huge mosaic of multicoloured dolphins, Cassius successfully detached himself from the girls, thus avoiding an encounter with their father. Once the governor's party was safely inside the dining room he joined the queue. Just ahead was the vast bulk of Magistrate Quarto. He seemed jovial; laughing and joking with the men around him.

Scaurus hurried past, hauling a pet leopard by a leash, reprimanding various servants who trailed along in his wake, trying not to get too close to the big cat.

Cassius suddenly felt something dig into his left arm. He looked down and saw a bronze viper head.

'Sorry,' said Antonia. 'Any progress?'

Cassius matched her whisper. 'No. You?'

Antonia took a small mirror from her purse and examined her make-up. 'Possibly. I'll tell you when we're seated.'

The senior attendant knew Antonia by sight and they were swiftly escorted to their places. The marble that covered the dining room floor and walls was striped with sea green. Not far from the doorway was another huge statue – a silver rendering of the Tyche. Beyond, three lines of tables had been arranged to form a U facing the statue. Antonia and Cassius were seated to the right, not far from a doorway through which sweating slaves brought platters of food from the kitchens.

Cassius tucked Antonia's high-backed chair in behind her, then sat down. He thought he saw a bread roll on the floor but then realised it was part of an ingenious mosaic, designed to

232

look like abandoned food. All the crockery on the table was silver, including a ruby-encrusted goblet for each diner. Cassius drew Antonia's perfume into his nose as she leaned close to him. It was delightful.

'This Octobrianus is quite the enigma,' she whispered. 'Drusilla's washer-woman's brother works at his stables. Apparently he's refused three potential marriages in the last few years.'

'Perhaps women are not to his taste.'

'On the contrary – there's hardly a maid at his villa he's not tried it on with.'

As they spoke, Cassius and Antonia washed their hands in the bowls of scented water in front of them.

'Anything else?'

'He often goes out alone at night, sometimes not returning until close to dawn.'

Cassius elected not to mention the procurator's possible Palmyran connections. If Antonia knew of anything, she would surely have said so.

'It's always the quiet ones,' she observed, gazing across the room. Octobrianus was sitting almost exactly opposite them. He was leaning back in his chair, dictating to a slave who knelt nearby, nodding continuously as he wrote.

'Certainly works hard,' observed Cassius.

'How pretentious,' scoffed Antonia. 'Probably a shopping list.'

She pointed at the Gordio twins. 'It seems you've made quite an impression on the girls.'

They were sitting next to their father, who had been been placed close to the centre of the middle table, as had General Ulpian. The girls waved. Cassius waved back. Thankfully, Gordio was busy talking to his wife.

'I must concede that they seem convinced of your gentlemanly qualities,' said Antonia with a slight smile.

'And you?'

'I'll tell you at the end of the evening.'

Having dispensed with the leopard, Scaurus strode back into the dining room, a huge goblet in his hand. A servant in his path dodged quickly out of the way, losing his grip on the heavy bronze dish he was carrying. The dish was empty but struck the floor with a thunderous clatter. The servant quickly picked it up. Before he could get away, Scaurus put a hand on his shoulder.

The boy was perhaps fourteen. Cassius had seen frozen expressions like the one on his face many times – the neutral visage of those who couldn't be sure how best to react, and therefore chose not to react at all. The boy was tall, and Scaurus had to reach high to grip the back of his neck and turn him towards the seated guests. Everyone stopped talking and the other servants suddenly became still.

'Clumsy oaf, this one,' said Scaurus, 'almost tipped a steaming bowl of water on me yesterday. What shall we do with him?'

Nobody said anything.

'Perhaps I should feed him to my lampreys?'

Several men – Magistrate Quarto among them – laughed.

'No,' continued Scaurus, his tone softening, 'I like to think of my slaves as my children. They must not only be disciplined but educated, and cared for.' He was now stroking the slave's hair with his fingers. 'Go,' he said quietly. 'Be careful next time.'

The boy walked away, shoulders stiff with fear.

'My guests, later we shall have more entertainment, and we shall drink and toast as never before.' Scaurus spread his palms towards the tables. 'But I have had my chefs working on this lot for weeks, and some of it is getting cold. So eat! All of you eat!'

Having lived on simple fare for the past month, Cassius found he had rather lost the taste for rich food but there was no mistaking the quality of what was on offer. Ignoring the endless varieties of seafood, the hams, the sausages and the fatted liver, he settled for a plate of scrambled eggs with some salted cheese. He also took some bread from one of the identical loaves within reach of every guest. On top of each loaf, written in a white glaze, were the words *Unshaken, Unthrown*.

'What's that about?' he asked Antonia.

'The city's motto. During the reign of Caligula there was a terrible earthquake here. A seer named Deborius created a talisman to protect the city against further disaster – a porphyry column; and written upon the base was that phrase. It was struck by lightning during Domitian's time. The column was destroyed but the base was left standing.'

'You're glad this latest disaster is over with, I presume?'

Antonia – who had hardly eaten a thing – picked at a stork wing and put some of the pale, thready meat on her plate.

'I remember the Persians. Compared to that, one might not even have known the city was occupied. I will say I enjoyed seeing their arrogant bitch of a queen knocked off her perch, but we should be glad she fled instead of trying to making a stand here.'

The servants began to remove the first course, and others hastily refilled glasses. The wine was hardly watered at all, and Cassius reminded himself to drink slowly; he had to keep a clear head. Before the second course arrived, Scaurus summoned the drummers to the dining room. He arranged them in front of the statue of the Tyche, then addressed his guests once more.

'As promised, a little more entertainment. Trust me when I tell you that you will not believe your eyes. A word of warning, Quarto: stay in your seat and keep your hands to yourself!'

The magistrate laughed along with the rest of the guests, his rolls of fat undulating under his tunic. Scaurus turned towards an anteroom.

'I give you – the dancing girls of Cadiz!'

As the drummers struck up a pounding beat, a troupe of dark-skinned, half-naked young women filed into the room. They had clearly been selected for their similarly shapely physiques and were wearing far more jewellery than clothing. Beaming, eyes wide, the girls formed a line in front of the drummers and began to move. Scaurus, clapping along in time, gleefully observed the reactions of his male guests. Ignoring Antonia's disdainful tutting, Cassius watched, transfixed, as the girls moved in perfect time with the drums, swaying their hips and making shapes in the air with their fingers. Scaurus went over to the nearest girl.

'My favourite!' he shouted above the din of the drums. He gazed down at her full, jiggling breasts, then darted forward and licked one of her dark brown nipples. The girl laughed gamely, not that she had a great deal of choice.

A few of the guests cheered or applauded. Many people – Cassius and Antonia included – turned quickly to gauge the governor's reaction. Gordio took care to make no obvious expression at all. His wife looked appalled.

Scaurus's display set the tone for the rest of the evening. As Abascantius had suggested, the Antiochenes did indeed seem ready to enjoy themselves. The diners left their seats and mingled; and, as lamps and lanterns were lit, the sound of urgent, light-hearted conversation built gradually to a tumult. The host alternated the drummers with the other musicians and was throwing food to his leopard by the time the fifth and final course was served. It included truffles, the arrival of which triggered the usual discussion about what they actually were. The guest sitting to Cassius's right was a firm adherent to Plutarch's theory: that they were made of mud cooked by lightning.

A few moments after a slave announced the third hour of night, Scaurus – now decidedly unsteady on his feet – went and stood by the statue. As he rubbed the Tyche's leg, then leaned against it, Cassius noted more than a few disapproving looks. The host completed a number of toasts, including a mention for both Marcellinus and Gordio. The governor was now accompanied only by his wife; the twins had left after the third course. Magistrate Quarto then gave a short, slurred speech praising Scaurus which met with rapturous applause.

The final toast was to the Emperor himself. The host had his guests stand and he walked past each of the tables to ensure everyone had a full goblet, then announced they would take a drink for every letter of the Emperor's name. Lucius Domitius Aurelianus contained no fewer than twenty-four and the more committed drinkers needed refills to complete the task properly. With that, Scaurus announced that the evening's formalities were over. He summoned a rotund, plainly dressed individual and announced that he was the funniest man he'd ever met.

'A comedian,' Cassius said to Antonia behind his hand. 'How novel.'

'Consider yourself lucky. I remember the year he read us some of his poetry.'

Scaurus sat down next to Magistrate Quarto and they were joined by General Ulpian, who also seemed to be enjoying himself. Octobrianus, meanwhile, was speaking to another man, still maintaining the neutral expression he had displayed all evening. Governor Gordio was again talking to his wife.

Cassius thought of what Abascantius had asked him to observe. Did the fact that both Quarto and Ulpian seemed so relaxed suggest they couldn't possibly be involved with the theft of the banner? Gordio and Octobrianus appeared – by comparison at least – more tense and preoccupied. Did that suggest they might be? Or did each man's behaviour simply reflect his nature? Cassius wondered if anything at all could be learned simply by watching the men. Abascantius clearly thought so.

The comedian began with a few vulgar quips, several of which were at the expense of promiscuous older women, eliciting yet more tuts from Antonia. He then moved on to mocking the Palmyrans, Zenobia and her lackeys in particular, and the guests responded with some zeal. When he ran out of related material and the laughs died down, Scaurus bounded up and whispered in his ear.

The next few jokes were all aimed at Quarto, largely to do with his weight. The comedian seemed wary, but was clearly even more concerned about defying his employer. In any case, the magistrate seemed too drunk to care, and laughed along merrily. Then there was a crack about the governor, centering around the apparent impossibility of removing him from his post. It was tame stuff – almost complimentary in fact – but the guests seemed unsure how to respond. Even the host seemed nonplussed by the awkward silence.

'Scaurus has gone too far,' whispered Antonia.

Governor Gordio looked around at the sea of faces, then smiled benignly and raised his goblet. This prompted a cheer, and a long round of applause. Gordio took a drink and put his arm around his wife's shoulder. She seemed thrilled by the way he'd handled it.

'He's popular,' said Cassius.

'Very,' replied Antonia, still clapping. 'And why not? Everybody loves a survivor.'

Scaurus took the hint and dismissed the comedian. He and his cronies – Quarto and Ulpian included – then began some highly convoluted drinking game. Within a few moments, Gordio and his wife left, only stopping to offer a brief thank you to Scaurus. Many of the older guests took this as their cue to depart. Antonia nudged Cassius and nodded across the room. Octobrianus was already on his way out.

'A prior arrangement, perhaps,' she suggested.

Cassius stifled a yawn.

'I don't think we're going to learn much else here tonight,' Antonia continued.

'I agree. Shall we?'

'I'll go and say goodnight to Scaurus. Meet you at the front door?'

Cassius nodded, bade farewell to his fellow diners, then walked back through the villa. He stopped by a window and looked down at the river. A pair of tribunes had lured the dancing girls outside and they were all splashing around in the water. Had he not been hung over and under orders to keep a low profile, he might have thought of joining them. Antonia caught up with him and took his arm as they walked back in to the reception room.

'Well?' he asked.

'They're drunk.'

Heading for the door, they passed several couples canoodling in the shadows. One lady sounded like she was enjoying herself greatly.

'A lively city, Antioch,' said Cassius.

'You should see the Maiouma,' replied Antonia.

'The what?'

'Maiouma. Old cult festival. Celebrated every three years. Next one is in the spring. Bascially it's an orgy.'

'I must remember to get my leave request in early.'

Antonia smiled as they headed down the steps towards the street. To their right, carriages were lined up in rows. One well-dressed individual was rambling incoherently and having to be manhandled into his litter by his attendants. Antonia waved to her driver and, after a good deal of manoeuvring, he pulled up in front of the steps.

'Gods, it's as black as Hades out here,' she said. 'I'd have thought Gordio would have had all the street lanterns going again by now.'

'Ah yes, the famed lights of Antioch.'

'Olive oil prices apparently,' Antonia explained. 'Would you like a lift home?'

'Much obliged.'

Without Indavara in tow, Cassius had no desire to walk back through the darkened city alone. He helped Antonia up, then took a seat next to her.

'Your shawl is there, madam, if you need it,' the driver said over his shoulder.

'Yes, Vedrix. I have it.'

Though there were several layers of cushions, the combination of the carriage's iron wheel rims and the uneven city streets made the journey a noisy and uncomfortable one. To Cassius's amazement, Antonia fell asleep on his shoulder just moments after they crossed Hadrian's Bridge.

He'd never met a woman quite like her. She was so confident and assured; witty too. These were not typically female attributes, and in truth it was no surprise she wasn't married. Even so, Cassius admitted to himself that he liked her, and he could see why Abascantius valued her so highly.

━█8█►

Antonia's villa was close, just a stone's throw from the eastern bank of the Orontes. She awoke as the driver pulled up.

'We're home?'

'You are,' said Cassius.

The driver got down and stood beside the horses, subtly remaining out of sight.

Antonia sat up and checked her diadem was still in place.

'Well, young man. I must admit you do seem quite the gentleman. Evidently not all of Abascantius's people are as unpleasant as him. Remind the pig to pay me promptly this time, would you?'

'I shall.'

Antonia put her hand against Cassius's chin and tilted it up. 'You have a wonderful profile.'

'Thank you.'

She squeezed up close to him. 'If you ever need to relax, get away from whatever awful job he gives you, come and see me. I'll help take your mind off things.'

The thought of this, which might have seemed rather distasteful to Cassius earlier in the evening, suddenly seemed almost attractive.

'I shall remember that.'

Antonia put her hand on his face again, and turned him towards her. She kissed him full on the lips, and flicked her tongue inside his mouth.

'Goodnight, Cassius.'

'Goodnight, Lady Antonia.'

'Vedrix will drive you home.'

240

XXI

A note arrived just as Cassius was dressing the next morning: Abascantius wanted to see him at his villa at the tenth hour and suggested he spend the day investigating whatever else he considered to be a priority. Taking an apple from a fruit bowl in the atrium as he passed, Cassius wandered outside and found Simo and Indavara already in the courtyard. The Gaul was sweeping dust out of the corners. Indavara was exercising; he was wearing only a loincloth and doing press-ups at a frankly ridiculous speed.

'Morning,' said Cassius.

Indavara nodded as he sprang to his feet and embarked on a series of stretches.

'How was the dinner party, sir?' asked Simo.

'Rather entertaining actually; drummers from Ethiopia, dancing girls from Cadiz. And the food' – he nodded at Indavara – 'well, you'd certainly have enjoyed yourself.'

Indavara shook his head. 'I have to eat less. I'm putting on weight.'

'You're thickset, that's all.'

'I'm getting fat. Weak too.'

'Weak? Gods, man, you look like you're carved out of rock compared to me.'

Indavara continued to stretch as he spoke. 'When I was in Pietas Julia, all we did was train, eat and rest. Every day that passes I get fatter, slower. I've no one to practise with, no way of staying sharp.' He looked genuinely depressed.

'Well, you can start by getting dressed and fetching your sword,' said Cassius. 'We've a busy morning ahead.'

Indavara went inside.

'Simo, when you're done with your jobs here, feel free to take some time for yourself. I'm sure you're eager to visit your father. I shall take the spare keys, just make sure you lock up properly and be back by dusk.'

The Gaul grinned and went about his sweeping with a new vigour.

Cassius had three leads in mind, and he hoped to make initial enquiries regarding each of them before meeting Abascantius. First stop was Antioch's basilica. It was on the eastern side of the city's central plaza, where the Avenue of Herod and Tiberius met the other colonnaded street that ran west to Hadrian's Bridge. The plaza was oval, two hundred yards across at its widest point, and also housed the forum, the meeting hall for the provincial assembly, and the capital's largest theatre. In an open area on one side of the forum, a class of teenage students sat on benches, listening attentively to their teacher.

The centre of the plaza was dominated by three enormous statues: one of the beloved Tyche, one of Tiberius and one of Caesar. The Tyche was surrounded by locals, either on their knees praying or leaving offerings at the statue's base. Market stalls had been set up too, though Cassius noted they were highly regimented and monitored by a dozen of Quarto's sergeants.

He and Indavara jogged up the wide steps and under the open arched doorway of the basilica. The two legionaries flanking the entrance nodded respectfully to Cassius, who was in full uniform, including his helmet and scarlet cloak. This was unquestionably an occasion for formality.

Inside the rectangular, well-lit hall, scores of administrators worked at tables on either side of the central aisle. There was a quiet sense of urgency about the place; a few senior men in togas strolled up and down while the clerks bent over their work. Cassius was afforded gracious assistance by the first man he approached, who told him where to find Antioch's military records office: it was housed in anteroom number eighteen at the rear of the basilica itself. Outside the room was a single legionary who took a long look at the spear-head and an even longer look at Indavara before allowing Cassius to enter. Indavara had to wait outside.

The room was in complete chaos. Mounted on three of the walls were scores of empty wooden racks and the tiled floor was covered with piles of boxes, writing tablets and rolls of papyrus. The clerk on duty sat in the middle of it all, facing away from Cassius.

'Morning.'

The clerk turned round, then stood up. He was about thirty; a thin man with dark, wavy hair and an angular chin.

'Corbulo, Imperial Security.'

'Petronax. Archivist.'

'With plenty to archive, I see.'

'It's a disaster. The Palmyrans had their people in here – made a right mess of everything. Nothing's where it should be and I'm not getting any help until next week. Anyway, what can I help you with, sir?'

'It's a bit of a long shot. I'm after a man missing his thumb and two fingers on his right hand. It occurred to me that if he is or was a legionary, there might be a record of it.'

'It's possible, sir, but if he was injured like that, he would probably have left service.'

'But some injured men stay on, if they're able to continue other duties. And if he was invalided out, a record of the injury might have been made.'

'True.'

'What records do you have here?'

'I'm told that everything in here is from the Third and Sixteenth Legions – last twenty years.'

'And there'd be a file on every legionary?'

'There should be. But some officers are more conscientious than others. It's likely that every soldier's name would crop up somewhere: when recruited, if given special duties, or when retired or killed. But to find something on injuries or distinguishing marks you'd need their personal file.'

'And those are here?'

243

'Some. Mostly copies. The originals stay with the legion. These are for the governor and the provincial administration.' The clerk pointed to a wooden tablet just like the ones Cassius had seen in Palmyra. 'Usually on these.'

'So there must be thousands of them.'

'Oh yes. We've a full room next door too.'

'And how are they organised?'

'By cohort and by century.'

'Then I'd have to go through them one by one.'

'I'm afraid so.'

Cassius stood there for a moment, looking at the mountains of tablets and papers. He felt Petronax's eyes on him. When he glanced back at him, the clerk looked away.

'All right, I don't think there's much point in pursuing this at the moment. Just do this for me, would you: keep the personal files separate from the rest. I may well come back to check what you have.'

'Of course, sir.'

'Thank you.'

'It was my pleasure,' said Petronax with a rather suggestive smile.

This wasn't the first time Cassius had had such an encounter and he doubted it would be the last. Well, if the clerk thought him attractive, so what? He might well need his help again.

Second stop was the Beroea Gate. After some more enquiries at the basilica, Cassius discovered that Tribune Bonafatius – the officer who could authorise a check on the gatehouse records – had an office in the forum next door. Cassius found him there, snowed under with paperwork, and – once he'd seen the spearhead – Bonafatius hurriedly scribbled the authorisation, not even bothering to ask the purpose of his enquiry.

As they marched back along the Avenue of Herod and Tiberius, Indavara pronounced himself hungry and bought some dates.

'I thought you were watching your waistline,' Cassius remarked,

Another guard stood close to the owner, who was lounging on a pile of cushions in one corner, reading a book. The sturdy shelves that covered every wall were laden with silverware – a Syrian speciality. Behind the counter were two glass boxes containing gold ingots of various sizes and grades. Hanging from the wall was a long sheet of papyrus with exchange rates listed in Greek; it seemed the proprietor was a money-changer too. Upon spying the spear-head, he scrambled to his feet and threw the book to one side.

'Good-day, sir,' he said, pressing down the front of his wine-stained tunic. 'What can I do for you?'

'Officer Corbulo, Imperial Security. Just a few questions. Your name?'

'Gallio Barrius Bulla.'

Bulla clasped his hands behind his back, and thrust out his chest, as if signalling he had nothing to hide.

'Have you been offered silver or gold ingots in the last few weeks?'

'No. None.'

'Nothing at all?'

'I can check my ledger but I'm pretty sure I haven't been offered anything since the spring. People are still holding on to what they have. Prices have been all over the place, what with all the uncertainty.'

Cassius wasn't sure he believed this but there was a certain logic to it.

'Tell me: if one wanted to offload a big pile of silver and gold quickly and quietly, how would one go about it?'

'It wouldn't be easy. You'd have to spread the sale around to avoid unwanted attention. How big?'

'Very big.'

'Not many people have that amount of coinage just lying around. You could exchange for gems, I suppose.'

Cassius reached into his satchel and retrieved the sheet with the sketches of the Palmyran jewellery.

'What about these? Seen anything like them in the city?'

Bulla carefully studied each sketch in turn.

'Unfortunately not. Lovely pieces though. We'd hoped some Palmyran stuff would turn up, but it looks like the Emperor grabbed it all.'

Bulla laughed nervously, realising he'd spoken out of turn. Cassius couldn't really have cared less, but he rather enjoyed being seen as a defender of the Emperor's honour so glared at the dealer until he looked away.

'All right, that's it. For now.'

There were six more stores to visit but it didn't take long because all the dealers said the same. Cassius knew there were any number of reasons why they might not disclose their true dealings to a Service man; but all had seemed disappointed that so little Palmyran booty had found its way to Antioch, and he was inclined to think they were telling the truth.

'Another dead-end,' he muttered as they made their way back along the avenue.

'Excuse me,' said a voice. They turned to see a young man behind them. Cassius recognised him: a slave who'd been at work cleaning jewellery in the fifth store.

'May I talk to you for a moment, sir?'

'You may.'

The youth darted between two passers-by and into a narrow alley. He went and stood behind a pile of rotting vegetables and gestured for them to join him.

'A bit further on if you don't mind,' said Cassius, holding his nose as he pointed further up the alley. They stopped twenty feet from the avenue.

'Can I see those sketches?' asked the slave, wiping sweat away from above his mouth.

Cassius reached into the satchel and showed him the sheet.

After a few moments, the slave pointed at a necklace. 'That's it – the pearls, and the gold links shaped like wheat.'

'Your employer was offered some of these?'

'No. But I've seen one.' The youth cast an anxious glance towards the end of the alley.

'Where, man?'

'I shall tell you, sir. But on two conditions. First, my master must not find out that I spoke to you. Second, I want four denarii.'

'Demanding little wretch, aren't you?'

'I know how valuable information can be, sir.'

'All right, but you're only getting two denarii.'

'I need the four, sir.'

'Two. Or I can have my ex-gladiator friend here beat the information out of you.'

The slave looked at Indavara. 'All right, two. I'll take it now.'

Cassius reached into his money bag and handed over the coins. The youth bent down and tucked the coins into the back of his sandals.

'Start talking.'

'I saw a necklace just like that in an inn over by the Wall of Tiberius two nights ago. There was a man there, drunk, showing it off to his friend. I knew what it was but he denied it was Palmyran, said it was Arabian or something. After I asked about it, he put it away and left.'

'This man – you know him?'

'No, but I got his name from one of the serving girls. He's called Nabor. I thought I might be able to get in touch with him and arrange a deal for my master.'

'Where does he live, this Nabor?'

'She didn't know. But he works at the glass factory south of the Daphne Gate.'

'Anything else?'

The slave shook his head.

'All right. You may go.'

'You promise you'll not tell my master of this?'

'I'll not promise anything to the likes of you. And remember – we know where you work.'

The youth hurried away down the alley.

'Not an entirely wasted morning, then,' said Cassius. 'Come, looks like we've a bit of a walk ahead of us.'

XXII

'We should have ridden,' Indavara said wearily as he and Cassius trudged along the side of the road.

'I told you, I'm not going on a horse for at least another week. Anyway, I thought you wanted some exercise.'

Though the city was beginning to quieten down again for the afternoon, the factories and workshops south of the Daphne Gate were still busy. They had passed iron and bronze casters; rush-weavers and wool-cleaners, tanners, fullers and potters. The next track leading off the road turned left to a large dye-works. At least two hundred workers – mainly women – were dunking sheets into vats of red and orange dye and hanging them out to dry on wooden racks.

'Why are these places so far out of the city?' asked Indavara.

'The stench for one thing. Risk of fire for another.' Cassius pointed up at the slopes of Mount Silpius, where a high aqueduct ran parallel to the road. 'Plus they can get plenty of water; well, at least when the rains come again.'

At the far end of the dye-works was a ditch, then an area of open ground dotted with pits and piles of sand. In the middle of the mess was a big, stone-built factory. The building faced the road, and as they drew level with it, Cassius spied the glow of furnaces inside.

'Looks like we're here.'

Indavara tightened his belt. Upon hearing they might have to apprehend this man Nabor, he had insisted on bringing along his bow as well as his sword and stave.

'Now listen,' Cassius continued. 'If Nabor's here, we'll need to question him first – make sure we've got the right man. But he might try to run, so be ready.'

They turned on to a path littered with broken glass and wood shavings. Ahead of them was a lad leading two horses to a stable. The horses' load had been a broad cart, now at rest in front of the factory. Two workers were shovelling broken glass out of the back into barrels below. They stared at the strangers.

Cassius had left his helmet and officer's cloak back at the villa and now wore a light cape over his tunic. The spear-head was wrapped up, though one end of it stuck out of his satchel. He reminded himself not to let Indavara weigh himself down with weapons in future; it attracted too much attention.

Rounding piles of firewood, they came to the factory itself. A sturdy, middle-aged man was squatting in the shade, reading a waxed tablet.

'Officer Corbulo. Governor's staff. Your name?'

The man stood and let out a long breath before replying.

'Juba. Foreman.'

'Excellent. I'm looking for a man named Nabor, apparently he works here. Nothing serious. Just a few questions.'

'Nabor's been away. Haven't seen him for a long time.'

Juba's reply was rather too quick and definitive for Cassius's liking.

'I see.'

Cassius wandered over to the factory and looked inside. Indavara followed him, Juba too. Eight men sat at stools in front of small, domed, clay furnaces, focused intently on their work. They were all wearing thick leather gloves and long aprons and their skin shone with sweat. The worker closest to them stood, then carefully eased an iron pipe out of the furnace. Attached to the end of it was a molten chunk of glass the colour of a newly risen sun. The worker put the pipe to his mouth and blew. The glass wobbled, then began to expand. Cassius had heard of the process but had never seen it done before. Indavara moved closer, utterly entranced. Cassius turned to the foreman.

'Do you know when he'll back?'

'Didn't say.'

'Do you have an address for him?'

'Don't think so.'

'You don't have an address for one of your employees?'

'Why would I? He comes, he works; I pay him, he goes.'

Having now blown the glass into a five-inch globe, the worker walked slowly to the other side of the furnace. He removed the globe from the pipe with a second rod and delicately placed it in another chamber.

'You won't mind if I talk to some of the others?' Cassius said, nodding towards the factory. 'See if anyone knows where I can find him.'

'You can't go in there. It's dangerous.'

'Misleading members of the governor's staff can be equally perilous,' said Cassius.

He and Indavara watched as the worker removed another globe from the second chamber and placed it on a wooden rack with a dozen others.

A miniature reflection of Juba gesticulating to someone suddenly appeared in every globe. When Cassius and Indavara turned round, the foreman stopped, then shrugged. They heard a metallic clatter from the factory. One of the glass-blowers at the back had dropped his pipe. The man tore off his apron and dashed away into the bowels of the building.

'Go!' Cassius shouted, dropping his satchel. 'Go!'

Acrid fumes filled his nose as he sprinted after Indavara. Once past the glass-blowers, they came to a wooden partition. Indavara already had his sword in his hand. Cassius drew his own blade, then followed him through the wide doorway.

On one side of the second section were boxes full of glass beads, on the other stalls full of sand. Another worker had just entered, dragging an empty hand cart. He darted out of the way as Cassius and Indavara hurried past, swords held aloft.

The last section of the factory was filled with long, high shelves laden with glassware. Beyond the narrow central aisle was open ground and, in the distance, the dye-works. Light bounced around the room, half blinding them as they charged on. There was no sign of Nabor.

Cassius glimpsed movement to his right; and suddenly one of the shelves was toppling towards them. Indavara stopped and tried to turn but Cassius ran straight into him. Before they could take another step, glass objects rained down on them. Both men got their hands up to cover their heads, but then the shelf struck, knocking them to the ground. It wasn't heavy enough to do much damage but they landed on a floor already strewn with broken glass.

Cassius cried out. He lifted his left arm to find a triangular shard of glass protruding an inch below the veins at his wrist. He looked up and saw a lean, dark-haired man already outside and running.

Indavara grabbed the shelf with both hands and pushed it off them. He picked up his sword and darted out of the workshop after Nabor.

Cassius got to his feet and pulled out the glass, releasing a rivulet of blood. There were other, smaller fragments embedded all over his hands, arms and legs. Trying to ignore the pain, he loped outside. Nabor was already fifty yards away: he had jumped the ditch and was heading for the dye-works.

Indavara stopped at the ditch. He reached over his shoulder and pulled the bow from his back. Eyes still fixed on the fleeing figure, he plucked an arrow from the quiver.

'Indavara! No!'

Belatedly realising he'd lost his sword, Cassius ran for the ditch.

Indavara held the bow out in front of him and fitted the arrow against the string.

Cassius splashed through a puddle.

'Indavara! Don't!'

The bodyguard cocked his head to one side and pulled back the string.

Nabor had reached the dye-works. He was running between two lines of women who had stopped work to stare at him.

Cassius struck Indavara's elbow with his hand just as he released the string. With a loud twang, the arrow shot high into the sky over the road. Indavara spun round.

'What are you doing?' he bellowed, eyes blazing.

'What in Hades are *you* doing?'

'He tried to kill us!' Indavara jabbed the bow towards the dye-works.

Nabor had just untied a horse and swung up into the saddle.

'We need him alive.'

'I was going for his legs.'

'From here? You might have hit one of those women.'

'No chance.'

They watched as Nabor kicked out at a man trying to stop him, then whipped at the horse with the reins, driving it towards the main road. Once there, he turned right in the direction of the city and within moments, both rider and horse had disappeared.

Cassius noticed a piece of green glass sticking out of Indavara's neck just below his ear. It was moving up and down with each breath. He pointed at it.

'Er, you have a—'

Indavara reached up and wrenched out the glass, along with a substantial chunk of skin. The wound began to bleed.

Cassius looked back at the factory. Juba and several others had gathered in the storeroom.

'I guarantee the foreman knows where Nabor lives. If we can get an address out of him and commandeer a couple of horses, we might get to his place before he can lose us for good.'

Indavara nodded and marched back towards the workshop, holding the bow in one hand.

'Just remember – nothing too excessive,' Cassius said as he hurried after him.

There were eight workers with Juba. They all watched Indavara approach. Without breaking stride, he whipped one end of the bow against Juba's arm. The foreman cried out as he fell to the ground. The workers scattered. All except one man: a broad fellow still holding his iron pipe.

'Juba's my brother,' he said as he moved in front of Indavara. 'You'll have to go through me.'

With a casual second swing of the bow, Indavara lashed it against the side of the man's head, striking him full on the ear. The Syrian dropped to his knees. The look on his face suggested disbelief at the level of pain he was experiencing.

'My ear!' he screeched. 'Why did you hit me in the ear, you barbarous piece of shit?'

'Because it hurts,' replied Indavara, before delivering a kick to the man's chest. He fell on to his back and was dragged away by the others.

Cassius recovered his sword from the floor and took up a position between the workers and Indavara. The bodyguard grabbed Juba by his tunic, dragged him to his feet and shoved him outside. The foreman stumbled on the uneven ground, then fell again. Indavara dropped the bow over his head and twisted it until the string was tight against the Syrian's neck.

Cassius came after them, but kept one eye on the workers. 'We need that address, Juba.'

The foreman took a look back at his brother and set his teeth. 'Go to Hades.'

Indavara twisted the bow tighter.

The foreman's face turned from pink to red. He clawed at the string.

'Address!' yelled Indavara, bending over him, turning the bow with one hand.

The foreman's eyes widened. His jaw began to shake, then his whole head.

Cassius thought of Estan, that night in Palmyra.

'All right, that'll do,' he said, grabbing Indavara's arm.

The bodyguard reluctantly untwisted the bow. Cassius loosened the string and pulled it off over Juba's head.

'Talk fast or I'll let him go to work on you again.'

The foreman cast a hateful look at them both, then spoke: 'Jewish Quarter. Apartment block next to the Fountain of Tiberius. Number twenty-four, I think.'

Cassius helped the foreman to his feet.

'That's more like it. And as you're now in a more cooperative frame of mind, I'm sure you won't object if we borrow a couple of your horses for the afternoon.'

With one hand still at his throat, Juba waved the other in surrender.

'Good man.'

The Jewish Quarter was just north of the Daphne Gate, an enclave about half a mile across. They found the fountain and left the mounts at a nearby stable. The apartment block was only four storeys high, but with the ramshackle balconies built on to the front, it seemed almost to bend over the streets below. Many of the ground-floor rooms were store-fronts.

'The people here look like any other people,' observed Indavara as they searched for the entrance. 'What are Jews anyway?'

'I've never been entirely sure. There are a lot of them here because we're not that far from Jerusalem. They're a bit like Christians – though they don't seem to get on with them very well. One god and all that. Maybe I should consider converting.'

Indavara frowned. 'Why?'

'Despite the fact that they're good at making weapons, their religion forbids them to work on one day of the week, so they're exempt from military service.'

'Ah.'

'I could avoid things like being strangled by my own cape, or sharing underground pits with dead bodies, or having people throw shelves full of glass at me.'

Cassius looked down at his arms. The skin was dotted with multicoloured specks of glass. There'd been no time to get it all out.

'I think we're here,' Indavara said as they arrived at a narrow staircase that ran up to the first floor. Outside sat an old woman presiding over an impressive stock of kitchen utensils.

'Can we get to number twenty-four through here?' Cassius asked her.

'Turn right at the top of the stairs.'

Indavara reached for his sword.

'Perhaps your stave this time,' suggested Cassius. 'I'd like to avoid any fatalities if possible.'

He followed Indavara up the dank, dark staircase. It stank of urine.

'Gods, what a hole.'

Just as they reached the top, a dog hurtled past them, closely followed by two young boys. Indavara leaned against the wall, peered round the corner, then stepped into the corridor. Cassius followed him. It was a narrow space, perhaps only five feet across, and the roof was only an inch or two above his head. A couple in one of the rooms were firing colourful insults at each other in Greek, providing some useful cover noise. The flimsy wooden doors were incredibly close to one another. Some had numbers illustrated with paint or bronze numerals; many had figurines nailed to the wall above them.

Twenty-four was close to the far end of the corridor. There was no number on the door. Indavara, who hadn't – or couldn't – keep track, was all set to walk past it when Cassius grabbed his tunic. The bodyguard stopped and turned round.

'This one,' Cassius mouthed, before pointing down at the bottom of the door. There was an inch between it and the floor. If Nabor was inside and watching, he would see their shadows.

Cassius didn't want the satchel and spear-head getting in his way, so he took the bag off and laid it carefully against the wall. Indavara took the stave from his shoulder. It was a five-foot length of timber with leather wrapped around the middle section and both ends.

The door was equipped with a solid-looking bronze lock, but the frame looked weak. Cassius pointed at the stave, then at a spot midway between the hinges. Indavara stood well back from the door, holding the stave in both hands. He lined the weapon up, then drove it forward.

The blow knocked the door clean off the hinges and into the middle of the room. Indavara leapt in after it. Cassius came in behind him, hand on his sword hilt.

The apartment was empty. It was a single room, only seven or eight yards wide, with one window facing the street. Under the window was a narrow, unmade bed. Next to the bed were a chest and a bedpan. To the left of the door was a set of shelves containing some clothes and a few glass items.

Cassius investigated the chest. The lid was open but there was nothing inside.

'Looks like he's gone. Let's see if we can find anything.'

There was little else to search. Once they'd checked the shelves and every corner of the bed, they stood there, staring blankly at each other.

The noise came suddenly: shouted orders in Greek, then the heavy footfalls of a group of men coming down the corridor.

'Draw your sword,' said Indavara, picking up his stave.

Cassius had only just done so when three city sergeants burst into the apartment. They were wearing mail-shirts and bronze helmets and wielding their clubs.

'Drop your weapons,' ordered the shortest and oldest of the three. Two more men arrived and pressed into the room behind them.

'You first,' Indavara replied. One of the sergeants had already advanced far enough for his liking so he swung lightly at the man's club with his stave. The weapons barely touched but the men spread out and advanced.

'Get out of my face,' Indavara snarled.

Cassius sheathed his sword and held up his hands.

'All right, that's enough. Let's *all* put our weapons down.'

The older man turned to Cassius. 'Who are you to order us around, son?'

'Corbulo, Imperial Security.'

'Prove it,' said the man sourly.

'My spear-head is just outside the door there. May I?'

'Stay there.'

The sergeant ordered one of his men to fetch the satchel. He took it from him and inspected the contents for himself. Then he returned the bag to Cassius.

'All right, men. At ease.'

They reluctantly lowered their clubs.

'I'm Master of Sergeants Congrio. My men and I work for the magistrate.'

'I know who you work for.'

'What are you doing in here?'

'Looking for a man named Nabor. He lived here.'

'Well, you need look no longer. He's just been found. Dead.'

Cassius and Congrio marched along the street, with Indavara and two of the sergeants behind them. The other men had been left behind to search the apartment, then stand guard.

'Someone knew his face,' said Congrio. 'Told us where he lived. When we got to the apartment block the old crone downstairs said you two were already in there.'

'Can't blame you for assuming the worst,' replied Cassius.

'Why's the Service interested in him?'

'I can't discuss that, I'm afraid. He was known to you?'

'I didn't recognise him, nor his name. We get bodies turn up all the time.'

Congrio pointed across the street to a low-walled enclosure full of overgrown bushes and trees. A group of women – rag-pickers with woven baskets on their shoulders – made way as Congrio hurried into the enclosure and along a gravel path. They passed an ornamental pool that was no longer very ornamental. Cassius doubted if any water had flowed in the little sanctuary for years; it had probably been established by some generous benefactor who'd died or fallen on hard times.

A group of young boys and girls had gathered where the body lay, chattering in Hebrew and Greek. Some of them had climbed up on to a fountain to get a better look over the shoulders of

Congrio's men. The children – and to a lesser extent the four other sergeants there – were dwarfed by the hulking figure of Magistrate Quarto. Congrio accelerated when he saw his superior there. Quarto turned round and stared down at the new arrivals with bloodshot eyes.

'Ah. There you are, Congrio.'

Quarto's beard and multiple chins completely obscured his neck.

'I haven't sent a runner yet, sir,' said Congrio. 'How did you—'

'I was down on the avenue. One of these brats came past jabbering about it.'

'This gentleman is with Imperial Security, sir; we found him at the dead man's apartment.'

Quarto took a step closer. Cassius was six feet tall, but the magistrate towered over him. His mouth seemed to be set in a permanent sneer.

'You one of Pitface's then?'

All things considered, Cassius didn't really feel the magistrate was in a position to be picking on the physical deficiencies of others.

'If you mean Officer Abascantius, the answer is no. I work directly for Chief Pulcher, though I do liaise with Abascantius from time to time.'

'What's your concern? What were you doing at this man's apartment?'

'Looking for him.'

Quarto scratched at his beard. 'Why?'

'I can't discuss that.'

For a moment, anger flashed in the magistrate's eyes. But then he shrugged. 'Then you shall receive no assistance from my office. If Pitface has a problem with that, tell him he can come and see me.'

'May I at least look at the body?'

'You have until the cart arrives.'

Quarto turned to Congrio. 'Anybody see anything?'

Congrio shook his head. 'The children found him.'

'You're in charge; get this mess tidied up quickly.'

Tucking his thumbs into his belt, the magistrate sauntered away past the fountain. Cassius could see a servant waiting with an enormous horse on the other side of the sanctuary.

He walked over to the body. Nabor was lying on his back next to a row of flowerless bushes, his arms and legs splayed wide. Cassius recognised the dark hair and lanky frame. His eyes were shut, his lips twisted in an eerie half-smile. Blood had soaked most of his neck and the top half of his tunic. On his belt was a knife, still sheathed. Cassius looked down at the wounds: two ragged punctures in his throat.

Indavara and Congrio joined him.

'Dagger, probably,' observed Indavara.

'Was anything else found here?' Cassius asked Congrio.

'I'm not supposed to cooperate with you.'

'Believe me, I wish I could be open with you, but my hands are tied.'

Congrio stared at Cassius for a moment, then turned to one of the sergeants and gestured to him. The man picked up a small sack with a length of twine around it. He handed it to Congrio, who showed it to Cassius.

'Just this. Clothes. No money, nothing else.'

'It was like this when you found it?'

'No, the clothes were all scattered around.'

'Thank you.'

Cassius and Indavara moved away from the body, under the branches of an apricot tree.

'They were looking for the necklace,' said Indavara.

'Yes, and I expect they found it. How long since we were at the factory? Two hours at the most. Didn't waste much time, did they? I imagine he thought they would help him. His last mistake.'

XXIII

The expression on Abascantius's face seemed to suggest anger and dismay in equal measure. He scratched his head and stared up at the ceiling.

Cassius and Indavara sat on a couch opposite him. Shostra had just brought them cloths and hot water. Indavara was picking shards of glass out of his leg, then cleaning the little wounds.

'This could have been avoided,' said Abascantius, pointing at Cassius, 'if you'd taken him alive at the factory. When you go to apprehend a suspect in a building, always send a man to the rear. That's elementary, Corbulo.'

'Yes, sir.'

Cassius knew he had been stupid; and now a man was dead. It was a horrible feeling – to know one's actions had precipitated such a thing, but he refused to allow himself guilt. He had neither the time nor the energy for it; certainly not for a stupid thief who'd been betrayed by his own kind. He watched Indavara remove a blue sliver of glass from his shin.

'This necklace,' continued Abascantius. 'You're sure it came from the cart?'

'I can't be entirely certain, sir, but from what the dealers said there have been no other new pieces like that on the market. It's unlikely to be a coincidence.'

Abascantius tapped his fingers against the side of the couch. 'Well, I can't deny you've made progress today. This killing is a setback but you must press on. We need to find out more about this Nabor. Don't be afraid to throw some money around. Now, what about last night?'

Once again, Cassius divulged everything except a single

incident; in this case Antonia's kiss. Abascantius seemed very interested in what she'd found out about Octobrianus and was also surprised to hear of Scaurus's behaviour. He whistled when he heard about the comedian's jibe and questioned Cassius about every detail of the governor's reaction.

'Scaurus was lucky,' said the agent. 'Ordinarily, Gordio would have taken exception to such an affront. Evidently he has other matters to concern him.' Abascantius hunched forward. 'A man was seen visiting his home in the early hours of this morning – the second such incident this week. A Persian, no less.'

'What do you think it means, sir?'

'Gordio's always been ambitious. Aurelian's a long way away now. And Marcellinus is out of the city.'

'You don't think he'd move against the Emperor?'

'Someone has the flag. And that someone now has a lot of leverage.'

Abascantius looked up as Shostra reappeared carrying his master's cape. He was with a big, grizzled man of about fifty, who was armed with a long sword and a wooden cudgel tucked into his belt.

'Message just arrived, sir,' said Shostra. 'He'll meet us as planned.'

'Good.'

Abascantius stood up and pointed to the stranger. 'That's Major, by the way. Bodyguard I use from time to time.'

Major offered a barely noticeable nod.

'Any other progress, sir?' Cassius enquired as he and Indavara stood.

'More hearsay and speculation. I am looking into the affairs of the most powerful men in this city. Each has his fair share of enemies; there are any number of people with good reason to incriminate them.'

Abascantius pressed his fingers against his brow, then rubbed his eyes.

'It's getting dark. Get yourselves home and cleaned up. At dawn I want you back in the Jewish Quarter.'

Abascantius walked up to Cassius and prodded him in the

chest. 'And don't set foot back in here unless you have something solid for me. Understood?'

▬8▬

As they walked back to the villa, Cassius felt the need to distract himself: not only from the nagging pain in his hands, arms and legs, but also from the mounting pressure of the investigation. All things considered, Abascantius had been lenient. Finding Nabor had been largely down to luck; losing him had been simple ineptitude.

As there was little likelihood of Indavara striking up a conversation, Cassius mentioned a matter that had been at the back of his mind since the previous evening.

'Tell me, what's your upper limit? As far as women go.'

Indavara shrugged. 'I don't know, I think any more than two is a bit stupid really. Another fighter I used to know said that with three girls or more a man really needs two—'

'No, no, you misunderstand me. I mean in terms of age. How old a woman would you go with?'

'I don't know.'

'Well, how old are you?'

Indavara shrugged again.

'Gods, numbers aren't your strong point, are they? I reckon you're about my age. So what's the oldest woman you would sleep with?'

'Thirty, maybe.'

'Yes, thirty. That's usually what I say.'

'Why?'

'Let's just say I'm thinking about revising my upper limit.'

Indavara suddenly dropped back, and concealed himself in the shadow of an ivy-covered wall.

'What's up with you?'

The bodyguard beckoned Cassius closer then pointed across the street. Descending from the slopes above was a party of men. There were two legionaries at the front, two at the back. In the

266

middle was the slight figure of General Ulpian, and just behind him his African bodyguard. The legionary was a good foot and a half taller than the general, and even at that distance Cassius could make out the bulging muscles of his arms and legs. The group disappeared behind a temple, heading for the centre of the city.

Indavara exhaled loudly. 'Didn't think I'd ever see him again.'

'The African? You know him?'

'Not exactly.'

'But you've met him?'

'Yes. In the arena, several years ago. He's the man who took my ear off.'

Simo didn't greet them when they arrived back at the villa, so Cassius assumed he was still out. As he was thirsty and Indavara was hungry, they made straight for the kitchen. They found Simo there. He was sitting at the table, facing away from them, head bowed. He was weeping.

'Best stay in there for now,' Cassius said. As Indavara withdrew to the atrium, he stood over Simo.

'What's the matter?'

Simo wiped at his face with a handkerchief, then stood.

'Sorry, sir.'

Cassius put a hand on his shoulder. He'd never seen the Gaul so upset; and imagined he must have heard terrible news. There had been little contact from his family while they were in Cyzicus. Just a letter or two from Simo's brother: a freedman who'd relocated his family to Tarsus just before the Palmyran occupation. The Gaul's mother was long dead. Only his father had remained in the city but he was illiterate, so there had been no way for Simo to stay in touch.

'Sit down. And tell me what's happened.'

Cassius waited for Simo to sit, then took a chair beside him. Simo wiped at his eyes again.

'I shall tell you, sir, but there is something I must explain first – something about me.'

Cassius was pretty sure he knew what was coming. 'You're a Christian.'

Simo looked surprised. Then he nodded.

Cassius sat back in the chair. 'I suppose I've known for a while. Hardly a great mystery. I've never once heard you utter the name of Mars or Jupiter or Fortuna. Those times I couldn't find you in Cyzicus. You were visiting one of your temples, I suppose.'

'A church-house, sir, yes.'

'Why did you never tell me before? I think you've known me long enough to appreciate there was nothing to fear.'

'Honestly, I'm not sure, sir. Why did you never ask?'

Cassius shrugged. 'Perhaps we both thought it more convenient to say nothing. What does this have to do with your father anyway? He too is a Christian?'

'Yes.'

'He's alive, then?'

'I think so. I went to his house and found it empty. One of his neighbours told me he'd been taken to the city prison.'

'What? Why?'

'You've heard of Bishop Paul, sir?'

'Of course.'

Though few people could have maintained less of an interest in religious affairs than Cassius, the reputation of Antioch's Christian leader had spread far and wide. Paul of Samosata had been the city's bishop for more than a decade but he had acquired a reputation as a fame-hungry narcissist who liked to surround himself with beautiful young women. He had also enjoyed the support of Zenobia, but shortly after her defeat his rule was challenged by the Church authorities. Aurelian had granted them the power to make their own decision and Paul was deposed.

Simo looked at the floor as he spoke. 'My father and several others were at the bishop's residence when the city sergeants came. They tried to resist and were arrested. They've been locked up while the governor decides what to do with them.'

'And what news? Has anyone been able to visit?'

'I don't know, sir. But I found out there's a meeting at a church-house tonight. An elder – a friend of my father's – will be there. He may know something.'

'I see.' Cassius stood up. 'When is this meeting?'

'The second hour of night, sir.'

'I shall come with you. And I'll do my best to get you into that prison. The spear-head should help.'

Simo clasped his hands together. 'My thanks, sir. Truly. I wish only to see him.' The tears started again.

'All right, Simo. That's enough of that. We'll find a solution. Can't have my manservant in such a state – you'll be useless to me.'

Cassius's father had taught him that a wise man tried to solve his slave's problems, especially if they were likely to hinder his work. But that wasn't the only reason he wanted to help. The big Gaul had made the most difficult period of Cassius's life a lot easier. He genuinely cared about his master, Cassius knew that and – though he would never speak of it openly – he welcomed the chance to repay that debt.

Simo was still drying his eyes.

'Why don't you keep your mind off things by preparing some dinner?' said Cassius. 'What about that Gaulish dish with the tripe and onions? I could do with a good feed. But first I need you to pick some glass out of me.'

Simo frowned. 'Glass, sir?'

'Don't ask.'

The church-house turned out to be a woodcarver's workshop that backed on to the city walls just west of the Beroea Gate. Simo hadn't been there before, and had to ask for directions several times. He was careful who he approached; apparently there had been a few violent clashes between followers of Paul and Bishop Domnus, now the official leader of the Christian community in Antioch. As they walked along a darkened alley towards the rear of the workshop, Indavara asked the latest in what Cassius considered to be a series of inane, annoying questions, most of which he'd been unable to answer.

'So Christians and Jews both believe in one god?'

'Yes.'

'Is it the same god?'

'Yes. No. I'm not sure. Why are you asking me?'

Indavara hurried after Simo, who had stopped near a wooden door. Cassius put a hand in his way.

'Not now.'

Simo knocked on the door. After a while it opened a few inches and a middle-aged man carrying a candle peered out. He looked over Simo's shoulder. Cassius tried to look friendly. Simo had tactfully suggested that he wear a normal tunic and belt: the meeting was being held in secret, and a Roman Army officer was unlikely to meet with a favourable reception.

Simo exchanged a few whispered words with the sentry, who then closed the door again. When he returned, an older man was with him. This man smiled solemnly at Simo then opened the door wide and let them in. The sentry locked the door behind them as the older man led the visitors into a cramped courtyard. Most of the space was taken up with stacks of timber, the rest by pieces of furniture. Through an open doorway, Cassius saw a group of people inside the workshop.

'Who are these men, brother?'

'My master,' answered Simo. 'Cassius Quintius Corbulo. And his bodyguard, Indavara.' Simo gestured to the old man. 'This is Elder Nura, sir.'

'Good evening,' said Cassius.

Nura was still inspecting him and Indavara.

'You look worried,' added Cassius. 'But you needn't. I'm with the army but I have nothing to do with the city authorities. I am simply here to help Simo.'

Nura smiled warily. 'The Lord tells us that we should look for the good in all men. Come, we shall talk inside.'

While the sentry remained at his post, Nura took another candle and led them through the doorway. There were in fact a dozen people stuffed into the small room, some on chairs, others standing, all listening to another older man, who sat reading quietly in Aramaic from a small book. Cassius was surprised to see there were more women than men. Wherever Paul of Samosata had found his young beauties it evidently wasn't here – they were a dowdy, serious-looking lot. Though no one said anything as they passed, a couple of the men seemed to recognise Simo.

The next room was a store-front with a wide, shuttered window. Nura found some stools and Simo helped him arrange them around a table. As the others sat down, Nura lit an oil lamp. He was a very slight man, with bushy eyebrows and a patchy beard of grey and white.

'Have you seen your father?' he asked Simo.

'No. I only found out about what happened today.'

'I wish there were better news,' Nura said as he too sat down. 'The last time we were allowed in to see the prisoners was almost two weeks ago.'

'How was he?'

'He had been struck about the head several times during his arrest, but he seemed well enough, and in good spirits.'

'You've heard nothing since?'

'No. There are ten of them in there, and some have decided not to eat. Do you remember Brother Albar?'

Simo nodded.

'He seems determined to martyr himself.' Nura lowered his voice. 'Though I sometimes wonder whether it's truly the glory of God he wishes to honour. We went to the prison with food, but the women became hysterical – crying, hurling themselves against the bars. I should never have let them go. The guards threw us out and no one has been allowed back since. I thought of appealing to the governor, but I suspect we have become a troublesome inconvenience for him.'

'And what about this Bishop Domnus?' asked Cassius. 'Surely you could appeal to him?'

Nura turned to Cassius. 'Never, sir.'

'Clearly I'm no expert in these matters,' Cassius replied, 'but there seems little chance a ruling allowed by the Emperor himself will be reversed. Surely you people would be better off accepting Domnus as your leader.'

'I'm afraid there's rather more to it than that, sir,' said Simo.

'This is not simply a matter of leadership,' added Nura. 'Domnus preaches ideas that we do not – and cannot – subscribe to.'

To Cassius, it seemed rather ridiculous that followers of a cult that had suffered persecution in recent years – and might easily face it again – could not even agree among themselves.

'Such as?'

'We, the followers of Bishop Paul, contend that our Lord Jesus Christ was a man, not a god.'

'What was he, then? A priest?'

Nura grimaced.

'An oracle?'

'Not exactly.'

'It's rather complicated, sir,' observed Simo.

Cassius glared at him. 'I'll manage.' He turned back to Nura. 'Go on.'

'Christ was God's son – his divine representative, the essence of God in human form. Yet he was not a god himself.'

'But Christ has been dead two hundred years. If he was so precious and powerful to you, why is he not considered a god now?'

'He is now one – with God,' explained Nura.

'Ah yes – the one god thing. I was forgetting. So Domnus disagrees with this?'

'He considers it heresy. As does most of the rest of the Church.'

'Wouldn't it be wiser just to give in? You've lost your leader and you seem to have lost the argument. You're here meeting in secret, half your number in prison. Why not simply alter your beliefs?'

'Sir.'

'People do it all the time, Simo,' Cassius snapped impatiently. He nodded towards the other room. 'Was every man and woman in there born a Christian?'

'No,' admitted Nura. 'Neither was I.'

'So you changed your beliefs. Why not change again?'

Nura leaned forward. 'Would *you*, sir?'

'If it meant avoiding prison, or death? Absolutely.'

Nura continued, apparently assuming Cassius wasn't serious. 'Bishop Paul taught us that a man cannot aspire to be God. But our Lord Jesus Christ showed us how a man might live the best life he can; so that when he faces the final judgement, he might be permitted to join the righteous in the kingdom of eternal joy.'

'I presume that your Bishop Paul set a similar example, and that all the tales I've heard about him are mere slander?'

'Evil lies, spread by our enemies. I can assure you that there is no such thing as "mere slander" for a man in such an important position.'

'And where is he now?'

'We don't know.' Nura sighed. 'But we pray that he be returned to us.'

'Then you seem to be on your own.'

'No. Our Lord and his angels are forever with us, even in our darkest hours, when the black demons try to divide and destroy us.'

As Nura was beginning to sound like one of those men who harangued passers-by in town squares, Cassius decided he'd heard enough.

'Where is the prison?'

'On the east side of the island, not far from the hippodrome.'

'We shall go there tomorrow.'

'Please, see how they all are,' asked Nura. 'And would you take some food for them? The guards might allow it.'

'I shall take as much as I can carry,' said Simo.

They stood. Nura put out the lamp, took the candle and led

them back through the building. The others were talking about marriage. They halted when Nura stopped.

'Brothers, sisters. This is Simo, Abito's son, and his . . . friends.'

The Christians all offered a greeting. Cassius and Indavara nodded to them.

Nura put a hand on Simo's arm. 'Will you stay a while and pray with us?'

Simo glanced at Cassius.

'You may.'

Nura shifted his gaze to Cassius. 'What about you, sir?'

'I'm afraid it's all a little complicated for my taste.'

'As you wish. We shall pray for you too.'

'You needn't,' said Cassius with a smile.

'We shall. We pray for every soul; for every man; that he might eventually find salvation.' Nura took a step closer to Indavara, and gazed keenly up at him. 'What about you, brother, do you seek the light?' He seemed to take Indavara's silence as a signal to continue. 'Would you like to join the righteous in the kingdom? Where we might dwell for ever in the warmth and the light with our loved ones. Who have you lost? Who would you like to see again?'

Indavara glanced at Cassius, then suddenly pushed past him and hurried towards the door.

XXIV

The second hour of the day had just begun when Cassius, Indavara and Simo returned to the Jewish Quarter. They found the door to Nabor's apartment open. The landlord was inside, awaiting a prospective new tenant. The only information he could offer was that the dead man had been a prompt payer and in the apartment for two years.

Cassius decided to start knocking on doors but many of the residents had already left for work. When a door did open, he took care to identify himself, and had Simo hold up the spearhead; but he swiftly realised his uniform was sufficient to command attention.

The smell of urine in the first-floor corridor was even worse than the previous day. A fuller's mate had been collecting the liquid contents of bedpans, and though he'd just left with a full barrel, the stench remained. Cassius's mood was not enhanced by the useless responses of the first five people he spoke to. The sixth, however – a young man who lived at number sixteen – said he'd known Nabor. He was about Cassius's age: a ruddy-faced, unkempt fellow named Valgus.

'How did you meet him?' Cassius asked.

'Don't remember exactly. Saw him on work crews, the odd festival, at the inn now and again.'

'Which inn?'

'The Wheel. Two streets south. Though I'd not seen him there in a while.'

'And these festivals? Jewish affairs?'

Valgus shook his head. 'No, I mean the big festivals – the ones for the lads. Saturnalia and all that.'

'And work?'

'Last time would have been a while back. Year or two maybe. Water-carrying. That was a big crew. Fifty of us plus two hundred slaves.'

'Did you work with Nabor on any other jobs?'

'Don't think so. He went to the glass factory after that.'

'Do you remember anything else? Family or friends? Girls even?'

Valgus pursed his lips. 'You see I knew him – to pass a good-day to, or have the odd drink with – but not that well. Not really.'

Cassius gave him two sesterces.

'Thank you, sir,' said Valgus with a humble nod.

'If you think of anything else, or come across anyone who might know more, direct them to me.'

'Very well, sir. Where would I find you?'

Cassius had to think about that. It didn't seem wise to give out the address of either his or Abascantius's villa.

'You can contact me at the basilica. There's a man works there by the name of Petronax. You can leave a message with him. Petronax – can you remember that?'

'I can, sir. Good-day.'

Valgus had almost closed the door when he suddenly spoke again. 'Ah. There *was* a girl. I know he was sweet on her – I remember him buying her flowers a few times. Don't remember the name though.'

Enquiries in the rest of the apartment block yielded nothing else of note.

'To this inn then, sir? The Wheel?' asked Simo as they left the dank shadows of the stairwell and strode into the warmth of the early morning sun.

'Not just yet,' Cassius said, cradling his helmet under one arm. 'Nabor had nothing to cook with, kept no food in the apartment, and hadn't been to the inn for a while. But he had to eat somewhere.'

276

Cassius gestured down the street – there were five or six vendors in sight. The first had set himself up with a marble counter on which he served food cooked on a charcoal-fired grill. His four male customers sat on stools, eating sausages.

'I heard about it, yes,' said the vendor, when asked if he knew of the murder.

'Did you know him?'

'Not really. Never said much. I suppose he got bored of my grub – he hadn't bought anything off me in months. He preferred Marta's fritters.'

The vendor wiped coal dust off his hands and nodded down the street.

The trio negotiated a gaggle of children playing with sticks and a ball and came to the next vendor. The set-up was almost identical, but run by a plump woman with a mass of grey curls tied above her head. Marta's customers – ten of them – took their breakfast on tables and chairs. She scooped a fritter out of a blackened pan and on to a plate.

'Cheese and herbs,' she announced.

A man grabbed the plate and returned to his seat.

Marta looked surprised when she saw who her next customer was. 'Oh. Good-day, sir. Are you hungry?'

'No.'

'I am,' said Indavara.

Ignoring him, Cassius spoke in a low voice: 'Did you know Nabor, the man who was killed yesterday?'

'I did. Poor boy.'

'Do you know of any family or—'

Simo tapped Cassius on the shoulder and pointed towards the street. Standing there alone was a young woman, anxiously fondling the big beaded necklace she wore over her tatty tunic. She was pale and alarmingly thin.

'Are you the man asking about Nabor, sir?'

'I am,' Cassius replied, walking over to her.

'I knew him. I knew him quite well.'

Cassius looked around for somewhere with a little privacy but the street was busy. There was, however, a shadowy room behind Marta's stall. He placed two sesterces on the counter.

'May I use your room there for a moment?'

'Of course, sir.'

Indavara put down another sesterce.

'And I'll have a cheese fritter.'

Still ignoring him, Cassius gave the girl an encouraging smile.

'We can talk in there.'

The 'room' was barely five feet square but there were at least a couple of stools. Cassius proffered one to the girl. She sat down, then rearranged her tunic over her knees.

'What's your name?' he asked, sitting down beside her.

'Bacara.'

Cassius took care not to get too close. There were wide pink sores along her forearms, smaller ones on her fingers.

'Well, Bacara, it's my job to find out who killed Nabor. I hope you'll be able to help me.'

'I wonder if his family even know.'

'They're local?'

She shook her head. 'From the desert.'

'Do you know anything about them?'

'Only that. I hadn't actually seen him in months. He really was nice. He used to sing to me and we would take walks down by the river. He said that one day he might have enough money to buy my freedom.'

Cassius imagined this was a promise more often given than fulfilled.

'What about his friends? Men he worked with?'

She shrugged. 'It was usually just us. Mistress would tell me the days when I could have a break. There was his brother though.'

'Do you remember the name?'

'Silus. He wasn't as nice-looking.'

Cassius watched Indavara attack his freshly served fritter. The bodyguard burned his mouth twice before deciding to wait.

'Do you remember anything about him?'

'He worked with Nabor before he went to the glass factory.

They were guards for a tax collector – in case there was ever any trouble. He was strong and tough, Nabor. He didn't look it, but he was.'

'This tax collector. You don't remember *his* name?'

Bacara shook her head.

'How did he die?' she asked suddenly.

'He was stabbed.'

Bacara began fiddling with the necklace again.

'You've not seen this Silus recently?' asked Cassius.

'Now and again. But I've no idea how to find him. I wish I could. He needs to know what's happened.'

'Did you ever actually see this tax collector? Do you know what he looks like?'

'No. He was good to Nabor and Silus though. He paid them well; said they were reliable lads. Mistress says *I'm* reliable.'

Cassius stood up. 'Well, thank you, Bacara.'

He made sure Simo wasn't watching, then retrieved a denarius from his money bag and handed it to her. Bacara stared at the coin in disbelief for a moment, then took it.

'Thank you, sir, thank you. I did see his house once, by the way.'

'Whose?'

'The tax collector. Nabor showed it to me on one of our walks. It was a nice place, just by the old walls. Big oak tree in the garden.'

'Could you find it again?'

Bacara thought about this for an excruciatingly long time.

'I think so, yes.'

After two hours of traipsing around the maze of streets south of the Avenue of Herod and Tiberius, Cassius finally lost his patience.

'Caesar's balls!' he yelled, lashing a boot against a wall as Bacara decided – for at least the tenth time – that they were not in fact on the right street. Cassius felt like slapping her and reclaiming his denarius. He thought about abandoning the search and returning to the Jewish Quarter. Perhaps someone in this inn – the Wheel – might know something more.

Bacara didn't dare look at him; she simply gazed down at the ground, her lank hair covering her face. Simo went over and spoke to her. Indavara – who was staring at some colourful graffiti on the pavement – yawned loudly. Cassius looked up at the high, crumbling walls that overshadowed the street. According to Simo, they'd been built on the orders of Seleucus I, one of Alexander the Great's generals and the son of Antiochus himself; that made them over six hundred years old.

Simo led Bacara over to Cassius.

'She says she will know it when she sees it. If it means helping you find the men who killed Nabor, she's happy to keep looking. If you are, sir.'

Cassius cleared his throat. 'Of course.'

To retain his own sanity and the girl's safety, Cassius decided to stay in the shade while the Gaul led her into the next street. This was an area of medium-sized villas; housing for professionals like teachers, doctors or engineers.

Indavara was looking at a poster nailed to a tree. Cassius tried to imagine what it was like – not being able to read. The bodyguard just saw lines of ink; he didn't know it was a notice about a lost cat. Cassius suddenly thought of those last moments at the church-house.

'You didn't seem too keen to stay with Simo's friends last night.'

Indavara kept looking at the poster as Cassius continued.

'It's rather clever, I suppose – all that stuff about the kingdom and seeing the dead again. Everybody's lost someone, after all. I mean, one can see the appeal.'

Indavara turned to him. Before he could say anything, Simo called out to them. Cassius and Indavara jogged up the street. The Gaul was pointing over a low wall.

'The oak, sir.'

At the rear of the property was a luxuriant tree with thick, sprawling limbs.

'You're sure of it?' Cassius asked.

Bacara nodded her head rapidly up and down like a child.

Simo leaned over the wall. 'Excuse me.'

Cassius joined him and saw there was an elderly slave watering flowers. The slave put down his bucket and ambled over to them at what looked like his maximum speed.

'Yes?' he croaked.

'Who lives here?' asked Cassius.

'Master Gratus Celsus, sir.'

'What is his occupation?'

'He is an architect.'

Cassius looked at Bacara, who was frowning.

'Has he ever worked as a tax collector?'

'No, though my last master did. I come with the house, you see.'

'And his name?'

'You will know it. He has gone on to great things: Gallio Novius Octobrianus.'

Abascantius smiling was a rather alarming sight, all yellow teeth and gleeful eyes.

'So, our esteemed procurator has connections to a murdered man seen with this stolen necklace. By the gods – if he really is in league with the Palmyrans . . . good work, Corbulo. Good, good work.'

Shostra had shown them through to the kitchen, where Abascantius sat at a large table. A middle-aged serving woman had just brought him a bowl of foul-smelling soup. The agent took a pinch of pepper and sprinkled it on to the thick, green liquid.

'Cabbage. My doctor says I must have it as my main meal for two weeks. To clean out my innards, apparently. Want some?'

'No thank you, sir.'

'You?'

Indavara shrugged, then nodded.

Abascantius caught the woman's eye and waved at Indavara. 'Soup for this one.' He turned back to Cassius. 'Did you get anything else out of the girl?'

'No. But I told her how to reach me if need be.'

Abascantius frowned as he took the first taste of soup. 'Needs garum.'

As Abascantius opened a nearby jar, Cassius braced himself. The smell of cabbage was nothing compared to garum, a condiment made up largely of decomposing fish intestines. He had never been able to understand why people ate it.

There was a knock on the kitchen door. Shostra was there with two men behind him: the bodyguard Major and another man.

'Wait outside. Be with you shortly,' said Abascantius. As the trio withdrew, he continued: 'Taken with what Antonia found out about his nocturnal habits, it seems evident we need to keep a close eye on Octobrianus.'

Cassius cast a look towards the woman. Surely Abascantius was far too trusting of his staff.

'Don't worry about her,' said the agent. 'She's deaf.'

'Ah.'

Cassius resisted the temptation to hold his nose as the smell of garum wafted towards him. He sat back in his chair.

'My other men are busy shadowing Gordio,' said Abascantius. 'You two can find out what exactly Octobrianus is up to with these night-time forays. I'll give you his address, you watch from a distance, and follow him if he goes out. Just don't get too close. Understood?'

'Sir.'

'Perhaps a rest this afternoon. I need you fit and alert – could be a long night.'

'No such luck,' said Cassius. He told Abascantius about Simo's father. The agent's curious expression turned to one of amusement when he heard about Nura's defence of Paul of Samosata.

Cassius was intrigued by this man. He had engendered such hatred from the rest of the Church, yet such loyalty from his followers; he knew Abascantius would have a view on the matter.

'Even before he enjoyed the queen's favour during the occupation, there was talk of his ties with Palmyra. I was never particularly concerned by it, but I recall I did have someone look into his affairs. Certainly not what one might think of as a typical Christian man.'

'Excuse me, sir,' whispered Simo as he left the kitchen.

Abascantius took a sip of soup and nodded at the departing Gaul. 'They're a sensitive lot, like the Jews. I saw Paul a few times around the city myself. He was always surrounded by a gaggle of maids and hangers-on. He'd have the girls sing his praises before he gave a speech. Some of them lived with him. Virgins, apparently.' Abascantius smirked. 'I wanted to dig up something on him, just in case I might need it later. My man tried to get one or two of these tarts to tell what really went on in that big villa but they wouldn't spill a thing.'

'He sounds like quite a character.'

'Handsome bastard too. Dressed like a prince. One wonders what the simple man from Nazareth might have thought of it all.'

'Indeed.'

'Well, you best get going. The bridges will be heaving. There are races this afternoon.'

Abascantius was right; it took them almost an hour to get to the island. After stopping at a market for Simo to buy food, they made for the Beroea Gate, then crossed the Orontes using the northernmost of the five bridges. Cassius had heard that the hippodrome could accommodate a hundred thousand people, and it seemed as if every one of them was using the same route to get there. The city sergeants were out in force, in pairs or trios stationed along the main routes, monitoring the rowdy supporters clad in the colours of their teams. Whenever groups of the Reds or Greens or Blues encountered each other, insults flew and the odd skirmish broke out.

Cassius detested crowds and he was highly relieved when they finally escaped the horde, taking a right turn from the bridge down to the almost deserted road that ran around the north-east corner of the island.

Away to their left were the high walls of the imperial palace and the hippodrome, dwarfing all the other structures nearby. The east side of the island, however, resembled a construction site, with abandoned buildings in various states of disrepair and endless piles of rubble. Simo pointed at a building to the left of the road. It would once have been an imposing structure: three storeys high and a hundred yards long, with grand arched windows and doors. But it had been left to rot; one section had collapsed entirely, and there were gaps in the brickwork everywhere. Only the tower attached to the right side looked in good condition.

For now, master/servant convention had been forgotten, and Simo led the way, hurrying towards the building, a big basket of food in his hand. As they approached the tower, and the two legionaries leaning against the wall outside, Cassius reached into his satchel and took out the spear-head. The legionaries stood up straight.

Simo stopped to let Cassius past.

'At ease,' Cassius said casually. 'Corbulo, Imperial Security. I'm here to question a man in your custody.'

'We were told all the questioning was done with, sir,' said the elder of the two soldiers. He was a chubby, squat individual, with the stomach of a man who spent too much time on guard duty.

'I'm telling you otherwise,' Cassius replied in his most imperious tone.

The legionary frowned and turned to his partner. 'They took a few of them away last week. And one died, didn't he?'

'Think so,' said the other guard.

'What was the name?' asked the older man.

Simo had grown visibly paler, but he managed to speak. 'Abito.'

The guard went inside the shadowy doorway that led into the tower. He returned with a waxed tablet and ran a finger down one side as he read. The wait seemed interminable. Simo stood absolutely still, his unblinking eyes fixed on the legionary.

'He's here.'

Simo let out a breath and looked up at the sky.

'But he's one of the Christians,' said the legionary. 'You don't want to speak to one of the collaborators?'

'No,' replied Cassius. 'This man Abito.'

'Why?'

'Remember your rank, man. I'm not obliged to disclose such information to you. Now take us inside.'

'I know my rank, sir. I'm an optio. And I'm in charge of this prison. They're not supposed to have any visitors.'

'From their fellows. Do I look like a Christian to you? This man might have vital information for the Service.'

The optio glanced at the basket of food. 'To loosen his tongue, I suppose.'

Cassius nodded.

'You can't take it into the cell. They get hardly anything – the smell of fresh bread will send them mad.'

'We shall need a private room. I'll question this Abito in there.'

The optio was clearly wavering.

'I do not have all day,' Cassius continued. 'If it will make you feel better, I shall drop a note to your superior later, telling him of my visit, and absolving you of any responsibility. What is your name? And his?'

'Herminius. And it's Tribune Bonafatius.'

'Ah, yes, I know the man. I shall have a message to him within the hour.'

'Very well, sir.'

Leaving the other guard outside, Herminius led them inside the tower and up the circular staircase. The interior was in a poor state: dirt and dust covered the floor and paint was peeling from the walls. They walked around and around, up and up, past small, grilled windows, until Cassius guessed they were sixty feet from the ground. They smelled the cell before they saw it – a noxious mix of stale sweat and urine.

The top of the tower had been split in two, with walled rooms to the right, the single cell to the left: a semicircular space enclosed by iron bars sunk into the floor and roof. Two more legionaries were on duty here. Simo pressed forward to get a look at the occupants of the cell. Cassius subtly moved in front of him and nodded at the rooms.

'We can use one of these?'

Herminius went to the second room along and opened the door. Cassius could see a table and chairs inside.

'Fine.' He turned to Simo. 'Take the food in there.'

Simo hesitated, then did so. Herminius led Cassius and Indavara past the other guards and towards the cell. Here the smell was at its worst, and when he saw the state of the prisoners, Cassius could see why. There were at least thirty of them, all sitting or lying down, all unshaven, their skin and clothes equally filthy. Cassius was wondering what they used for a latrine when he spied a hole under the large grilled window at the rear of the cell. Next to it was a bucket of water.

One man got to his feet. He came close to the bars and gazed curiously at Cassius and Indavara. He seemed especially interested in Cassius's spear-head.

'You're from the Governor's Office. Has he made his decision?'

'That's right,' said Herminius. 'You're to be set free.'

Hope shone in the man's eyes. He gripped the bars.

'Set free into the arena,' Herminius continued. 'Where the crowd will cheer as wild dogs tear you limb from limb.'

The other guards laughed as Herminius aimed a kick at the bars. 'Get back, traitor!'

Herminius turned to Cassius as the prisoner withdrew, head down.

'Palmyra-lover. Spied on the governor for their whore queen.' Herminius gestured for Cassius to follow him. 'Your Christian's over here.'

286

The men on the right side of the cell were in fact in a far worse state than the others. Several were lying flat and hadn't stirred. Others could barely summon the energy to turn and examine the visitors. Close to the bars, two men lay on thin, holed blankets. One was very old – pale and emaciated; he looked close to death. The other was no more than thirty. His face was wet with sweat and he was rambling in Aramaic, pawing at the blanket. A third man was sitting between them, holding a damp cloth.

'We were glad when this one decided to stop eating,' said Herminius, nodding at the young man. 'Loud-mouthed bastard never shut up. I think that one's Abito.'

For one awful moment, Cassius thought he meant the old man, but it was the third individual who glanced up. Cassius saw instantly that he was Simo's father. Though a far smaller man, he had the same thick hair as his son – albeit a slate grey – and the same kind eyes too. He got to his feet.

'Officer here needs to question you,' said Herminius.

One of the guards unlocked the door at the right-hand end of the cell.

Abito looked at Cassius but said nothing. Across his forehead was a nasty gash surrounded by a yellow and purple bruise. He walked to the door and out of the cell. Some of the other Christians spoke up.

'Strength, brother.'

'The Lord is with you.'

Herminius grabbed Abito roughly by the neck and pushed him towards Cassius.

'He's all yours.'

Cassius took Abito's arm. It was thin, like a child's. He could feel the man shaking as he escorted him to the room. He whispered to him as they rounded the corner: 'I'm a friend. I have your son here. Do not cry out when you see him.'

Cassius took Abito inside the room, and Indavara quickly shut the door behind them.

Simo rushed forward and embraced his father, who hadn't

even a chance to speak. Cassius and Indavara moved away as Abito gripped his son's broad back.

'My boy. My boy Simo.'

Abito began to cry, his tears running down his face and on to his son's tunic. After a time, Simo held his father out in front of him. He kissed him once, then examined the wound on his head.

'It's not bad,' said Abito.

'Tell me you're eating,' said Simo. 'Tell me you'll have some food.'

'Gladly.'

The Gaul embraced his father again.

'I knew you wouldn't give up. I knew it.'

'I told the others,' announced Abito, turning to Cassius and Indavara. 'My boys lost their mother before they could speak. I always said I'd not leave them on their own.'

Cassius nodded but raised a finger to his mouth. Herminius or one of the other guards might easily have drifted back towards the door to listen in. Indavara turned away and went to the window, staring contemplatively down at the river.

Simo gestured to Cassius. 'My master, Father – Cassius Quintius Corbulo.'

Abito bowed.

'And that's Indavara, his bodyguard.'

Abito bowed again, though Indavara kept his back to him.

Simo went to the basket and brought out some bread and cheese, and a gourd of water.

'Sit, Father, sit,' he said, pulling out a chair.

A distant cheer from the hippodrome drifted across the island towards them.

Simo laid out a cloth for the food on the table.

'Do the guards give you anything to eat?' enquired Cassius, sitting down on the other chair.

'Nothing for five days. They said it's a waste – because we don't want it.'

'All the other Christians have refused food?'

'Not all. I and three others have tried to make them see sense.

There might be more chance now that Albar is so weak. He was the most determined.'

Abito tore off a piece of bread and swallowed it down, then grabbed a lump of cheese.

'Slowly, Father,' advised Simo.

'You must keep your fellows alive,' Cassius continued. 'Letting them die just provides the governor with a convenient solution.'

'Albar said Gordio is under the power of the demons,' replied Abito. 'Domnus too.'

Cassius sighed. 'The governor is under the power of the Emperor. Which is why he had to act against your bishop in the first place. I'm sure he couldn't care less about Domnus or Paul, or this split. He is simply doing his job – trying to keep the peace.'

Simo passed his father the gourd, then turned to Cassius. 'Do you think Master Abascantius might be able to help, sir?'

'Even if he was inclined to – which I doubt – certainly not at the moment.'

'Then what can we do?'

Cassius pointed at Simo's father. 'Your group could write a letter to Bishop Domnus pledging your allegiance. I imagine that might be enough.'

Abito sat higher in his chair. 'We cannot, sir.'

Cassius shook his head and turned to Simo. 'Would you see your father die in here? Talk to him.'

Simo seemed to be about to speak but then stopped himself.

Cassius slapped the table with his hand and stood up. 'This ridiculous misplaced loyalty.' He paused a moment, reminding himself to keep his voice down. 'Where is your precious Paul now? Where is he in your time of need?'

Simo looked down at the floor.

Abito smiled. 'He came to me. In a dream. He told me—'

'Oh, spare me, please,' said Cassius. He leaned over Simo's father. 'You have a simple decision to make, Abito. Which is more important to you: your faith or your life? If it's the former, I don't see that I can help you any more.'

Another roar from the hippodrome.

Cassius tapped Indavara on the shoulder and pointed at the door. 'Simo, we shall give you a few moments alone. Think about what you want to say to your father. You may not get this chance again.'

Indavara followed Cassius to the door and shut it behind them. Cassius walked back round the corner to where Herminius stood with the other guards.

'It's true you're not feeding the Christians anything?'

Herminius shrugged. 'What's the point if they won't eat it?'

'Did your tribune authorise that?'

'Not exactly.'

Cassius stared down at him.

'No,' the optio admitted.

'Then you provide food for every man in that cell. If some of them don't want it, the others can take it. And make sure they have enough water to drink. I shall mention all this to Bonafatius. Ensure that it is done.'

Sneering, Herminius pointed at the Christians.

'Two weeks back – at festival time – we gave them a little *extra* food, so they could make an offering to Jupiter. They threw it back at us. They disgust me.'

'They should burn, sir,' added another of the guards. 'Every one of them.'

Cassius took a step backward, and when he spoke, addressed the guards as a group. 'You men would do well to remind yourselves of your station. It is not your place to make decisions that rest with your superiors.'

Herminius gave a reluctant nod.

Cassius turned towards the cell. 'These men are zealots. Idiotic, stubborn zealots admittedly, but that's all they are. Not robbers, not murderers, nor even traitors.' He looked back at the guards. 'Remember that.'

XXV

Cassius was about to doze off for the third time when Indavara gave him a sharp nudge in the ribs. They were sitting on a bench between two clumps of bushes, in the grounds of a small temple devoted to the mountain god Dolichenus. Cassius had struggled to stay awake throughout their two-hour vigil opposite Octobrianus's house – a surprisingly modest villa not far from Hadrian's Bridge.

He peered across the street. A servant carrying a lantern had appeared. They heard the key turn as he unlocked the gate and opened it. Octobrianus stepped out on to the pavement. He was wearing a long cloak with a hood, which he now flicked up over his head as he hurried away. Once more, Cassius was struck by how utterly unmemorable the man was. He was physically small, and his manner gave no suggestion of his status, nor the power he wielded in the city.

Indavara vaulted over the stone wall in front of them and dropped quietly on to the street. Cassius clambered after him, shaking his head to try to wake himself up. He was wearing a pale blue tunic and a non-military belt with a fine silver buckle. It was a warm night and – knowing they might have to move quickly – he hadn't bothered with a cloak or cape. He and Indavara were armed only with their daggers.

Octobrianus set a quick pace. With the streets quiet, their footsteps seemed alarmingly loud so they kept well back. Cassius soon realised the procurator was heading towards the Orontes. As they got closer to the river, the quality of the housing decreased, as did the width of the streets. At one point, they passed two shifty-looking characters in an alley. Indavara's hand went to his dagger, and he made sure he was between them and Cassius, but the men stayed in the shadows.

They eventually came to a street that bent around to the left, running parallel to the river. As the procurator approached the bend, a dark shape seemed to lift off the wall beside him. They heard a voice. A woman's voice. Octobrianus tried to pull away but it seemed she had hold of him. Struggling to get free, he looked back along the street.

'Keep walking,' Cassius told Indavara, hoping the procurator would get away before they reached him. The woman was pleading for money. Octobrianus reached into a purse and handed over a coin. She let go and he made his escape around the corner.

Cassius exchanged a relieved glance with Indavara. They kept to the right – well out of the beggar's way – as the street opened out on to a broad square divided from the river by a low wall. Beyond the wall was a wooden jetty where skiffs and rowing boats were tied up. On the other side of the river, several barges lay at anchor on the edge of a marsh. A strong breeze was blowing. Furled sails and lines flapped, and the boats bounced against their moorings.

Here and there were small groups of men, either sitting in the boats or standing on the jetty. There was enough moonlight to see by; and it caught the glass of the bottles some of them were holding. Others were still hard at work, ferrying barrels off the boats and up to the square.

Cassius and Indavara stopped by the wall and continued to watch Octobrianus, now striding purposefully along the other side of the square, hood still covering his face. There were at least ten different establishments facing the waterfront. Cassius knew some would be inns, some brothels, some both. Song, laughter and the hum of conversation spilled out from the windows.

The procurator nodded to a doorman before hurrying inside a two-storey building with a striking sign above the door; the erect phallus was at least two feet high. Cassius grinned speculatively as he turned to Indavara.

'Half an hour I've been on here. It's always the same these days. Half an hour twice a day adds up to a lot of wasted time.'

'I suppose so. Tell me, friend, do you know if Helena is working tonight?'

'Haven't seen her. Though I think she usually uses the rooms on the other side.'

'Ah, thank you. I shall check over there. Hope you can get away soon.'

The man nodded ruefully as Cassius left.

After some subtle enquiries in the other corridor, he established that Helena was indeed busy, and unlikely to be available any time soon. Seeing no sign of the procurator on the other side of the room, he concluded Octobrianus was occupied.

Indavara had been joined by three girls. One of them was urging the bodyguard to flex his biceps. Unaware that Cassius was behind him, he did so. Each of the girls had a turn at touching his arm and it took him a while to notice he was being watched. Cassius grinned as he sat down. Indavara pulled his arm away and shook his head irritably as another of the girls played with his hair.

'Leave us a moment, would you, ladies?' said Cassius. The girls reluctantly complied, one giving a parting stroke to Indavara's neck.

'Have you chosen your favourite yet?' Cassius asked.

Before Indavara could answer, one of the doormen walked past carrying a large candelabra which he set down in the middle of the room. A serving girl came along to light the candles, and was joined by another holding a flute. Some of the men left their seats and gathered round. An extremely statuesque young lady then made her way gracefully into the circle formed by the men. She removed her robe and threw it to the serving girl. Underneath she was wearing only a thin belt with little chains hanging from it. Her nipples had been tipped with silver paint. The flautist began playing, and the girl swayed to the music. The men looked on in lustful silence.

Cassius recognised a couple of familiar faces from the House of the Dolphins, including the newly arrived and unmistakable figure of Magistrate Quarto, dwarfing the men either side of him. Cassius alerted Indavara then indicated that they should turn away. It would hardly be a disaster if the magistrate saw them there, but he would prefer they remain unnoticed.

'Well? Which girl are you taking?'

Indavara shrugged.

'They not to your taste? Plutarch said: *When the candles are out, all women are fair.* Wise words.'

'It's not that. They're beautiful. They're all beautiful.'

'Don't tell me it's your first time. What about when you were a fighter?'

Indavara chose to drink rather than reply.

'Well,' Cassius continued, 'I'm going to spend my token. We need to be done before Octobrianus comes out, so if you're intent on doing the same, I suggest you hurry up.'

As Cassius stood, Indavara locked a hand on his wrist.

'Wait.'

Cassius shook his hand away.

'Sorry,' continued Indavara. 'It's just . . .'

He sighed and brushed his hair away from his face. Cassius sat down again.

'There were women. But it was all so . . . rushed. I never knew when they were coming. Or *who* would come. Then they would disappear. I never had a chance—'

' —to get good at it.'

Indavara shrugged.

Cassius waved a hand at him. 'That's natural. It takes time, training – just like anything. Listen, these girls are professionals. You're in capable hands. In any case, don't feel you have to go all the way, so to speak. I won't be. They may look like goddesses but they can carry all manner of pox. My cousin got the most awful fright when – well, perhaps it's best not to go into that.

Let me put it this way. There's no need to sheathe the sword, but that doesn't mean the blade can't be touched. See what I mean?'

Indavara nodded.

Cassius stood again, then leaned closer to him.

'Don't take too long to choose. The ones you reject will be angry. And don't forget to enjoy yourself.'

Cassius still hadn't made up his own mind; so it didn't particularly concern him that when he arrived back at the room, the voluptuous girl was alone. She was sitting in front of a lamp, examining her face in a mirror. Cassius held the token up. She smiled and came to him, then led the way back down the corridor to another room. As Cassius went inside, she turned and locked the door. The room was small, half its space taken up by a substantial bed covered in fine cotton sheets. The only other features were an oriental-looking rug and a hexagonal wooden table. On the table was a pile of clean towels and a large bowl of water. While the girl lit a lamp by the bed, Cassius bent down, untied his boots and took them off. The girl then led him over to the table. She put his hands in the perfumed water and began to wash them. He looked down at her and reflected that he'd perhaps judged her a little harshly. Her face was too chubby ever to be considered beautiful but she was certainly pretty, with a full mouth and big brown eyes. She glanced up at him and smiled. She had finished washing him, and now examined his fingers.

'Someone looks after you well.'

'My attendant.'

'He attends to all your needs?' she asked with a provocative smile.

'No. For that I need a woman. What's your name?'

'Athena.'

'That's your real name?'

'Does it matter?' she replied, unbuckling his belt.

Cassius shrugged as she laid the belt on the table.

'And your name, sir?'

'Cassius.'

Athena ran a finger down his chest. 'Well, Cassius. What are we to do tonight?'

'I shall tell you. I shall tell you precisely what to do and when to do it. You can start by helping me undress.'

Cassius bent forward. Athena took hold of the tunic and pulled it off over his head, leaving him in only his loincloth. He always wore underwear if there were likely to be attractive women around – to avoid embarrassing bulges under his tunic. Athena took off the loincloth and dropped it on the table with a smile.

'Now go and sit at the end of the bed,' Cassius told her.

'Shall I take my robe off?'

'Did I ask you to?'

Athena smiled. As she walked away from him, Cassius stared at the transparent cloth clinging to her bottom. He waited for her to sit down, then joined her at the bed. He lay down, and adjusted the pillows until he was comfortable.

'Now, come and sit on my chest.'

Athena clambered along the bed, then lowered herself on to him. She pushed her dark tresses of hair away from her face.

'Pull your robe down.'

Athena loosened the robe and eased it down over her shoulders, first one, then the other.

'Further.'

Now the robe cut a line across the swell of her breasts.

'Slowly.'

Cassius watched the hem as it descended past her cleavage.

'Stop there.'

He reached up, took the material in both hands, then slid it down, revealing as fine and full a pair of breasts as he had seen.

'Ah,' he said. 'Antioch.'

Indavara returned to the table just after Cassius. He slumped down in the chair, a bottle of wine in his hand. It was almost empty. He looked more relaxed, more at ease with himself, than Cassius had seen him.

'I hardly need ask, but how was it?'

Indavara shook his head and grinned. 'She's so lovely. Her skin's so soft.'

Just as he spoke, what Cassius had previously thought were two separate groups of men stood up together and made for the back of the room. As well as Magistrate Quarto there must have been a dozen others. They filed out through the right-hand corridor, moving quickly and quietly, strangely purposeful.

Indavara was staring into space over Cassius's shoulder. He took a hefty swig from the wine bottle.

'Are you drunk?'

The way in which the bodyguard's eyes took time to re-focus was all the confirmation Cassius needed.

'No. I just – her skin, it was –'

'Yes, yes, so soft. I heard you the first time.'

Cassius took the bottle of wine and placed it on the far side of the table. 'That's quite enough for you.'

Indavara nodded towards the rear of the room. 'There's Octobrianus.'

'What's he doing?' asked Cassius without turning round.

'Just kissed a girl. Now coming towards us. I think he's leaving.'

'Then try to reclaim your wits, bodyguard, because in a moment so are we.'

XXVI

By the time they got outside, Octobrianus had vanished. They ran back down the street to the corner. The procurator was there, thirty yards away, swiftly retracing his steps. As they followed, Indavara stumbled off the kerb.

Cassius tutted. 'Don't tell me I'm going to have to teach you how to drink too.'

'I'm fine.'

Octobrianus turned another corner. They sped up; and had almost reached it when a large group of men appeared out of the darkness ahead. Cassius spied several well-dressed figures and numerous attendants and bodyguards behind them. Like the men in the brothel, they too were silent and seemingly intent on reaching their destination quickly.

Cassius cut right into an alley. 'Quick. In here.'

'What are you—'

'Quiet.'

Cassius turned to face the street, knelt down and untied one of his boot-laces. He was retying it as the group passed and was able to get a good look at them. He saw Ulpian's huge African bodyguard, then the general himself. Neither was in military attire. A couple of the bodyguards took a cursory glance at Cassius and Indavara but said nothing. The group turned left into a side street behind the square.

'Was that—'

'Yes,' replied Cassius. 'Ulpian and your dark friend.'

'We should hurry – Octobrianus.'

'Chances are he's going home. I'm rather more interested in

where the general and his friends might be headed at so late an hour with so great a sense of purpose. Come.'

Cassius led the way down to the side street. The men were just passing the back of the brothel, where the group from inside had already gathered. After a few hushed greetings, they all moved off together, now swollen in number to twenty or more.

'Curious,' Cassius whispered. He and Indavara had to move carefully as they followed; there was only the moonlight to guide their way, and all manner of refuse in the side street to avoid. Cassius made sure they kept their distance. There would be serious consequences for himself, Abascantius and the investigation if they were discovered following Ulpian's party.

Thankfully there wasn't far to go. After crossing two more streets that ran down to the river, the men came to a stop by a gate at the front of a high-walled villa. Cassius and Indavara got as close as they dared, then waited and watched. They heard the chime of a bell, then a few murmured comments. A lantern appeared, illuminating the gate and the faces of the twenty-six men Cassius counted filing inside. The lantern-bearer walked out on to the street, took a brief look around, then joined the others, locking the gate behind him.

'Most curious,' said Cassius. 'We shall make a circuit of the walls.'

The left side of the villa ran along the street they had just crossed. They started up the shallow slope and, about fifty feet along the wall, came to a second gate. They kept walking until they reached another large, walled villa. Unlike the first building, it was flanked by a row of high poplars.

A bark of laughter from behind them; and they turned to see two men emerge from an alley. The laughter faded quickly as the pair hurried across to the gate.

Cassius tugged on Indavara's tunic and nodded at the trees. They ducked through the stiff branches and soft leaves into cover. Once again they heard a bell ring. Cassius made his way back down the slope, rounding each tree carefully in turn. Indavara followed; and just as they came to the last poplar, a light appeared. The elongated shadows of the two new arrivals stretched back across the street.

'State the number,' said an impassive voice from behind the gate.

'7-6-9-1-3-5.'

'Enter.'

The shadows disappeared, then the light. The gate clanged shut. Indavara was already whispering the number to himself.

'Relax,' said Cassius quietly. 'I've got it.'

They tiptoed back up the street.

'So – we going in?' asked Indavara.

'We can't risk it,' replied Cassius.

'But we heard the code. They didn't even ask for names.'

'Perhaps they know their faces. Whatever's going on in there, I doubt surprise guests will be welcome.'

'I can take care of the guards,' said Indavara.

'I'm sure. But then what? We walk up to the front door and ask what's going on? And we have to get back out.'

'Let's at least try it. If you didn't want to know what's going on, you wouldn't have followed them here.'

'You seem very adventurous,' said Cassius. 'I think you're still drunk.'

'Not at all.'

'What if we do get in and something goes wrong? You can't use your dagger.'

Indavara held up his fists.

'All right,' said Cassius, 'but listen. We're going in there to find out what this lot are up to, not for you to practise cracking heads. Understood?'

Indavara nodded.

'Leave the talking to me. If we run into trouble . . . do what you do.'

Upon reaching the gate, Cassius looked through the bars and saw a faint light behind some trees. In an alcove by the gate hung a small bell on a string. He rang it. Indavara moved up next to him but Cassius gestured for him to take a pace backward.

A man carrying a lantern pushed his way through the trees, closely followed by another. They came up close to the gate and inspected the newcomers. Both had clearly been selected with intimidation in mind; they were broad six-footers with short hair and light beards. Even without the century tattoos on their forearms, Cassius would have known them for ex-legionaries.

'State the number.'

'7-6-9-1-3-5.'

One of the guards produced a key and unlocked the gate. As he opened it, the other – an older man – whispered something to him. The guard with the key stopped, the gate still only half open.

'Is the number incorrect?' Cassius asked.

'No,' said the younger man.

'Perhaps you hesitate because you haven't seen me here before.'

The guards said nothing.

'My uncle seemed to think the number would be sufficient. I thought names were not usually given here. Well, I'll be prepared to make an exception as this is my first time. Titus Rufus Ulpian. Does that help you?'

The guards looked at each other. The older man shrugged, then nodded. The younger man opened the gate and stood aside. Cassius went in first.

'Thank you.'

The branches of the trees formed a natural barrier that hid the villa from the street. The guards shut the gate, then held the branches out of the way so that Cassius and Indavara could pass through.

'The main door is that way, sir,' said the older guard, pointing along a tiled path that ran across open grass to the front of the villa.'

Cassius led the way with a purposeful march, glancing left at the dim lights inside the villa. Only when the darkness had swallowed them up again, did he come off the path and make for the corner of the building. The main gate was twenty feet away, with two more guards milling around in the glow of a powerful lantern.

Cassius leaned back against the wall. 'I can't believe they swallowed that horseshit.'

'So now what?'

'We can't go anywhere near the front. Let's double back along the villa and try to get round to the other side. Slow and careful.'

Cassius got down on his hands and knees – well below the level of the windows – and crawled across the dry, prickly grass. They heard nothing from the guards, nothing from within, and soon arrived at the rear of the building. Cassius got to his feet, wiped his hands on his tunic and looked round the corner. A single lit lantern hung over an arched doorway. Opposite it was a small outhouse with a thin wooden door secured by a chain.

Cassius slid along the brick wall. There was a plaque mounted under the lantern: *GUILD HOUSE OF THE SONS OF ANTIOCH.*

'What does it say?' whispered Indavara.

'Quiet.'

Keeping well clear of the lantern, Cassius continued past the doorway to the other side of the villa. There was no sign of any more guards or another entrance. Cloaked by the darkness, he made his way out across the turf, then turned when he had a good view of the building. Indavara arrived beside him and they stood in silence, watching events inside unfold.

Of the eight windows, only the first five were lit. The front half of the villa seemed to be one room and contained little furniture and few signs of decoration. The main gate clanged shut and more men arrived. Servants collected robes and cloaks. Cassius examined the men's faces. There were few greetings, fewer smiles.

'What did that sign say?' Indavara asked.

'This is a guild house. Remember the group at the inn on the river? A kind of club for men in the same trade. But this one is called the Sons of Antioch. Rather vague.'

'What do you mean?'

Cassius didn't answer. He realised that the servants were not just collecting robes; they were handing some out. Now lights appeared beyond the darkened windows. The men gathered, then followed two servants towards the rear of the villa, leaving the bodyguards and attendants in the big reception room. The men hurried past the sixth window, but didn't appear again at the seventh.

'Where did they go?' Indavara whispered.

'It's a one-storey building – so I think it's safe to assume down.'

'You mean underground?'

'The Sons of Antioch are an interesting group indeed. Come, let's have a look at that outhouse; there's a little light coming from it now.'

Again staying well clear of the windows and the lantern, they walked through high weeds and came to the outhouse door. On closer inspection, they saw that the chain had merely been wrapped around the latch. Cassius glanced back towards the side gate.

'Perhaps we should just leave.'

'It'll look suspicious,' replied Indavara. 'We've only just arrived.'

'All right. Take it off.'

Indavara went to work on the chain; and though he undid it carefully, Cassius winced at every slight clink of metal. Once the chain was free, Indavara eased the door open. Inside was nothing but a shadowy stone staircase that led down at right angles to the door, then turned towards the villa. Cold air drifted up, reminding Cassius of the mine.

Indavara put a hand on his dagger. 'I'll go first,' he said.

'No. I will. If anything happens – we run.'

'And the guards?'

'We're the ones trespassing. I'll say it again – no blades.'

Cassius went inside and started downward. Twelve of the narrow, slippery steps took him to the turn and there he stopped. Squatting low, he looked around the corner. Beyond the last step was a narrow passage that led to a wider corridor. Mounted on the wall of the corridor was a lighted torch. Cassius continued on to the bottom. Once there, he could hear men moving around. Someone began speaking, but the words were indistinct. Indavara came down the steps. There was barely enough space for them to stand side by side.

Cassius slowly advanced down the short passage until he could see along the corridor. To his left was an alcove piled high with firewood. To his right were two doorways on opposite sides of the corridor. One led right, into a small anteroom. To the left was a chamber of unexpectedly large dimensions, where four men could be seen. They were standing still, facing the other end of the chamber, all holding up miniature spears about eight inches long.

Indavara came up behind him and they pressed themselves against the wall next to the torch. They looked into the anteroom and saw a table covered with ornate wooden cups, plates and bowls, each adorned with carvings of snakes and birds.

'What is this place?' Indavara whispered.

Cassius didn't answer, though he now had a fairly good idea. A woody, aromatic smell drifted out of the big chamber. More talking; and he heard the four men move away. He edged up to the doorway and peered around the corner. The men were walking along a central aisle between three rows of benches. The chamber was huge: at least seventy feet long, twenty wide. On each side were seating platforms covered with cushions. The walls and the arched roof looked like rock, yet the walls outside the chamber were compacted earth. Cassius decided it must be some kind of plaster facing designed to resemble rock. Glowing braziers illuminated the yellow stars painted on the walls and the sky-blue roof. The other end of the chamber was more brightly lit; and here stood all the men – thirty at least – arranged in neat rows, facing a raised platform with steps on either side. Cassius could make out the main features of a large sculpture mounted on a central altar: a cloaked figure leaning against a bull's flank, pulling its head back as he cut its neck with a knife. He turned to Indavara and spoke in a whisper.

'Cultists – worshippers of Mithras.'

'I know the name.'

'It's a mystery religion. Secret.'

Cassius turned back, and saw that a man had appeared next to the altar. He held something up in the air then began to chant.

'Come, we can get closer now.'

Indavara looked less than enthusiastic about entering the chamber. 'What's that noise? What are they doing?'

'I don't know – it's all a lot of dressing up, code words and so on; my uncle followed it for a while. Nothing to fear. But I need to see who's here.'

Cassius checked that the men were all facing forward, then crawled beyond the doorway until he was in deep shadow behind one of the benches. Indavara followed, casting wide-eyed glances at the other end of the chamber. Cassius sat up and examined the figure by the altar. The man held up his hand once more and Cassius realised he was in fact holding a long whip.

'Welcome, Soldiers. Now, I, Runner of the Sun, call forth the Lions, so that our noble fraternity can await the Father together.'

Cassius recognised a voice he'd heard rather a lot of two days previously; and a second look at the thick black curls, round face and portly frame confirmed that the Runner of the Sun was indeed Kaeso Scaurus. He lashed his whip against the platform.

'Come forth, Lions!'

With that, men clad in red cloaks appeared from the darkness beyond the altar and filed past either side of it. Cassius spotted more familiar figures immediately: Centurion Turpo with his withered arm; then one of the gold merchants they'd spoken to. Last – and most distinctive of all – Magistrate Quarto. He had to duck as he entered the chamber and the lines of his cloak were distorted by his immense belly.

Indavara nudged Cassius.

'I know,' Cassius breathed.

Once the 'lions' had settled themselves, Scaurus took the whip in both hands and held it out in front of him.

'Now we demonstrate our respect for the Father.' He lowered himself on to one knee. The 'soldiers' and 'lions' did the same. From behind the altar came a smaller man clad in a long black cloak and a strange triangular cap. In one hand he held a bowl, in the other a staff. From his slow movements, and stooped posture, Cassius gathered he was rather old. The Father moved closer to the altar and the candles illuminated his face. At first Cassius thought he was getting carried away because of the others he'd recognised but there was no doubt about it: the Father was none other than General Ulpian.

Five familiar faces. But what did it mean?

Ulpian spoke: 'Runner of the Sun, Lions and Soldiers – stand!' He struck his staff against the platform as the others got to their feet. Scaurus moved back, and stood at the older man's shoulder.

'Hail Sol Mithras Invictus!' Ulpian cried.

'Hail! Hail! Hail!' repeated the men as one, their cries echoing around the chamber.

'Who here has passed the most mysterious and sacred of tests?'

'I! I! I!'

'Who here has been transformed, so that he may be accepted, and united as one with the men who stand beneath the ground, servants of the All Powerful Kosmokrator; He, Born of the Rock; He, Slayer of the Bull, the Almighty Sol Mithras Invictus?'

'I! I! I!'

There was an undeniable power to this rhythmical exchange; and no mistaking the fire in the men's voices. Combined with the overpowering scent of what Cassius now realised was pine smoke, and the flickering shadows created by the braziers, the very air inside the chamber seemed to crackle with some other-worldly energy.

Cassius turned round. Indavara was staring at a painting of the cult image on the opposite wall. Here, dogs and serpents licked the blood dripping from the bull's neck as Mithras slit its throat.

Ulpian continued: 'Who will stand, awed, beholding the Giver of Life as he shows us his true and everlasting power?'

'I! I! I!'

Ulpian struck his staff against the ground again. Silence. 'Who? Who has been honoured with the privilege of firing the bow?'

'I will fire the bow.'

Ulpian beckoned to a young man at the back. 'Come forth.'

Cassius and Indavara ducked down as some of the others turned to watch the 'soldier'. As he made his way to the front, Scaurus put down his whip, then disappeared behind the altar. The young man waited in front of the platform and Ulpian came down the steps to stand next to him. Scaurus returned holding a small bow which he carefully presented to the 'soldier'.

'Show us, Lord,' continued Ulpian, still facing the sculpture. 'Show us the moment when you gave life to the world! Show us the everlasting wonder of your eternal spirit!'

Ulpian and Scaurus moved out of the way as the youth raised the bow and aimed it at the sculpture.

'Show us your power, Lord! Show us!'

The men joined in, repeating the chant ever louder. 'Show us! Show us!'

Embedded in the sculpture above the bull was a stone snake's head with jaws wide open. Suddenly water began to flow from the snake's mouth.

Indavara gave a sharp intake of breath as the eyes of Mithras himself seemed suddenly alight. They turned yellow, then orange. Indavara turned towards the doorway.

Cassius gripped his arm. 'Don't even think about it,' he hissed. 'It's just a trick. Lit coals, nothing more.'

But when Cassius looked back at the altar, the way the fiery light seemed to shine out into every corner of the chamber made him doubt himself; and for a moment he felt certain they would be discovered. Indavara stayed where he was but Cassius could feel his arm shaking.

'Is he here?' Ulpian asked in a low, breathy voice that nonetheless reached the back of the chamber.

'He is here!' answered the men. The eyes grew brighter than the candles around them. A dazzling, fiery red.

Indavara wrenched his arm free and scrambled to the doorway, inadvertently striking a bench. The bench knocked against a brazier and several coals fell to the floor. The men in the back row turned round.

'Look there!' shouted one.

Cassius hauled himself to his feet and sprinted away. Shouts were already echoing around the chamber.

'You bloody idiot!' he yelled, finding Indavara standing in the corridor, staring blankly back at the cavern. 'Go! Go!'

Cassius pushed him towards the staircase and rushed after him. He slipped on one of the steps, banging a knee against the unforgiving stone, then used his hands to propel himself upwards. He could hear men close behind as he scrambled up the last step.

Thankfully, Indavara seemed to have recovered his senses. As Cassius darted out of the outhouse, he shut the door behind him. Picking up the chain, he ran it through the latch and tied it into a knot. The door rattled as someone tried to pull it open.

They ran across the darkened lawn towards the gate.

'Leave this to me,' Cassius said, slowing down as the guards came forward.

'Ah,' he said, trying to sound normal. 'Would you be so kind as to—'

Shouts rang out from behind them: 'Guards! The side gate! Stop them!'

Indavara barged past Cassius just as the closest guard reached for his sword. Without a moment's hesitation he chopped a hand up into the taller man's windpipe. The guard dropped the lantern in his hand, then fell next to it, choking noisily.

Indavara was already closing on the second man but the ex-legionary had drawn his blade quickly. Cassius managed a half-hearted attempt to grab the guard's other arm as he swung at Indavara. The sword hadn't travelled far when Indavara clamped both hands around the guard's wrist. He drove a knee up into the man's gut then twisted round, trying to wrench the blade free, but his foe somehow held on. As they struggled, Indavara nodded at the fallen man.

'Get the key!'

The first guard was on his knees, hands clutching his neck. The lantern was still alight and Cassius could see the key on a ring attached to his belt. He grabbed for it but the guard swatted his arm away and pulled out his sword.

Cassius went for his dagger but his hand never made it there. *No blades.* He'd said it himself. He couldn't kill this man.

The guard – holding himself up with one hand on the ground – swung his sword in a wide arc. Cassius leapt backwards, and was still trying to think of a way to get the key when Indavara – dragging the second man along with him – landed a hefty kick on the back of the guard's head. The blow sent the man face first into the grass at Cassius's feet.

'Get the bloody key!'

The guard was still. Cassius knelt down and reached for the key. He could see men rushing out of the front of the villa, guards with lanterns leading the way.

Indavara decided he would let the man keep his sword. He freed his right arm and drove his elbow back into his foe's face. Catching him between the eyes, he sent him several yards backwards and into a tree. The guard slid down between the branches: unconscious, but still gripping his sword.

Cassius tore the key ring off the belt and ran through the trees, closely followed by Indavara. He found the lock with his fingers, slid the key in and turned it. Together they wrenched open the gate and bundled through on to the street. Cassius set off and had already reached the trees when Indavara turned back and shut the gate.

'What are you doing?' Cassius bawled.

Indavara reached through the bars and grabbed the key ring. He tugged on it hard, snapping the key close to the lock. Two guards charged through the trees. Skidding to a halt at the gate, they reached through the bars, flailing hands missing Indavara by inches as he turned and bolted away.

There were already more men coming round the corner from the main entrance as Cassius and Indavara sped past the poplars. Grateful he was without his sword, Cassius set a fearsome pace, driven on by pure terror. After what Indavara had done to the guards, he knew retribution would be violent and swift if they were caught. He had nothing with him to confirm his identity; and they had violated the inner sanctum of a secret cult whose leader was one of the most powerful men in Antioch.

'I can't believe you're in the army,' Indavara yelled.

'Shut up and run!'

The streets were quiet; and Cassius knew their pounding footfalls and the cries of their pursuers would soon draw attention. He hoped there were no city sergeants close by.

With his long stride and rangy frame, he'd always been a strong runner, but he was surprised to see the stocky bodyguard match him as they charged along street after street. They headed east, and soon came to the old walls. Cassius slowed. He could hear shouting; but the guards and whoever else had joined them were still some distance away.

'We mustn't get trapped against the walls,' he said. 'This way.'

He jogged up a curved road they'd been on that very morning while with Bacara. It passed through a gap in the walls and intersected a street parallel to the Avenue of Herod and Tiberius.

They came to a convoy of empty carts emerging from a courtyard and heading up to the avenue. Cassius hurried over to the last cart as it turned on to the road. He hailed the man holding the reins, who brought the vehicle to a stop. Next to him was a lad with an oil lamp on his lap.

'Which way are you going?' Cassius demanded.

'What's it to you?'

Cassius might have sworn at the man had he not needed his cooperation. He took out two denarii and held them next to the lamp.

'I'm in need of some transportation. No questions asked.'

'We're heading out of the city. Beroea Gate.'

'Drop us off at the Parmenios River?'

The driver nodded. Shouts sounded from the other side of the walls.

'They after you?'

Cassius added two more denarii. The lad stared at him in amazement. The driver scooped up the coins.

'Get in. Lucius, chuck them that cover.'

By the time Cassius and Indavara had hurried round to the back and climbed into the cart, the lad had unfolded a thick square of leather. They grabbed it as the driver got the vehicle under way. The wooden timbers of the cart were filthy with mud but they lay down and pulled the cover over them. Indavara was breathing hard.

'You're labouring, bodyguard.'

'You're quick. Handy – considering the way you fight.'

'Shut up.'

'You're *really* in the army?'

'I said shut up.'

XXVII

Abascantius was busy with other visitors when they arrived the next morning.

The cart-driver had been true to his word and dropped them off at the river; and from there they'd made their way back to the villa where a very concerned Simo let them in. After collapsing into bed, they were woken just three hours later by the Gaul, who had orders from Cassius to do so. He had to see Abascantius without delay.

As they waited in the atrium, two stern young men in togas strode in from the courtyard. Fixing Cassius and Indavara with contemptuous glares, they hurried past them and out the front door. Abascantius came inside. His face was red.

'Governor Gordio's men,' he explained. 'Warning me off. The operatives I had watching his villa were discovered.'

He waved at the couches. 'It does seem, however, that we can strike him from our list.'

'Sir?' Cassius enquired as they sat down.

'I suppose I should have remembered, but it was so long ago. During the last Persian invasion – what was it, ten, eleven years ago – Shapur took hundreds of hostages back with him, anyone he found interesting or thought might be useful. One of them was the governor's brother: an engineer – very talented man. I imagine Gordio had long ago given him up for dead. But with the change of regime, some of these people are being allowed back. This mysterious Persian visitor is a friend of the brother. It seems he might be able to arrange his return.'

'Ah,' said Cassius.

Abascantius nodded. 'But we must tread even more carefully

now. The governor is in a rather emotional state. At least they assumed I was simply monitoring things for the Emperor. Gods – if they knew the real reason.'

Cassius wasn't exactly sure how Abascantius might view the events of the previous evening, but doubted he would characterise them as 'treading carefully'.

'Did you learn anything useful last night?'

'I believe so, sir, yes. But not about Octobrianus.'

As Cassius described what had happened, he once more found himself observing the changing expressions on Abascantius's face. The agent's eyes grew wide as he heard about Cassius's gambit to get them inside the guild house, and when it came to their escape and the fight with the guards, his brow set into a stony frown.

'You fool,' he said when Cassius had finished. 'You young fool.'

'But, sir, we have learned something of great use—'

'What? What have we learned?'

'Ulpian is presiding over a secret sect, the members of which are perfectly placed to transport and sell a large amount of gold and silver secretly. As I said, there was this merchant, then Centurion Turpo to help get it in and out of the city, and Scaurus, and Quarto to ensure—'

'You speak as if I know nothing of this. Half the army follow Mithras and a good proportion of the wealthy and influential men of this city belong to the Sons of Antioch. I'll admit I'd thought it was no more than a trade guild, not a cover for a sect, but these meetings have probably been going on for years.'

'But why so secretive, sir?'

'All Mithran sects are secretive!' Abascantius dropped a fist on to the couch, then sighed and shook his head. 'All right – they may well be up to no good. But I cannot concern myself with that now. This Nabor had a material connection to what we seek; and Octobrianus is the one linked with Nabor, not Ulpian. You were supposed to stay with him.'

'He was going home, sir, I'm sure of it.'

'Well, we'll never know now, will we?'

Abascantius propelled himself to his feet with surprising agility. He ran a thumb and finger down the sides of his mouth.

'And masquerading as the general's nephew? By the gods.'

Cassius looked down at the floor.

'He did actually have a nephew by the way,' Abascantius continued. 'Was very fond of him. Boy died of the plague.'

Though he blanched when he heard this, Cassius thought it rather obtuse of Abascantius not to acknowledge what an admirable piece of quick thinking that had been.

'We're lucky Quarto's men aren't at the door right now,' added the agent.

'It was very dark, sir,' Cassius replied. 'I don't think anyone got a good look at us.'

'Oh, you better hope not,' snapped Abascantius. 'Because you're a pretty memorable pair: a one-eared hard-arse and a well-groomed beanpole who looks like he should still be in school. And Quarto has met you! Some of the others too. Gods, Corbulo, you were supposed to help me solve this problem, not create a new one.'

Abascantius suddenly pointed at Shostra, who was lurking in a corner. 'Do you know nothing of my mood after all these years? Wine – at once!'

Cassius glanced at Indavara, who shrugged. At that moment, Cassius could quite happily have broken one of Abascantius's vases over the bodyguard's head. He summoned some courage.

'Sir, I'm not sure it's entirely fair I take all the blame. If Indavara here wasn't so damned credulous, we might have got out without a fuss. A few conjuror's tricks and he was shaking like a baby.'

Abascantius walked around the table between the couches and stood over Cassius. He jabbed a finger at Indavara.

'He gets paid to fight. And it sounds like he did it damn well as usual. You get paid to make decisions. You made a bad one when you elected to follow those men, a very bad one when you elected to go through that gate and an appalling one when you went down into that cave.'

Cassius's face had grown hot. He could accept that he'd been unwise but he was convinced that what they'd discovered was significant.

'Sir, I apologise. But I really think we should turn our attention to the general, to Quarto even. He did nothing to help us investigate Nabor, after all.'

Abascantius snatched the large glass of wine from Shostra and took a long swig before replying.

'Why would he? I already told you we can expect nothing from him. No – we stay with Octobrianus. We'll keep on him night and day. He'll slip up sooner or later.'

'But the general, sir. Ulpian fought the Persians. Surely that's motive enough to disrupt the treaty. The army – or sections of it – might not wish to see this peace.'

'And Octobrianus – a man I know has betrayed the Empire before?'

'His villa is small, modest. He dresses as if he were still a tax collector. He doesn't strike me as the type to organise a robbery.'

'And what if he's still acting for the Palmyrans? This is an investigation, Corbulo. We follow the evidence. The evidence points to Octobrianus.'

Abascantius paced around the room, sipping his wine.

'What would you like me to do now, sir?' Cassius asked after a while.

'At this particular moment, I couldn't care less. Just stay out of my sight. And stay away from here. The less contact we have, the better.'

'Sir, I could at least go back to the records office. Look through the files for this two-fingered man.'

'You can't get in too much trouble there, I suppose. If I need you, I'll get in touch. But I meant what I said, Corbulo. If those guards did get a good look at you, these people won't take long to find you. Stay sharp and stay together.'

Cassius lasted four streets before his frustration got the better of him.

'Congratulations, I thought you managed to come out of that rather well. It seems a policy of silence can be very effective at times.'

Indavara shrugged. 'Like he said, I'm just a bodyguard.'

'Indeed you are. I've yet to see a single other string to your bow.'

'What's that supposed to mean?'

Cassius stopped. 'Listen – in five days this whole affair will be settled one way or the other. You will be a free man, and I will probably be off to Thessalonica to take up my post as prison governor.'

'What?'

'Personally, I would be quite happy for us to go our separate ways right now – I expect you feel the same – but the truth is I could be in real danger after last night. So let's just see out these few days. We don't even have to talk to each other, just do our respective jobs and hope to Hades we get out of this city alive. I think I can tolerate your company for that long. Can you tolerate mine?'

Indavara nodded.

'That's settled then.'

They continued on towards the villa.

'What did you mean before?' Indavara asked after a few moments. 'Conjuror's tricks?'

'At the Mithraeum last night. What you believed to be manifestations, signs of the god – the water and the glowing eyes.'

'Yes?'

'They were tricks. The eyes were no more than lit coals, like I said. Probably put there by the same man who poured the water from the snake's mouth.'

'What man?'

'Hiding behind the altar.'

Indavara shook his head. 'It was their god. They asked him for a sign and he showed them – the water came.'

320

'It's not intended to be interpreted literally. They don't really believe it's Mithras himself. It's more like a . . . recreation.'

'They don't believe it? Then why were they there?'

Cassius threw up his hands. 'All right – it was Mithras! What do I know?'

Indavara didn't speak again until they were close to the villa.

'So you think Abascantius is wrong about Octobrianus?'

'Not necessarily, but I fear his determination to nail the procurator has blinded him to other possibilities. Between them, Ulpian and Quarto control just about every armed man in the city, and with this handy little cult they have all the contacts they'd need.'

'So we're going to the basilica?'

'Soon. First the baths. I need to think.'

Simo was off visiting Elder Nura – to tell him what they'd seen at the prison – but he'd already given Cassius directions to the Baths of Julius Caesar. They were just a quarter of a mile from the villa, further up the slopes of Mount Silpius.

Knowing they would be busier in the afternoon, Cassius was pleased to find the baths quiet. Passing through the colonnaded entrance, they entered a narrow but high-roofed reception room. The only people there were a woman at a table and a team of artisans working on a mosaic of Caesar. Cassius paid the woman. She aimed a thumb over her shoulder at the door behind her.

The baths were relatively small, with no facilities for women, so there was only one dressing room. Inside were benches and shelves where patrons could leave their clothes. There were two doors, one straight ahead labelled *WARM ROOM*, the other to the left, labelled *COLD POOL.* The only occupant was a scrawny old man who had just pulled his tunic off over his head. He nodded at the new arrivals.

'Good-day.'

'Good-day,' replied Cassius.

The old man pulled a face. 'Not even a slave to look after our clothes.'

'Too early, I suppose.'

'Probably just as well. Thieving bastards every one.'

The old man opened the door to the warm room. Steam swirled in before he shut it behind him. Cassius put down the bag Simo had left for him. Inside were his bath oils and two towels. Normally he wouldn't have permitted the humiliation of having to look after himself, but it seemed only right that the Christians should hear how their imprisoned fellows were faring – even if the news wasn't good. He hadn't yet asked what Simo had said to his father, but he feared the Gaul had ignored his advice.

Cassius sat down and quickly untied his boots. He couldn't wait to get in the water. In Cyzicus it had been rare for him to spend less than an hour a day at the local baths. It wasn't just the pleasure of cleaning off the dirt and smell of the city, it was the whole experience. A good bath gave one's body a chance to recuperate, one's mind a chance to relax; and he was in dire need of both.

Indavara was still standing by the door.

'Not getting undressed?'

'I thought I was standing guard.'

'You are. But you can't walk around inside there clothed. It's simply not done. You can use one of my towels to dry off later.'

Indavara looked uncertain.

'Another new experience?'

'We were allowed to bathe sometimes. But it wasn't like this.'

Not for the first time, Cassius felt sorry for him. He was so capable and powerful in the physical realm, yet so ignorant of the ways of the world. It was a curious combination.

'Well, last night's new experience with the girls worked out well, didn't it? You might find you enjoy this too.'

Indavara shrugged and removed his boots.

Cassius took off his belt, then his tunic. Now naked, he put his bag, boots and clothes on one of the shelves. Feeling chilly, he rubbed his shoulders.

'Come on, I want to get into that warm room.'

'Go ahead then,' replied Indavara as he unbuckled his belt.

Cassius shook his head. 'You may not like it and I certainly don't like it, but I want you no more than five yards from me at any time over the next few days.'

Indavara removed his main belt and his sword belt and placed them with his boots on another shelf. Then he took off his tunic.

Cassius looked at him. He really was an impressive specimen, but any appreciation of his condition was forgotten when Cassius saw the marks upon him. He had noticed the brand before, and all the scars on his foreams and legs, but now he saw the full extent of the damage Indavara's young body had sustained. Between his shoulder blades were three identical red circles. And below this, line after line of welts; scar upon scar.

'By Mars, you've been through it.'

Indavara turned to him. 'What?'

Cassius pointed at his back. 'They whipped you.'

Indavara said nothing.

'As if it's not enough to make a man fight for his life.'

Indavara nodded at the door behind Cassius. 'I thought you were cold.'

The warm room was on the small side, but Cassius adjudged the temperature to be about right. The furnace would be directly beneath the next chamber – the hot room – but some of that heat was redirected to the warm room, radiating up through the floor and out through the walls, preparing the patrons' bodies for the high temperatures to come.

The walls had faded from red to pink and there were some damaged mosaics on the floor. Only the ceiling retained its original grandeur, with ornate leaf and flower patterns swirling around the four high windows.

Already inside were the old fellow – who was sitting on a bench – and a large man lying face down on a table, attended by a trio of slaves. Two were oiling and scraping his broad back, while the third read a letter to him.

'So now what?' queried Indavara as they sat down on the bench.

'We wait, warm up a little, then it's the hot room.'

'We just sit?'

'No. Usually I would be being oiled but as my attendant spends more time dealing with his own problems these days, I shall have to just sit, yes.'

'Pretty boring.'

'Even more so if some fool is engaging you in mindless conversation. Hush, I came here to think.'

Indavara rolled his eyes and stared down at the nearest mosaic. The big man began dictating his reply to the letter. It sounded like he was some kind of architect. Cassius tried to turn his thoughts to the investigation but he was soon distracted: the architect could barely string a sentence together yet insisted on ignoring his slave's literary advice. 'As you wish, sir,' the slave would say every time his master overruled him. On the eighth 'As you wish, sir,' Cassius stood up.

'Come on.'

They passed through the open doorway into the hot room. Back home there would usually have been an adjoining exercise area, but Cassius knew from his time in Cyzicus that the eastern provincials did things their own way. He wasn't overly concerned, having never particularly embraced the habit of exercising before a bath anyway. He did, however, hope the cold pool was big enough for a good swim.

'Ah, yes,' he said, enjoying the soothing heat rising up from the floor and out from the hollow walls. Dead ahead was a high, round basin full of steaming water. From here, the chamber led to their left, down a set of wide steps to the hot pool. Sitting on the steps was a slight, middle-aged fellow missing both legs below the knee. His slave, a powerfully built young man with the colouring of an Egyptian, sat beside him.

As Cassius made his way past them down into the water,

another man came into the chamber. He had a wild head of hair and was clad in the roughly cut tunic of a slave. The invalid called to him but he disappeared towards the cold room.

'Useless. Bloody useless.'

Cassius acknowledged this with a brief nod, then lowered himself into the water up to his neck. He didn't want to get involved in a conversation but couldn't resist the pool. He closed his eyes as the heat enveloped him, then dunked his head under. As he re-emerged and ran his hands through his hair, the man was already talking.

'. . . thirteen functioning bathhouses in Antioch. The eight best are on the island and of the remaining five, only one is worse than this place. I use it because it's close.' The man nodded down at the stumps of his legs. 'I have to consider these things now.'

As there seemed little chance of avoiding talking to him, Cassius replied.

'It happened recently?'

'Last year. I was out at Daphne. A snake startled my horse, we fell into a ditch and the damned thing landed on top of me. They both had to come off. At least I have my wealth. A poor man couldn't afford a slave to carry him around all day.' He offered his hand. Cassius swam around his big attendant and shook it.

'Titus Plotius Otho.'

'Cassius Oranius Crispian. Are you a local man, Otho?'

'Well, I came here as a youth but that was nigh on forty years ago now, so yes, I suppose I qualify.'

Indavara was still back at the basin, washing his face. Cassius splashed water on to his shoulders. He decided the conversation need not be a complete waste of time.

'So you know a little of city society?'

'Not as much as I used to,' Otho said sadly. 'But yes, a bit.'

'This may seem rather forward, but I am in need of advice. I'm new here. It would be useful to hear the view of a longtime resident. A rather sensitive matter.'

'Speak, friend.' Otho nodded at the slave, who was gazing

thoughtfully down at the water. 'My lad knows not to repeat a word of what he hears.'

'I am in the army, attached to the governor's staff. It's been communicated to me – via several sources – that if I wish to advance myself while here in Antioch, it would be to my advantage to join one of the local Mithran sects.'

'Indeed? Well, these sources might be right. Do you object to such a prospect?'

'Not at all. It has always seemed to me to be a most worthy religion.'

'You are pledged to other gods, then?'

'No, it's not that either. It's just that this particular sect seem very secretive. They almost seem to enjoy creating an air of mystery around themselves.'

Otho nodded gently, then glanced at Indavara, who had just sat down on the far side of the steps, with only his feet in the water. 'This fellow is trustworthy too?'

'Absolutely.'

Otho glanced over his shoulder to check they were still alone. 'You are talking about the Sons of Antioch.'

Cassius nodded. 'Do you think it would be worth joining?'

'Oh, I should say so. From what I've heard, the ceremonies get shorter every year, and the trade talk gets longer. Perhaps that's what comes of pretending to be no more than a guild – a self-fulfilling prophesy. There's certainly no shortage of esteemed members. You know who their leader is?'

'I do.'

'Not a young man.' Otho smiled. 'When he steps down, they may do away with the religious stuff entirely.'

'He is – for want of a better expression – a true believer then?'

'From what I've heard, yes. It may be that he has enjoyed the benefits of such an organisation over the years, but I think he was the founder, or at least one of them.'

Cassius nodded. 'Interesting. You never considered it?'

'No. My mother was a Jew – she would never have forgiven me. And frankly, I'm not sure I would have got through the initiation. But you must make up your own mind, young man. Did I help at all?'

'Indeed. Thank you.'

In fact, Otho's information had done little to clarify things. The general was thought to be truly devout, yet the Sons of Antioch had become more like a guild under his leadership. Had someone exploited their contacts within the organisation to carry out the theft? Ulpian himself? Quarto? Both of them? Someone else? And was the fact that these men associated in this way even significant? Abascantius clearly didn't think so.

Cassius was occupied by these questions while he exchanged small talk with Otho. As they spoke, he began a leisurely breast stroke that took him in circles around the pool. The old man came into the hot room and joined them. Otho knew him and introduced to him to Cassius: Tiburs was his name, and the two Antiochenes soon launched into a long-winded conversation about the respective merits of the city's chariot-racing teams.

Despite Cassius's entreaties, Indavara refused to put anything above knee height in the pool. Cassius could never understand people who didn't like the water, but he knew it was common among the lower classes. He left the pool and went to stand in the middle of the room, directly over the furnace; he wanted to build up a good sweat before finishing off in the cold room.

When Tiburs announced he was moving on to the last chamber, Cassius and Indavara joined him. Otho said he'd be along presently. Just as they left, a powerfully built, square-jawed man with a head of thinning black hair strode in. With a cursory glance at the others, he went to the basin.

Cassius cursed Simo for forgetting to pack his sandals. His feet – wet with water and sweat – slipped on the stone floor as he walked through a short passageway into the cold room. They had come around in a circle, or rather a square, and to their left was the door leading to the dressing room.

The cold room was three times larger than the other chambers, and far more impressive. Octagonal in shape, it was well lit by four glassed windows in the high roof. The far wall was lined with wooden shutters to help regulate the temperature and today these were open. Outside was a dense line of trees.

The circular pool dominated the space: it was twenty feet wide, with steps all the way around. The water was slightly cloudy, but considering the season, Cassius was just relieved there was enough to fill it.

Tiburs hesitantly negotiated the steps.

'I'm hungry,' said Indavara.

'You're always hungry. We're too early for the vendors.'

'It's cold.'

'Any more complaints, Grandma? It's supposed to be cold. If it wasn't, then one couldn't do this.'

Cassius took two steps forward and dived into the pool. He felt himself smile as the icy shock lit up his skin. He stayed under and a few long strokes propelled him to the other side. He surfaced, pushed off the cool stone and paddled around in the centre. The sides of the pool sloped steeply; he couldn't touch the bottom.

Indavara sat down on the highest step. He dipped his toe into the water, then swiftly removed it. Cassius grinned, and began swimming back and forth across the pool. Though he could barely get up to a good speed before having to turn around, he felt calmer than he had in days. The last few weeks aside, he generally enjoyed riding (running too, in the right circumstances) but swimming was his preferred form of exercise. It always seemed to clear his mind; and he hoped he might gain some some fresh insight on the investigation.

After ten swift widths, he stopped and noted two new arrivals in the room. The square-jawed man was just stepping down into the pool and the wild-haired slave had returned too; he was standing by the door to the dressing room, hands behind his back.

Tiburs, standing waist-deep on one of the steps, yelled at him. 'Hey! Master Otho called out to you and you ignored him. Get in there and see if he requires some assistance.'

The slave hurried into the hot room.

Square Jaw dived gracefully into the water.

'You know him?' Cassius asked Tiburs while the stranger was still under water.

'Never seen him before. Strapping fellow.'

'Indeed.'

Indavara stood up. 'I'm going to get changed.'

Cassius gestured for him to wait a moment. He lowered his voice. 'Just keep me in sight. Understand?'

Indavara nodded and walked away towards the dressing room. Now Tiburs climbed up out of the pool.

'A pleasure, sir. Enjoy the rest of your swim.'

'You're leaving already?'

'I can't take too much cold at my age. Good-day to you.'

'Good-day.'

Cassius looked over the lip of the pool at the dressing room. Indavara was standing in the doorway, drying his hair with a towel. Cassius turned round. Square Jaw was powering smoothly around the pool. The wild-haired slave reappeared. He had a net in his hands and started fishing out the leaves that had blown into the pool from the trees outside.

Cassius leaned back against the steps and stared down into the water. He tried to gather his thoughts but found he still couldn't concentrate. Square Jaw had stopped opposite him. He flexed his shoulders, then pushed off and glided across the pool, his dark eyes just above the water, fixed on Cassius.

Cassius raised one foot on to a higher step, ready to move if he had to.

With a flick of his feet, Square Jaw altered direction. He waited until his fingers struck the edge of the pool, then climbed up the steps.

'Good-day,' he said cordially.

'Good-day,' Cassius replied, watching him walk away. Indavara was still at the doorway. Cassius shook his head. He was letting his imagination run riot; he needed to keep swimming.

Circling the pool, he concentrated on keeping his movements fluid, his breathing even. The slave was now reaching one-handed with the net to retrieve the leaves in the middle of the pool but he made sure he kept out of the way.

Cassius decided he would complete ten circuits; and with that established he went over the events that had occurred since their arrival in Antioch, starting with that busy first day. He was so busy recalling every incident that he barely noticed the net until he almost swam into it. He slowed, then stopped, treading water.

The slave just stood there at the edge of the pool. He was a strange-looking man; as well as the straggly thatch of hair, he had a heavily lined face that didn't fit with his athletic frame. And now he was smiling. Cassius was about to ask him what in Hades was so funny when his gaze dropped to the pole. The right hand gripping it was missing a thumb and two fingers.

Before Cassius could shout or move, the man flicked the net over his head. He was dragged forward, then momentarily driven under the water. When he surfaced, Two Fingers pulled in the loose material of the net and twisted the pole, tightening the rough ropes of the net around Cassius's face and neck. Then he drove the pole down again.

Cassius tried to grab a breath, but he took in more water than air as his head was forced under. Flailing at the pole, he shut his mouth and scrabbled desperately with his feet. His toes scraped against the bottom of the pool. He kicked out and managed to break the surface for long enough to snatch another breath. Two Fingers pushed him under again.

Where is Indavara?

Cassius finally got hold of the pole, but his foe was keeping him out in the middle, and without purchase for his feet he could bring no force to bear. He thrashed his legs, trying to move back and pull the man off balance. Through the foaming water he saw Two Fingers come down another step. His arms were taut with the strain, his face set in a pitiless grimace.

Cassius clawed at the rope itself, trying to free his neck.

Where is Indavara?

Two Fingers shook the pole. Cassius didn't know if he was trying to throttle him or force his mouth open. He clamped his mouth tighter and bit into his lip. Tasting blood, he tried to touch the bottom again but if anything he was further out now.

He was just floating. Struggling. Dying.

Indavara!

The assassin came down another step; pushed Cassius further out, further under. He shook the pole again. The rope was crushing Cassius's nose and snagging on his bottom lip. Icy water rushed into his mouth. He tried not to swallow but his entire body was being wrenched from side to side. The water was bitter in his throat. Suddenly he had to get it out. Though he was a foot below the surface, and he knew what it meant, all he could think of was getting it out.

Don't open your mouth! Don't open your mouth!

He stopped thrashing around. The shimmering light from the windows above the pool had merged into a single yellow glow. It looked warm. Inviting.

Indavara – who had taken only moments to change into his tunic and pull on his belt – returned to the doorway just as Otho's Egyptian slave slammed into the wild-haired man holding the net. He dropped the pole and was knocked flying, landing a full ten feet away before sliding across the floor and into one of the shutters.

The Egyptian was all set to chase after him when his master – lying prostrate on the floor – yelled at him and pointed at the pool.

The wild-haired man struggled to his feet, then stumbled away – through the open shutters and between two trees.

Indavara ran across the cold room as the Egyptian splashed down the steps and into the pool.

Darkness faded from Cassius's eyes, and he found himself staring at square, red tiles. Sharp pain surged through his chest as he coughed up what felt like a barrel full of water. The ropes of the net were pulled from his face. Two strong hands gripped him under the arms and hauled him out of the water. His chest burned again as he was lowered face down on to the steps.

'Hit him. Hit his back!' shouted a voice. One of the hands struck him. More pain. But not from the hand; from the water that continued to pour out of him. It felt like his entire throat and chest had been cut with glass.

Finally he looked up; and saw Otho lying at the side of the pool. Behind him - standing still and staring open-mouthed at Cassius - was Indavara.

XXVIII

Cassius awoke. He was lying in his bed at the villa, propped up on two pillows, covered by a single sheet. The room was empty, the villa quiet. He gazed at the opposite wall, determined to stay awake and dispel the images that had forced themselves upon him as he lay there, slipping in and out of consciousness.

The grim face of the two-fingered man as he went about his deadly work.

Water bubbling around him, pouring into him.

The tempting light above.

The moments. That's how Cassius thought of them.

These were the new ones; the ones he was condemned to relive and live with. There were others, and he knew they would never truly be gone, though these days they returned with less frequency.

A lone legionary hacked to pieces by a dark warrior in a purple cloak. That same warrior marching towards Cassius, cloak billowing behind him as he raised his sword . . .

Stay awake!

Cassius sat up. He coughed, and felt a stab of pain in his throat. He touched his neck, and the bandage wrapped around it. He remembered Simo putting it on just after he had fallen through the door and into the Gaul's arms.

It had taken quite some time to recover himself at the baths. He had thanked Otho, refused his offer to send for the city sergeants, then returned to the dressing room. Indavara had trailed after him, apologising again and again for his error. Cassius had ignored him as he'd hurried back to the villa, coughing and retching every step of the way.

'How are you feeling now, sir?' asked Simo as he walked in.

'Are the doors all locked? Did you check outside?'

'Indavara is out there, sir.'

Cassius snorted dismissively.

Simo continued: 'He asked me to tell him when you woke up, sir. He—'

'Simo, I told you already. I don't want to see him. Keep him away. What about Abascantius?'

'No reply yet, sir.'

'How long's it been since I got back?'

'About four hours, sir.'

'He obviously has more pressing matters to attend to.'

Simo checked the bandage. 'Is this too tight, sir?'

'It's fine. How bad?'

'The skin was still tender from what happened at Palmyra and there's a couple of nasty cuts, but nothing too serious.'

Simo sat on the side of the bed, and put his hand on Cassius's arm.

'You've had a terrible shock though.'

'The latest in an increasingly long line.' Cassius felt tears forming in his eyes. He coughed again and pulled his arm away.

'A drink perhaps, sir,' suggested Simo. 'Water?'

Cassius glared at him.

'Ah. Sorry, sir.'

'Do we have any milk? It might be easier on my throat.'

'We do, sir. I shall fetch it at once.'

Simo rose and headed for the door. He stopped when Cassius called out to him.

'Wait. Pass me my figurines. They're in that little hardwood box.' Cassius nodded at the shelf where Simo had placed his belongings. The Gaul gave him the box then went for the milk. Cassius opened the lid and pulled it closer so he could look at the twelve tiny models mounted on two racks inside. Each represented one of the Olympians, the great gods: Jupiter, Juno, Mars, Venus, Apollo, Diane, Ceres, Vesta, Mercury, Neptune, Minerva and Vulcan. Dust had somehow got inside the box. Cassius brushed it off the faces.

He couldn't recall the last time he'd looked at them. His mother had given him the box on his tenth birthday and made him promise he would keep it for ever. When he'd left for Syria, she'd said she would feel happier knowing he had the great gods with him, to watch over him so far from home. In the last letter she had written to him in Cyzicus she'd asked if he'd set up a proper shrine and displayed the figurines there. He lied and said he had, intending to do so; but then another letter arrived – this one from Syria – and there had been no time.

It was the classic mark of the fickle worshipper to turn to the gods when dangerous or difficult situations arose but Cassius felt he had to. Somebody wanted him dead. If he was to survive, he would need all the help he could get, especially as he clearly couldn't rely on Indavara. Cassius replaced the figurines in the box as Simo returned. He would offer a prayer later, when he was alone.

'Master Abascantius is here, sir,' Simo said as he handed Cassius the glass of milk.

The agent appeared at the doorway with Shostra, Major and Indavara in tow.

'Leave us,' said Abascantius. 'All of you.'

Simo and the others departed. Abascantius grabbed a chair, carried it over to the bed and sat down.

'You look better than I thought you would.'

'I wish I could say I felt it, sir. I suppose you want to know what happened.'

'Actually I just got the basics from Indavara.'

'Ah yes – my "bodyguard".'

'He was only gone for a few moments.'

'A rather important few moments from my perspective. Looks like you were right, sir. Clearly somebody did identify us last night. And it seems the Sons of Antioch do not respond well to unauthorised visitations.'

Abascantius tilted his head to one side. 'It might have been them, I suppose. But they would want to know who you were, what you were doing there. And if they did want to kill you – which I doubt – they wouldn't make such an amateurish attempt.'

'It felt pretty professional to me.'

'But if Ulpian knows your identity, why not simply have Quarto arrest you? Or come to me?'

'No reason. Unless he wishes to avoid official involvement entirely.'

Abascantius didn't look convinced. 'All we know is that this two-fingered piece of shit killed Gregorius and now he's tried to kill you.'

'Which someone ordered just hours after what happened at the guild house.'

'But what if he's been on to you for a while? What if your trip to the baths just provided a useful opportunity?'

Cassius drank the milk. It hurt less than he thought it would. 'Have you made any more progress, sir?'

'Two more of Octobrianus's ex-employees have gone missing recently. Perhaps they also took their share and disappeared. Or, like Nabor, became more trouble than they were worth. We're also trying to turn one of the clerks from the procurator's office; he's been with Octobrianus for years, does most of his paperwork, probably knows him better than anyone.'

'Sir, what if I could find a link between Ulpian and Two Fingers?'

Abascantius gave a crooked grin. 'You still think I'm wrong, don't you?'

Cassius sat higher in the bed. 'You did tell me I should keep an open mind, sir. If Two Fingers was a legionary, maybe he served with the general. Which legion was Ulpian with before becoming prefect of the garrison?'

'He was cavalry commander of the Sixteenth.'

'I'll go back to the records office.'

'You're happy to risk the streets, even after this morning?'

'Far from it, sir. But I should be all right at the basilica. In any case, it now seems I will be unable to consider myself safe until we resolve this affair.'

Abascantius stood up. 'Best get used to that feeling. I've spent the best part of two decades worrying who might be creeping up behind me.'

A chill ran down Cassius's spine when he heard that, yet it

hardened his resolve. He pushed the sheet away and reached for the clean tunic Simo had left at the end of the bed. Abascantius wandered over to the window and looked up at the sky.

'If we can't recover the banner before Marcellinus returns then I shall simply have to go to him and tell the truth. Gods, what a mess.'

Cassius pulled on the tunic.

'Then there's no time to waste, sir.'

'Good lad. But you should take a carriage. And keep Indavara on a lead.'

Cassius shook his head. 'Sir, I don't want him anywhere near me. Can't you find someone else? Someone reliable? I'll pay whatever it costs. I've done all you've asked of me, and I shall continue to do so. But I'll not put my life in his hands again.'

Abascantius sighed as he turned from the window. 'I've hardly the time for this.'

'I know, sir, and I'm sorry.' Cassius buckled his belt. 'But I almost died in that pool today.'

'I have a solution. Major is outside. We shall swap. He can accompany you and I shall take Indavara off your hands.'

'He's good?'

'Getting on a bit but as street-smart as they come.'

'Perfect,' Cassius replied as he attached his dagger to his belt.

'I shall be in touch later,' said Abascantius. 'And I'll get the word out about Two Fingers now we know he's in the city. Doesn't ring a bell with me but someone might know of him.' Abascantius pulled a sheet of papyrus from a pouch on his belt and showed it to Cassius. 'Indavara gave me a good description – anything to add?'

Cassius checked it. 'No. That's all accurate.'

He pulled his sword belt over his shoulder as he followed Abascantius to the door. Simo met him there.

'You're up, sir?'

'Send for a covered carriage. Then get me some food.'

Abascantius knocked a fist lightly against Cassius's shoulder. 'I do believe you're rediscovering a bit of that old Alauran spirit, Corbulo.'

'Not really, sir. But whoever is behind this, they seem to consider me a threat. Hardly the time to retreat. I would rather find them than wait for them to find me.'

Despite these words, Cassius was immensely relieved to reach the records office without incident. It only took half an hour to get there but it was difficult to think of anything other than who exactly was trying to kill him, what they knew, and what they might try next. He did at least feel reassured by the presence of Major. The veteran seemed capable and conscientious and had asked several questions about the danger they might face – the two-fingered man in particular. Leaving the bodyguard at the door, Cassius and Simo hurried inside. The room was looking rather more ordered now, with paths made through the piles of boxes and tablets.

'Afternoon, sir,' said Petronax, stepping out from behind a shelf. 'I was beginning to think I wouldn't see you again.'

'I've been rather occupied,' Cassius replied, stepping over a box as he approached the clerk.

Petronax looked at the bandage. 'Are you all right?'

'It's nothing.'

'Thank the gods it wasn't your face.'

'What about these records then?'

'We've still only scratched the surface but I separated all the personal records out as you asked.' He pointed at two distinct piles close to the door.

'I don't suppose you'd have anything on General Ulpian?'

'Records for senior officers are kept at the governor's office.'

'I'm interested in someone he may have served with in the Sixteenth.'

Petronax nodded and led Cassius to one of the piles by the door.

'This is the Sixteenth stuff that's been sorted out so far. The most recent records are from two years ago, the oldest are' – Petronax examined a small piece of papyrus glued to the pile – 'twenty years old.'

'Ulpian was a cavalryman. We'll start with them.'

'Cavalry are in the box on the top there.'

Cassius looked around. 'Is there a space where we can work?'

'There's a clear table next door. Go and make yourself comfortable and I'll bring the boxes through.'

'Thank you, Petronax.'

The clerk smiled; he seemed to enjoy hearing Cassius use his name.

With Major on guard outside the second storeroom, Cassius and Simo sat opposite each other at the table. Stacked in front of them were all the records from the cavalry detachment of the Sixteenth Legion. Petronax had been able to find out that Ulpian had left his post as cavalry commander ten years previously. Cassius initially thought about discounting all the records compiled after that date, but if the two-fingered man had served with Ulpian, he could still have been invalided out of service after the senior man had moved on.

'Cavalryman Eborius,' said Simo, reading from a sheet of papyrus. 'Invalided – injury. Doesn't specify what, sir. Height: five feet, ten inches.'

Having estimated Two Fingers to be between five feet five and five feet eight, Cassius had decided to discount any potential match that didn't fit this parameter.

'No.'

It was a while before either of them came to another file of interest.

'Cavalryman Juncus,' said Cassius, reading from a waxed tablet. 'Invalided. Hand injury. Height not listed but age . . . he would be forty-two now.'

With that strange, lined face of his, Two Fingers was difficult to age; Cassius reckoned he could be anything between thirty-five and fifty.

'Possible.'

He added the sheet to the smaller pile next to the main stack.

A few moments earlier, a slave inside the basilica's main hall had announced the beginning of the eleventh hour. According to Petronax, at the end of the twelfth, the entire building would be locked up.

'You can start copying details from the ones we have, Simo. Note everything. Especially the addresses if they have one.'

Simo nodded and stirred the ink Petronax had brought in for them. Addresses weren't normally listed on the legionary records, except for some of those who'd retired due to injury – to assist with payment of the military pension.

As Simo started writing, Cassius thought about what he would do with the list of names once it was compiled. They could try the addresses but what about those without? What other way was there of tracing ex-soldiers? Perhaps the stores that supplied equipment and weapons. Many legionaries kept accounts there. Presumably, cavalrymen did the same.

They worked on in silence. Cassius went through another twenty files and found nothing of interest.

'Last night there were thirty people at the church-house, sir,' Simo said suddenly. 'They prayed for those at the prison. Elder Nura is sure our Lord will answer.'

'Keep writing, don't get behind,' Cassius told him as he discarded another file. 'Most would say a believer must demonstrate his commitment to a god. Shouldn't you show it somehow – a sacrifice or something?'

'Our Lord always hears us, sir,' Simo replied, without looking up.

'Yet often ignores you.'

Simo stopped momentarily, then continued writing in silence.

'My point is, it's all rather out of your hands,' added Cassius. 'Except of course that every one of those men could be free – if they took the wiser course of action. What did you say to your father when I left you alone there?'

Simo put down his pen.

'I considered what you said, sir – about him pledging his loyalty to Bishop Domnus, and you might well be right. It could work.

340

But I couldn't ask that of my father. He introduced me to the faith. It's not my place to question him, or tell him what to do. You would understand that, I think.'

Cassius didn't particularly like the tone of that last remark – it was rare for Simo to speak to him in such a way – but he let it go. And once he'd said nothing, he knew it would appear weak to admonish him later. But there was another reason why he remained silent. Simo was right. He did understand.

They carried on until they had to leave, by which time there were nineteen names on the list. As papers were put away and doors locked, and the last of the administrators filed out of the basilica, Cassius hurried down the steps, Major by his side. Simo had been sent ahead to find the carriage driver, and the vehicle now stood at rest ahead of them, one of a long line picking up late-working bureaucrats. To the left a small crowd had formed around a pair of drummers, to the right were a noisy group of toga-clad young men; students perhaps. Major edged closer to Cassius as they passed between the two groups. They were almost at the carriage when a female voice called out.

'Master Corbulo, sir.'

The voice seemed to have come from the left, but when he looked that way, Cassius saw only a stocky man hurrying towards him. He had a large, sheathed dagger on his belt. Major darted in front of Cassius and drew his knife.

Then a girl stepped out from behind the man. Bacara.

'It's all right, Major,' Cassius said. 'I know her.'

'And him?' asked the bodyguard.

Bacara pushed past her friend. 'Master Corbulo, this is Silus – Nabor's brother. He knows who killed him. And he knows all about the silver and gold.'

Cassius took a moment to absorb what the girl had said. He looked around, unsure what to do. It would be unwise to stay in this crowded, open place for long, he knew that much.

Silus was about thirty, and carried himself with a certain swagger; he didn't seem overly concerned about the big man with the knife standing three paces in front of him.

'Put the blade away, Major,' Cassius said.

The bodyguard did so.

'We need to talk,' Cassius told the girl.

'Not here,' said Silus.

'Agreed. Simo, you go up with the driver. Back to the villa.' He turned to Bacara and Silus. 'You two: get in.'

Cassius opened the door to the carriage. Silus helped Bacara up then climbed in himself. Major gestured for Cassius to go first, then clambered up behind him. The carriage was designed for four; but with the three big men inside there was little space. With a cry, the driver set the horses off and the carriage bumped away down the street.

'Well, speak up,' said Cassius, looking first at Bacara, then Silus.

'Like she said, I know who killed Nabor, I know who has all that treasure, and I know where it is.'

Cassius tried to keep his expression neutral but excitement surged within him. After all the trails, dead-ends and guesswork, was this the break he and Abascantius so desperately needed?

Silus continued: 'I'll tell you what I know because I want revenge for my brother. But I have conditions.'

'Go on.'

'I had a part in it myself. I want a written guarantee that I cannot be punished for my involvement.'

'I'll have to—'

'There's more. Once I've told you all I know, you must let me go immediately and pledge not to try to find me again. I will be in danger, and I must leave Antioch. The girl too.'

'If you really know all you say you do, I'm confident accommodations can be made, but I cannot authorise any of that myself.'

'Then take me to someone who can.'

XXIX

Abascantius wasn't at home. Shostra had let them in, and he now stood in a corner of the courtyard, watching Silus and Bacara, who sat together on one of the stone benches, occasionally exchanging a hushed word. Simo was wandering the orchard, inspecting the trees. Major had picked an apple and was now slicing it up with his dagger.

Cassius had been unable to settle; first sitting down, then pacing around, and he was on the verge of insisting that Silus tell him what he knew when Abascantius finally returned. Shostra went to meet him and his master came straight outside.

'Well, who are they?' the agent whispered, looking over Cassius's shoulder.

'The girl is named Bacara – the one who led us to Octobrianus's villa. The man is Nabor's brother Silus. Says he knows all about the silver and gold. And that he was part of the scheme too.'

Abascantius's eyes widened; but before he could step past, Cassius held up a hand.

'Sir, he has some demands.'

Abascantius nodded. 'Let's hear him out.'

Silus and Bacara rose as the agent approached but he waved them back down. 'Stay, stay there. We shall be here a while.' He dropped his cape on to the other bench then sat down next to it.

Indavara appeared in the doorway, looking out at the courtyard. Cassius ignored him and sat next to Abascantius, who pointed at Simo and Major.

'You two inside. And you, Indavara.' He waited for the trio to disappear, then hunched forward, hands clasped together between his knees.

'You know me?'

Silus shook his head.

'You know my name? Aulus Celatus Abascantius.'

Silus nodded.

'Then you know the power I have. If all you tell me is true, I'll do my best for you. If not – if you mislead me – the consequences will be serious.'

'All very interesting, sir, but it is I who will dictate terms.'

Abascantius scowled at this but he listened to Silus's demands before replying.

'Men have been killed. Good men. You admit to being part of this scheme and yet you expect me to guarantee your freedom from prosecution or punishment?'

'There's no blood on my hands. The only dead man I know of is my brother. I didn't steal the treasure. I just helped to unload it.'

'It's here? It's still in the city?'

'You're getting ahead of yourself,' Silus said calmly. 'I need a written agreement before we go any further.'

'We've got a smart one here, eh, Corbulo?' said Abascantius. 'Let's see if you know as much as you claim, young man. What has all this treasure been stored in?'

'If I answer correctly, you'll give me what I want?'

'You have my word.'

'Eighteen small barrels.'

Abascantius yelled at Shostra to bring papyrus and a reed-pen. The four of them waited in silence until the attendant came, also carrying a wooden writing block which he placed on the table. As Abascantius put the sheet on the block, Shostra handed Cassius two rolled-up sheets tied with twine.

'I forgot. These came for you. One late last night, one this morning.'

The first of the letters had been sealed and although most of the wax had worn away, Cassius assumed it was from Prefect Venator; nobody else knew to contact him at this address. He opened it and – momentarily forgetting about the code – was bemused to see the apparently random series of letters. He put it to one side for a moment.

Abascantius had written out a simple signed declaration agreeing to all of Silus's terms. He grinned slyly as he handed it over.

'Shall I read it for you?'

'I know my words well enough.'

As the young man checked it, Cassius wondered how much legal weight such a document might have; or whether Abascantius would feel even vaguely obliged to honour it. The agent hunched forward again.

'Now tell me. Who has it?'

Silus glanced briefly at Bacara, then up at the darkening sky, and finally at Abascantius.

'Procurator Octobrianus. All eighteen barrels are neatly piled up in a warehouse at the back of the imperial mint.'

For a moment, Abascantius said nothing, apparently unable to accept that the man he suspected really was behind the theft. He scratched at his chin.

'You're sure of this?'

'I'm supposed to be there again this evening – for another job.'

'Did you see anything of a standard – a large, jewelled flag?'

'No.'

'Start at the beginning.'

'Nabor came to see me, said Octobrianus wanted us for some special job, even though we'd not worked for him in years. The money was good, so I agreed.'

'When was this?'

'About two weeks ago.'

Abascantius turned to Cassius, who had already made a few calculations – about a week after the cart was ambushed. He nodded.

'Go on,' instructed Abascantius.

'We met him at his villa at midnight, then the three of us went to get this cart. It was behind some warehouse up in the hills. There was a man there.'

'Did you get a name?'

'No. But he was funny-looking. Sort of old before his time.'

'Lined face?' Cassius interjected. 'Wild hair?'

Silus nodded.

Abascantius gave a grim smile. 'And his hands?' asked the agent. 'Did he have any fingers missing?'

'I didn't notice. It was night, and he left once we took the cart.'

'Continue.'

'I drove. Octobrianus followed some distance behind on his horse. He told us that if we came across any city sergeants, we were to keep quiet and let him handle them; but we never saw anyone. It wasn't far to the mint. He unlocked the gate and we took the cart around to a warehouse at the back. Then we started to unload the barrels. They were small but heavy – very, very heavy. We could only just lift one together. To start with Octobrianus watched us, then he went to check the gate. One of the barrel lids came off and we saw the old coins on top. Nabor had a look underneath – that's when he took the necklace. There was another barrel coming apart; we saw the silver and gold, though we made sure Octobrianus didn't know it. When the barrels were all unloaded he paid us twenty denarii each and said he would need us again soon for another job. He told us what to expect if we told anyone. We left. I told Nabor he'd been an idiot but as usual he didn't listen. I hadn't seen him for a few days, then I saw Bacara here and heard what'd happened to him.'

Silus took a breath and shook his head. Bacara put a hand on his arm.

'Octobrianus must have found out,' he continued. 'Apparently the fool had shown off the necklace in half a dozen inns. Then yesterday I get this note, asking if Nabor and me can come to the mint again for this job today, asking where Nabor is – like he didn't know. He said he really only needed me – I'd get all the money. I dare say he planned to knock me off too once I'd done what he wanted.'

'When are you supposed to be there?'

'The second hour of night.'

'What's your profession?'

'At present I work a furnace, like Nabor.'

Abascantius turned to Cassius, who was already nodding.

'The Palmyran brands,' said the agent. 'He means to have them taken off the ingots. Then he can sell them on. Gods, we can catch him there red-handed. Crafty son of a bitch – the mint's not been used since the occupation.'

'Is there anything else you can think of?' Cassius asked Silus.

'No. What will happen to him?'

'He'll hang. Or burn,' replied Abascantius.

'Is that a promise?'

'Oh, it's a guarantee.'

'Can we leave now?'

'You may.' Abascantius stood up. 'Shostra, see these people out, then find my sword. And send Indavara and Major out here.'

Bacara and Silus followed the servant out of the courtyard.

'Don't worry,' Abascantius told Cassius quietly, 'I'll have them followed, just to be sure.' He glanced down at the letter. 'Who's that from?'

'Prefect Venator,' replied Cassius. 'But we need a cipher book.'

'I don't.'

Abascantius grabbed the letter and sat down again, studying it intently. Cassius unrolled the second letter. It was not encoded and had been sent by the Chief Clerk of the Fourth Legion at Zeugma, on the instructions of Venator. Transcribed below the brief message was a copy of a personal record. Cassius knew the name.

'You were right,' announced Abascantius. 'Centurion Tarquinius went missing from Zeugma six days ago.' The agent stared across the orchard, tapping the letter against his leg. 'He must be working with Octobrianus. This two-fingered character too. What's that there?'

'Tarquinius's record.'

Though Cassius was staring down at it, his thoughts were racing too fast to absorb what was written. He forced himself to focus on the words. Tarquinius had been in the army for twenty-two years, but only five of them with the infantry. He had started out as a cavalryman and spent seventeen years with the mounted detachment of the Third Cohort, Sixteenth Legion.

Cassius opened his satchel and found the list they had started at the basilica. Abascantius looked over his shoulder as he read. There was only one cavalryman there who'd been invalided out of the Third Cohort; and he had joined long after General Ulpian had moved on.

He had, however, served at the same time as Tarquinius. Cavalry detachments were comparatively small – the men would have known each other. Justius Pythion was the cavalryman's name; and the description of the injury that had forced him to leave service four years previously was pleasingly precise: *Lost three digits on right hand.*

There was even an address listed: an apartment in the southeast of the city.

Abascantius slapped the page. He and Cassius spoke simultaneously: 'Two Fingers.'

Abascantius spent the next half an hour doling out orders at a prodigious rate. Shostra was instructed to send messages to three operatives telling them to arm themselves and meet Abascantius at an inn close to the mint within the hour. A fourth man was tasked with following Silus. He was to observe any contacts he made and apprehend him at once if he seemed to be leaving the city. Indavara was told to fetch his sword and wait by the front door.

'And me, sir?' Cassius asked. 'Shall I fetch my sword, too?'

Abascantius placed a hand on his shoulder.

'That's probably a good idea, but you shan't be coming with us. I need you to go after our two-fingered friend. Start with this address.'

Cassius couldn't believe what he was hearing. 'But we've found it, sir. We've found the silver and gold, probably the banner too.'

'Until I have that accursed thing in my hands, I'm taking

nothing for granted. If the gods are with us you might be right, but if something goes wrong I don't want all our eggs in one basket. Two Fingers didn't go with them last time, so he probably won't this time either. If he gets word that we're on to them, he'll make his escape. Don't tell me you're happy with the idea of him getting away?'

'Of course not. But I want to see this through to the end, sir. I've chased those damned barrels across half this province. I want to be there.'

Shostra had by now returned with Abascantius's sword and belt. The blade was an expensive piece, the hilt studded with blue gems.

'I understand, lad,' said the agent as Shostra slipped the belt over his shoulder. 'But there's no time for debate. Take Major, and if you do find him, get a message to Shostra here.'

'But, sir, that address is four years old.'

'If he's not there, do what you've been doing so well: track him down. He's in the city somewhere.'

Cassius could think of nothing else to say. He was still struggling with the notion that Abascantius had been right all along. He wondered now why he'd been so determined to ignore the signs of Octobrianus's involvement that he himself had uncovered.

Abascantius ran his sword in and out of the scabbard a couple of times then picked up his cape.

'Don't think I'm not grateful, Corbulo. We wouldn't have got to this point without you.'

Cassius nodded vacantly, then followed him back into the villa.

Abascantius hurried over to Major, then pointed towards the door. 'Go and organise a carriage.'

'Covered?' asked the bodyguard in his deep, gruff voice.

'No. Something quick.'

Abascantius turned to Cassius and grinned. 'It's getting dark but you've no need to hide yourself now anyway. The hunter has become the hunted.'

He gripped Cassius's shoulder again. 'I'll meet you here later. Good luck, Corbulo.'

Shostra had reappeared holding his master's spear-head. It was identical to Cassius's apart from some extra strands of gold thread hanging from the top. Abascantius took it and strode towards the front door. Indavara waited for him to pass, then, after a brief glance back at Cassius, followed him outside.

The apartment block was a quarter of a mile from the Daphne Gate. They had to leave the carriage three streets away. It was the Festival of Apollo and thousands had turned out to celebrate. By tradition, hawks and other birds were sacrificed, and many Antiochenes were carrying them around impaled on the end of sharpened sticks. As if this wasn't dangerous enough, the bow was the weapon most associated with Apollo and the addition of errant arrows fired by drunken revellers made it one of the most perilous days of the year.

Cassius had stopped off at the villa to fetch his sword. He had also left his helmet and the spear-head there and changed into a plain tunic.

The apartment block was a little more respectable than Nabor's: the recently painted interior was lit by oil lamps and smelled only of cooking. They were looking for number one hundred and three; and they found it on the third floor, close to the stairs.

Major stood in front of the door, Cassius and Simo to the right. Cassius flexed his fingers, and reminded himself to act quickly if the need arose. Major slipped the cudgel from his belt.

'Now,' whispered Cassius.

The big bodyguard raised his left hand. Before he could knock, another door opened further down the corridor. Out stepped a young woman. She was rather lovely – wearing only a simple tunic and sandals, but with an hourglass figure and a lustrous head of dark brown hair. She gazed curiously at the trio as she neared the stairs. Cassius raised a finger to his mouth. She smiled as she passed him.

Reproaching himself for being even momentarily distracted,

Cassius turned back and nodded again. Major knocked on the door. They heard slow, careful footsteps. Cassius brought up his sword. He waved Simo out of the way to give himself space.

'Who's there?'

The voice of a woman; an old woman.

Cassius put a hand up before Major could reply.

'We're from the magistrate's office. Just a few questions.'

He doubted the woman would have heard of the Service; but almost everyone in the city would know of Quarto and his men. The latch came up and the door opened. Cassius saw white hair, a leathery face and a curious green eye.

'Where are your clubs then?'

Major tapped the cudgel against the door close to the woman's face. 'Will this do?'

'Open up please,' Cassius said. 'Like I said – just a few questions.'

The door opened another inch. Major slammed his hand into it, knocking it open. He stepped inside and neatly caught the door as it swung back towards him. The old woman – who had retreated with impressive speed – swore at him. Major ignored her and looked around.

'Just her, sir.'

Cassius and Simo followed him inside. The Gaul shut the door behind them and went to speak to the old woman.

The apartment was quite large but packed full of furniture, barrels and sacks. Opposite the door was a grilled window; and barely a few feet away were the walls of another apartment block. To the left was a doorway covered by a tatty curtain. Major hurried over to check the second room.

Simo had by now worked his magic, and the old woman had already lowered her voice. She tapped Cassius on the arm.

'This is about my wretched son, I suppose?'

'If his name is Justius Python, yes.'

Major reappeared. 'No one.'

The old woman sighed and sat down. 'Been up to no good again, has he?'

'You could say that,' answered Cassius as he sheathed his sword. 'Do you know where he is?'

'Hah! He never tells me a thing.'

Cassius stepped closer and leaned over the woman. 'Magistrate Quarto takes a very dim view of those who obstruct our investigations.'

'He went out a couple of hours ago – took his big bag with him – who knows when he'll be back?'

'You have no idea where he might be? What are his usual haunts?'

The old woman placed a finger against the side of her nose and cleared one nostril.

'He eats, he sleeps, he goes! I tell you I don't know. Never held down a job since he left the army but somehow he's always got a few coins. Only the gods know where he gets them. I hope you catch him – a good stiff lashing might whip some sense into him.'

Cassius wondered what Pythion's mother might have said had she known the real consequences her son faced. Even putting aside his other crimes, by attempting to kill an officer of the Roman Army he had assured his own death if caught. Cassius's testimony alone would be enough to see him executed.

He pointed at the curtain. 'That's his room?'

'It is.'

'I'd like to search it.'

The old woman cleared the other nostril and shrugged.

Cassius gestured for Simo to join him, then caught Major's eye. 'You watch the door.'

Cassius pushed aside the curtain, and stepped into the cramped room beyond. Again the walls were lined with all manner of objects; there was army gear: packs, belts, boots, even a saddle; and boxes of cheap washing lotions and mass-produced religious figurines. Lying below the single window was a low bed.

'We shall have to go through all this,' Cassius said morosely. It was hard not to think of Abascantius striding into the mint, clapping Octobrianus in chains and reclaiming the banner. What annoyed him most was that Indavara and Abascantius's other men would be part of it. What exactly had they contributed?

'Are we looking for something specific, sir?' asked Simo.

Cassius shrugged, then wandered over to the window. A group of men not far away were singing a song about the Whites; apparently they'd been victorious at the hippodrome that day. Cassius looked at the wall above the head of the bed. Nails had been hammered into the plaster; and hanging from them was a variety of weapons and tools. There were several daggers, two little axes, spikes, rods and a saw. Two of the nails had nothing on them. Sunlight had faded the paint to form tell-tale shapes where the missing objects had been. One was a long, narrow blade; perhaps Python's old cavalry sword. The other was shaped like a spear; except it was too small to be of any practical use – it was only about eight inches long.

'Woman. Come here!'

Cassius pointed at the outline as soon as she came through the curtain. 'What do you know of the little spear he keeps there?'

'Oh, he's taken that, has he? Must have one of his meetings. Perhaps he'll be back after all.'

'What meetings?'

'I don't know – some kind of club, I think. Usually on a Wednesday.'

Cassius looked back at the outline. Wednesday. Yesterday.

He hurried back into the main room. Major was standing in the doorway, watching the corridor.

'You know the quickest route down to the river from here?'

The bodyguard nodded.

'Come, Simo, there's no time to waste.'

Ignoring the old woman's entreaties not to do too much harm to her son, Cassius set off towards the stairs at a run.

XXX

Full grey clouds rolled in over the darkened city; and scattered drops of rain soon became a light drizzle. Indavara pushed himself off the uneven stone wall and brushed his wet hair away from his eyes.

He was standing in an alcove, just behind the others. They had waited at the inn for the last of Abascantius's operatives to arrive, then marched through the streets to the rear of the mint. Indavara only recognised one of the men – from the agent's house when he'd eaten the soup. He was almost as fat as Abascantius and his name was Salvian.

The mint was a large, red brick building with several high chimneys, surrounded by a substantial wall. Opposite the alcove was a narrow iron gate. With a tap on the shoulder from Abascantius, one of the men scurried across the street and hunched over the lock. Abascantius shouldered his way between the others and came close to Indavara.

'He won't be long. You come in last and keep an eye out behind us. Draw your sword.'

The agent returned to the side of the street. Indavara eased his sword from the scabbard, then went and stood beside him, idly tapping the tip of the blade against his leg.

He reckoned tomorrow would be his last day in Antioch. He wasn't exactly sure what was going on but matters were clearly coming to a head. He was glad, because once he'd been paid, he could decide what to do next.

It seemed best to keep moving: partly because when he stayed in one place too long things took a turn for the worse; partly because he wanted to see more of the world. Travelling east, the lands seemed only to become hotter, drier and more bleak. Of all the terrain he'd seen since leaving Pietas Julia, it was green fields, rivers and hills that most appealed to him – they seemed so peaceful, so permanent. He would go north, or return west.

But before leaving he would spend some money on that girl. Galla was her name and he'd thought of her often since their time together. He would ask her to go for a walk with him; that's what men and women who liked each other seemed to do. And if she didn't want to, he could at least ask her where she thought he should go next.

Or he could ask Simo when he went to fetch his things from the villa. He liked Simo. He seemed kind, and he didn't ask questions all the time. Indavara thought he might even miss him a bit.

Simo's master, on the other hand, he wouldn't miss at all. Indavara knew he'd made a bad mistake at the baths, and it was no surprise that Corbulo was angry about it. Fair enough. It wasn't this that annoyed him, more the character of the man. Indavara found it difficult to respect someone who couldn't fight, couldn't stand on his own two feet.

And Corbulo was arrogant too. Indavara could see he was intelligent; he knew a lot about the world, he spoke well, and he would sometimes argue with Abascantius, even though the older man gave the orders. But he seemed to have little time for anyone else. He did listen to Simo sometimes but Indavara thought that was just because they'd been together so long.

Corbulo had probably had an easy life: a family to look after him, money for an education and all those expensive clothes. He knew nothing of what Indavara had been through; what he'd endured simply to win his freedom – to walk free of chains, and walls and the whims of a man like Capito.

Indavara had seen men like Corbulo at the games. Rich men. Comfortable men. For them someone like him would only ever be useful for either entertaining them or protecting them. Indavara didn't want to work for men like that any more. He would have to try to find another way of earning money. He was free now – free to choose the company he kept.

355

But it was a pity; because Simo really did seem like someone who might make a good friend. Yes, he would probably miss him.

A jaunty whistle from the other side of the street.

'Now.'

Abascantius drew his blade and led the others across the street. Indavara checked first left, then right, then followed them to the gate. There was no sign of anyone approaching. The lock-picker waited for the others to come through, then quietly pulled the gate to behind him. One of the men was carrying a shuttered lantern, which he now opened a crack as they made for the rear of the mint. The lock-picker hurried past Indavara to a second gate and went to work again.

Indavara turned round. Above the walls he could see several lighted windows on the higher floors of the forum and the basilica. He heard a dog growl. It sounded close – like it was on the street beyond the wall. Then the dog barked. Abascantius came and stood by him, staring at the gate. They saw nothing but heard another bark, then a man cursing. Then a long moment of quiet. When the dog barked for the final time, it was some distance away.

Abascantius exhaled loudly and returned to the gate; and a few moments later it was open. Indavara was last inside. The chilly room was dark but he could tell it was a large space. Abascantius took the lantern, opened the shutter a little more and led them further into the building. The air was stale. Dust went up Indavara's nose. He squeezed it and managed not to sneeze. They entered a narrow passageway, then stopped. He looked over the shoulder of the man in front; there were lights up ahead.

With Major leading the way and Simo behind him, Cassius barged through the dense stream of revellers thronging down the slope towards the river. A sizzling piece of animal skin fell from a torch on to his shoulder. Cursing, he flicked it away as he reached the comparative safety of the street that led to the guild house.

Though he still had no idea what this new development might mean – or how it might tie in with Octobrianus – his initial hunch had been right: at least one member of the Sons of Antioch was involved in the theft of the imperial banner.

'Where now?' asked Major.

'This way.'

Cassius hurried past him along the street. He waited for another group of festival-goers to pass, then approached the guild house gate. Beyond the bars lay only darkness; there were no lights in the grounds or at the villa. Cassius tried the gate. It was locked. He ushered Major forward and drew his sword. There was a bell just like the one at the side gate. Without a second thought he rang it, somehow certain that no one would emerge from the darkness.

Apart from the light patter of the rain and the noise of the festivities, the only sound was the rustling of the high trees swaying in the breeze.

'Simo, go to that inn on the corner. I need a ladder and a lantern; pay whatever you have to. Hurry, man. Major, follow me.' As Simo ran towards the inn, Cassius started along the wall to the corner. A boisterous gang of youths strode past them, singing and drinking. Cassius went on up the slope to the side gate and looked inside. No lights, no sound. He rang the bell and again no one came.

They retraced their steps and saw Simo emerging from the inn, a lantern in his hand. Not far behind him was a small fellow with a ladder under his arm. Cassius sheathed his sword and took the ladder.

'Thank you. Now back inside,' he said.

'You're not going in there, are you?' asked the man, nodding at the guild house.

'That's none of your concern. Back to the inn.'

'We'll return these presently,' said Simo.

'For what you paid, you can keep them,' said the man as he left. 'Just don't tell anyone I helped you get into that villa.'

Cassius laid the ladder up against the wall next to the gate.

'We must be quick – there'll be plenty of sergeants around tonight.'

He climbed to the top then clambered on to the rough stone wall. 'Now you two. Hurry.'

He steadied the ladder as first Major, then Simo followed him up. The wall was two feet wide and there was plenty of space to manoeuvre as they hauled the ladder up then lowered it over the other side. Once it was firmly set on the ground, Cassius climbed down. Stepping off the last rung, he drew his sword again. The thick branches of the trees ahead completely obscured the villa.

'Come on.'

Once the others were down, he took the lantern from Simo and led them towards the villa, pushing his way through the branches until he was on open grass. When the dark bulk of the building was close, he stopped and listened. The noise of the festivities down on the waterfront seemed distant now. The villa was silent.

Major came close and spoke in his ear. 'What is this place?'

'A guild house. And something more.'

'I don't like it. It's too quiet. Why are we here?'

'I'll worry about why we're here. You worry about whether anyone else is.'

Cassius ventured close to the arched front door. He opened the lantern shutter and handed it to Major. The door was latched but not locked. Dread dried his throat as he put his hand on the latch but the fear didn't halt him. He wondered what it was that drew him onward. Curiosity? Or simply a desire to bring this whole accursed affair to a close? It hardly mattered. But he had to see inside.

He raised the latch slowly then eased the heavy door open. Major stepped up next to him, the lantern held high. They stared into the huge room that took up the front of the villa. There were a couple of oil lamps alight; pockets of murky yellow in the pitch black.

Cassius stepped inside, followed by Major, then Simo. The room was even more bare than it had looked from the outside, with only a few bits of furniture and some well-worn rugs. Several capes and cloaks had been left on a table. Cassius continued forward, sure that if he stopped he might not take another step.

He reached the far end of the room. To the right was a wide corridor leading to the rear of the house, to the left was a wall. In front of it a steep staircase led down to a door that had been left ajar. As he descended towards it, Cassius was assailed by a smell he now knew well. The smell of blood; the smell of death.

Indavara was surprised: first because he'd expected Abascantius to advance slowly, not speed up; and second because there was not a small group ahead but at least a dozen men.

The passageway emerged into a big warehouse with high walls and a domed roof, lit by several giant braziers. Piled up around the edges of the warehouse were innumerable pallets and equipment that reminded Indavara of the glass factory. The men were gathered around a big wooden table. Whatever lay on top of it had been covered by a single white sheet.

The men all turned to examine the new arrivals striding into the warehouse. Indavara noted no fear or anxiety on their faces. They just seemed surprised. He recognised only a single face: Octobrianus.

The procurator was standing next to a tall, lean man wearing a purple cloak over his toga. Four of the other men looked like clerks or attendants. The other eight were legionaries and they now moved up to shield Octobrianus and the tall man, pushing their cloaks away and gripping their sword hilts. One was a centurion, wearing a red-crested helmet like Corbulo's.

'What in Hades are you doing here?' asked the tall man, narrowing his eyes as Abascantius came to a stop by the table. The agent was now holding one spear-head.

'I might ask you the same thing, Governor Gordio.'

'By the gods, man, you're already on thin ice with me as it is. Sheathe your weapon, tell your men to do likewise, and answer me: what are you doing here?'

Abascantius replaced his blade in the scabbard and gestured for the others – Indavara included – to do the same.

'You will recall that I was asked to deliver a rather valuable cargo to the capital.'

'Of course,' said Gordio impatiently.

'Information has come to me suggesting that the procurator here is responsible for its theft.'

Octobrianus laughed.

'What?' snapped the governor. 'It's been stolen? When?'

Abascantius nodded approvingly. 'Very good, Governor. Almost convincing.'

'This is preposterous,' hissed Gordio. 'First you accuse me of being in league with the Persians, and now this outrage.'

Abascantius glanced at Octobrianus and continued calmly: 'I'm certain of his involvement. What interests me now is your role in all this, Governor. You may as well forget the theatricals; your bluff is admirable but not even you will survive a part in this conspiracy.'

Gordio coloured. The centurion had fixed Abascantius with a stony stare and was tapping his thumb against his sword.

'By Jupiter you've a nerve,' said the governor. 'I've no idea why Marcellinus entrusted you with such a task. How I wish the Palmyrans had caught you – we would have been spared your ineptitude and deranged imaginings.'

'Thanks to that little shit they almost did,' Abascantius retorted, nodding at Octobrianus. 'In any case, there's one simple way to establish what exactly is going on here.'

He darted forward, gripped the sheet and whipped it off the table. As it fluttered to the ground, every man present stared down at the glittering gold that covered the table. Indavara saw no silver, nor any jewellery; only rows of coins in furrowed wooden racks.

Abascantius stood still for a moment, then picked up one of the coins.

'Indeed there is,' replied Gordio, glaring at the agent with imperious disdain.

Octobrianus placed his hands on the edge of the table. 'The

first true Roman aurei produced in Antioch for almost three years. Prototypes – they were finished yesterday. Rather good image of the Emperor, don't you think?'

'Why wasn't I told?' Abascantius asked shakily.

'Why in the name of the gods would you imagine that you are important enough to be told?' Gordio bellowed. 'Your inflated ego and tawdry methods have sullied the reputation of my staff for long enough. You will surrender your spear-head at once. I am placing you under house arrest until Marcellinus returns. He can decide what to do with you.'

Abascantius looked first at Gordio, then at Octobrianus. The procurator gave a slight smile.

'You. You arranged this to discredit me.'

Octobrianus shook his head. The mocking smile remained.

Abascantius dropped the spear-head and launched himself across the corner of the table, reaching for the procurator's neck. Gordio got in front of the smaller man and blocked his way. Abascantius only had time to shove the governor once. The centurion was quick; Indavara didn't even see the dagger coming out. The soldier held the glittering blade close to Abascantius's throat.

Twelve men reached for their swords.

'Nobody move!' barked the centurion. With his spare hand he gently eased the governor back and away from Abascantius. He looked down at the agent, still sprawled across the corner of the table. 'If those blades come out we're going to have a bloody mess in here. My boys outnumber your lot two to one. Tell them to stand down, surrender their weapons and come quietly.'

Indavara could see only the back of Abascantius's head.

The centurion inched the blade closer. 'Well?'

Indavara turned. If he ran now, he could probably get out. But what chance of ever getting his money if he abandoned Abascantius? And what might be the consequences of resisting the soldiers?

'All right,' said the agent. 'Do it.'

Indavara hadn't been particularly impressed by Abascantius's other three operatives and he wasn't surprised when they immediately undid their sword belts and dropped them to the floor. Four of the legionaries advanced towards Indavara, whose hand was still on his sword.

'You too, One Ear,' ordered the centurion.

'Do as he says, Indavara,' said Abascantius without turning round. 'You'll get your weapon back later. This won't last long.'

Indavara took off the sword belt and lowered it to the ground.

The centurion backed away from the table but kept the dagger in his hand as he nodded at Abascantius's sword belt. Abascantius straightened up and removed it, then picked up the spear-head.

'Forget house arrest,' growled Gordio, rearranging his robe. 'You can go to the prison tower with the rest of the scum.'

'What?' Abascantius said through gritted teeth.

'Quite apart from the fact that you dare to lay your grubby hands on me, do you think I'm going to leave you and your lackeys on the loose with the Persian delegation arriving in the morning? You've already done enough damage. You shall tell us exactly what happened and I shall charge General Ulpian and Magistrate Quarto with recovering what you've lost. You better pray it's not too late.'

'Nothing's been lost. It was stolen. You can't use Ulpian or Quarto — it must have been one of them.'

Shaking his head, the governor reached out and took the spear-head from Abascantius. 'I've no idea why you think it necessary for Octobrianus to discredit you — you've done an immaculate job of that yourself.'

Gordio turned to the centurion. 'Get him out of my sight.'

Like the walls of the cavern, the tunnel had been faced with plaster and moulded to resemble rock. The pool of light from the half-shuttered lantern ran over the undulating surface as Cassius led the way down the shallow slope of the tunnel. He turned every few moments to make sure Major and Simo were right behind him. The smell was growing stronger, the cold too.

The tunnel suddenly widened out. Directly ahead was the rear of the Mithras sculpture, and beyond that the darkened expanse of the cavern itself. Only two braziers were alight, close to the benches at the back. Cassius stopped; and the three of them stood in silence behind the sculpture, listening again. A faint, whistling wind blew through the cavern. Cassius noticed the holes behind the eyes of the god. Inside each one was some kind of glass or crystal. Behind was ash, where the hot coals would have been placed. There was also a jug of water on the floor below the snake's mouth. Cassius wished Indavara could see it; and admitted to himself that, though Major seemed capable enough, he wouldn't have minded having the ex-gladiator by his side.

He peered round the side of the sculpture, the back legs of the bull. The front of the cavern was inky black. He stepped out on to the platform, knowing he would be a clear target for anyone concealed by the darkness – but nothing happened. He walked in front of the sculpture, the lantern still in his hand.

Two green dots caught the light. Eyes – staring up at him from in front of the platform. He shrank back towards the sculpture.

'What is it?' asked Major.

'I saw . . . something.'

'By Hades, that smell,' said the bodyguard.

Cassius walked forward again. He sheathed his sword and pulled back the shutter on the lantern. The iron was warm under his fingers. The light spilled out, filling the cavern.

Lying in the space between the front row of benches and the base of the platform were at least twenty bodies. Feeling Simo's hand on his arm, Cassius nonetheless advanced, lantern held high.

The men hadn't just been killed; they had been smashed to pieces. The eyes Cassius had seen belonged to a man lying against the platform. The bottom of his face – mouth, chin and jaw – had been mangled into a soggy mess of pink flesh and jutting bone.

Cassius's stomach burned hollow. Major threw up, the vomit splashing noisily against the floor. Simo backed up against the sculpture. The Gaul turned, and saw the implacable expression on the face of the god Mithras, staring skyward as he cut the bull's neck.

'Who could have done this, sir? Why?'

Cassius went to the right side of the platform and down the steps. He half-wondered if there was anyone alive, but once he'd passed more of the bodies he realised the killers had left no chance of that. Most of the dead had been struck above the neck at least twice; crushing impacts that left deep wounds in their faces and skulls. His boots squelched on blood as he stepped between the corpses.

He spied a red tunic and held the lantern over the dead man. The face was battered beyond recognition but then he noticed the withered arm. Centurion Turpo. Not far away was the gold merchant. Cassius still couldn't remember his name but he recalled the ostentatious collection of rings on both hands. The killers had left them.

Beyond the main mass of bodies was a smaller group of four. They had fallen between the first and second row of benches. One was a woman, lying face down, a ragged gash in the top of her head. Cassius knelt beside her and picked strands of hair from her face. Bacara's eyes were open but the pupils were surrounded by black blood.

On his back next to her lay Silus; the entire right side of his face had been torn open.

Another man was lying on his side, fingers still gripping a long cavalry sword. The unkempt hair was unmistakable. There was little blood on him, just a wide hole in his tunic and a puncture in the flesh over his heart. Justius Pythion – Two Fingers – had been the only one with the time, awareness or wit to get out his weapon and try to defend himself.

The last man's sword was still sheathed. Etched on the handle was a dedication to Mars. Cassius looked closer at the man's belt buckle. It was silver, with a name engraved upon it. Tarquinius. Cassius moved the light past the ugly rent in his neck and saw a handsome, rugged face topped by a fine head of greying hair.

Cassius straightened up and again noted the position of these four bodies. Had Tarquinius and his old comrade Pythion – along with Bacara and Silus – looked on as the others were butchered, only for the killers to turn on them?

He walked to the rear of the cavern and leaned against the wall, feeling the heat of the braziers close by. Simo and Major were talking but Cassius didn't hear a word of it. He gazed at the morass of bodies. There was no sign of the aged frame of Ulpian, nor the distinctive bulk of Quarto. Had he been right all along? Had one or both of them taken the banner and the treasure? Used the cultists and the others for their own ends, then dispatched them once they'd ceased to be useful?

Whoever it was wanted to cover their tracks; tie off all the loose ends in one murderous frenzy. And their attempt to divert Abascantius had succeeded. Cassius cursed himself for his part in it. He had swallowed every word of what Silus had told him about Octobrianus, without even attempting to confirm or corroborate any of it. He wondered what his and Bacara's real names had been. Not that it mattered now.

He lurched out of the cavern and into the anteroom, looking for some water. There was only a dusty old wine bottle. But he had to drink something; fill the bitter void in his guts.

Before he could pick it up, he heard a metallic clang. Stepping outside, he now noticed that the woodpile that had occupied the other end of the corridor had been pulled down. Timber lay scattered across the floor. Beyond was a darkened tunnel. The sound had come from there.

Major and Simo arrived.

'Gods, they were just here,' Cassius breathed. He pushed past the others and started at once along the tunnel. It sloped downward for about forty paces, then became level as it curved to the right. Cassius smelled the tang of river water; it was heading back towards the Orontes.

From the footmarks in the grey mud that lined the floor, Cassius guessed there must be at least five or six of them. When he saw light ahead, he shuttered the lamp and stopped.

'We shouldn't follow,' whispered Major as he came up behind him.

'Sir, I think he's right,' added Simo. 'You saw what they did.'

Ignoring them both, Cassius pressed on. Another fifty paces and he spied a gate. The light was in the distance, on the other side of it. The tunnel was low here and he had to bow his head.

He came up to the gate; and saw that the tunnel emerged just above a jetty. The light was a lantern swinging in the hand of a man at the back of the group. In a moment they were gone, striding along the jetty back towards the square. Cassius could hear the festival-goers singing and shouting.

He opened the lantern shutter and examined the gate. It was locked and had been set deep into the walls.

'They're there,' he hissed as Major and Simo caught up. He gripped the bars of the gate and shook them. 'They're right there!'

He turned and pushed past the others once more.

'Come on!'

When he later recalled that night, Cassius remembered nothing of charging back up the tunnel and across the cavern, then through the villa and out into the garden. Nor did he recall clambering up the ladder or dropping down to the street. But he could always picture the scene that faced him after he sprinted down to the waterfront.

Every single square foot seemed to be occupied. The rain had now stopped; and torches bobbed above the heads of the revellers as they threw dried flowers in the air or danced to the cacophony of uncoordinated drumming. Gangs of young men drank from bottles of wine, laughing and singing and pushing each other around.

Cassius darted to the side of the street and leapt up on to a barrel. He looked out into the sea of bodies and faces. There must have been close to a thousand people there. If the killers were heading back into the city, they would have to pass through the crowd.

Major was next to arrive. He had sheathed his sword and was breathing hard. Simo was still trotting down the hill, hand on his chest. Cassius had left the lantern on the ground. Major stopped right next to it; and as Cassius jumped down, he noticed the blood on the bodyguard's boots from where he'd twice crossed the cavern. His own boots were in a similar condition.

'They'll have blood on them too,' he told the others. 'They'll be in a group, carrying weapons.'

Without a second thought, Cassius picked up the lantern and hurled himself into the crowd. He forced himself left, squeezing past body after body; and in moments he was covered in wine and flowers.

His eyes were drawn to two figures about twenty feet ahead, close to the river, ploughing through the mob with lanterns held high. Cassius pushed a slight, older man out of the way to gain a better view. There were others behind the front two, also moving purposefully, clearly not part of the festivities.

Cassius steeled himself and shoved his way forward once more. It was difficult to make progress but his height helped him see over the crowd and follow the lanterns. The man at the front turned and yelled something at the others. Then he changed direction; towards the street and the city beyond.

Cassius tripped. Flinging his hands out as he fell, he dropped the lantern. It smashed as he landed, and he found himself stretched out on the ground, staring at the shards of glass flickering with the light from the torches above. He got to his knees. Then a big man standing nearby grabbed his belt and helped him to his feet.

'Here you go, mate.'

'Thank you.'

'Take a swig for Apollo!' said the reveller, offering a bottle of wine.

Ignoring him, Cassius moved away. He looked over the sea of heads and saw the group passing left to right just in front of him. He squeezed past two men singing at the top of their voices, and suddenly found himself right in the path of the leader. His face was set with grim determination as he led his fellows through the crowd.

Cassius stopped as the man passed within a yard of him and noted his thick belt and well-maintained scabbard. The others were similarly attired. Cassius looked down at their hobnailed boots. There was not a trace of blood, nor the grey mud of the tunnel. The squad of legionaries continued on their way.

He turned in every direction, searching desperately for some tell-tale sign. How long had it been since he'd seen the men leave the tunnel? Were they already past him? Could they have got through the crowd even before he'd arrived?

Then he saw the staves – three of them. He couldn't see the men holding them but he followed anyway. His way was soon barred by a group of twenty or more standing in a circle. In the middle was a drummer. The others had linked their arms and were kicking their legs up in time with the beat.

Cassius tapped one of the men on the shoulder. 'I need to get through!'

The reveller shook his head. Cassius tried to force his way through anyway. The man shoved him in the shoulder.

'Go around, fool!'

Cassius got up on his tiptoes. The staves were moving to his left, away from the river. He ducked down, and tried to burrow between two of the men. He thought he was through but then felt himself being hauled backwards by his belt. He twisted round and saw the same man staring at him. The Syrian was short but well-built; and he suddenly looked very, very drunk. He grabbed Cassius by the tunic with his left hand, then drove his right fist into his stomach. Winded, Cassius staggered backward. He couldn't catch his breath. He fell on to his backside.

Then he felt hands under his arms.

'I've got you, sir.'

Simo helped him to his feet and held him up while he recovered himself. Major appeared too, which was enough to drive the drunk swiftly away through the crowd. The bodyguard cleared a path as Simo helped Cassius towards the river. There was a little space at the edge of the square, by the wall above the jetty. Simo helped Cassius sit down on a wide stone bollard.

'Stay here a moment, sir.'

'Those men with staves—'

'Wait to catch your breath, sir.'

Cassius tried to stand, at least to try and point, but Simo put two hands on his shoulders.

'No – Simo – They could be – ' Cassius bent forward, wincing at the pain as he took deep breaths.

'That's it, sir.'

After a moment, Cassius raised his head and looked down at the jetty. Moored against a pontoon twenty yards away was a long rowing boat. At the end of the pontoon, three lanterns had been hooked on to a wooden post. Below it, four men were kneeling, washing their hands in the river. They were identically attired in black loose-fitting trousers and sleeveless tunics.

'That's it, sir,' said Simo. 'Slow, deep breaths.'

One of the men had taken off his boots. He dunked them in the water, wiped the soles with his hand, then put them on again. He stood up and joined the others as they clambered down into the rowing boat. All had heavy sacks across their shoulders which they deposited in the bottom of the boat before grabbing an oar.

Cassius stood up.

'Sir? What is it?'

Ignoring Simo – and with his hand pressed against his aching gut – Cassius hurried along the wall towards the pontoon.

Two of the men had taken lanterns with them into the boat. The last was lifted off the post by a fifth figure, who waited for the others to get settled, then climbed down into the stern. The men untied the mooring ropes and pushed off. They then took up their oars and gently propelled the boat away from the jetty.

The fifth man was holding the lantern on his lap, and even as the boat neared the main stream of the river, Cassius could still see his face quite clearly.

'Kaeso Scaurus.'

XXXI

The covered cart was stuffy and hot. The legionary sitting to Indavara's right was dozing, the man to his left drinking noisily from his canteen. Abascantius's men sat in a row opposite him. They had barely stopped talking since leaving the mint.

'Ten years I've worked in this province. And this is my reward?'

'I reckon old Pitface has lost it this time. I told you we were looking in the wrong place. Octobrianus doesn't have the balls for something like this.'

'Enough, you two,' said Salvian, who as well as being the largest of the three, was also the oldest. 'This isn't over yet by a long way. Gordio's overstepped the mark.'

'I'm not so sure. Aba used up all his favours a long time ago. Marcellinus and the rest will be more than happy to see him disgraced. And where does that leave us?'

Salvian spoke up again: 'I've known him a lot longer than you. He's come through worse than this. I reckon he'll have us back on the streets by dawn. Now shut it.'

Indavara took heart from this last comment, but when the cart stopped and they were manhandled outside, he realised he was back at the tower where Simo's father was being kept. As they were escorted up the stairs with spears at their backs, he felt a rising sense of panic. And when he smelled the foul stench of the prisoners and came close to the iron bars, he was suddenly sure that if he let himself be put inside that cell, he would not get out.

Herminius was on duty again. With a curious glance at Indavara – the last in line – he unlocked the door and opened it wide. The others went in quietly. A push in the back from one of the legionaries sent Indavara to within a foot of the cell. He turned round.

'I'm not going in there.'

'Don't tell me: you're an innocent man,' said Herminius with a sneer.

'I can't.' Indavara wiped away the sweat running down his forehead. 'I can't go in there.'

The guards laughed.

'It's funny, you don't look the craven type,' added Herminius. 'Get in.'

'I tell you I can't.'

Another of the guards jabbed his spear towards his face. 'You heard the man.'

Herminius shoved Indavara in the shoulder. He didn't move an inch.

'I'll take pity on you and assume that because you've only the one ear, you don't hear so well. Last chance. Inside!'

Herminius lashed out again. This time Indavara grabbed his hand, or, more precisely, two of his fingers. With a single flick of his wrist, he bent the fingers back on themselves, snapping them just below the knuckle.

Herminius loosed an agonised screech and staggered away, staring down at his hand.

Two of the guards struck out with their spears. Indavara had nowhere else to go but back. He tripped over the bottom of the gate, and fell into the cell. One of the guards swung the door. As it clanged shut, another man came forward and locked it.

'You one-eared whore-son,' Herminius spat. 'You'll pay for that. By the wrath of the gods you'll pay!'

Indavara got to his feet. He barely noticed the other prisoners as he retreated across the cell to the window. He turned and looked out at the black sky.

'Caesar's balls,' said Cassius. 'Then we'll just have to steal one.'

Having dispatched Simo with orders to find Abascantius and tell him everything they'd seen, Cassius and Major had spent the last few moments scouring the jetty for a manned boat, but to no avail.

Alongside the last pontoon was a rowing tender about twelve feet long. Cassius ran over to it and knelt down, searching for oars. He found a pair stowed under the middle of the three seats.

'No rowlocks but it'll do. Major, untie that rope.'

Cassius climbed down and pulled out the oars from under the seat. The bodyguard threw in the rope then clambered in after it. Cassius pushed off and passed an oar back to Major.

'We shall have to paddle – you take the right.'

The little boat lurched alarmingly as the two men got settled, Cassius on the forward seat, Major to the rear. Realising his sword belt would hinder him, Cassius wrenched it off over his head.

Then he took up his oar and dug deep, propelling the boat out into the river. He was relieved to see the tide was ebbing; it would have been a struggle to row against the water and keep pace with Scaurus's craft. Cassius reckoned the boat was about a hundred yards away but with the lanterns still alight it wouldn't be difficult to follow.

On they went, until Cassius could feel his arms burning and sweat on his back. To their left were high banks of reeds, to their right the scattered lights of the city. Occasionally a snatch of singing would drift across the water towards them.

Kaeso Scaurus. He could hardly believe it. The ostenatious host, this vulgar, almost comical man – a robber and murderer? Cassius reminded himself that Scaurus was a slave-trader. It hardly defied belief that he held human life in such low regard, or that he might be prepared to use anyone – and dispose of anyone – to get his way. There had been that moment at the dinner party with the young slave when his cruel nature had been there for all to see. And Antonia felt he had given up on obtaining office in the city, been unusually rude and impolitic; had he known his days in Antioch were numbered?

And what of the banner? If he was acting alone, did he even understand the true significance of the object in his possession? If he was working with others, why did they want it?

Forcing himself to focus on the job in hand, Cassius put in a few wide strokes to keep them on course. Major was powering them along well from the rear, and he had to keep his concentration to compensate.

They passed an area of the river bank lined with sections of the old city walls, then followed the eastern channel as the Orontes split around the island. Once or twice, Cassius heard heavy splashes close to the shore – rats, he guessed. He looked up and saw that Scaurus's boat was pulling away. He increased his stroke.

Soon they were passing under the arches of the closest bridge, past the smelly, salty weed that clung to its bricks. Now there were more river craft: a few rich types being rowed home by their attendants, and some noisy drunks on a moored barge.

Then the broad arches of Hadrian's Bridge loomed out of the darkness. Cassius slowed down and watched Scaurus's boat clear the bridge, then put in next to the galley at his private dock. Cassius nodded to the left; and they made for the wall of the nearest arch. He shipped his oar and put out his hands. His fingers touched only slick stone covered with weed, but then he found an iron ring which he used to pull the boat in. He soon realised there was a line of the rings, and he and Major hauled the little vessel along to the front of the arch. Leaning forward over the bow, Cassius peered out at the dock.

It was well lit by more than a dozen lanterns. Scaurus was already out of the boat. He had a brief conversation with a guard standing close to the bow of the *Radians*, then strode towards the House of the Dolphins. The other four – still with their heavy bags over their shoulders – weren't far behind.

Cassius turned round. 'Let's take a closer look.'

They cast off from the bridge and let the tide take them down past the dock, using the oars only to keep away from the main stream. Cassius examined the galley. He guessed the *Radians* was eighty feet long, perhaps twenty wide. The sail and the yard were lying on the deck and eight ranks of oars now rested in their holes. Several barrels had been tied down behind the deckhouse. The galley looked ready to sail.

As they drifted past the stern, Cassius spied a second guard. Sculling gently with his oar, holding the boat in place, he stared hard at the hull. Were there other barrels below decks? The eighteen small, heavy barrels he had tracked across Syria?

'We shall go alongside,' he whispered.

'What?' replied Major.

Cassius almost wavered then. It would be so easy to let the boat float away downstream. Major certainly wouldn't complain. But the same determination that had possessed him at the villa was with him again. If he could confirm the banner and the treasure were aboard the *Radians*, this whole affair might be resolved in a matter of hours. He had to know.

Cassius dug his oar in deep again and made for the ship. Major let out a long breath but did his part. They approached the galley slowly, easing closer until they were just yards away from the high hull. Manoeuvring between two of the long oars, they came alongside with a slight bump. Cassius reached for the rope and tied it around the oar just above his head. He indicated that Major should hold them off with his arm, to avoid the hulls banging together.

Cassius looked down at his sword belt and thought about putting it on, but he knew it would get in the way or knock against something. He still had his dagger. He clambered back to the middle seat, facing Major.

'If anything goes wrong, tap on the hull,' he whispered. 'I'll get back here as soon as I can.'

Cassius stood up on the seat, a hand on the galley to steady him. He placed one boot into the oar-hole, launched himself upward and gripped the side rail with both hands. He then climbed over it and hunched down on the deck. It was still wet from the rain.

He had come aboard close to the mast. He stood up for a moment and saw that the guards were still keeping station at either end of the ship. Towards the stern, in the middle of the deck, was a dark square: the main hatch, he guessed. He got down on his hands and knees and crawled towards it, feeling ahead for any obstacles.

Once there, he raised his head and looked along the lighted path that led to the southern wing of the villa. Away to the right, the grass sloped down to where he had stood just days ago, watching Scaurus's antics and talking to the governor's daughters.

Ducking down, he rounded the edge of the hatch. Reaching the first of the wide steps, he descended slowly on his backside, step by step. He could smell pitch; perhaps the galley's hull had been freshly lined for a long journey.

By the time he reached the bottom, he could see barely a yard in front of his face. But as he crawled towards the bow and his eyes adjusted, he found he could use the dim light from the oar-holes to measure his progress. Beyond the last pair was a short set of steps leading downward. He continued on and saw an open hatch that admitted enough moonlight to illuminate the forward hold. He got to his feet and began his search.

He moved slowly and carefully, so as not to dislodge anything and make a noise. To the left of the hold he found only sailing gear: spars, rope, blocks, piles of sailcloth. By the bow were water barrels and trays of food. There could be no doubt now: the *Radians* was going somewhere.

To the right a large square of canvas had been laid over something. Cassius gently pulled it away and knelt down in front of the objects underneath. He put out his hands and found the first of the small barrels. It seemed about the right size. He gripped each side and tried to move it. Heavy. Very heavy.

He tried the lid but it had been nailed down. There were more barrels behind it and to the side. He counted as he touched each in turn and was up to ten when he found one with a loose lid. He tried to open it with his fingers but a few nails were still in place. He pulled out his dagger and finished the job, slowly prising up half the lid. When he had an inch of clear space, he wedged the lid open with his knife and put his other hand inside.

His fingers slid over the cold, tightly packed coins. He took one, then stood and held it up by the hatch. This coin was in excellent condition. Even in the moonlight, he could see both the crossed swords commemorating Artaxata and the portrait of

Marcus Aurelius. Cassius put the coin in his money bag and smiled in the darkness. It was hard to resist the temptation to look for the banner, but he set off straight away.

He was halfway back to the main hatch when he heard footsteps and voices. The ship shifted slightly as several people came on board. Cassius ducked down by an oar but it soon became obvious the party were heading for the stern. He heard several items thump down on the deck and prayed to the great gods that the men would leave their loads and return to the villa. He carried on to the hatch and waited at the base of the steps, staring upward. He could hear them – servants by the sound of it.

'Just here will do.'

'Not that way up.'

'Should we tie it on?'

'Nah, that's sailors' work.'

'Come on, let's get back to the kitchen. That Helena's bringing the vegetables tonight – I want to get another look at her.'

'Hold on. I need a piss.'

Two men passed the hatch. Cassius heard them step off the galley, then heard the third man relieving himself into the river.

'Hey!'

The servant stumbled back past the hatch and jumped on to the dock.

'There's a boat there!' he shouted. 'Guards! There's a boat there. And a man!'

Cassius charged up towards the deck. He was almost at the top when one of his feet fell between two steps. He recovered himself and clambered out of the hatch. The guard at the stern had just climbed on to the galley.

'One here too!'

He ran at Cassius, blade up.

Cassius didn't move. If he could get out of the way of the sword, the man's speed might take him down into the hatch. Crouching low, he was ready to dive out of the way when something struck the guard in the face. The man's feet went from under him and he landed on his back right in front of Cassius.

'He's yours!'

Major sprang past as the second guard jumped up on to the galley. The three servants were running up the path to the villa, shouting for help.

Cassius smashed his fist down into where he thought the guard's stomach was and connected with yielding flesh. The guard grunted but was still able to bring up his sword. As Cassius scrabbled forward to take it off him, his right hand brushed against a hard, rounded object lying on the deck. Major's cudgel – the object he'd thrown at the guard.

Trying to ignore the clanging of swords to his left, Cassius picked up the cudgel and slammed it down – again into the stomach. The guard's breath flew from his mouth but he struggled on. Cassius struck again, lower this time. The guard groaned, and rolled over on to his side.

Cassius plucked the sword from the guard's fingers. He stood and stepped over him.

Major jabbed his blade at the second guard. His foe parried, then swung himself but he slipped and pitched forward, knocking Major's sword aside. Too close to use their blades, the men grappled, grunting as they slid on the slippery deck.

With the sword in one hand, the cudgel in the other, Cassius looked for a way to help Major, but the struggling pair lurched away from him.

Shouts from the path. The men who'd been with Scaurus were out in front. They reached into their bags as they ran and pulled out long, heavy clubs, then cast the bags aside.

Cassius was about to take a swipe with the cudgel at the guard's head when the battling pair crashed to the deck. Major recovered first. He smashed his sword handle down on to the man's head, knocking him out cold.

'Let's go,' he said between breaths.

Major still hadn't seen the advancing men. He stood up.

'Major, look out!'

The first of the club-men launched himself off the dock and leapt clean over the side rail. Boots thudding across the deck, he swung the weapon just as Major turned. The bodyguard didn't even have time to get his arm up.

Bloody flesh splattered Cassius's face as the club connected, virtually decapitating Major. Head lolling from his neck at forty-five degrees, his limp form collapsed, blood spewing from the gaping wound. Cassius stood there, frozen.

The club-man glanced at him then looked down at his handiwork. One of his comrades came to a halt next to him. He looked down at what was left of Major and said something. They laughed.

Cassius retreated, wiping a soggy chunk of skin from the side of his mouth. He turned and ran. He was almost at the side rail when something struck his legs. He fell; and heard the crack of his head striking the deck. He pressed his hands against the timbers, trying to push himself up, but he couldn't move an inch. Pain seared his head. Dazzling white. Then nothing.

XXXII

By taking a route he knew would be largely clear of revellers, Simo made good time, arriving at Abascantius's villa in three-quarters of an hour. He wiped his wet brow as he rang the bell and waited. A little way up the street stood a carriage. A young lad was feeding the two horses from a bag of hay.

Shostra emerged from the shadows with his hand on his dagger. Simo could see a woman behind him, her face obscured by a hood.

'You,' said Shostra. 'Where's your master?'

'I don't know exactly. But I need to see Master Abascantius.'

Shostra unlocked the gate, then opened it. 'You better come with us.'

As the woman hurried past Simo, he glimpsed a young, fair face. Once Shostra had locked the gate, he and Simo joined her in the carriage. Talking to the horses in Aramaic, the lad jumped up and took hold of the reins.

'On we go, boy,' Shostra said over his shoulder. 'To the island.' He turned to Simo as they set off. 'Well? What's going on?'

'I think I'm supposed only to talk to Master Abascantius.'

'That may be easier said than done. Word's just come to me that he's been taken to the prison tower.'

'What? Why?'

'None of your concern. What's happened to that young fool *you* call master?'

Though mention of the prison inevitably sparked thoughts of his father, Simo forced himself to concentrate and began with the visit to Pythion's apartment. By the time he'd finished, they were crossing the Avenue of Herod and Tiberius.

379

'It's lucky you got back before we left,' said Shostra. 'Master Abascantius must hear of this immediately.'

'But how will you get word to him?'

Shostra gave a lascivious grin and glanced at the young woman beside him. 'There are ways.'

Indavara sat at the rear of the cell, with nothing to look forward to but a beating. Herminius had gone to get his fingers attended to, promising revenge when he returned. Indavara was certain of one thing. When the guards came at him again, more of them would get hurt.

A few moments earlier, Abascantius had been brought in by the centurion from the mint, along with two legionaries and a clerk carrying a leather case. The five men were now in the same little room Corbulo had used the previous day. Salvian and the other two operatives stood close together at the front of the cell, deep in discussion.

Indavara was so lost in his thoughts that he barely noticed Simo's father had walked over to him.

'You were here with my son.'

Indavara nodded as Abito sat down.

'Do you know where my boy is?'

'No.'

'Why have they thrown you in here?'

Indavara shrugged. 'I was in the wrong place at the wrong time. As usual.'

'I'm sure your Master Corbulo will have you out of here in no time.'

'He's not my master.'

'Friend, then.'

'Nor that.'

Indavara tapped the wall above his head. 'The plaster around the window – looks pretty weak, yes?'

'It does.'

'As if it might easily be pried away?'

'This whole place is falling apart. But even if one could take it off, there's a sixty-foot drop outside.'

Indavara shrugged. 'There is that.'

'What was your name, again?'

Indavara told him.

'Unusual. Where does it come from?'

Abito received no reply.

'Will you pray with me, Indavara? We both need a little help, I think.'

'To your god?'

'We believe there is only one.'

'Would he listen to me? Help me?'

'He listens to all men.'

'Then why has he punished you?'

Abito looked over at the other Christians. The only lantern was close to the guards' room, casting a dim glow over the men. They lay in a line; some asleep, others staring up at the ceiling.

'I don't think he is punishing us. Testing us, perhaps.'

'Testing what?'

'Our faith in him.'

Indavara tilted his head back against the wall. 'If he won't help you, he definitely won't help me.'

Abito picked at the crumbling clay floor with his fingers. 'Perhaps this is not his work. Perhaps it is the beast Satan.'

'Satan?'

'Our Lord's enemy. His demons are loose in the world – they are the ones that unleash pain and cruelty on us.'

'Are they men? These demons?'

'I don't know,' said Abito quietly.

'I think they're men.'

━━◆8◆━━

Half an hour later, the door to the little room opened. First out were the centurion and his clerk, followed by Abascantius, then the two legionaries. While the clerk and the soldiers waited, the centurion led Abascantius over to the cell and ordered the guards to open up.

One of the prisoners sitting to Indavara's right got to his feet. Despite the fact that most of the others were sleeping, he clapped his hands.

'Gods be praised! If it isn't Pitface himself. Perhaps there is a little justice to be found in Antioch after all.'

Some of the other prisoners stirred, looking on as Abascantius entered the cell.

'Have a good night,' the centurion said drily as he and his men left.

As Abascantius turned from the bars, the loud-mouthed man came towards him.

'So all your underhand tricks and lies have caught up with you at last,' he said smugly.

'Hello, Dexippus,' Abascantius replied. 'Haven't they hanged you yet?'

'Now that you find yourself in here, perhaps you will beat me to the noose. Tell me, who did you set up this time? Whose life did you ruin?'

Salvian moved forward to cut off Dexippus, but Abascantius waved him away.

'Do yourself a favour, Dexippus. Shut up and sit down. I'm not in the mood.'

'Oh, you're not in the mood? Well, I wasn't particularly in the mood for having my life destroyed. I wasn't particularly in the mood for—'

Abascantius took one step forward and landed a solid boot between Dexippus's legs. The man hit the ground hard, squirming and groaning.

'Never did know when to keep his mouth shut,' muttered Abascantius as he joined his men. They stood between the Christians and Indavara, and had only just started talking when Herminius came up the stairs, his fingers now bound. He walked straight into the guards' room and emerged brandishing a long, thick cane in his good hand. He came close to the bars and peered into the gloomy cell.

'You, One Ear. Come here.'

Indavara stared back at him.

'All right,' Herminius said, nodding at the door. 'Bring him out.'

Two of the guards grabbed their spears. Another took the key from a hook.

Abascantius came over to Indavara. 'I'm assuming you're responsible for that bandaged hand?'

Indavara nodded.

Abascantius walked back to the door and faced the chief guard through the bars. He glanced down at Herminius's hand and shrugged. 'He can be a little excitable at times.'

Herminius tapped the cane against the floor. 'Me too. As he's about to find out.'

'The thing is,' replied Abascantius, 'I really can't have you attacking my men. I could perhaps offer you a little compensation for the pain, but that's all you'll get. Put the cane down, have a bit of wine.'

The man with the key still hadn't unlocked the door. Herminius exchanged glances with him and the other guards, then turned back to Abascantius.

'I must confess I didn't expect ever to see you here but you *are* my prisoner, Master Abascantius. As is your young friend.'

'What's your name, legionary?'

The chief guard rolled his eyes. 'Optio. Herminius.'

'Well, Herminius, listen a moment. You are free to ignore me, of course. As you say, I am your prisoner. But you'd better be confident that I will remain on this side of the bars. Personally, I doubt I shall be here much longer than tomorrow, but if you know something I don't – go ahead, please. Make an enemy of me if you wish.'

Herminius now looked considerably less sure of himself. Before he could reply, a legionary came jogging up the stairs. He hurried over to Herminius and whispered in his ear. After a moment's

thought and a brief glance at Abascantius, the chief guard put
his cane on a table and went down the stairs.

Simo had been told to stay by the carriage with the lad. Shostra
and the woman – her hood still covering her face – were waiting
outside the door to the prison tower. Simo recognised the rough
features of Herminius as the chief guard stepped outside. Shostra
showed him a letter and they began talking. Herminius shook his
head several times.

Then, at a word from Shostra, the woman pulled down her
hood. Simo saw that she was indeed fair, with pale, delicate features
and long tresses of glossy blonde hair – features rarely seen this
far east. Herminius and the two sentries were transfixed. The chief
guard dragged his eyes away long enough to examine the letter
again. With a last glance at the girl, he nodded, snatched up the
letter and returned inside. Shostra sent the girl after him and they
both disappeared into the tower. Shaking their heads, the sentries
returned to their posts on either side of the door.

Shostra walked back to the carriage with a triumphant smirk
on his face.

A quarter of an hour later, Herminius and the girl came out of
the tower. The girl already had her hood back up as she trotted
towards the carriage.

'Nighty night,' called out Herminius, before disappearing up
the stairs.

'Where's that wine?' the girl demanded as she climbed into
the carriage. Simo detected an unusual accent; he was certain
she came from some distant western province.

'Under the seat,' answered Shostra.

Simo looked on as she found the bottle, pulled out the cork
and took a long swig. He had never seen such a thing.

'What are you staring at, Fatso?'

'Apologies, madam.'

Shostra snorted. 'I wouldn't worry. She's no lady.'

He pulled out some coins and gave them to the girl. She put down the wine and counted her money.

'Take her home,' Shostra told the lad. 'Then come back here.'

As the boy turned the carriage around, Shostra chuckled at Simo's expression. 'You needn't look so shocked. Your master's a grain man too – better get used to dirty dealings.'

'Now what?' asked Simo.

'We wait.'

'What for?'

'Orders.'

Abascantius had continued his discussions with his men but his attention switched to the chief guard when he saw the sheet of papyrus in his hand. Indavara sidled along the wall towards the front of the cell; he wanted to know what was going on. Herminius came up to the bars once more.

'You have some persuasive friends.'

Abascantius nodded at the letter. 'That's for me?'

'I was ordered not to admit visitors for you. Nothing was said about letters.'

'I'm glad you're seeing sense.'

'You mentioned compensation. I have a figure in mind.'

Herminius gestured for Abascantius to come closer and a whispered conversation ensued. At the end of it both men nodded, and Herminius passed the letter through the bars.

'Your man's expecting a reply. You have half an hour.'

Abascantius waved the others away and leaned back against the wall as he read the letter. After only a moment he cursed and lashed a kick at the floor. Then he took a few deep breaths and finished reading. When he was done, he asked Herminius for a pen. The chief guard brought one and a pot of ink from the guards' room and passed them through the bars. Salvian took them and started filling the pen with ink. Abascantius knelt down on the floor, turned the sheet over and pressed it down on to a piece of reed matting.

Indavara went over and squatted next to him. 'What's going on, sir?'

'Not now.'

'Bloody thing,' said Salvian, shaking the pen to get the ink flowing. 'Won't be a moment.'

Abascantius sighed and turned to Indavara. 'Looks like Corbulo was on the right trail after all. He may have found out who has what we're after.'

'Do those men know? The governor and—'

'No. Nor can I risk telling him. There's no way yet to know who else is involved. But if I can get this information to the right person, we still have a chance.'

'So where is he? Corbulo?'

'We're not exactly sure. And that lying rat Silus and his whore girlfriend have vanished into thin air too. I hope Corbulo hasn't got in over his head. He's no hope of handling this on his own.'

'What if I told you I could get us out of here?' said Indavara. 'With a little help.'

'After all the mistakes I've made in the last few days, I suppose I should be open to suggestions. Go on.'

When Indavara had finished explaining what he had in mind, Abascantius gave a grim smile.

'Why in Hades not?'

Simo and Shostra held on tight as the lad urged the horses on through the city streets. Midnight had just passed when the reply came down from Abascantius and they had instantly set off back across the island. As far as Simo could gather, there was some kind of coded message within the letter, which Shostra had been studying for quite a time. Eventually, he spoke:

'You should know what I'm doing in case you do find that master of yours. I am to fetch Lady Antonia and ride north with a message. Apparently Marshal Marcellinus is on the Tarsus road. My master believes he will listen to her and take charge of the situation.'

'And what am I to do?' asked Simo.

'I shall tell you in a moment – a most unusual task. But first we must check something. Stop here!'

They had just started across Hadrian's Bridge. As the horses slowed, then halted, Shostra jumped down from the cart and looked over the wall. He spat a curse and smacked his hand against the rough stone.

'We must move quickly.'

'What is it?' asked Simo, joining him at the wall. Below was the dock of the House of the Dolphins.

'Scaurus's ship – it's gone.'

XXXIII

They began early, while the other prisoners and the guards slept. Indavara had claimed the space next to the window and been joined by Abascantius and his men. After the incident with Dexippus, the other collaborators had stayed well clear of the new arrivals, lining the wall on the other side of the cell. The Christians were closer but Abito had given assurances they would do nothing to interfere. Indavara's main concern was that Dexippus or another troublemaker might notice what they were doing, but there were at least a few heavy snorers to cover the noise of their work.

The grille was a six-foot iron grid that had been nailed around the window. The plaster was old – dry and rotting; and with some coordinated effort the nails could be levered out. Without their daggers, Indavara and the others used whatever they could find: belt buckles, coins, even an old fork. And by the time the very first traces of red appeared on the horizon, the job was done. To the casual eye, the grille would look precisely as it had the previous day, but it was in fact held in place by only six nails: two at the bottom, two at each side.

Abascantius kept watch; and had already decided he would leave the escape bid to the younger, more athletic members of his group. They had all been briefed to try to intercept Scaurus, or at least track him until help arrived from Marcellinus. Salvian had elected to stay behind too but Indavara had gained a little more respect for the agent's men; they had toiled for several hours.

The guards and the other prisoners were already stirring when Abascantius finally agreed there was enough light to go ahead. Indavara and the other two men quietly readied themselves, tightening their boots and belts. Abascantius and Salvian were just getting into position when a loud voice split the silence.

'What are you doing?'

One of the prisoners – a slight, sly-looking man who'd been sleeping next to Dexippus – was staring down at the small mounds of plaster and dust below the window. Salvian was closest, but he couldn't quite get there before the man cried out to the guards. A moment later, Salvian's right fist struck his mouth, sending him sprawling to the floor, blood leaking from a split lip.

'Now!' shouted Indavara.

Abascantius and Salvian reached for the grille.

Herminius burst out of the guardroom, still doing up his belt. He looked inside the cell.

'Get your spears!' he cried as he plucked the key from the hook and ran for the door.

Abascantius and Salvian were having trouble; some of the nails were stuck. Indavara ran over to help. He gripped the edge of the grille with both hands.

'Get away from that window!' barked Herminius as he opened the door. The other two guards piled past him, spears at the ready. Though they had almost freed the grille, Abascantius and Salvian let go. Indavara turned to find the guards right behind him.

'I don't know why you're trying to get out of a window this high up, but in my book that's an attempted escape,' said Herminius. 'I shall have to take action.' The chief guard picked up his cane and aimed it at Indavara. 'Starting with you. Lads, bring him to me. Stick him if he tries anything.'

The guards closed in on Indavara. He darted to his right, dodged past a spear blade with six inches to spare, and ran for the door.

But in an instant, Herminius had kicked it shut behind him. He raised the cane as Indavara charged forward.

One of the Christians was between them. He scurried out of the way, dragging his blanket with him; the blanket on which Indavara's left foot had just landed. Indavara stumbled past the chief guard and slammed into the unforgiving bars.

As he tried to get up, Herminius lashed the cane against his shoulder: a heavy, stinging blow.

'Nice try,' snarled Herminius. 'Over here, you two.'

Indavara grabbed the bars and pulled himself to his feet. By the time he'd straightened up, the guards had surrounded him.

'Going to come quietly this time?' asked Herminius.

Indavara took a moment to appraise the two men in front of him; they were holding the spears horizontally, points aimed at his stomach. Then he looked across the cell at Abascantius.

'Do you trust your servant?'

Abascantius's eyes narrowed for a moment, but then he gave an enigmatic half-smile. 'Yes.'

Herminius frowned.

Indavara looked over at Abito, who was now on his feet and looking on. 'Do you trust your son?'

Abito took rather longer to answer, but the reply was even more definitive. 'Absolutely.'

Indavara kicked out at the closest guard, striking the hand gripping the top of his spear. As the weapon flew upward, Indavara grabbed the shaft and drove it into the guard's face, striking him on the nose. As the guard let go and fell, Indavara swung the weapon to his right, catching the second guard on the forehead with a dull slap. Arms flailing, the guard staggered backwards into Herminius.

Abascantius and Salvian wrenched off the grille and threw it to the floor.

Eyes fixed on the bright square of light, Indavara ran between them and leapt feet first through the window.

In the brief time it took him to drop sixty feet, he closed his eyes. If there was nothing beneath him, he hoped his neck would break; he wanted to die quickly.

But he landed flat on his back, and made such a hole in the mountain of straw that when he opened his eyes, the pile was already falling in on top of him. He was winded; but nothing was broken.

'You all right?' cried a familiar voice from somewhere to his right.

He spat out a piece of straw. 'Yes!'

'What about the others?'

'Just me. Go!'

As the cart rumbled away, Indavara slid to his left and almost off the back. He threw up his hands and gripped the side of the cart as his legs hung over the rear edge. He dragged himself forward and hung on as the cart juddered across the rough ground. Looking ahead, he glimpsed Simo's broad back. The Gaul was hunched over with one hand on the reins, the other holding the side of the cart.

Only when they reached the road was Indavara able to move. He crawled through the straw then clambered up on to the seat next to Simo. The Gaul – his face flushed and wet with sweat – looked back towards the prison.

'It's all right,' said Indavara. 'No one's following. They have no mounts there.'

Keeping the horses at a trot, Simo turned on to a wider street, heading directly away from Hadrian's Bridge, west across the island. Though the route passed close to the sprawling walls and high towers of the imperial palace, there were only a few people up and about.

'Thank the Lord,' said Simo, patting Indavara on the arm. 'I must have moved that cart twenty times. Every time the horses twitched my heart almost stopped.'

'You did well,' said Indavara. 'But slow down. We're attracting enough attention as it is.'

Thanks to their speed, most of the straw was now gone, but they were still leaving quite a trail on the road.

'Ah,' said Indavara. 'Good.' He glanced down at the collection of weapons and equipment Simo had strapped to the seat.

'Your bow and quiver. I found you a sword and dagger too. Plus Master Cassius's armour.'

'Water?'

'In your bag.'

Indavara found the gourd inside the leather sack and took a long drink. Passing the imperial palace, they saw a squad of legionaries and six curtained litters being carried towards the gates.

Before long they came to the bridge on the western side of the island, where four city sergeants were gazing down at a boat passing underneath. When they heard the approaching cart one man hurried into the road, waving at Simo.

'Go,' ordered Indavara. 'Speed up.'

'Oh my.'

Simo lashed at the horses and the cart rattled around the guard and on to the bridge. The sergeants shouted at them but stayed at their post. Indavara hung on tight as they sped over the river.

'Are they following? Are they following?' jabbered Simo.

'Relax and use your eyes. They don't have mounts either.'

Only when they were across and on to the wide road heading west did Simo slow down. He turned to Indavara.

'Did you see my father?'

'I did. He's well. In fact he helped us.'

'I might find myself beside him soon,' said the Gaul, gripping the reins with one hand so he could wipe his brow with the other. 'I too shall be considered a criminal now.' He turned and looked back at the bridge.

They passed several small hamlets; and a few farmers and traders heading into town for market, then came to a junction.

'This road runs parallel to the river,' said Simo. 'I pray they've not made it to the port yet.'

He guided the horses to the left.

Indavara held up a hand. 'Stop here.'

'What? Why?'

'Just stop.'

Simo reined in, and the cart trundled to a halt.

'We can't waste time here,' said the Gaul impatiently. 'Abascantius wants you to go after Master Cassius. He was following this man Scaurus and his ship has gone. Shostra believes he'll be headed downriver, trying to escape.'

392

'I'm not going after any ship,' replied Indavara coolly.

'But that's why all this was arranged.'

'I arranged it. So I could get free. Now I am.'

Indavara turned to look at the signpost by the junction. 'What does that say?'

Simo didn't reply; he was still staring at Indavara in disbelief.

'Well,' said Indavara as he untied the weapons, 'if this road leads to the coast, I shall go the other way.'

'What about your money?'

Indavara jumped down to the ground. 'I have a little left.'

He swung his bow, quiver and bag over his shoulder and took the sword and dagger.

'You can't just leave him,' said Simo. 'You were supposed to protect him.' The Gaul clambered down and hurried after Indavara, meeting him at the rear of the cart.

'Corbulo decided I wasn't up to the job, remember? And I'm glad of it. He did me a favour. Why should I risk my life for a man who cares only for himself?'

'There's been no word from him. This man Scaurus is evil. We found a cavern full of bodies. Full of blood.'

'Then your master's probably dead too.'

Simo's head dropped.

'Anyway,' Indavara continued, 'do you even know what all this is about? What it is we've hunted across Syria? Can anything be so precious that so many men must die for it? Leave these rich idiots to their games. Why not just come with me?'

'I cannot,' the Gaul said quietly.

Indavara offered his hand. 'Then I shall say goodbye, Simo.'

Simo ignored the hand, but he spoke: 'I know you may not have seen his best side, but Master Cassius is a good man and I'll not abandon him. If he's alive, then he's alone and he needs help.'

'I wonder – would he do the same for you?'

'I believe he would.'

'That is where we disagree. Goodbye, and good luck.'

Indavara set off in the opposite direction.

393

Simo watched him for only a moment. He hurried back to the front of the cart and climbed up, then set the horses off along the river road.

—8—

Indavara tried to stop someone, find out where he was walking to. The drivers of the first three carts kept going; perhaps, he thought, because of the weapons he was carrying. The fourth cart belonged to an old man, who halted only long enough to tell him that the road led to the city of Alexandretta. Indavara had never heard of it.

He walked on; and soon came to a milestone. As he stood there, trying to make sense of the letters and numbers, four boys emerged from the marsh at the side of the road. They walked past him, headed for the river. They were carrying fishing rods and nets and one was leading an unsaddled horse along. They weren't speaking, but were taking it in turns to kick a stone ahead of them. Indavara put his bag down by the milestone, then laid the weapons on top of it. He squatted down on his haunches and watched the boys ambling towards the water.

Back in Pietas Julia, he had always taken great care not to make friends, because gladiators measured their lives in weeks and months, and never knew when they might face each other in combat. He had outlived every last man. From the moment he had heard of Capito's deal, he had thought only of that twentieth contest. For six long years, he had done nothing but train and fight.

All he could do – all he had ever done – was look after himself.

He watched the boys a moment longer, as they began running towards the river.

Things were different now. He was free; free to do what he wanted. But that meant he had choices, and whether he liked it or not, the choices he made today had consequences for others. What if Corbulo was alive? And what if Simo tried to save him on his own? They wouldn't stand a chance.

Indavara looked back at the junction.

It was one thing to be forced to fight. It was another to choose to.

At the top of the river bank was a well-trodden towpath usually used by slaves hauling barges up and down the Orontes. The path was smooth and wide, and Simo made good time. He knew there were fifteen miles of river between Antioch and Seleucia. Without knowing when the galley had left, it was impossible to guess where the ship might be.

For the first hour, he passed only small vessels going downriver and three big grain freighters coming up. He came to an unmanned loading dock and was delayed while he took the road that ran round it.

Another hour; and the path followed the meandering river through a wooded area thick with insects. The horses were fading fast. Simo was on the verge of stopping and unshackling them from the cart, when they passed the last of the trees and he spied a vessel up ahead.

The galley was moving quickly, the sixteen oars dipping in and out of the water at speed, leaving a thick trail of foaming wake. Simo slowed the horses as he came up behind the ship. Below the sternpost was a bronze plaque. Shostra had told him the vessel's name and there it was: *Radians*. One man was operating the tiller, another – the captain perhaps – stood next to him. Six other sailors were on deck, coiling ropes. They soon noticed Simo, and watched him as they worked. The captain looked up at the bank too.

Simo kept his head facing forward, but his eyes stayed on the galley. As he passed each rank of oars, he could make out the dark, muscled forearms of each slave beyond the port-hole. There was no sign of anyone else. He passed the bow and drove the exhausted horses onward. He could see the cranes and warehouses of the port a couple of miles ahead.

'Dear Lord, grant me strength.'

XXXIV

It was the shivering that woke Cassius: a sharp, icy chill that ran up his spine and across his shoulders. Raising his hands to rub his eyes, he realised his wrists were tied together. He shifted and felt a fiery pain on the left side of his skull. He could hear a rhythmic beating sound coming from somewhere ahead of him. He made himself stay still. Slowly, the pain receded.

Where am I?

A bright light somewhere above. He was sitting with legs stretched out in front of him, his back against a hard surface. He moved his neck and felt something sticky on the left side of his neck – dried blood, he guessed.

Dreams? That pile of mutilated bodies in the cavern? Major butchered in front of him by that laughing warrior?

Water dripped on to his lap. He looked up and saw blackened timbers, then a square of bright blue sky. Clouds too; and a gull swooping by on the wind. That noise. The beating. A drum for oarsmen. He was on the ship.

A key turned. The door in front of him swung inward, and Kaeso Scaurus walked in. The smile on that cherubic face seemed so innocent, so genuine, that Cassius almost smiled back.

'Ah, you're awake at last.'

Scaurus was wearing a simple long-sleeved tunic, with only the finger-rings and a gold-plated belt buckle to mark him out as a man of means. He was armed with a long, narrow dagger. He stood over Cassius and looked down at his head.

'Ouch.'

Running a hand through his curls, Scaurus leaned back against a thick pile of sailcloth.

'I have some questions.'

'Me too,' replied Cassius. He was struck by the strangeness of his own voice; it sounded thin and weak.

Scaurus smiled again. 'I'm afraid I will have to insist on accurate answers.'

'Me too.'

Scaurus chuckled and looked Cassius over. 'You are rather pretty, grain man. I do like your face. But be under no illusions – I will get what I need from you.'

Cassius thought of Simo; remembered sending him to Abascantius. It was morning now; that had been hours ago. Why had no one come to help him?

'What does he know?' asked Scaurus.

'Who?'

'Pitface.'

'I have no idea. The last time I saw him he was headed for the imperial mint. But I suspect you already know that.'

Scaurus shrugged. 'Don't suppose he needed much encouragement to finger his old friend the procurator, did he? It seemed wise to keep the fat swine occupied. I heard from Quarto that Octobrianus was unveiling some new coins to Gordio there last night. I imagine there was quite a scene.'

Cassius's head was clearing. He ran over the events of recent days.

'It must have started with Nabor, I suppose. The misdirection.'

Scaurus nodded. He seemed rather proud of himself. 'You had a narrow escape there. Python wanted to kill you right away – as soon as you started sniffing around – but that would have invited too much attention. Better to put you on another trail. How did you come to Nabor by the way?'

Cassius told Scaurus about the merchant's slave and tracing Nabor to the glass factory.

'You were lucky.'

'Perhaps,' said Cassius. 'But you didn't control your people.'

'Python's mistake, not mine.'

'Who were the others? The men who took the cart.'

'Whoever he could get. Brigands, mercenaries. Even a few ex-legionaries, as I recall. There wasn't time to be too picky.'

'And Silus? Bacara? Or whatever their names were. You wouldn't find a talented pair of actors like that just anywhere.'

'True, true. They had done a few jobs for me before. Do you know how I first met them? They tried to con me out of five thousand denarii with a property scam. They were lovers. A shame really.'

'But they had outlived their usefulness. Just like the others. Turpo. Tarquinius. Even Pythion.'

Scaurus nodded approvingly. 'You've been to the guild house again.'

'We followed you from there. Do you have even an ounce of regard for human life?'

'You seem to have answered your own question.' Scaurus pushed himself off the sailcloth and came closer. 'But what interests me is whether you got a message to Abascantius. Or your one-eared friend. I don't like surprises.'

'I'll tell you – because I've seen enough to know what you'll do to me if I don't. But will you satisfy my curiosity about a few things first?'

Scaurus shrugged. 'Quicker than torturing you, I suppose.'

'Quarto and Ulpian. They know nothing of all this?'

'Those two idiots? Hardly. I took them out for a sail just a couple of days ago. They were standing on the deck above this very spot, drinking my finest Falernian. How I would love to see their faces when they find out.'

'And the Sons of Antioch?'

'A useful charade. And not only for myself, I might add. But it has been especially beneficial in the last few weeks.'

'And what happened at the baths? You said you'd decided not to kill me.'

'Once Pythion heard about your first visit to the guild house he panicked. And when he found out you were with Abascantius he took it upon himself to act. Could be a little impetuous at times.'

'How did you know him?'

'Oh, he was my half-brother. He and our father shared an unfortunate inability to control themselves.'

Cassius shook his head; such ruthlessness was hard to comprehend.

'He was always on about some money-making scheme or another,' Scaurus continued. 'Told me one of his old soldier mates knew about this stash of Palmyran treasure. I said I wasn't interested at first. Then I began to think about it . . .'

Scaurus shut the door.

'It's best they don't see what I have here. Wouldn't want a mutiny on my hands.'

He walked over to the barrel Cassius had half-opened the previous night. The lid had now been removed. Scaurus scooped out handfuls of coins, then retrieved a slender ingot of gold. He held it up to the light shining in through the hatch. Cassius could make out the Palmyran brand.

'Look at that beauty. And there are a hundred more like it. A hundred!'

Cassius took a deep breath. 'What about the Persian banner?'

'Yes, I wondered what that old thing was. Couldn't ask anyone about it of course, so I had to send one of my clerks to the library.'

'It's here?'

'No. I burned it.'

Cassius let his head fall back against the barrel. He hadn't even found the flag. Major had died for absolutely nothing; and now he faced the same fate.

'Only joking,' said Scaurus with a gloating smile. 'It's here somewhere. Don't see why the Persians think it's so special. I do like the gems though.'

Scaurus replaced the gold in the barrel.

Cassius shook his head and sighed with relief. 'But you are already a rich man,' he said. 'Why?'

'I *was* rich. I was the richest man in Antioch. But I ploughed most of it back into the city. They always wanted another temple, or another statue, or another bloody wall. And for what? A few cheap bronze plaques and a pat on the back. But never any real power. Not for a half-Jewish legionary's son.' Scaurus cast an eye across the barrels. 'I did some calculations. Even with all the slaves and the property – it was barely a third of what I have here. And this I can take with me.'

'But it wasn't just about the money, was it?'

Scaurus shrugged again.

'The fame?' Cassius continued. 'Or rather the infamy?'

'Oh the former, I think.' Scaurus opened his palms wide. 'This is the greatest robbery of all time, grain man. Everyone from here to Britannia will know *my* name.'

Cassius looked up through the hatch at the sky – it was so bright, so benign. Just another day, yet here he was, a prisoner on this ship, conversing with this murderous madman. So many lives lost. And for what – some twisted desire for notoriety?

Scaurus came close to him again.

'I've indulged you long enough, pretty boy. Now, what does Abascantius know? You must have got word to him.'

'I sent a message telling him about the cavern below the guild house and the dead men; and that you were responsible.'

'When?'

'About the fourth hour of night.'

'Ha, he really has lost his touch, hasn't he?' A relieved grin spread itself across the spherical face. 'We'll be at sea within the hour. There's nothing he can do now.'

'And then what?' countered Cassius. 'Abascantius is the least of your worries. Half the eastern fleet is stationed at Seleucia. They'll send the navy after you.'

'Possibly. But I'll have a good start. Rufus Bolanus is the commander of that fleet – a personal friend of mine. He's currently enjoying a week of leave at my villa in Paltus.'

'Even if you do get away, Marcellinus and the Emperor will hunt you to the ends of the earth.'

'They shall have to, for I am headed to Africa. There are lands there beyond a great desert where no man has been. I will find a way across it, and with all this I can build my own city, my own armies. No one will give a damn about my lineage there. And one day I may return.'

Cassius knew he had to keep the conversation going as long as he could; find a way to make Scaurus let him live.

'If I'd made it off this ship, you would never have got out of Antioch.'

'Ah, but you didn't, did you?'

'But I got close to stopping you – you must admit that.'

'Closer than Pitface, certainly.'

'Listen, Scaurus, I've only been with the Service a few months. My father made me join the army. I detest it; and there seems to be no prospect of returning to my former life. I'm not a fighting man, but I've more intelligence than most. I could be useful. Why not let me join you?'

Again, that wide, beatific smile.

'A well-framed gambit, grain man, but a desperate one. You know my business – I trade in slaves. I have spent most of my life dealing with people who hate me, who'd like to see me dead. And try as you might, you can't hide the disgust in your eyes. No, you shall die too. Stand. I don't want to make a mess in here. That big friend of yours bled like a pig; made a horrible stain on my deck.'

Cassius stayed where he was.

Scaurus eased the thin blade from the sheath. He walked over to Cassius, bent over him, and placed the tip of the knife just inside one of his nostrils.

'I said stand.'

Cassius slowly did so. Scaurus kept the blade where it was, then ran his other hand up Cassius's thigh and between his legs. He left his hand there for a moment, then continued on, up his chest and neck. He reached Cassius's mouth and pressed a single finger against his lips.

'Perhaps you *could* be useful to me.'

Scaurus lowered the blade and stepped away. 'But no, I mustn't let myself get distracted. I'm not quite safe yet.' He moved aside and gestured towards the door. 'I shall slit your throat and drop you over the side. You should be grateful – a swift death.'

'More than you'll get,' Cassius said as he passed him. 'I hope they crucify you.'

'What's your name, pretty boy?'

Cassius raised his chin. 'Cassius Quintius Corbulo.'

'Well, Cassius Quintius Corbulo, I, Kaeso Scaurus, am going to kill you now.'

He opened the door and shoved Cassius outside, then placed the tip of the blade against his neck. Cassius heard him locking the door behind them. The cold blade pushed at his skin.

'Up you go.'

Cassius went up the three steps and found himself staring at sixteen African slaves. Naked save for loincloths, the oarsmen were the darkest men he had ever seen. Though their upper bodies rippled with muscle, their legs seemed rather undeveloped in comparison. Each man was shackled to a longer chain that ran along the floor.

A seventeenth slave sat close to the hatch, beating out a slow rhythm on a drum between his legs. The oarsmen were taking long, steady breaths between strokes. Cassius could see they were an experienced, well-trained crew; though their chestnut skin shone with sweat, every man looked well within himself. A couple of them glanced curiously at him, then looked away.

An overseer with a long cane tucked into his belt was patrolling up and down the aisle between the slaves, sipping from a wooden mug. He made way for Cassius and looked him up and down as he and Scaurus passed. Next to the hatch, opposite the drummer, was a table around which four men sat, playing dice on a board and drinking wine.

The men from the jetty: the men who had slaughtered Major and laughed about it. The men who did Scaurus's killing for him.

They looked to be from lands either east or south of Syria. One was older – bald, probably in his forties; the other three about Cassius's age. All stocky and powerful, they were still wearing their black tunics and heavy leather boots. Propped up against the table were their four clubs. The head of one had been embellished by metal studs hammered into the wood. Another had two spikes sticking out of it. Cassius examined each face in turn but had no idea which of them had killed Major.

'Need a hand there, sir?' asked the older man casually, in passable Latin.

'I think I can handle this one, Alikar,' answered Scaurus. 'Take it easy on the wine.'

'Yes, sir.'

Cassius slowly made his way up the steps.

'Palestinian mercenaries,' explained Scaurus, his hand on Cassius's arm. 'I've bought and sold every kind of warrior imaginable. There are none better.'

Cassius stepped up on to the deck and bowed his head against the sunlight glinting off the river.

'Come, grain man.'

Scaurus led him towards the stern. Two men were there, one with both hands on the tiller, the other standing beside him. They were both wearing a pale belted tunic with trousers – standard sailor attire. The older man had a vertical blue stripe on his tunic. He was standing next to the deckhouse, a solidly built shelter that offered protection from the elements when at sea.

'Bit of rubbish,' Scaurus said, nodding at Cassius. 'Needs to be disposed of.'

The helmsman suddenly pointed forward. 'Sir, look there.'

The captain stared along the river, then moved right to see around the mast. His jaw dropped open. He ran forward and bellowed down into the hatch.

'Oars up! Oars up!'

Simo had prayed; and he believed God had answered.

Just half a mile downriver, he'd come across three old barges tied up to a decrepit jetty. One of the barges was full of water and listing badly, but the other two were still afloat. They were little more than wooden shells with posts close to the bow for a tow rope. The vessels were narrow but long – long enough for what Simo had in mind.

Having left the cart and the horses on the towpath, he'd cut some rope from the sunken barge, then used it to connect the other two via the towing posts. He then cut all the ropes except a line holding one of the barge's bows against the jetty.

Seeing how close Scaurus's galley was, he pushed the stern of the other craft out into the river. The ebbing tide did the rest, pulling both vessels out into the channel, until the far end of the second barge swung into the thick bank of reeds on the other side of the river. For one terrible moment, Simo thought the tide might pull it through but then both craft came to a rest, blocking the entire width of the river.

Now the big Gaul ran back along the jetty and jumped down on to the muddy path that led up to the road. He crouched down and peered through the reeds at the *Radians*, still cutting along the river at speed. Three sailors were running towards the bow.

'Back the oars!' yelled the captain. 'Now!'

He held out his arm to the right. The helmsman hauled on the tiller.

Scaurus was still gripping Cassius by the arm. In his other hand was the knife.

Cassius watched the oars spin around, then drop into the water just as the galley struck the middle of the first barge. The entire ship shuddered as the prow smashed into the rotten timbers.

Unlike the sailors, Scaurus hadn't taken the precaution of holding on to something solid and he and Cassius were thrown forward. Though his wrists were tied in front of him, Cassius at least managed to twist in the air so that he landed on his side. Scaurus fell too but swiftly scrambled back to his feet.

'What in Hades?' he yelled.

The captain ignored him. 'Centre the rudder,' he told the helmsman before striding forward.

Cassius lay where he was, his face an inch from the deck. He could smell the oil in the pitch-coated timbers. Next to the main hatch was a little square box affixed to the deck. Inside were two sponges, some lengths of cloth, and a rope-spike.

'Very good. So now what?'

Simo turned to find Indavara standing behind him, breathing hard. The bodyguard took his bow and quiver from his shoulder and laid them carefully on the ground. He had also attached the sword and dagger to his belt. At the top of the path was an unsaddled horse. Simo stared at it.

'Cost me every coin I had,' Indavara explained. 'Time to earn some more.'

The Gaul couldn't help smiling. 'Master Cassius is alive. He's right there.'

'I know. What's the plan?'

Simo gestured towards the barges. 'I hadn't thought much further than this.'

Indavara came up next to him, and peered through the reeds at the galley. 'I had a feeling you'd say that. Go and get Corbulo's mail-shirt.'

Simo started back up the path, then stopped. 'What are you going to do?'

'There are a lot of men on that thing. Let's see if we can even the odds.'

Cassius looked up at the helmsman. The sailor was staring forward and didn't even notice when Cassius rolled over on to his front and crawled across the deck towards the box.

Indavara took three arrows from the quiver and examined the ship. He could see no sign of Corbulo at the stern now. In fact there seemed to be only one man there.

The prow of the galley had embedded itself in the barge. Small chunks of timber continued to fall off both vessels and float away. The other sailors were gathered there, leaning over the side rail, examining the damage. A chubby older man was walking along the deck towards them. He was holding a knife.

'That's him,' said Simo as he returned with the mail-shirt. 'That's Scaurus.'

'Quickly. Before they realise this was no accident.'

Indavara raised his hands and squatted down. Simo lifted the mail-shirt and lowered it on over his head. Indavara stuck his head through the collar, then shoved his arms into the sleeves. The shirt got stuck over his chest.

'It's very tight,' Simo said as he heaved it down.

'It'll do.'

Indavara turned back to the river. 'What about bodyguards? Any fighting men?'

'I don't know. There were some with him earlier.'

Indavara picked up the bow and an arrow. He moved out on to the path to give himself a clear shot and got down on one knee. He checked the flight of the arrow then slotted it against the string. Drawing it only halfway back, he aimed for a point close to the *Radians'* prow, a foot below the deck.

He fired; and hit exactly where he wanted to. One of the sailors was so surprised he stumbled backwards and fell over. The others looked up at the jetty, then the bank. Some of them saw him. Indavara wasn't worried about that.

He already had the second bolt ready. He waited for the men to scurry back along the deck, then fired the second one into the mast. The sailor at the head of the group stopped. The others – Scaurus included – piled up beside him.

Indavara took the third arrow, aimed low, and fired straight into them, catching a man on the thigh. As he fell, some of the sailors ran back across the deck, jumped into the water and swam for the opposite bank. Others leapt off the bow into the barge and scrambled away. Left alone, the injured man decided he too would abandon ship, and rolled himself off the deck. Scaurus scuttled back towards the stern, head down as he ran.

Indavara turned to Simo and nodded down at the quiver. 'Bring that.'

He walked down the path and on to the jetty.

Cassius's fingers closed on the handle of the rope-spike. He was about to pull it towards him, when a booted foot landed on his wrist. He turned and stared up at the dark face and light eyes of the mercenary Alikar. He was holding his club by his side. Cassius could see notches on the handle. There were at least forty. Alikar screwed his boot into Cassius's arm. Cassius let go.

The Palestinian reached down with his spare hand, grabbed Cassius by the hair and dragged him up, then towards the stern. Cassius's boots slipped on the deck as he tried to stay on his feet. The mercenary deposited him in a corner by the deckhouse.

'Stay.'

Indavara walked along the narrow siding of the barge until he came to the prow of the ship. The swiftest of the sailors had already made it to the reeds and were dragging themselves up the bank. He turned to Simo and handed him the bow.

'You stay here. Any of them come back towards the ship – shoot them.'

Simo looked anxiously down at the weapon in his hand.

'Will you do it?' Indavara demanded. 'I need you to watch my back.'

Simo nodded.

'Then ready an arrow.'

Indavara reached up to the prow and hauled himself on to the galley.

━●8●━

Cassius watched the other three mercenaries hurry out of the hatch. When Scaurus reached them, he struck one across the shoulder.

'Go! All of you! It's just one man.'

Alikar said something to the others in their own tongue. They raised the clubs and started towards the bow.

Scaurus ran to the side rail and bellowed at the fleeing sailors. 'Come back, you cowards! Come back!' He spat into the water. 'Whore-sons, every one!'

He turned round as Cassius got to his feet and looked to the bow.

'Yes – your one-eared friend. But I fear he's bitten off a little more than he can chew this time.'

Scaurus still had the narrow blade in his hand. Crouching, his face flushed, he advanced towards Cassius.

'Now, where were we?'

XXXV

When he saw the size and weaponry of the four men striding towards him, Indavara gave serious thought to running back to the barge and grabbing the bow from Simo. But they were ten yards away and closing fast; they'd be on him before he could string an arrow.

He looked despairingly down at the blade in his hand. The short sword was perhaps his favourite weapon but it would be virtually useless against the clubs. And as there was no chance of obtaining a long spear or a heavy shield in the next few moments, his options were limited.

The oldest of the club-men barked an order and they spread out across the width of the deck. Indavara stopped a few feet forward of the mast. Lying behind it was the yard – the forty foot length of timber from which the sail would hang. The sail itself was bundled up in a long, leather sack. The leader and two of his men were to the left of this obstacle, the other man to the right. This warrior was also fractionally ahead of the others.

Indavara didn't like the idea of losing his main weapon but there was no time to hesitate. He took a couple of steps to the right, put both hands on the sword's hilt, drew it back over his shoulder, and let fly.

Caught completely by surprise, the mercenary gazed down at the quivering sword now sticking out of his chest.

The other three were staring too; and not one of them had moved when Indavara sprang forward and plucked the club from the warrior's hands. His face still frozen in shock, the mercenary pawed at the sword then toppled backwards. As he hit the deck, a glob of blood shot from his mouth and splattered his face.

Indavara left the sword where it was; fighting with a type of weapon he had handled perhaps only five times in his life was enough of a challenge.

The mercenaries still looked stunned. Then the older man gave a war-cry and they came around the mast at a run.

Indavara retreated past the fallen warrior. He couldn't believe the weight of the weapon. Looking down at the head, he saw that a thick metal band had been affixed an inch below the top. He adjusted his grip on the sticky leather wrappings and raised the club.

The mercenaries slowed down. The first man was dead by the time they passed him. The younger two looked down at the body. The leader did not.

Indavara had already decided there was no point trying to take on the three of them at once. He withdrew as far as the end of the yard, then backed around it towards the other side of the ship.

With a word from the leader, the two younger warriors came after him. The older man retraced his steps and hurried around the mast so as to surround his prey.

With his back to the side rail, Indavara turned one way, then the other.

The mercenaries advanced.

Sunlight sparked off Scaurus's blade. Cassius tried to shut out the noise of the slaves shouting down below and the sight of the sailors hauling themselves out of the river on the southern bank.

Scaurus darted forward, forcing Cassius back between the rear of the deckhouse and the stern. Though his hands were still tied, Cassius looked around for a weapon. To his left were the barrels that had been lashed to the deck but there was nothing else he could use.

Scaurus reached the corner of the deckhouse, cutting off the route along the right side of the ship.

Cassius was running out of space. He didn't know how he would fare in a fast-flowing river with his hands bound, but – if it came to it – he'd have to go over the side.

Having split up the mercenaries, Indavara imagined they would expect him to go for the single man, but he could see how edgy the death of their comrade had made the younger warriors. Spike and Bolt – as he'd named them – were twenty feet away and spitting curses as they came closer, eyes bright with hate. Enraged men didn't think. The leader's movements were calm and measured. They had made the choice for him.

With the club in his right hand, Indavara sprinted towards the stern.

Bolt was closer to the side rail. Spike moved away from him. They raised their clubs.

Indavara drifted left. He was five feet away when Bolt came out to meet him, club poised.

Indavara feinted right then leapt nimbly up on to the side rail. It was no more than six inches wide, but he danced along it and was already past Bolt when the warrior launched a clumsy swing. He hit nothing but air.

Indavara swiped one-handed into the back of his head: not a strong blow, but enough to send him tottering forward. As Indavara jumped down on to the deck, Spike attacked.

Towering over his foe and unleashing a bestial roar, the mercenary swung the club down from over his head, giving Indavara time to spring aside and watch as the weapon smashed into the side rail. One of the spikes sank two inches into the seasoned timber. Incredibly, Spike kept his hands on the club, trying to pull it out.

Indavara was more concerned with speed than power but his downward blow snapped the warrior's right arm just below the elbow. A jagged shard of bone tore out of the skin. Spike was still screaming when Indavara's second swing connected with his mouth. The bottom half of the mercenary's face shattered in a pink cloud of teeth, flesh and blood.

Indavara was moving forward before he fell to the deck. The older man was charging towards him.

Bolt was still dazed, facing the water, club hanging from one hand. He looked to his leader and cried out; but the breath was driven from his lungs by the blow that struck him between the shoulders. He flew over the side rail, crashed through an oar and plunged into the water.

The leader slowed, staring past Indavara at what was left of Spike.

Indavara didn't turn round, but he could hear the uneven, bubbling breaths of a man close to death. Out of the corner of his eye he noticed something stuck to his cheek. He plucked it off with his spare hand: a perfectly preserved – and remarkably white – tooth. He threw it over the side.

The mercenary spoke to him in Latin. 'This is how you will die.'

Cassius was just inches from the stern of the ship. He got ready to dive into the river. The bank wasn't far away. If he could keep his head above water, he reckoned he could make it.

Scaurus closed in, knife up – and Cassius wondered why he hadn't struck out at him yet. And then he realised. Scaurus was scared. He had a knife, but his opponent was younger, bigger and stronger than him. He daren't risk getting too close. He was a vicious bastard, but he was no soldier.

Cassius realised something else. He hated this man. He wanted to see him beaten and hurt.

Even so, he wasn't entirely sure he would stand and fight until he spied the object on a rack attached to the stern: a boathook.

Alikar used his club like a sword.

Indavara saw that it was longer than the others and – without the metal additions – lighter.

The mercenary held the weapon in both hands, out in front of him, thrusting it towards Indavara, who could do little more than block and evade. His club was shorter and heavier, and he was no master of it.

Considering his age, Alikar's footwork was immaculate. He stood in a fighting hunch: constantly on the move, constantly changing the point of attack.

He swiped at Indavara's head, then pushed at his face. The club slid off Indavara's weapon and smacked into his nose. It didn't break, but he tasted blood on his lips. He felt strangely weary – the club was so heavy, so unwieldy.

A flurry of thrusts and sweeps. Alikar struck at his flank.

Indavara couldn't get his weapon down in time. The club slammed into his side and the rings of the mail-shirt bit into his skin. Winded, he stumbled backwards, staring into the pale, raging eyes of the man before him.

If he didn't do something soon, the mercenary would wear him down, then look for an opportunity to finish him off. He lifted the club again. It was so heavy, so difficult to defend with.

He had to attack.

Scaurus hadn't taken another step forward once Cassius snatched the boathook from the rack. It was a six-foot length of wood topped by a bronze head. Even with his hands bound, he could wield it well enough.

Scaurus looked around for help. On the southern bank, a few of the sailors looked on.

'You men, get back here. I command you!'

But the men did nothing. Though not shackled like the Africans below, Cassius wondered if they too were slaves. They certainly idn't seem overly concerned about returning to help. In fact, most had already run away.

Scaurus retreated past the side of the deckhouse towards the main hatch. Behind him, Indavara and Alikar circled each other. The mercenary seemed to have the upper hand.

Cassius swung the boathook into Scaurus's shoulder – a thumping blow sufficient to make him drop the knife and reach for his arm.

'I'll have you torn limb from limb for this,' he hissed, spittle dripping down his chin.

'I don't think so, Scaurus.'

Cassius altered his grip and smashed the boathook into his foe's right thigh.

'That's for Major, you murdering bastard.'

'I swear by all the gods, I'll have you torn apart!' Scaurus yelled, his face scarlet.

Cassius's third blow caught Scaurus just above the ear, sending him tottering backward towards the hatch. He tried desperately to keep his balance but slipped on the top step. He seemed to freeze in mid-air for a moment before falling head first through the hatch, his body thumping against the wood all the way down.

Cassius came forward and looked into the gloom. Scaurus lay motionless next to the table. Seventeen pairs of eyes stared out from the darkness at their fallen master.

'And that's for Gregorius.'

Cassius looked up.

Indavara was just feet away, between the hatch and the side rail.

Alikar lunged at him.

Indavara didn't dare let him get close again. He took two swift steps back to give himself space, then launched a wide sweep at the mercenary.

Alikar parried solidly; and the impact sent convulsive tremors up Indavara's arm. He barely kept hold of the weapon, but saw for the first time a flash of doubt in the older man's eyes. He lashed out again, this time aiming low.

Alikar saw it coming and leapt backwards. Indavara missed him completely – and almost lost his balance – but he pressed on, raising the club over his shoulder once more. He took a deep breath, planted his front foot on the deck and twisted into a full-blooded swing at his foe's head. Alikar had no choice but to block.

The clubs met with a shuddering crack. Both men lost their grip: Indavara's weapon flew from his hands and smashed into the deck, Alikar's wheeled into the air.

Before it had even hit the ground, Indavara reached for his dagger.

Alikar went for his own blade.

Indavara's fingers closed on the handle. He plucked the blade from the sheath.

Alikar was fumbling. He looked down.

Indavara plunged the dagger straight into his foe's heart, sinking the blade in deep.

Alikar's hand was still on the handle of his knife.

Indavara forced the blade in another inch.

The mercenary's entire body quivered and he let out a gasping sigh. His hands came up around Indavara's neck. Indavara tried to push him away but Alikar pulled him in close and locked him into a bear hug. He staggered backwards, dragging Indavara with him.

Cassius dropped the boathook, picked up Scaurus's knife, and rushed towards them.

Two more stumbling steps and they were at the side rail. Indavara's arms were pinned. He tried to get a knee into the Palestinian's groin but they were too close.

He smashed his head into Alikar's nose just as the mercenary gave a final heave.

They pitched over the side rail and into the river.

Water exploded against Indavara's face. He shut his eyes as he sank, then opened them as he began to rise. He thought Alikar still had hold of him but then realised his arms were free. His head broke the surface and he saw the big body drifting away between the ship and the jetty.

For the first time in his entire life, Indavara found himself floating in water. The feeling of a liquid void around and beneath him panicked him like nothing before. He kicked out to try to stay afloat but the river seemed to be sucking him down.

He went under again, swallowed water, came back up, spat it out, thrashed around, swallowed more.

Under again and this time he didn't come back up. The mail-shirt seemed to have tripled in weight. He tried to pull it off him but it didn't move an inch.

He sank lower.

A dark shape in front of him. He reached for the ship, trying to halt his descent, but his fingers slid down the smooth planks of the hull.

He fell further into the green mist. Tendril fingers slithered over his legs, pulling him lower. He shut his eyes again.

This is how I will die.

XXXVI

'Cut, damn you!'

Kneeling by the side rail, with Scaurus's knife wedged between his knees, Cassius ran the ropes on his wrists up and down the blade. He was already through one but needed to cut another to get free.

He took long, deep breaths to get some air into his lungs. It seemed an age since he'd heard the last splash. Indavara had been under a long time already. But he was so strong. He could hold on.

Cassius saw movement to his left: Simo – running along the barge towards the jetty.

'Simo, he can't swim! The armour! He can't swim!'

Finally the knife was through. Cassius shook the rope off his wrists and wrenched off first one boot, then the other. He got up on the side rail. All he could see below was a thin trail of bubbles.

He dived into the river.

The shock of the cold faded quickly, as did the power of the dive. He felt himself rising again and kicked downward as he opened his eyes.

Nothing but murky green. Wide, arcing strokes took him deeper. Pain stung his ears.

There, impossibly far below him, something glinting in the darkness. He kicked again. Fifteen feet down. Twenty. Pressure in his lungs and throat.

Twenty-five feet. Then he saw him. Indavara's face was no more than a blur. Everything below the silvery mail-shirt was obscured by thick clumps of undulating reed.

Cassius kicked towards him. When he was close enough, he reached between Indavara's flailing arms for his belt, catching an elbow in the neck for his trouble. Cassius hauled the belt upwards. Indavara moved a couple of inches but then stopped. The reed seemed to have wrapped itself around him. The disturbed water cleared. He looked like a child, terrified and helpless.

Cassius felt the slippery reed licking at his legs. He locked both hands on the belt and heaved upwards again but Indavara was stuck there.

He came for me.

I can't leave him here to die.

Cassius's chest was on fire; and the fire was moving up to his throat. He knew he had only moments of air left.

He let go of Indavara. Instinct took over. He began to drift upwards.

Sensing something behind him, he turned.

A dark shape above, a big hand coming towards him, then a broad face set in a steely grimace.

Despite his size, Cassius knew Simo to be a strong swimmer. The Gaul ploughed past him and took Indavara's left hand. Cassius reached out and took the right, interlocking their fingers. Simo started upward. Cassius shut his eyes and kicked out with every ounce of strength he had left.

Indavara shifted, then suddenly was free.

Legs thrashing, they rose swiftly, accelerating up towards the dark bulk of the ship.

The fire was through Cassius's throat and into his mouth. His eyelids flickered open and shut. Darkness closed in around him. He was blacking out.

Shimmering sunlight above. Yellow spots flashed in his eyes. His body felt light, hollow. He wasn't even kicking any more.

He reached up. His fingers broke the surface. And then he was there.

Spluttering as he sucked in air, he let go of Indavara's hand, barely noticing the other two surface three yards away.

'Sir!'

Cassius could do nothing to help. He reached out for the ship, then realised it was too far away. But as he drew in more air, his vision began to clear. He turned to see Simo struggling to keep Indavara's head above the surface. The bodyguard's eyes were shut. He was coughing up water.

'There,' cried Simo, nodding at the thick timbers that supported the jetty.

Cassius could move now. Between them, he and Simo manoeuvred Indavara over to the nearest support. They propped him against it, then wrapped their legs around the wood. The three of them just hung there, recovering.

After a time, Indavara's eyes opened. He stared blankly forward, his breaths coming in convulsive gasps. Simo smacked him on the back a couple of times to clear all the water out. The bodyguard couldn't even keep his grip on the support. Cassius and Simo put their arms under him to keep him out of the water and he laid his head against the wood.

Cassius had no idea how long they stayed there. At some point he realised he could hear the slaves, still shouting to each other in their own language. And once he turned towards the ship, he thought of Scaurus and the barrels; and the imperial banner. He had to know.

'You all right, sir?' Simo asked. A thick clump of weed lay across his forehead.

'I will be,' replied Cassius. He turned to Indavara. 'Can you move?'

Indavara nodded.

Again they took one of his arms each, and swam to the bank. They hauled themselves up through thick, clinging mud until they were above the level of the jetty. Then they collapsed on to a bed of reeds and lay out on their backs for a moment, eyes shut against the sun.

'By the great gods,' breathed Cassius. 'To think I used to love swimming. After today and yesterday, I don't ever want to leave dry land.'

'Me neither,' spluttered Indavara.

It was the first thing he'd said; and Cassius and Simo laughed long and hard, mostly out of relief.

Indavara turned on his front and continued to spit out water. He looked as if the river had washed all the colour out of his face.

'Can you take this off?' he said.

Simo crawled over to him and, after several attempts, managed to wrench the mail-shirt off over his head.

'Thank you,' said Indavara. 'Both of you.'

Cassius dragged himself to his feet. 'Our pleasure. Come, you two, I hope to show you what this terrible affair has been all about.'

Walking along the jetty, they could still see some of the sailors – now all running back towards Antioch. A glance along the northern side of the river confirmed why they were leaving at such a pace. About half a mile away, a column of horsemen with a standard-bearer leading the way were riding along the towpath.

'About time,' said Cassius. 'I wonder who they are.'

'Marshal Marcellinus's men probably,' suggested Simo. 'Shostra was to take a message to him.'

'Better late than never, I suppose.'

They made their way back out along the barge – Indavara taking special care – and on to the galley. The slaves were still babbling away to each other below.

They passed Indavara's first victim. The bodyguard went to recover the sword, and was barely able to summon the strength to dislodge the blade.

Cassius retrieved Scaurus's knife from the deck and tried not to look at the second fallen mercenary.

'Careful,' he said as he led the way down the hatch. 'This could be dangerous.'

Lying next to the still motionless form of Scaurus was the overseer. The slaves had somehow overcome him but were all still shackled. One man was stretching for the key on the over-seer's belt as Cassius came down the last step.

'We should free them,' Indavara said.

'Why?' Cassius asked.

'Look at them. What life is this for a man?'

'The life of a galley slave.'

Indavara looked again at the Africans; and when Cassius saw

the expression on his face, he lost interest in arguing about it. He took the key off the overseer's belt and passed it to him.

'All right, Spartacus, do as you wish. But tell them to head for the south side of the river or the legionaries will round them up. And don't blame me if they turn on you.'

Cassius checked Scaurus and the overseer. They were both still breathing. He found Scaurus's key in a bag on his belt.

The slaves strained at their chains, trying to get close to Indavara.

Cassius pointed at the two unconscious men. 'Drag them out of the way, Simo.'

He hurried past the slaves and down the steps to the forward hold. He unlocked the door and went inside. Using Scaurus's knife, he set about taking the lids off the barrels. As he worked he heard the cries of the slaves; then Indavara and Simo trying to talk to them; then their footsteps as they hurried up the stairs, across the deck and on to the barge.

He had opened nine of the barrels – scooping aside the old coins to see what was underneath – before he came to one that didn't contain either silver, gold or jewellery.

The flag had been rolled up and stuffed into the barrel. Cassius pulled it out and spread it across the floor. The gems had been removed and the purple had faded, but he recognised the star in the middle and the swirling patterns of golden thread from the sketch Abascantius had given him. He smiled as he ran his hands across it.

'Now I understand,' said Indavara as he walked into the hold and gazed down at the barrels. He picked up one silver ingot and one gold and weighed them in his hands. Then he glanced quizzically at the imperial banner.

'What's that old thing?'

'Just a flag.'

'Worth anything?'

Cassius nodded. 'Priceless.'

XXXVII

The old man could barely walk. Despite the attendants either side of him – each with a hand on an elbow – every step seemed to require a huge effort. His head was bent so far forward that his chin touched his chest, and the parched skin of his hairless head was marked by liver spots and freckles. His pale robes reached down only as far as the knees of his gnarled, nut-brown legs.

Coming to a stop by the table, he rested his hands on the edge and took a few breaths. The attendants moved aside. He raised his head a little and looked around. There were no pupils in his eyes: they were milky white.

Sliding a bony hand across the table, he grabbed a handful of cloth and dragged the flag towards him. He ran his fingers down one side, then let his hands wander over the material. He traced the patterns of the thread, the faces of the recently restored gems.

Ten paces behind him, the small Persian delegation looked on: four middle-aged ministers in modest robes and – standing slightly ahead of them, looking over the old man's shoulder – the young Emperor himself, Hormizd Ardashir. The delegation's presence in Antioch was a secret so he had forgone regal apparel, and wore only a dark cloak over his tunic; yet he somehow still projected the composed confidence of a man born to power. He was tall and slender, and his sleek black hair hung far below his shoulders.

On the other side of the table were the Romans. They too were dressed in normal attire, with only Governor Gordio in a toga. He glanced nervously at the imposing figure next to him. With his cropped brown hair, bronzed skin and compact physique, Marshall Marcellinus looked every inch the man of action. Only the purple edging on his tunic hinted at his status as Aurelian's second-in-command.

To his left were General Ulpian, and the slight, rather incongruous figure of Procurator Octobrianus. Both men looked on anxiously. Magistrate Quarto completed the party, hands clasped together over his stomach as he peered down at the old Persian. The only other men in the meeting chamber were five Persian soldiers, eight Praetorian guardsmen, and one African bodyguard.

The old man seemed to have checked every last inch of the flag. He laid it flat on the table; pushing down each fold, straightening each edge. Then he turned round and nodded.

Hormizd smiled. Marcellinus started clapping. The rest of the party joined in; and then Marcellinus and Gordio came forward to talk with the Persian Emperor and his ministers. At a click of the fingers from Octobrianus, two clerks came trotting in carrying a leather case and writing equipment.

Abascantius turned from the scene below, mimicked wiping sweat from his brow, and grinned. He moved away from the thick column he and Cassius had been standing behind and tiptoed towards the doorway at the corner of the first-floor gallery. He was – by his own standards – dressed smartly, in a largely stain-free tunic and a light cape.

He had insisted they both take off their sandals, and not a word was said as they made their way down the stairs, then sat down and put them on again, watched impassively by two more Praetorian guardsmen. A long, empty corridor took them to the door at the rear of the forum, where another guardsman let them out, locking the door behind them. Abascantius tapped his fingers against his belt as he looked up at the cloudless blue sky.

'Thank the gods.'

He glanced at Cassius as they started away along the street.

'You did well, Corbulo. It's a shame you won't ever be able to tell anyone about this little venture, but by Jupiter you did well.'

'Thank you, sir. I wish I could say it's been a pleasure but this has quite easily been the second worst month of my life.'

Abascantius chuckled as he led Cassius around a corner. It

was mid-afternoon and the warm city streets were quiet. He shook his head. 'A robbery. A simple robbery.'

'Not that simple, sir.'

'You know what I mean. I was so convinced we were investigating some dire web of intrigue, I couldn't see the wood for the trees. Perhaps I've been in this job too long. How's the head?'

Cassius touched the hard bump and scabbed skin on the left side of his skull. 'Your surgeon friend seemed to think it will heal well, sir. Thank you for sending him along. He gave Simo an entire page of instructions.'

'You've a good man there, Corbulo – Christian or not.'

'I know it, sir.'

'You must at least be a little refreshed after a few days of rest. What did you do with yourself?'

'Slept mostly. Indavara too. He's been even quieter than normal. I think being dunked in the Orontes shook him up more than taking on those Palestinian brutes.'

'He really is quite exceptional. Alikar and his men were notorious, known in every city from here to their homeland. To think he took them on alone and came out on top. And jumping out of that tower window – by the gods – he must have balls the size of ostrich eggs. I do hope we can keep him on.'

'What about Scaurus, sir?' Cassius asked as they ducked under a low awning. 'I heard his execution has been announced.'

'He'll be lunch for the beasts at the next games. Quarto and Ulpian are personally taking charge of the arrangements – wild dogs, I gather. Would you like a ticket? I'm planning to make quite a day of it.'

Cassius's stomach churned. He wouldn't spare a moment to sympathise with Scaurus, but he'd had more than his fill of violence and death over the last few weeks.

'No thank you, sir. I must say I was surprised Marshal Marcellinus decided not to keep the whole affair quiet.'

'That would have been difficult. Better to tell nine-tenths of the truth. Only the issue of the standard is to be kept secret. Our Persian friends have no idea there was even a problem.'

'And how does the marshal view the Service's part in all this, sir?'

Abascantius looked at Cassius as they rounded a sprawling fruit stall, then hopped back on to the pavement.

'Diplomatically put, Corbulo. But let's be honest: I was roundly outwitted by Scaurus. If not for your efforts, I've little doubt I'd be on my way to that mine in Thessalonica I threatened you with. But he made fools of Ulpian and Quarto too, and I hear Gordio got a fairly substantial slap on the wrist from Marcellinus for putting me behind bars. As long as Chief Pulcher has the ear of the Emperor, I should think my position is secure. I shall simply have to keep my head down for a bit.'

'And Octobrianus?'

Abascantius spat on the ground. 'I had to write a letter of apology, would you believe? But he'll put a foot wrong sooner or later. And I'll make sure I'm there when he does.'

'Er, sir, where exactly are we going?'

Abascantius smiled as he led Cassius down a narrow side street. 'This way.'

Standing outside a dingy arched doorway was a bulky individual picking his nose. Abascantius threw him a coin and hurried past him through a beaded curtain. The inn was a grimy little place, with a bar in one corner and half a dozen patrons gathered round a large table, playing dice. One man gave a roar; the others groaned.

Seeing Abascantius arrive, a small man hurried out from behind the bar and silently led them past the gamblers to another door. He produced a key from a pocket on his apron and opened it for them.

'Still got that ten-year-old Nomentamum?' Abascantius enquired as he led Cassius through the doorway.

'I have.'

'Bring some. And six of your best glasses.'

The innkeeper nodded and shut the door behind them. The narrow corridor was lined with empty bottles of every possible size, shape and description. Beyond a stack of stools was another door on the right. Abascantius rapped on it. Shostra opened up.

They entered a small, murky room lit only by a skylight, around which were perched several birds, chirruping away merrily. Sitting at a table facing the door was Lady Antonia. She was as well turned-out as ever: skin flawless, hair piled high; and wearing a hooded green cape over her stola. She cast an impatient stare at Abascantius, but her expression softened into a smile when she saw Cassius.

Simo was sitting opposite her. He stood and hurried over. 'What's this all about, sir? Shostra fetched us from the villa.'

Cassius shrugged and looked past the Gaul at Indavara. He was standing in the corner, one foot up against the wall, arms crossed. Under his sleeveless tunic, Cassius could see the bandages Simo had wrapped around the welts on his side.

'Have a seat, Corbulo,' Abascantius said, gesturing to the table. 'You too, Indavara.'

They sat down: Indavara opposite Abascantius, who remained standing; Cassius next to Simo. Shostra shut the door, retrieved a wicker basket from below the table and placed it in front of his master. There was a cloth across the top.

'Are we going for a picnic?' asked Lady Antonia.

Cassius laughed.

Abascantius took the jibe in good heart and removed the cloth. 'All will be revealed, my dear.'

'Quickly, I hope. I've been waiting in this hole for half an hour.'

'If you're happy to make our association public, we can of course choose another locale.'

Antonia nodded begrudgingly.

Abascantius leaned forward and planted his hands on the table. 'It's unfortunate that I cannot share with all of you the precise details of the events we've been involved in, but everyone here has been of great help to me in the last few weeks. And I was in very great need of help.'

'My, my,' interjected Antonia. 'Humility. I do believe you're mellowing in your old age, Aulus.'

Abascantius continued undetered: 'In stopping Scaurus, you not only prevented one of the most audacious crimes ever committed against the Empire, but you may also have helped secure peace in this region, possibly for years to come. I have dispatched missives describing what occurred to both Chief Pulcher and the Emperor himself, and I have no doubt that they will add their profound gratitude to mine. Now – some tokens of that gratitude. Never let it be said that the Service doesn't reward those who do their duty.'

Cassius felt rather thrilled by what he heard. Not thrilled enough to make any of the nightmarish last few weeks seem worthwhile but proud nonetheless. He imagined returning home to a hero's reception back in Ravenna, the warm congratulations of family and friends. No such luck.

Abascantius reached into the basket and pulled out three silver ingots. He passed one to Lady Antonia, one to Indavara, and one to Cassius.

'I checked the prices this morning. Those are worth over two hundred aurei each. They are unmarked.'

'And how did you reward yourself, Aulus?' asked Antonia.

Abascantius placed his hand on his heart. 'The privilege of serving the Emperor is reward enough,' he said, with a gusto that bordered on convincing.

Antonia smiled.

'Now – for you,' said Abascantius, glancing at Simo. He took out a folded sheet of papyrus from the basket and handed it over. 'Your master told me what you did.'

Simo stood and bowed.

'Read it.'

As the Gaul did so, Abascantius caught Cassius's eye.

'A pardon for his father. Him and only him, I'm afraid, but he's free to leave the prison. He'll have to do some time on a work crew but no charges will be brought, and he need not pledge his allegiance to Domnus.'

'And the others?'

'That's up to Gordio.'

427

'You think he'll leave?' Cassius asked Simo.

'I don't know, sir. But I shall certainly tell him that he should.' The Gaul turned to Abascantius. 'Thank you, sir.'

Cassius slid his silver ingot back across the table to Abascantius. 'Sir, would you give this to Major's family for me?'

'I told you I'd take care of that.'

'The man gave his life, sir.'

Abascantius examined Cassius's face for a moment, then took the ingot. 'Very well.'

A knock at the door. Shostra opened it and took the tray from the innkeeper.

'One for all of us,' ordered Abascantius as the attendant poured the wine.

A rich, fruity aroma reached Cassius's nose.

'Not for me,' said Lady Antonia as she stood, leaving the ingot on the table. 'I can see the dust on those glasses from here.'

'Come, Antonia – drink with us,' implored Abascantius.

'Aulus, it's the middle of the afternoon. I should be asleep.' She nodded down at the ingot. 'Thank you for that though – an unusually timely and generous payment. But I shall not carry it around with me. Have it sent over later, would you?'

'Of course. And entirely well deserved it is too. Who else could have persuaded the Emperor's deputy to halt his column and come to our aid?'

'Emperor's deputy or not – a man is a man.'

'May I?'

Abascantius took Lady Antonia's hand and kissed it.

She walked towards the door.

Cassius stood up.

'Good-day.'

'Good-day.'

Antonia leaned in close and whispered in his ear. 'Don't forget my offer. I have my carriage outside. I shall only wait for a few moments – no longer.'

Cassius reddened as she left. He tried to ignore the speculative glint in Abascantius's eye as he took his drink.

Simo declined his glass of wine.

'No, no. I insist,' said Abascantius.

Simo took a glass, as did Indavara.

'To success!' declared Abascantius.

They raised their glasses and drank. Cassius savoured the sweet, powerful wine. Nomentamum was one of his father's favourites; it was extremely expensive, and very hard to come by outside Italy.

Another knock on the door. It turned out to be Salvian; and the portly operative was carrying a letter. Abascantius went over to speak with him.

Cassius turned to the others. Indavara put down his already empty glass.

'Well,' said Cassius. 'As this seems to be an occasion for giving gifts – Simo.'

The Gaul reached into Cassius's satchel, which was hanging from his chair. He pulled out an object a little longer than his hand, wrapped in cloth. He passed it to Cassius, who then presented it to Indavara.

'For you.'

Indavara took the object and unwrapped it carefully. It was an immaculately rendered figurine.

'Fortuna,' Indavara said.

'Silver leaf. Best you can buy,' stated Cassius.

'I shall still keep the old one.'

'Of course.'

'Thank you,' said Indavara with an awkward little nod.

'Quite literally the least I could do. I wouldn't be here if not for you.'

'Me neither if you two hadn't fished me out of that river.'

Cassius shrugged. 'Let's call it even.'

'Not quite – don't forget the inn at Palmyra.'

'But what about the baths?'

Cassius kept up a serious expression for a moment, as did Indavara, but then they both cracked into broad smiles.

'Fair point,' said the bodyguard. 'Even it is.'

So what are your plans?' Cassius asked.

Before Indavara could reply, Abascantius spoke up. 'Gentlemen.'

They turned round. The agent was holding up the letter.

'It seems we have a slightly problematic situation developing in Cilicia.'

Cassius let out a breath and rubbed his brow. 'Oh no.'

'Don't worry, Corbulo; a trifling matter by comparison with this last outing. But I fancy you might be well suited to it. You'll need your man Simo, of course, and a bodyguard wouldn't go amiss.'

Abascantius cast a speculative glance at Indavara, who said nothing.

'Well, you needn't give me an answer now,' continued the agent. 'Perhaps a little later.'

'No,' said Cassius. 'I shall be otherwise occupied for the rest of the day.'

Abascantius grinned. 'Prior engagement, Corbulo?'

Cassius ignored him and turned to Indavara. 'What do you think?'

Indavara still had the figurine of Fortuna in his hand. He gazed down at the pale, delicate features of the goddess's face, then looked up as Cassius asked again.

'Well?'

HISTORICAL NOTE

As before, I though it worthwhile to comment on the historical background to this story and mention a few points of interest.

Gladiators often fought in pairs and invariably specialized in a certain fighting style, but those who staged the contests (emperors included) showed a remarkable capacity for invention, so I think the challenge concocted by Capito is within the realms of possibility. A few fighters did manage to win their freedom – through the favour of their owner, the crowd, a local governor or even the emperor himself. Logic and the information available suggests that only a few would have achieved victories in double figures but grave inscriptions do attest to a select band who defeated astonishing numbers of foes. The most impressive of these honours one Asteropaeus, who is credited with no less than one hundred and seven victories.

The emperor Aurelian did conclude some sort of an accommodation with the Persians in 272. Although hostilities were renewed within a few years (possibly even towards the end of Aurelian's reign) the arrangement was undoubtedly crucial in restoring stability to the Roman east during this period.

Faridun's Banner is just one of the many names given to the royal standard of the Sassanid kings. The flag (most commonly referred to as the Derafsh Kaviani) was as revered and significant as I have suggested and remains an important symbol in Persian/Iranian culture. There is not – as far as I know – any record of its theft but the Palmyrans did reach Ctesiphon in about 262, though there is disagreement about whether or not the city was captured.

Regarding the rather 'undramatic' siege of Palmyra, I have tried to reflect modern thinking on what actually occurred when the Roman forces reached the city. In truth, victory had effectively already been assured by the triumphs at Immae and Emesa.

The tales of the dog-killing at Tyana and the shooting of the Palmyran defender by the Persian archer come from Roman historians.

We do know that much of Palmyra's treasure was claimed by Aurelian – primarily to fund the cost of the campaign – and that much of it was returned to Rome.

There are few specific details about which legions were involved in the fighting. In this story, what I have called the Fourth Legion is tasked with keeping watch over Palmyra and eastern Syria. The *Legio IV Scythica* seemed a logical choice because it was based at Zeugma in the first century and was still there in the fourth century. Similarly, the Sixteenth Legion (*Legio XVI Flavia Firma*) was based at Samosata during the reign of Hadrian, and was still in Syria in the time of Diocletian.

The figure of Marcellinus appears in the Roman histories. 'Marshal' is simply a convenient term but does something to convey the breadth of his command over the eastern empire.

It was Marcellinus who informed the emperor of unrest in Palmyra the following year – 273. The small garrison of Romans left to watch over the city had been killed by rebels, possibly under the leadership of a Palmyran named Apsaeus (who may have had some familial connection to Zenobia). It is not clear exactly what the rebels hoped to achieve but - for the second time in a year – Aurelian marched on Palmyra. The uprising was swiftly defeated and the emperor abandoned his earlier restraint. The city was sacked, the defences dismantled; and Palmyra never recovered. The remains of the city – including the huge Temple of Bel – survive to this day.

Although most historians agree that Zenobia was taken to Rome and presented to the people as part of Aurelian's triumphal parade, we cannot be certain of her eventual fate. It is probable that the emperor spared her life. According to *Historia Augusta*, he even provided her with a villa in Tibu (modern Tivoli), where she lived on with her children.

As mentioned in the historical note for *The Siege*, the background information concerning what I have called the Imperial Security Service is accurate. The term 'grain-men', or *frumentarii*, relates to the organisation's original purpose: supplying the legions with grain. Nothing (as far as I've been able to discover) is known of the role its agents played before, during and after the conflict with Palmyra. However, given Aurelian's commitment to strict military discipline and purging of 'disruptive' elements within the Senate – it's hard to believe he didn't rely on his *frumentarii* as much as his predecessors. Historians have presented differing interpretations of how 'the service' functioned within the military and provincial hierarchies, but given that the organization was headed by a senior centurion in Rome – who was directly responsible to the emperor – I imagine the agents often acted with considerable autonomy.

There is general agreement that the *frumentarii* were widely disliked for their shadowy activities, and that in later years the organization was plagued by corruption and venality. I remain wary of accepting this characterization as 'the whole truth'. Alexander Severus (emperor from 222–235), for example, was praised for choosing only honest individuals for his 'grain men'. Additionally, when we consider that the agents were primarily dedicated to serving the emperor's interests, we might assume that their conduct often reflected the rule of the commander-in-chief: in the case of Aurelian, a strident – but by the standards of his day – relatively benevolent figure. It must also be acknowledged that rank corruption was virtually a defining feature of the entire army by the end of third century.

The representation of Paul of Samosata within the story reflects what it known from the sources. Historians disagree on the nature of his association with Zenobia but he was certainly Bishop of Antioch during the Palmyran occupation. The

sequent events were significant because it was the first time
: Church invited a Roman emperor to make a judgment on
leir affairs.

It should be noted that the Christian community featured
are seen generally from Cassius' point of view; that is to say the
point of view of an upper-class Roman. During these years,
Christians were not subject to the widespread persecution
carried out by earlier and later emperors, but life was rarely
easy for them. The Romans were well used to tolerating a
plethora of belief systems alongside their own, but they did insist
on some adherence to 'state religion', in particular the worship
of the emperor. It was the 'exclusive' nature of the Christian
faith that engendered such frustration and hatred.

Some other issues:

Symbolic spear-heads – or 'spear-standards' – like the one
issued to Cassius were exclusively the preserve of officers repre-
senting the governor's staff in a given province. Some actual
examples have survived. These officials were also often in possession of a *diploma*, an authorization document that enabled them
to use the *cursus publicus* – the postal system which allowed
officials to communicate messages along military roads. The
way-stations were established to facilitate this.

Although I have featured a single magistrate for the city of
Antioch, there were in fact usually several *aediles*, whose respon-
sibilities included the policing of roads, markets, baths and so
on. I have chosen not to use Latin terms in this series, so I
decided on 'city sergeants' for the magistrate's men. These were
of course the *lictors*, whose clubs or *fasces* (later the symbol of
Mussolini's Fascists) represented the magistrate's power to
punish.

I describe Lollius as 'legion quartermaster'. The correct Latin
term is *praefectus castrorum* (camp prefect).

The records office at the basilica may seem anachronistic but
historians have shown that Roman military 'filing systems' were

very sophisticated. There is clear evidence of cataloging, annotation and cross-referencing. It is probable that details on every soldier would have been recorded in some form or another.

It may seem odd that a city of Antioch's size had no permanent prison, but incarceration wasn't generally used as a form of punishment. Those behind bars would mainly have been awaiting either trial or execution.

Mithraism was indeed very popular amongst the military, particularly the lower ranks. Mithraeums like the one described can still be seen at numerous sites. They seem to suggest secrecy and mystery, but in fact many followers would have worshipped openly. After Constantine's conversion to Christianity, Mithraism suffered its own persecutions and eventually ceased to exist as a significant religious movement.

The mercenaries featured in the story are based on the Palestinian 'club-men' – the fearsome auxiliaries said to have played an important part in Aurelian's victory over Palmyra.

Novels such as this are not possible without the work of historians, and I am indebted to all those whose texts I used.

I have tried to be as accurate as is possible within the bounds of a fictional work. Any perceived mistakes or inaccuracies are mine.

ACKNOWLEDGEMENTS

The Imperial Banner was completed between January 2010 and November 2011, a much shorter period than the (rather excessive) five years it took to finish *The Siege*. It is a pleasure to acknowledge the professional and personal support I have received during that period.

Thanks again to 'the readers' – the people who took the time to look at early drafts and provide me with some very useful feedback – my dad Neil Brown, Adrian Smith, Becky Amiss, Matthew Amiss, Neil Harrison and Lindsey Roffe.

I must also mention some people criminally overlooked in the acknowledgments for the first book: David and Debs Brown, Mark Sanderson and Milena Pierscinska.

Once again, my agent David Grossman has provided sterling encouragement and guidance.

My editor, Oliver Johnson, was again massively helpful in ironing out literary wrinkles. His enthusiasm for the direction in which I wanted to take the series was, and is, much appreciated.

Credit is also due to Rosie Collins, who created the map of the Roman empire; and Larry Rostant, whose striking covers complement the stories so well.

Editorial assistant Harriet Bourton was meticulous, organised and patient throughout (even when I returned a late draft with over a thousand changes!). Thanks also to copy-editor Morag Lyall, especially for spotting the 'lost days'! The efforts of all those at Hodder & Stoughton who contributed is much appreciated.

Praise for Nick Brown's stunning debut

Agent of Rome: The Siege

'Brown has given this Roman military adventure story a great twist in having Cassius hail from the secret service ranks . . . Much more than a simple military story, *The Siege* is also a character study and offers a rare glimpse into 3rd century Rome and her occupation of Syria.'

Historical Novels Review

'Brown promises to be one of the most exciting sword-wielding writers in an ever-popular arena. In this, his debut, his principal is a 19-year-old fresh-faced officer commanding 100 men in defence of a Syrian stronghold against a vastly superior force. There are echoes of *Beau Geste* in this death-or-glory stand.'

Oxford Times

HODDER